DE-173

J G Bell

ISBN: 978-1-916696-71-6

PublishNation
www.publishnation.co.uk

Chapter One

Iraq 2008

Colonel Jack Marsters, British Army, and Major Ben Rhodes, US Marine Corp, were playing cards together in their tent as they had done for the past six months on this detachment. It wasn't the best, they'd both agreed on their first day, but someone had to do it. And they'd both been told in no uncertain terms that this would be their last posting if they so much as put a toe out of line.

Although they had been strangers, it seemed that they were cut more or less from the same cloth; they followed their instincts, if not always their orders, and it was for that reason they had been handed the task of overseeing the exhumation of the latest mass grave that had been discovered.

The Colonel was in his late thirties, good looking, with cropped fair hair, which was often covered by his sand-coloured beret. The beret was the only part of his desert camouflage uniform that related to his service in 22 SAS Regiment from which he was currently suspended after, in his words, 'a difference of opinion' with a superior officer. It had taken the best part of a bottle of Scotch for him to loosen up enough to tell Rhodes the truth, and it wasn't easy listening.

The intention of Marsters' last mission was to draw out local insurgents and give away their position ready for an airstrike; however, he had been told it was routine weapons targeting. Otherwise, he would never have accepted it. When Marsters realised what was happening it was too late; his unit was outnumbered and surrounded. When he called for backup, no ground troops were sent, and an airstrike was ordered instead. Only he and one other man survived to make it out. Upon his return to base camp, Marsters sought out the man responsible and put him in intensive care for three months.

This should have resulted in a court-martial, but Marsters was a highly respected and decorated officer. The mission was deemed a failure due to bad planning, and Marsters was sentenced, for want of a better word, to the coalition exhumation detail. To him, it was a burden he must accept; to the scientists and civilians on the team, they couldn't have hoped to be placed in safer hands.

He was a good man, Rhodes thought, as he looked at his superior officer. He never mentioned his private life, but then some guys liked to keep that separate. He probably would do so himself if he had someone special, which he didn't. Sure, there had been a few women, but nothing lasting. He was always looking for something that wasn't there and couldn't even explain it if he tried. He allowed his thoughts to wander now as he stared, poker-faced at the winning hand he held.

Marsters also considered the man opposite him. Ben Rhodes was in his early thirties with light-brown hair. He also wore the desert camouflage uniform and, although his rank of Major and the fact that he was a United States Marine was apparent, less so to non-military personnel was the fact that the webbing belt he wore around his waist was black and depicted that he was a black belt fifth degree. That meant that he was trained by the Marine Corp Martial Arts Programme (MCMAP). MCMAP was where marines were trained in the use of unarmed combat, rifle and bayonet, also weapons of opportunity and much, much more. This method of training was affectionately known as 'Semper Fu' taken from the Marine Corp motto 'Semper Fi'. A handy bloke to have in your corner, Marsters had thought to himself when they first met and even more so when their booze-soaked evening led to his explanation of events leading to his present posting.

Rhodes and his unit had seen some of the worst combat in Iraq, and they had been helped in no small way by their Iraqi interpreter. He had acquired information for them on countless occasions that had saved their – and many other service personnel's – necks. So, on the night the interpreter's wife was screaming at the sentry post that her husband had been dragged from their home by masked men, Rhodes and his team wasted no time preparing a rescue party. This, however, was quickly quashed by the base commander; he wasn't prepared to let them wander into an ambush.

The ensuing firefight, (Rhodes was never going to leave a man down) hostage rescue, and the safe return of all did nothing to assuage the ferocity of his CO's disciplinary action; he wanted a court-martial.

Rhodes spent two days in the brig awaiting a trial that never came. The next day he was assigned to serve under Marsters' command. He had a high-ranking guardian angel somewhere but had no idea who the hell it was.

The light outside the tent was fading now; it would be dark soon. Jack threw in his hand – it was a lousy one anyway. Ben looked at it and laughed as he pulled his winnings, a pile of pennies, towards him. He was about to speak when one of the exhumation team rushed into the tent. The bespectacled pathologist, Dr Hodges, was rambling excitedly but his strong Glaswegian accent was too complicated for Rhodes at the best of times.

'Colonel, see you hay a wee shufty at this,' he blurted out as he left the tent as quickly as he had entered. The two men followed him out into the half-light. The temperature would be dropping soon, but at least tomorrow they would be out of here; no more smell of decomposition or having to look at the tortured faces of the dead, those that had faces left, at least.

Jack wondered what the big deal was as they walked towards the pit where the exhumation crew was just tidying up now, all the bodies were gone. The two officers stopped at the edge as the doctor jumped in; it was only a few feet deep. They had been taking soil samples today; there were no remains left in the pit. But if that was the case…

'Doctor, what is that?' The Colonel pointed to a half-exposed skeleton. He was no scientist, but he could see that it had been buried deeper than the others, indicating it must have been in the ground longer.

'Come away in,' the doctor gestured to them as he spoke.

Both men jumped down. Ben looked at the half-buried remains. 'More mass burials,' he sighed. He'd thought his penance was almost over, but that hope seemed to be slipping away now; they could be here for months. He looked at his CO 'You're gonna need more pennies, sir!'

'We've scanned the whole area. He's the only one.' Ah, someone whose accent he understood, thought Ben. It was Dr Fraser from the American side of the team.

'So, what's the big deal, Doctor?' Jack asked.

'Well, apart from the fact that this man has been buried for over a thousand years, there's this,' as he spoke, Fraser removed a piece of cloth that had been covering the wrist of the skeleton.

'He's wearing a watch?' Ben gave the scientists a sideways look. 'Very funny, Doc. Now, let's wrap it up and get ready to leave in the morning,' Jack didn't find it the slightest bit amusing, but then he never understood the humour of academics.

As the two officers turned to leave, Dr Fraser stopped them, 'This is no joke, Colonel. The remains have been dated to within a few hundred years!'

Ben sighed and crouched down to take a closer look, 'The hands on the watch are moving Doc, c'mon, you gotta try harder than that.'

'What?' The doctor crouched as Ben stood, touching the watch with his trowel. The two pieces of metal sounded against each other, and suddenly it felt as if all the surrounding air had been sucked away and then quickly put back. In an instant, everything was normal again except for Dr Fraser. He was nowhere to be seen.

The three remaining men stood in silence for a moment until Ben laughed. 'Okay, Doc, now that was much better!' he turned to the Scot, 'How'd you do that?'

'It was nay me,' Hodges gasped, finally finding his voice.

'Joke's over, Doctor. You can come out now,' an uneasy feeling washed over Jack as he spoke.

The search party found no trace of the missing doctor. Jack made his report about the incident, and late that night, they called off the search ready to resume it again at first light.
Ben and Jack sat in their tent, planning the following morning's search. They sat opposite each other at the table as they had done earlier when they played cards. Ben fiddled with the watch they had found on the remains. It looked like an ordinary wristwatch, but on closer inspection, the face showed not only time and date but also the year, and the bezel looked like it was marked with degrees of longitude and latitude. It was clearly damaged.

He laid it on the table, and Jack picked it up, studying it with one eyebrow raised. It had stopped ticking when Dr Fraser had tapped it with his trowel. Jack stood up and dropped it back down; it landed with a dull thud and started ticking again. 'Fixed it,' he sniffed. But when Ben picked it up it stopped ticking instantly.

'You haven't got the touch, Major,' Jack smirked.

'Sir,' Ben's voice was a little hesitant.

'It was a joke, Major.'

'No, sir, not that,' Ben pointed over Jack's shoulder, 'that!'

Jack turned and stared at the crack where the tent flaps hadn't closed properly, 'It can't be!' he gasped.

'It is sir. Sun's up, it's morning!' Ben heard the words come out of his mouth, but he didn't believe them.

They raced out of the tent and stood in disbelief. The camp was busy getting ready to leave, and to their right, the search party was almost ready to move out. The two men exchanged confused glances and went back inside. Jack pointed at the watch on the table, 'What the hell is that thing?' To his surprise, his voice was level.

'You think it's a weapon of some sort?' Ben was as stunned as his superior.

'I dunno, but I've gotta call this in,' Jack scratched his head.

'And say what, sir?' Ben stepped back a little from the object.

'And say nothing!' A deep, authoritative voice commanded from behind them.

They both spun around and instantly stood to attention as they were now face to face with a US Navy Admiral. 'As you were gentlemen, I am Admiral Hennessey,' he was an Afro-American, early fifties; and maybe carried a little more weight than was good for him. He walked to the table carrying a small metal box, which seemed to have its own power source as it emitted a gentle hum. Holding his breath, he picked up the watch carefully and placed it inside, closing the lid quickly. 'That should keep it contained for now,' he exhaled slowly.

'Contain what exactly, sir?' Jack was still staring at the box. 'Don't bother to pack your gear, gentlemen. You're coming with me. We've a special flight to the U.S. waiting,' Hennessey spoke over his shoulder as he left the tent; clearly, there was to be no further explanation.

The two men stared at the tent flaps as they closed behind the Admiral, then Ben turned to his superior. 'Sir, what just happened?'

'No idea,' Jack muttered, 'but I'd say we're up to our necks in it, and there's not a damn thing we can do about it.'

'Now, gentlemen,' Hennessey barked, poking his head back inside.

That soon brought them round, and they followed him in quick time.

The flight back to the States was not through the usual channels. They were helicoptered out to a remote airstrip where a private jet was waiting for them. As they thundered up the runway and left the ground, neither man spoke; they just exchanged glances. The plane levelled out, and from the windows, on either side, they could see a fighter escort made up of British and American jets.

'Gentlemen, you may as well get some rest. Your questions will not be answered until we are in situ,' was all the Admiral said to them as he made his way forward.

Easy for you to say, thought Jack, his mind racing as he was sure Ben's was too.

Still, they slept and woke to hear the pilot announcing their descent, although to where was still a mystery. Ben looked out of the window; the Admiral was near the front of the cabin now talking on the phone. 'Well, it ain't Area 51, that's for sure!'

Jack turned and looked out of his window. The Major was right: they were approaching an American military installation surrounded by forest, not desert.

They landed, and the plane taxied towards a large hangar that stood alone and some distance from the other buildings that made up the base. An armed escort led them into the waiting hangar through a small door inside one of the huge outer ones. Neither man knew what to expect once inside, but probably not the sight that greeted them, it was utterly empty, entirely deserted.

Still maintaining his silence, the Admiral led them through another door to their right and into an empty office. Jack and Ben exchanged confused sideways looks.

This was where the armed escort left them to wait outside the door Hennessey was now closing. Satisfied all was well, he proceeded to what looked like an ordinary industrial metal light switch, flipped it upward and stared into its vacant space. A retinal scanner flickered over his eye; identity confirmed, he snapped the switch down as the floor beneath them began to slowly lower. Both men looked at one another again, both thinking the same thing: *Shit!*

As they descended further, a false floor overhead moved into place, making the room above seem as if they were never there. And in doing so, artificial light flooded their compartment. The ride ended when a panel in front of them slid open, allowing access to what lay ahead. Their silent journey continued along a dull, cream-painted concrete corridor; its blandness punctuated every now and again by a khaki green door.

Stopping outside one such door, the Admiral opened it and stepped inside. It appeared to be his office; it was just as bland as the corridor outside and was furnished with the very basic of furniture: grey metal filing cabinet, grey metal desk, not even a comfortable-looking chair for him, never mind the ones he offered them. The only thing in the room that could have given anyone a hint that it wasn't World War Two was the computer terminal that sat on the desk to the Admiral's left.

'Thank you for your patience. I can only imagine what's been going through your minds,' he began but was interrupted by a knock at the door.

'Come!' Hennessey's voice had a natural boom.

'Och, is tha' it?' A familiar voice spoke as its owner pointed to the box containing the watch; it was Dr Hodges. Both Jack and Ben spun around at the sound of his voice. 'Ah see you, yer allreet?' He grinned at them.

Jack was confused by the circumstances, not the conversation, but still nodded. Ben was confused by both, so just followed his CO's lead. Hennessey passed the box to Dr Hodges, who took it carefully and left the room at a more cautious pace than he had entered it.

From his desk drawer, Hennessey took out a large manila file from which he selected some photographs that he then handed to his subordinates. The first was that of a watch, possibly the twin of the one Dr Hodges had just taken away, except this one looked to be in pristine condition.

Hennessey explained, 'This timepiece was found at an archaeological dig in the east of England in 1933. It was brought back to the States by the man in charge, Professor James Smalley. He claimed that when wearing the device, he was transported to another time and place completely. He was dismissed as a madman, but it later transpired that he described the destruction of the twin towers on 9/11. To add to the theory of his madness, when asked to produce the timepiece for a demonstration he was unable to do so, stating that on the night of September 5[th,] 1933, a beautiful woman appeared in front of him, took the timepiece and just vanished.'

Hennessey presented them with a drawing, 'this is his sketch of her: blonde hair and blue eyes.' He showed them three more photographs which included the same woman during different periods in history, 'Dunkirk 1940, Korea 1951, and Vietnam 1974,' the Admiral pointed to each one.

'Sir, is this some kind of sanity test? cos, you know we're fine really,' Ben was having none of this, 'I mean, she's a beautiful woman and all,' he looked closer; 'wow, gorgeous, in fact, but...'

'I realise how difficult this must be for you to digest gentlemen, but just go with it please,' Hennessey's voice was firm, not commanding.

'How is it possible?' Jack was happy to still be in denial with Ben.

'Time travel, gentlemen. The same thing that happened to you and Dr Fraser back in Iraq, although the loss of the Doctor was unfortunate.'

'No, no, you want me to believe that?' Ben shook his head, 'no.'

'Believe what you will, Major, but it wasn't a guide that led us to that grave site. One of our military satellites picked up an energy reading. We had no idea what it could be, so we sent Doctor Hodges and Doctor Fraser to check it out,' he looked from one man to the other, 'the two of you were both handpicked for the task, we needed good men in position for this very reason. Otherwise, you would both be facing your own court-martials,' he waved his hand dismissively, 'all charges have been dropped for both of you, by the way,' he sat back in his chair.

The silence was broken as Dr Hodges knocked on the door once more. He did not wait for permission this time, just came straight in grinning like a Cheshire cat, 'Howay and hay a gleg.'

Hennessey and Ben looked blankly at the Scot as Jack interpreted, 'He wants us to look at something.'

Ben looked at the Admiral as they left the room, 'He really speaks like that, sir? I mean it wasn't just a cover?'

The Admiral sighed, 'Unfortunately, not, Major.'

They followed the doctor along the drab corridor and through yet another khaki door. This one opened into a vast laboratory where another scientist in a white lab coat like Hodges' was busy tapping away at his computer terminal.

Hennessey led them over. 'This is Professor Jennings,' he introduced them to the long-haired, skeletal academic.

Jack and Ben counted six armed guards in the room, all carrying semi-automatic weapons and side arms. *'Not your run of the mill lab then'*, Jack thought, as he caught the Major's eye. He knew Ben had spotted the same; he was a good marine, well trained.

The professor began typing on his keyboard again, 'We should be able to access the device with the software I've programmed,' he said arrogantly as Dr Hodges eyed him. Clearly, Jennings was a glory hunter and not one to share the credit.

'You know that thing's broken?' Jack piped up, but too late. The timepiece began ticking again. Both Jack and Ben took a few steps back, Dr Fraser still fresh in their minds. The room started to hum as the generators kicked in, then it happened again: the air was sucked out and forced back in, but this time the walls began to fade away, then disappeared entirely.

They were outside now in a forest where children could be heard laughing and playing, everyone was mesmerised until sparks flew from the computer terminal, bringing them all back to reality as the smell of smoke filled their nostrils, and once more they were all back in the lab, but they were not alone.

In the middle of the room, two small children clung to one another fearfully, a boy and a girl maybe four or five years old. They appeared to be Native Americans dressed in skins.

'It worked!' The professor was overjoyed.

'That's great,' Jack said slowly, 'now send them back!'

Ben walked over to the children and, with a calm voice, tried to comfort them.

'I can't, I need more time to work on the device,' the professor admitted.

Ben carried the young girl in his arms, and she buried her head in his neck. The young boy clung to his leg, terrified. Jack picked the small child up and tried to soothe him. Traumatised, he held on tightly, sobbing words in a language neither man could understand.

Hennessey opened his mouth to speak when there was a small blue flash from across the room; nothing big, just tiny and bright. And there she was, the woman from the photographs, she stood a short distance from where the two men still held the children, her outfit was brown leather: trousers with a short jacket which allowed a slight glimpse of a leather bodice laced at the front and secured with a halter neck; flat, knee-length boots finished the ensemble. She eyed the room warily as she stared down six-gun barrels.

'Stand down!' Hennessey gave the order. Immediately the soldiers lowered their weapons. The woman inclined her head in thanks, then she held out her hands and spoke to the children in what the adults assumed was their native tongue, as they began to wriggle free from Rhodes and Marsters, who gently lowered them to the ground. They ran to her and gripped her legs, she put her arms around them protectively, not taking her eyes off the other occupants in the room, constantly watching for a threat.

'Wait!' Professor Jennings ran towards her. He was stopped in his tracks, as from under her right sleeve, a twelve-inch blade extended in a second. The look in her eye told him she meant business. Then there was a small blue flash, and she was gone, taking the children with her.

The Colonel and the Major were given joint quarters later that evening due to limited space at the facility, and after events during the afternoon's experiment, Hennessey had informed them that they had been reassigned to the programme. Neither man was sure how they felt about that; Dr Fraser's disappearance still sat uncomfortably.

To help them get up to speed, they had both been given a pile of files to work through. They were marked classified, and you could have heard a pin drop as the two men sat in silence reading, now and then shaking their heads in disbelief.

They had already read the manila files on the table in front of them. One was marked *Project Rainbow,* and from under the cover, a black and white photograph of a U.S. naval vessel, the *USS Eldridge,* poked out. That file contained mostly what they already knew from conspiracy theories on late-night TV, although to them *Project Rainbow* was more commonly known as *The Philadelphia Experiment.*

The Philadelphia Experiment was an experiment into radar invisibility back in 1943. The aim was that using a strong enough current from generators placed on board; it would produce an electrical field and render the ship radar invisible; however, something went wrong, and the whole ship disappeared briefly, only to return a short time later. But all was not well on board, some of the crew were severely burned, some confused and disorientated; others returned physically joined with the metal of the ship, and some other poor souls didn't return. Those that survived were discharged from the Navy on mental grounds.

Although Marsters and Rhodes knew this already, they were still uncomfortable at having it confirmed as a fact, not fiction. They even had photographs of the ship as it was when it returned, with the sailors badly injured, burned and the dying melded to the bulkhead.

They were in unknown territory as they read the next file marked *Project Phoenix.* This told the story of how research continued after the war under the supervision of a Dr Reinhart, the man responsible for *The Philadelphia Experiment.* However, this new project was about mind control. A massive human study began at The Brookhaven National Laboratories on Long Island, New York. But alas, as with *The Eldridge,* the project went too far. Those in charge of *Project Phoenix* managed to enhance technology so well that a computer could in effect transmit a thought into the mind of a human being. Pushing the ethical boundaries too far, they used human guinea pigs and altered their DNA to enhance their physical and mental abilities.

Realising the sinister potential, Congress ordered the project shut down. However private concerns that had helped develop and fund the project did not follow Congress nor play by their rules. A secret group with deep financial resources and an unknown link to the military set up a new research facility at Camp Hero, an abandoned Air Force station at Montauk Point, New York, new scientists with a distinct lack of ethics were brought in to replace the originals, and by 1972, the project was fully underway despite having no military funding or intervention. Those in charge threw ethics out of the window and began tampering not only with mind control but dabbling in time travel too. It seemed that a few Phoenix agents only made one successful leap and that was into the future; unfortunately for them, it was to discover that time travel had been outlawed. Undaunted by this, they stole superior technology that would allow them to travel through and alter time to suit their own means.

The file ended with a note that for unknown reasons *Phoenix* was destroyed in 1983. The information was passed to Congress by anonymous persons with a warning never to meddle with time again.

The two men finished their reading at about the same time, Ben dropped his file on the table and ran his hands over his hair as he did when he was tired, his head was spinning with outrageous facts.

Jack threw his reading material down now too, and they looked at one another. It was Ben who broke the silence, 'So where do you think our time-travelling beauty is from?'

Jack shook his head, 'Can't be from the future if time travel is outlawed,' he pinched the bridge of his nose; his head was beginning to throb.

They turned in early, both exhausted by the past couple of days, but neither slept well as their minds turned over the information they had been expected to digest.

The following morning another test was scheduled so everyone was in the lab once more. Professor Jennings typed furiously on his keyboard, oblivious to anyone's presence other than that of Dr Hodges to whom he snapped out the occasional order.

'I thought we were told not to mess with this?' Ben was referring to the previous night's reading material.

Jack shrugged, 'Human nature, Major. It's never should we, always, could we?'

'And if other timepieces are out there, we should acquaint ourselves with the technology so as not to be left vulnerable,' Hennessey added dryly, as he stood at their side.

'That too, sir,' Jack cleared his throat.

The professor raised his head briefly and nodded to Hennessey, indicating he was ready to begin. 'Very good, Professor, please continue,' the Admiral said.

The familiar hum of the generator drowned out any ambient noise in the room. The professor stopped tapping his keyboard and looked up expectantly, no one spoke, mostly because the hum of the generator was getting louder now and because nothing was happening.

Ben folded his arms across his chest while Jack wrinkled his nose and started checking under his fingernails. Neither man liked the professor; they couldn't say why, but there was something about that guy they didn't trust. Then there it was again, the little blue flash and there she stood. The guards aimed at her and once more Hennessey stood them down, shouting over the din of the generators.

She nodded her thanks and cautiously kept her eye on Ben and Jack as she walked past them to the generator, she looked at it for a moment then reached forward and pulled the lever to turn it off. The room fell silent.

The woman turned to them. Ben stood closest to her, only a few feet away, 'Um, hi,' he smiled.

She returned the smile and was about to speak but was startled when the door burst open and in rushed armed troops, their weapons raised and ready to fire, instinct made Ben position his body between her and them.

'Captain Hackett, what is the meaning of this?' Hennessey bellowed at the young officer who led the intrusion.

'Following your orders, sir. If we had no contact from you for twelve hours, we were to assume hostile intent and send in a force,' Hackett recited.

'Captain, I spoke to you not thirty minutes ago,' Hennessey was furious, the woman might leave at any time – and now this.

'Sir,' Hackett bravely stood his ground and moved towards one of the computer terminals where he accessed the CNN website, turning the screen for his superior to see. He was right: the news headlines were beginning for the news at nine o'clock, but it was 2100 hrs now, not 0900 hrs as everyone in the room expected; some twelve hours had elapsed in a matter of seconds.

'Very good Captain, you may stand your men down,' Hennessey's tone was less harsh.

'Yes, sir,' Hackett saluted and gave his men the signal to clear out of the room.

Hennessey looked over Ben's shoulder and saw that the woman was still there, she moved to stand by the Major's side as Hennessey spoke to her, 'We travelled through time?'

She did not speak though; it was the professor who replied, 'Not quite, Admiral; we were travelling through time and if our guest hadn't shown up, we could've ended up anywhere.'

'With no way of getting back,' Jack surmised, he knew he was right by the sheepish look on the professor's face.

'We owe you a debt of gratitude, ma'am,' Hennessey began. 'Perhaps…' His sentence was cut short as Jennings pulled a dart gun from beneath his white lab coat, no doubt put there for this specific task, he quickly took aim at the woman and pulled the trigger. The dart found its target, hitting her in the side of the neck. She pulled it out instantly, but the drug had already been forced into her system, she stumbled a little as it began to take effect.

Both the Admiral and Jack shouted their condemnation of the professor's actions. While Jack wrestled the weapon away from him, the woman fell back as she fought to stay conscious.

Ben turned and quickly caught her, holding her up. Jack had the scientist bent over his desk in a painful arm lock; he looked at Ben holding the semi-conscious woman, then came the small blue flash that seemed to emanate from her chest, and she was gone again, this time taking the Major with her.

It was over in the blink of an eye, one second, they were in the lab, the next Ben could feel the warmth of the sun on his face. He quickly took in their surroundings, they were on a grassy hill, overlooking a clear blue sea, with a wooded area close by. She was out cold now as he swept her up into his arms and carried her to the shelter of the trees, gently laying her down. Removing his greens jacket he fashioned a makeshift pillow for her, then, un-holstering his sidearm, went to reconnoitre the area, frowning at the fact that he had no choice but to leave her there in a vulnerable state. He kept her in sight as best he could while he satisfied himself that they were alone and in a good position to be able to see anyone approaching from a long way off. Finally, he returned to where she lay and sat patiently waiting for her to wake up.

He looked at her as she lay peacefully sleeping, her shoulder length blonde hair swaying gently in the breeze. They must be around the same age, he pondered, and she was beautiful. He thought back to the photographs he had seen of her in the files the night before and tried to imagine where she came from.

Almost an hour passed before she began to stir, her hand went to her head as she opened her eyes and looked directly up into the branches of the trees above. Groaning, she tried to sit up; it was then that she noticed him. Startled, she tried to stand and immediately fell to her knees. 'Take it easy,' he calmed, 'you're safe.' She tried to stand again and fell against him. He held her up but at arms-length, 'If I meant you any harm, don't you think I would've done it while you were out of it this past hour?' He helped her to sit back down, then sat a respectful distance away; staying silent, allowing her a moment or two to collect her thoughts.

'Thank you,' she smiled a little nervously, her accent English. 'You're welcome,' he extended his hand to her, 'Major Ben Rhodes, United States Marine Corp.'

'Tannis,' she introduced herself as she shook his hand, 'and I'm sorry about this,' she gestured to their surroundings.

'Yeah, about that… Where are we? Or should I say, when are we? Or both?' he furrowed his brow in mock confusion.

'We are on what will be known as the Greek Island of Kefalonia, and the year is 5015 BC, so we shouldn't be disturbed for a while,' she said casually.

It was his turn to jump up now as he took in his surroundings again with fresh eyes, 'Oh, my God, really?' His excitement was contagious. She smiled and nodded as she too stood, now feeling fine. The effects of the drug had completely worn off.

'So, you can go anywhere you want, to any time you want?' He continued with his excited chatter for a moment before remembering the situation, clearing his throat, he calmed down as he stood in front of her, 'You know, back at the lab, the professor was acting alone, we really wouldn't do anything to hurt you,' his voice was gentle. She could feel herself relaxing with him as she nodded, 'I know, I saw what happened after he shot me with the dart,' she rubbed her neck, then realised she was dropping her guard, 'I should get you back,' she said stiffly.

'Will you stay for a while, this time?' As his eyes searched hers, he reminded himself that he knew nothing about her; but he found that he didn't care.

'I won't help you,' she sighed.

'You already did. You shut the power off, remember? Who knows where we could've ended up!'

'Then why?' her voice was full of frustration, 'why risk it all; Phoenix are finished, the Time War is over!'

'Because we have to be able to defend ourselves if the technology falls into the wrong hands again,' he said, his tone still gentle.

She shook her head; it seemed this was something they couldn't agree on. So, a mutually unspoken truce was declared, and as neither showed any desire to return to the lab just yet, they sat back down under the shade of the trees.

'Will you tell me where you're from?' He asked.

She wrinkled her nose, 'It's better if I don't.'

'Well, I know you're not from the future cos time travel is outlawed,' he tried to probe, but she didn't answer, 'ok, so are there any others like you who travel through time?'

She sighed, 'Major, please don't ask me things I can't tell you.'

'How're we supposed to get to know each other?' he fixed her gaze.

'We're not. I'll take you back, and that will be the end of it,' she seemed reluctant to the idea. Ben picked up on this and grinned, 'Well, I'll just have to keep messing with time, so you'll show up again.'

'And maybe I'll just leave you to it,' she bluffed.

'Nah, you'll come back. You're not the type of girl to leap through time with a guy and never call.' They laughed together, but Ben's tone was serious now, 'You know they're not gonna stop fooling around with that old timepiece they found until they work it out!'

Tannis went rigid, 'Timepiece? I assumed they were developing their own shoddy technology.'

'I thought you knew and that's why you came back, to take it away with you like in 1933. We found it on some remains in Iraq.'

'Was the strap metal?'

'Yes, just like the one you took back before,' he frowned, there was more to this, he thought.

'What colour was the bezel?' She closed her eyes, and her voice shook a little.

'Gold,' he thought back a moment, 'yeah, it's gold.'

Her hand trembled slightly as it went to her mouth, 'Have you dated the remains yet?'

He could sense her tension, 'Tannis, what's wrong? Did you know this guy? Was he one of yours?'

'It was male?' She gasped.

He nodded as she stood up and walked a few paces, her hands on her hips, her head down. Ben got up and went to her, 'Tannis, what is it?'

She raised her head and faced him, 'Yes I knew him,' she whispered, 'Cole went missing three years ago, Phoenix must've ambushed him.'

'Cole?' On a personal note, he didn't like the sound of that.

'He was my brother,' she said softly.

Ok, he liked the sound of that better.

'If you can get the soil dated, I can go back and save him,' she smiled, her eyes brimming with tears. He liked the sound of that even more as he put his thoughts into words, 'You'll have to come back with me, then.'

She took a deep breath and then exhaled slowly, thinking, 'Ok but I make no promises,' she warned him.

'Then let's go,' he was eager to experience another leap. She nodded and then bit her lip, 'Um we have to be touching for it to work.'

He took her hands in his and stepped closer until they were standing face to face, 'This, ok?' His voice was a little husky now as he pushed the thoughts, he was having about her to the back of his mind. His proximity made her feel things she had never felt before too. She didn't trust her voice to remain steady, so just nodded and they were gone.

They returned to the lab, but 24 hours later, Tannis hoped that the dust had settled a little from the day before. In what was becoming the norm, the armed guards raised their weapons to the incoming threat and were told to stand down by the Admiral who was standing alongside Jack and Dr Hodges. The professor was nowhere to be seen and Tannis was relieved to see that no more attempts were being made with the timepiece. They had appeared on the far side of the lab, she was taking no chances this time; still facing one another, her hands in Ben's when they returned, 'Now if I let go, you'll stay right here?' He smiled as she nodded and followed her gaze towards his superiors, 'Relax, they're good guys. The Colonel's bark is worse than his bite, although I'm not so sure about the Admiral,' he whispered, making her smile again.

Ben then led the way towards them with Tannis by his side. Hennessey and Marsters walked forward as well, and they met in the middle of the room.

'Admiral Hennessey, Colonel Marsters, this is Tannis,' Ben introduced.

'A pleasure, ma'am, and thank you once again for all of your help over the past few days,' Hennessey said, shaking her hand.

Jack and Tannis looked at one another, and then both extended a hand. His grip was firm, not overbearing like some men, 'Colonel,' she nodded curtly.

'Tannis,' he fixed her gaze, but could see no deceit in her eyes 'And it's Jack,' he liked her already, which was unusual for him, people earned his trust; it wasn't handed to them on a plate, one of the reasons he'd stayed alive so long.

Ben explained that Tannis thought the remains they'd found wearing the timepiece might be those of her missing brother and with their help in dating them, she could return and save his life.

'Let's discuss this further in my office, shall we?' Hennessey said as he began walking towards the door. Both Jack and Ben made to follow but stopped as Tannis started to show signs of doubt. Without question, she wanted to save her brother. But at what cost, she wondered? She didn't know these people. Yes, the Major had proved he could be trusted so far back when they were in Kefalonia, but what would they want in return for the information they could give her? She chewed her lip.

Ben turned to her, 'Hey, it's ok, just listen to what the Admiral has to say.'

Jack winked, 'You're alright, if you don't like it you get to disappear, we're stuck with it.'

That made her smile again and they set off together following in the Admiral's wake. It was odd, she thought, she had only just met them, but already felt at ease in their company.

The two men sensed she had the same thoughts they'd had when they had first walked down the dull corridors. She didn't say anything, but they knew.

Inside Hennessey's office, Tannis sat between Jack and Ben, but she moved her chair slightly.

She doesn't like having her back to the door; Jack noted, smart girl.

'Tannis,' Hennessey began, 'I have been in touch with the lab regarding dating the soil samples taken from around your brother's remains, they tell me that such an accurate dating will take approximately a month to conclude,' he steepled his fingers as he rested his elbows on the table, 'I have given the order for them to begin straight away.'

Tannis smiled, 'Thank you, Admiral,' she now waited for a list of requests that she knew she could never fulfil.

'I can see that we must earn your trust, so please accept the dating process as an act of goodwill,' he added.

'Really?' she sat forward in her chair, 'No strings?' She eyed him cautiously.

'No strings,' he assured her.

'I don't know what to say,' her mood lifted now, 'um, except, can you stop messing with Cole's timepiece? It's going to be leaking all over the place, and you're either going to end up blowing a hole in time, or leaving a trail of energy all through it as you pass.'

'Sorry?' Jack sat forward and looked across at her now, 'for those of us time travelling novices in the room, could you say that again slowly and in words with very few syllables?'

She pushed her sleeve up a little now and revealed a platinum bangle watch that she began to fiddle with idly, 'Cole's timepiece will be leaking energy, and if it ruptures it will cause an explosion big enough to tear a hole in time,' she thought of a way to explain, 'time will mix with itself, and it will take me forever to clean the mess up.'

'What about the energy trail?' Ben asked.

'Once I'm in a timeline like this one now, I can't leap from here to say five minutes into the future because the energy from this visit can linger for about 24 hours and it could cause a paradox,' she looked at Jack, 'Bigger bang very bad.'

'Got it,' he nodded slowly.

'So, that's your timepiece?' Ben pointed to her wrist as she fiddled with the bangle.

'Yes, I didn't like the men's ones,' realising she was saying too much she shut up.

'How many of you are there?' Hennessey asked.

'Not as many as before,' was all she was prepared to say.

He didn't push it any further but changed the subject, 'Well Tannis I must leave you with Colonel Marsters and Major Rhodes for now. If you'll excuse me, I have a scientist to throw off base.'

Jack saw that as their cue to leave, as he stood up and walked to the door, Ben followed him with Tannis close behind. Back out in the drab corridor Jack turned to her, 'Well, I would offer you the guided tour, but as you can see, they've had the atmosphere hoover out around the place.'

'The Colonel's right, but the Mess isn't far if you're hungry?' Ben offered.

'I'm thirsty,' she told him.

'To the Mess, then,' Jack grimaced, 'probably just as well you're not hungry. You'd think we were trying to poison you if you tasted any of that muck.'

They laughed as they made their way along the corridor. The Mess was empty inside, so Tannis chose a table where they could be alone if anyone else came in, but also near the door.

'What can I get you, sirs and ma'am?' a young man in kitchen whites asked.

'What do you drink?' Jack asked.

'Tea, Breakfast tea?' she looked up hopefully.

Jack shook his head, 'Sorry, love, there's only a brown sludge they call coffee or hot chocolate.'

She wrinkled her nose at the coffee, 'Chocolate, please Corporal,' she looked at the man in whites rank on his sleeve.

'Same for me and sludge for you Major?' He looked at Ben who nodded.

As the Corporal went to fetch their drinks Jack looked across the table and sighed, 'You know it's hard to think of anything to say to you; that doesn't involve a question you probably won't answer.'

'Sorry,' she shrugged, 'I'm sure the SAS taught you to be the same as did the Marines with you, Major.'

'So, you're military trained?' Jack tilted his head a little to the side.

'No, my father was in the Navy though,' she let slip.

'Which one?' He sat forward.

'One with boats,' she evaded.

'Ships,' Ben corrected.

'Whatever,' she wouldn't reiterate further. The drinks arrived, and the Corporal put them down and left.

'Ah now,' Jack passed Tannis her drink and sniffed his cautiously, 'let's see if you crack under torture,' he took a gulp of his and put the mug back down on the table. Ben drank his coffee without fuss, but Tannis didn't touch hers. Instead, she reached over and picked up Jack's and began to drink it, then shoved her untouched one towards him. 'You don't trust easily, do you?' he admired.

'The places I've been to and the things I've seen have knocked a lot of trust out of me, Colonel.'

'Well, we'll have to work on that won't we Major? And it's Jack,' he reminded her.

Ben looked at Tannis as he spoke, 'Yes sir, we will.'

The Corporal bought them some doughnuts, 'Compliments of cook sir's, ma'am.' Ben picked one up and bit into it. It was delicious. He nodded his approval to Jack, who in turn picked one up for himself; he bit into it, 'Mm, at last something edible,' he mumbled through a full mouth, and then he lifted the plate and offered it to Tannis, 'You don't want one I've just bitten, do you?' She licked her lips but declined, that was when Ben took another and tore a piece from it which he ate, then offered her the rest which she took and ate hungrily licking her fingers clean. 'You are hungry,' Ben frowned and made to rip a piece from another, but this time she took it from him whole and ate it.

'Not the type who watches her weight then?' Jack joked.

'Never know when the next meal is coming sometimes,' she told them, 'Can't be fussy, although these are good.'

'What's it like travelling through time?' Jack asked.

'Don't know any different,' she swallowed.

'It's amazing, sir,' Ben cut in, 'when we left the lab, we travelled back to 5015BC to a Greek island in a blink. It was unreal.'

She smiled as she listened to Ben's description of their trip, when they finished their drinks, Tannis fiddled with her timepiece again; Ben hoped she wasn't planning on leaving anytime soon, he was enjoying her company. Sure, it wasn't as good as being alone with her a few millennia ago, but it was ok for now.

'Colonel, would it be possible to see my brother's remains?' She stopped fiddling and looked at Jack.

'You sure you want to, love? He's been there a while you know,' he said softly.

'Please Jack, I've seen death before,' she used his name for the first time.

'Ok c'mon,' he wasn't sure it was such a good idea, but was interested to see how she handled it, so the three of them left the Mess and headed down the hall.

'How do you find your way around this place? It's all the same,' she frowned as she walked between the two of them.

'Good sense of direction, I guess,' Ben said, 'you must have one; you've had some training,' he observed.

'Not me, my brother Ned says I couldn't find my arse with both hands,' she muttered; both men gave a quick glance at her rear as they continued their journey, Jack jerked his eyes forward as she turned her head towards him slightly.

'So, that's two brothers,' he commented.

'Maybe,' she was evasive again.

They came to a stop outside the door to what Tannis assumed was the infirmary, as it was the only khaki door with a red cross painted on it. Jack opened it and switched on the light as he stepped inside. She looked through the open doorway as best she could, then over her shoulder at Ben; she was checking his position, then she went inside. It was a makeshift morgue; she guessed they never had much use for the real thing at the facility.

The table was in the middle of the room. A green sheet covered what lay beneath. She walked over and stood at its side, Ben picked up a clipboard from the foot of the table and began to read through it as Jack stood at the head and took the sheet between his fingers; he looked at Tannis, she nodded, and he slowly pulled it back revealing the skeletal remains. She didn't flinch, just stared then gently touched the skull it had been smashed in on one side. 'Oh Cole, what did they do to you?' she whispered. After a moment, Jack pulled the sheet back in place as she looked at Ben, 'What does it say?' she motioned to the report he had been reading.

'Wounds consistent with a fall from a great height,' he read aloud then added, 'there was a cliff above the grave.'

Tannis shook her head sadly, 'Thank you both.'

Ben led her out of the room and back into the corridor while Jack switched out the light and closed the door behind him. As the three of them stood there, she began to fiddle with her timepiece again. 'I should be going now, thank you again; I guess I'll see you both in a month, well, a month to you anyways,' she grinned, then stepped away from them slightly, but didn't leap, as the lights in the corridor dimmed for a moment, and then the base alarm sounded. Tannis looked at her timepiece, 'You're testing again,' she cried, 'after all, I told you!'

'Not us, love,' Jack yelled back over the din, then turned to Ben. 'Major, take care of Tannis. I'll find the Admiral and put a stop to this,' and with that, he raced down the corridor ahead of them.

Tannis turned to Ben as the lights flickered and then went out completely. He grabbed her hand in the darkness as he waited a few seconds for the emergency lighting to kick in, which it did, bathing the corridor in an eerie red glow. Still holding her by the hand he led Tannis in the same direction Jack had gone a moment ago, but they hadn't gone far when there was a loud explosion that brought the ceiling down just in front of them, the force was such as to knock them both off their feet. The dust hadn't settled as Ben was helping her up, 'Are you ok?' he coughed.

'Are we under attack?' Her question was answered for her by the sound of automatic weapon fire from above.

Ben un-holstered his sidearm and grabbed her hand again, 'C'mon.' They ran back the way they had come, pausing as they approached a blind corner. Pressing themselves against the wall, he looked cautiously around the bend, 'Clear,' he confirmed as they stepped out and continued, again only managing a short distance before shots rang out. Ben pulled her behind him and raised his weapon, but there was nothing to aim at, the corridor was empty 'What the...?' he couldn't understand it.

Tannis stood by the wall, she had shoved her finger in a small hole, 'Musket balls, Major.'

'From where?' he frowned.

'Them!' she shouted as four men dressed as colonial trappers raced towards them trying to reload their firearms. Ben took aim. 'No, Major, we can't kill them! We don't know who they are. We could alter history,' she yelled as she ran towards them.

'Damn it!' he cursed as he holstered his sidearm and ran after her.

Tannis reached two of the trappers and kicked out, knocking the first's weapon to the ground. Then she spun around, kicking out again, and sending him falling unconscious alongside it. When Ben reached his two, he grabbed the nearest man's musket, snatched it from him, and jabbed him in the face with the butt. One down; the second had reloaded and made ready to fire, but before he could discharge Ben ducked down and using the musket he still held, took the man's legs from under him, as he lay flat on his back, Ben jumped up and again jabbed his opponent in the face with the butt, game over. He turned to see how Tannis was getting on with her second target, but he was already on the floor out cold too. 'Where did you learn to do that?' he shouted, then raised his hands in mock surrender, 'don't say it; you can't tell me.'

He grabbed her hand, and they ran on to the lab, bursting through the door just in time to see Professor Jennings disappear holding the timepiece. As he did the alarm stopped and all fell silent except for Tannis, 'Shit!'

'I was more expecting I told you so, but either way, you said it all really,' Jack agreed as he walked towards them. Ben reluctantly let go of her hand as she stepped away from them now.

'I have to find him,' she said, looking from one man to the other, but stopped and looked around the room as did they all. The walls were disappearing around them again, as were some of the people and equipment this time. 'He's changing history,' Tannis told them as more people began to vanish from the room, 'all of this will cease to exist,' she took off her timepiece and reset it, then she grabbed Ben's hand and pressed it into his palm.

'No,' he tried to give it back to her, 'what about you?'

'I'll be fine. You grab the Admiral, then press this,' she showed him a button at the side of the timepiece, 'I'll get Jack out,' she shoved him towards Hennessey. 'Trust me, go!' she shouted. He reluctantly did as she asked and grabbed the Admiral's arm. 'Sorry, sir,' he pushed the button, and they were gone.

The ground beneath them grew unstable as Jack turned to Tannis, 'Now what? We're a timepiece short of a leap!'

'Hang on to me!' she yelled as she threw her arms around his neck. He grabbed her around the waist and felt himself falling backwards.

Crash! He landed on a hard, metallic surface, Tannis on top of him; they were nose to nose, 'Thanks for the soft landing, Jack.'

'Anytime,' he groaned as she rolled off him and onto her back. Looking up he could see Ben and the Admiral standing a short step away from them, their hands raised and looking towards a figure in the shadows. The only part visible of the person they were looking at was the handgun aimed at them.

'It's ok, Ned, you can put it away. They're friends,' Tannis closed her eyes, seemingly tired as she made no effort to get up. The weapon was lowered, Ben and Hennessey slowly put their hands down as out into the light stepped Ned. He looked a little sheepish as Tannis raised herself on to her elbows, 'Ned, my God!'

The visitors looked a little awkward too as Ned came into full view. He was wearing a black leather knee-length skirt, black knee-high boots and a red leather basque covered slightly with a black cardigan. He had also accessorised with diamond drop earrings and a diamond necklace, 'I didn't think you'd mind,' he mumbled, shamefaced.

'That necklace was a gift from Wellington,' she chastised as she got to her feet offering Jack a hand in the process.

'I know, but you let mine go down with the Lusitania,' he haggled.

'I had other things on my mind at the time!' she gave him a frank stare, 'oh, keep it anyway it looks better on you; besides, when would I ever wear it?' She kissed him lightly on the cheek and turned to their three guests.

'So, dear sister, would you like to fill me in on what the hell is happening? Your mission was to find out what they were up to and stop it, not invite them round for tea!' he glowered at her, 'and now it seems that all of history is changing.' As he said this Tannis looked over his shoulder at two monitors on the wall behind him and grimaced a little, then perked up, 'Oh, look! No Hitler,' then remembered herself. 'Oh, it's nothing, just some nut job,' she said excitedly. 'Ned, they found Cole's body, they can date the remains, and I can go back and save him!' her enthusiasm ran away with her a little.

Ned raised his hands to calm her but looked at the three men, 'Is this true?'

Hennessey nodded, 'It was up until our timeline ceased to exist.' Tannis remembered herself now and made the introductions.

Hennessey brought Ned up to speed with the preceding events, and he listened attentively, occasionally chastising Tannis with a glare as he was told about her accepting an invitation to discuss things with them in the Admiral's office, and even more so when he found out, she went to the Mess.

Ned was wary of strangers, but he gave them the benefit of the doubt. Tannis was a good judge of character, of that, he was sure. After all, he'd known her since she was born.

As the two men were talking, Jack and Ben took in their surroundings. They were on board a ship, Navy specifically, and it wasn't a modern one either. They seemed to be in the comms room, but it was not like any they'd ever seen before. As if to contradict the surroundings, most of the equipment was far advanced. For instance, the screens Tannis had looked at when Ned had told her about the time changes were both showing scripts, in English, one was constant, telling them what should be happening in the world, the other screen showed them what they assumed to be the changes that were taking place. Tannis joined them, keen to get away from Ned's narrow-eyed glances, she pointed to the screens and confirmed their suspicions, 'True timeline and altered,' she told them.

Ned and Hennessey moved over to them now, Ned possibly concerned how much she was telling them.

'So, Ned, now that the Admiral has filled you in, is there any chance you might tell us when and where we are?' Jack looked him directly in the eyes, 'I'm guessing Navy, U.S. by the looks of it.'

'Perhaps it would be easier to explain if we went up on deck gentlemen,' Ned offered, and he led the way. As they walked through the passageways and up the stairs, it became apparent that the ship was deserted.

Emerging up on deck it took a little while for their eyes to adjust to the bright sunlight. But once they did as they stood alongside the deck rail, they were afforded a stunning view of a small harbour, that was home to a handful of small fishing vessels, which upon as close an inspection as was possible were newly built, but to an old design neither man had seen before except maybe in history books. The houses around the harbour and nestled in the hills above looked like Roman villas.

Tannis looked at Ned who just shrugged, 'They'll never believe it.'
'After the day we've had, try us!' Hennessey cut in. Ned drew a deep breath, 'Ok gentlemen, this,' he gestured towards the harbour, 'is the island of Atlantis and as for the ship you're standing on...' he pointed to the nameplate mounted on the bridge behind them which read USS Eldridge. The three guests remained silent. 'Told you,' Ned raised a painted eyebrow at his sister. 'I think you'd better start at the beginning, Ned' Hennessey folded his arms.

They all went below decks again, but this time into a large dining room where there was enough space for them all to sit around a huge oval table.

'You're familiar with *The Philadelphia Experiment*?' Ned looked at them expectantly, and his audience nodded, 'well, when The Eldridge disappeared from the Navy Yard,' he held a hand out palm up, 'it reappeared here,' he held the opposite hand the same way now. 'To avoid being burned some of the crew jumped into the sea. As the local fishermen pulled them from the water, The Eldridge went back to 1943 leaving them trapped here.'

'There are crew here from The Eldridge?' Hennessey was intrigued. Ned continued, 'There were six of them in total Admiral, and when it became obvious, they would never return to their own time most of them settled down and married some local ladies. Between them they had seven children, Tannis and myself included.

We call ourselves brothers and sisters, but only Will and Em were biological siblings. We were all raised very close though.'

Jack looked across the table at the two of them as Tannis sat next to Ned, 'So, you're part American, part Atlantean?' He tried to get his head around it.

'No, Colonel, that brings me to the part where almost all of the crew married local ladies,' Ned looked at Tannis now, he knew she hated being talked about, especially what was to come; she bit her lip nervously. 'Tannis' father never bothered with the local women,' Ned shrugged, 'not sure what he was looking for I suppose until she showed up,' he thought to himself for a moment and then continued. 'The crew had been on Atlantis for about two years when Catherine arrived. She didn't make such a grand entrance as The Eldridge, she was more discreet, she had one of these,' he rolled up his sleeve to reveal his timepiece. Its design surprised the three men sitting opposite. It was masculine; Ned noticed their expressions as they looked at it, 'On missions, we all have to dress appropriately to time and place,' he was used to this by now.

Tannis smiled to herself, as the three men tried to shrug off Ned's comment casually.

'Anyway, the gorgeous gal bowled Tannis' dad off his feet, even when he found out the truth about her,' Ned leaned closer now, 'you see, Catherine was from *The Phoenix Project*. I assume you've heard of them too. But she was one with a bit of a conscience, though. She didn't hold with their plan for time domination; so, when the opportunity arose, she grabbed a timepiece and made a run for it, apparently locking on to the energy trail from The Eldridge. She thought she was going back to 1943 to stop the first experiment, therefore cancelling out Phoenix in the future, but she wound up here. Everything was rosy for a while, Tannis was born, life went on, and the years rolled by until a couple of Phoenix thugs showed up. There was a terrible fight, all but two of the crew were killed, my father and Tannis' were the only ones to survive. Tannis' mother, you see… Catherine had been trained well,' he felt Tannis stir uncomfortably at his side, 'she could handle herself in a fight. She had been subject to the full force of Phoenix's experiments, altered at DNA level, enhanced strength, stamina, her metabolism ran faster than normal so her body could heal itself quickly, but the sinister part was her ability to control people's thoughts and actions. There's a saying *if looks could kill*, well she had that power too.'

Tannis felt uncomfortable now as all eyes were on her, 'Where are your parents now?' Ben finally spoke.

'My parents along with Ned's father took it upon themselves to finish Phoenix once and for all, so they took the timepieces from the two dead agents and leaped to 1983. They destroyed *The Phoenix Project*, although some got away and hid in the past. We never saw our folks after that day.'

'Well, at least one of them made it as somebody passed on the file to Congress. So, where are they?' Jack looked from Tannis to Ned.

It was Ned who explained, 'Some of the Phoenix filth leaped to the future. Our folks followed them to try and put things right there too. Which they did but then wound up stuck there.'

'And to stop Phoenix making any more leaps into the future, the powers that be there altered the earth's electrical fields slightly in 2021 so that no one can leap forward anymore,' Tannis added.

'So how did The Eldridge end up here? Last I heard of in our time it was sold to the Greek Navy for scrap,' Hennessey questioned.

'Who knows, this could even be a copy,' Ned shrugged, 'all we know is that one day, there was a big blue flash, and Atlantis was removed from the real world and hurled three and a half thousand years into the future to run with the timeline you come from, and there was The Eldridge docked ready and waiting carrying seven timepieces, one for each of *The Eldridge Brats* with instructions from our folks telling us that we were now the caretakers of the past, and it was our job to take care of whatever Phoenix agents were left!'

'Where are the other four?' Jack had only accounted for three. 'Our brothers and sisters are all dead, only Tannis and I survived the final battle with Phoenix.'

'And that ended how?' Hennessey was direct.

'With them being blasted into another dimension with no way back,' Tannis snapped, agitated now, she got up and paced the room, 'I need some air, excuse me,' she said sharply as she left.

Making sure she was safely out of earshot Ned confided, 'It's still raw for her, and it doesn't help to talk about her mother, you see

Tannis got most of mommy's powers and then some, so she hates to be made to feel different, it's kept her alone all her life.'

'Mommy's powers and then some, care to elaborate on that?' Jack probed.

'Did you not wonder how she brought you back here when she had given Major Rhodes her timepiece?' Ned smiled.

'I dunno. I thought maybe she had a spare,' Jack muttered.

'The six of us needed our timepieces to travel with, Tannis wears hers to remember her parents. She doesn't need it.'

'Tannis has the ability to travel through time under her own volition?' Hennessey was aghast.

Ned sighed, 'In for a penny in for a pound,' he rubbed his hand over his mouth as he muttered, 'dimensions too.'

'Dimensions!' It was Jack's turn now.

'Can the timepieces do that?' Ben looked at Tannis' as he held it in his hand.

'No, only she can do that,' Ned paused for a moment, 'and she is only immune to Phoenix mind powers. She doesn't have the power to control or kill others. Tannis has had a hard time of it, gentlemen. You know if she may seem a little standoffish, it's because she's had to grow a thick skin. When people here found out about all this, she was treated like a freak for some time.'

Ben looked at the timepiece in his hand, how looks could be deceiving he thought, this little watch seemed so innocent, but look at what it could do; the same applied to Tannis it was a lot to think about.

'One more thing, Ned,' Jack piped up again. 'When we left the base, time was changing, so why is everything still the same here?'

'Well done, Colonel,' Ned admired his thought. 'An excellent question and one I'm afraid I cannot answer. I believe it has something to do with The Eldridge's power source, which is beyond my comprehension. Another gift from the future. It seems to have moved Atlantis from the world allowing us to exist alongside it; our timeline runs true no matter what happens in the real world, and it also only allows us to leap in and out. Phoenix can't touch us here.'

'Thank you for being so honest with us Ned, I realise how difficult it must be having strangers asking such personal questions,' Hennessey said genuinely, 'and now we have been read into the way things go on here; perhaps we can work together to put things right out there.'

Ned nodded, 'I'll show you the time screens then we should sit down and work back through history to see where the changes began.' They all stood to leave the room as Ned continued, 'You'll have to give me a brief background on the target, I'm only used to tracking Phoenix, and each one of them had their own annoying bloody habits to screw with time,' he grumbled as they headed back towards the comms room.

Once there, Ned explained the time screens to Hennessey pretty much the same way Tannis had done with Jack and Ben, but with a lot more technical banter thrown in. 'Seems straightforward enough,' the Admiral mused.

'Oh, this part's the not so bad bit, it's the killing and people trying to kill us that pisses me off,' Ned's sarcasm did not go unnoticed so Hennessey addressed Ben instead, 'Major Rhodes, perhaps you should find Tannis and return her timepiece, see that she is alright now.'

'Yes sir,' Ben answered his superior and as he walked along the passage towards the stairs that would lead him up on deck, he thought about Tannis, and all that Ned had told them. He had been attracted to her from the first time he saw her, but now things were different, and it had nothing to do with her powers; they were going to be working together, and that put a different complexion on things.

He blinked for a couple of seconds as he walked out on deck, then he saw her standing as far forward as she could get, looking out to sea, letting the breeze blow freely through her hair.

She knew he was behind her, but then he had made no effort to be quiet. 'Big pow-wow finished?' she asked over her shoulder.

Ben moved closer standing next to her now, 'The Admiral and Colonel Marsters are giving Ned a profile on Jennings to try and help track him down.'

'Ned'll find him!' Tannis said with complete conviction, 'and then we can go back and put things right, and all will be well with the world,' she sighed heavily as if bored with the task.

He held out his hand now to return her timepiece, 'Thanks for what you did back there.'

She looked at it and pursed her lips, 'He told you, didn't he?'
'Yeah,' he looked directly ahead now.

'So, you still want to keep messing with time, so I'll show up again?' she stared straight ahead too.

'We're gonna be working together,' he began.

'Thought not,' she said sharply as she turned and walked away. 'Oh well done, Major, you idiot,' he hissed when he heard her slam the hatch as she went below. He remained on deck looking over towards the harbour, the sun was sitting lower on the horizon now, and he just wanted to give her a chance to get back to the comms room before he followed. He allowed his thoughts to drift for a moment but was alerted to the sound of the door opening again.

'Major?' It was Jack.

Ben straightened up and turned to face his CO, 'Sir?'

'The Admiral said to check she was ok, not send her back down in a worse mood than when she left! What did you say to her?' he joked.

'I didn't say anything, sir,' he replied thinking that was the whole problem.

'Hmm, glad she's on our side,' Jack mused, 'she really could knock you into next week if she didn't like you,' he looked at his subordinate now as they both leaned on the rail, he wasn't blind, he'd seen the way the two of them had been looking at one another, the way they acted around each other, 'I want you focused on the mission Major, clear?'

'Yes sir,' Ben said firmly.

'Good, now come on, we'd best see what they've found out so far.'

The two men went below deck and joined the others, Ned and Hennessey were pouring over a pile of books on the table, still no further forward. Tannis was leaning her back against the wall, arms folded across her chest looking extremely bored.

Ned turned to her, 'Tannis, this is going to take the best part of the night, nip to mine and tell Elea I won't be home,' he turned back to the table, then as an after-thought, 'oh and get some grub.'

Tannis, still leaning against the wall raised an eyebrow, 'My life is so glamorous,' then the small blue flash and she was gone.

'That is so cool,' Ben whispered to Jack, who could only nod in reply.

'Hang on a minute; I thought you couldn't make multiple leaps in the same place?' Jack turned to Ned. 'Oh, here we can, another gift from The Eldridge, really handy, kids are never late for school. We can't leap back though in case we bump into ourselves, paradox and the like you know,' he mumbled as he buried his head in the book he was reading once more.

Ben walked over to the table now, 'Ned, the first time I made a leap with Tannis, I felt fine, but this time when I came through with the Admiral, I felt a little disorientated, nauseous even?'

'Me, too,' the Admiral agreed.

'And apart from having my sister land on top of you, you felt fine Colonel?'

'Well, yes,' Jack agreed.

'Tannis hardly ever uses her timepiece to leap. When she leapt with you both, she was using her own power. It doesn't have the same effect,' he looked at them all, 'don't worry, your bodies will soon get used to it. It's a lot like getting your sea legs.' Another thought struck him, 'Oh, one more thing, if she uses her powers too much, for example leaping to another dimension, it can drain her for a day or so, or like when she brought you back from a changing timeline Colonel, it makes her weak for a short time.'

The little blue flash a split second before she appeared again alerted them to change the subject, they turned to see her holding two huge hampers full of food and drink; Jack and Ben took one each, 'Thanks,' she smiled, then looked at Ned as he came over to check out the food, 'Elea says get your arse home a.s.a.p. when you're done. No leaping or she'll kill you herself, and your five youngest are in bed, and she sends you this…' Tannis stepped up and gave him a quick kiss on the lips, after which they both wiped their mouths with the backs of their hands, and Ned sat back down with the Admiral. Tannis followed Jack and Ben into the dining room where they had held their meeting earlier, the two men put the baskets on the table and began to unpack the cartons of food as Tannis laid out plates and glasses.

'So, Ned and Elea are married?' Jack tried to keep the surprise out of his voice.

Tannis nodded, 'Yep childhood sweethearts, married when they were nineteen,' she told them.

'So, if his five youngest are in bed, how many kids do they have?' Ben asked in surprise.

'Nine,' she replied politely enough, it wasn't his fault she thought; it was just life, she softened her tone towards him, 'Elea had a lot to put up with. Just after they were married, we were sent to fight Phoenix, and she went through hell not knowing if he was ever going to survive.'

'Did none of the others have anyone special?' Jack stepped back as she moved in front of him to reach in the basket.

'None of us expected to survive, so the others shall we say lived for the moment,' she busied herself once more.

'And you?' Ben was glad it was Jack who'd asked.

Tannis laughed, 'Colonel, my brothers and sisters were all between 19 and 21 when we were sent to fight Phoenix.'

'That would've made you…' Ben didn't have time to finish.

'I was 15 and had three really overprotective brothers,' she gave a small smile, 'and as I got older, I just couldn't see myself having flings with people I knew were going to die, or belonged in another time,' for a brief moment, she made eye contact with Ben.

'You were 15 when you made your first leap?' Hennessey was standing in the doorway with Ned now.

'No Admiral, Tannis was a toddler when she made her first leap, frightened the life out of her parents and kept them on their toes for years to come,' he grinned at his sister now, 'the teenage years were particularly entertaining. She blasted our brother Will into the next room when he read her diary.'

Tannis narrowed her eyes at Ned, 'And still can!'

'Big mistake reading your sister's diary, believe me,' Jack shook his head at a painful memory.

'Tannis, how do you blast someone?' Hennessey was always fact-finding.

She raised an eyebrow at him, 'When I lose my temper usually.'

'Tannis has had sound training over the years Admiral. It takes a lot for her to lose her temper big style,' Ned grinned at Hennessey, who seemed to be wondering if he was going to be the target of a demonstration.

Getting back to his question, Ben asked again, 'But you were 15 when you were sent to fight?'

She didn't feel comfortable with all the attention again, 'Yes.'

Ned sensed her mood, 'We were all trained by her parents from the moment we could walk and talk, didn't have a childhood did we, sweetheart, they had to teach us how to look after ourselves just in case, or more likely because they knew something was coming.'

'Not exactly an all-American upbringing,' Hennessey disapproved.

'I'm not all-American,' Tannis put in.

'Oh, I'm sorry, you see yourself as an Atlantean?' he asked her. 'Never thought about that. I suppose so, but what I meant was my mother is English. Phoenix recruited her from Oxford University.'

'Thank God, I was beginning to feel a bit left out,' Jack smiled his approval, 'but if you were such a pain in the arse to Phoenix, why didn't they just go back in time and kill your parents when they were kids, so you never existed?'

'Oh, they can't do that, we can't exist without one another. No experiment; no Phoenix or us. Even the slightest time change there could alter the future,' Ned explained.

The rest of the meal was, under the circumstances, a pleasant one. They all made small talk about their childhoods apart from the Admiral, of course, some distance had to be maintained.

Tannis poked at some of her food now, 'Oh God Ned have you been cooking again?' She dropped the container on the table and investigated further.

'I'll have you know my chocolate covered prawns went down well at the last party,' he huffed.

'They came back up pretty quick too if I remember correctly,' she shuddered.

'Philistine,' he took a drink to hide a smile.

She picked something out of the container with her fork, 'This is a weird baby sweet corn!' she held it up.

'That's because it's a tentacle.'

'That's disgusting,' she shoved the container away as their three guests cautiously checked their food.

'You're safe,' she told them, 'Elea marks the containers Ned's food is in,' she showed them the lid with a black spot on, 'should be skull and crossbones,' she grumbled then stood up.

'And where might you be off to?' Ned raised an eyebrow. 'Shoes,' she replied looking down at her bare feet. 'Because?' Her brother had an idea what was coming.

'Because I'm going to see what cake they have in the new timeline.'

Ned shook his head, 'Don't even think about it, not while we're the first, last and only…. Again!'

She folded her arms across her chest and raised her head defiantly.

'The words if it pleases your royal highness never come into an order,' he threw her another container, which she checked for a label and once satisfied, sat back down and began to eat.

Hennessey and Jack were both impressed how Tannis immediately stood down when given an order, she showed excellent strength of character.

After the meal, Ned and the Admiral made their way back to the comms room to continue their research. Before he left, her brother gave Tannis instructions to show Jack and Ben to the crew's quarters, adding that *'they should get some sleep before the mission.'*

'And remember we have guests, keep the music down, and preferably contained to your own room,' Ned called over his shoulder as he heard them making their way towards the crew passage once used by The Eldridge Brats.

Tannis just rolled her eyes and sighed as she led the way. A row of doors faced one another, 'Take whichever you like, seven's mine, though!' she called over her shoulder as she carried on a little further.

'Lucky seven?' Jack thought out loud.

'No just the baby of the bunch,' she rested her forehead against the door as the sadness washed over her.

'You live on board alone?' Ben was surprised.

'Yeah, big for one person, I know, but Ned has a family. He can't be expected to live on a boat.'

'Ship,' they both corrected her.

'Whatever, I stay on board just to keep an eye on things,' she sighed and folded her arms across her chest as she turned to face them, 'Not a peep in three years and then you lot go and throw a spanner in the works, goodnight,' she went inside, 'Eldridge playlist 9 please, and contain to my quarters,' as she closed the door *Crowded House - Don't Dream It's Over* began to play.

Jack took the first door and Ben the one next to it, they said their goodnights and turned in, although neither expected to get much sleep. Jack lay on his bed; his arms folded behind his head and closed his eyes as he exhaled slowly, 'Bloody hell, Jack, what have you got yourself into this time,' he said to himself. In the next room, Ben also lay down, he kept his eyes open and chewed the inside of his mouth, then shook his head and sat up, he couldn't even try to sleep.

An hour or so later, sleep still evaded him, he lay down and tried to close his eyes, but they flicked open as he heard movement in the passageway outside his door, he heard a quiet knock, then Ned's voice 'Tannis, dining room now!' His voice was harsh. Hearing Ned walk away and a short time later Tannis padding along too, he gave her the chance to get clear, then quietly opened his door, simultaneously it seemed with Jack, they both looked at each other.

'She's in for a bollocking for saving us,' Jack whispered. Ben nodded, and they both set off towards the dining room.

They could hear Ned as they got closer, 'What the bloody hell were you thinking bringing people back!'

'I didn't see you object earlier Ned, you were very forthcoming about what we do here, so don't tell me the same thought hadn't occurred to you either,' she raised her voice right back at him.

'I don't know what you mean,' he lied, 'I just want to help get Cole back.'

'No,' she cried 'I'm tired, Ned. I can't do this anymore. They're out there now experimenting with time travel. You know what will come next. Another time war with a new enemy. I can't fight on my own and I won't. Why can't we join with them or let them take over for all I care?'

'Our parents entrusted us with this job, how can you even think that,' he yelled back.

'Our parents abandoned us and condemned us to death, Ned!' her voice cracked, 'what happens when I'm killed out there? Who's left?' Tears ran down her face now.

Ned rushed over and wrapped his arms around her, she held on to him, 'I know' he soothed, 'I'm sorry.' They stood like that for a while, then Ned kissed her on top of the head, 'I'll think about it ok, let's just get this mission out of the way first!'

Jack knocked on the open door, and he and Ben stepped inside. Ned looked at them as he held his sister, then stepped away from her 'Gentlemen we need time to think,' he said as he left the room.

Tannis turned her back to them as she wiped her eyes, then faced them once more, she was in her pyjamas which consisted of loose-fitting cotton bottoms and a tight crop top, she shivered now and wrapped her arms around herself, 'Goodnight again,' she said quietly as she made for the door.

'Tannis,' Jack called after her, 'You think there'll be another time war?'

She turned back to them, 'Human nature Jack, the professor's already at it, it won't end with him; then the time will come again when we have to choose a side and fight,' with that she left.

Chapter Two

Next morning Jack and Ben made their way to the comms room, it was empty though, so the next port of call was the dining room where they found Ned and Hennessey eating breakfast. 'Good morning, gentlemen,' Hennessey greeted them as did Ned, 'Tannis is up on deck,' Ned told them, 'It's her favourite place right at the pointy bit as she calls it, she'll be along later, she said she was going to the Sim for a bit as she's grounded.'

Just as Ned finished his sentence *Elevation by U2* began to play loudly from somewhere forward of them.

'Hmm Spitfire would be her weapon of choice this morning then,' he muttered as he set to his breakfast once more.

'Sim?' Jack gave Ned a questioning look.

'Spitfire?' Ben was intrigued, he really liked those planes.

'Simulator,' Ned mumbled his mouth half full of bacon, he finished chewing and swallowing he continued, 'as you can imagine we had to learn to fly and drive most things,' he shoved his empty plate away, 'Eldridge, Sim on screen,' he commanded and instantly on the wall in front of them they saw Tannis flying a Spitfire, but it wasn't like any simulation they had ever seen, it looked as though she was actually flying the real thing, then suddenly her squadron came under attack from German Messerschmitt's.

Tannis broke right as her cockpit canopy was sprayed with bullets, she took a head wound, 'Bastard,' she cursed calmly as she opened fire on one of the attackers, sending him down in a ball of flames.

'She's hurt!' Ben couldn't help sounding concerned.

'She'll heal,' her brother looked at the three men in turn, 'the rest of us never had that luxury.'

'How real does it get?' Hennessey was riveted.

'Oh, just minor cuts and bruises, it's the Sim's way of making you pay attention, although I don't doubt Aunt Catherine had something to do with that,' Ned's reply was tinged with a hint of bitterness, which did not go unnoticed.

The three guests watched in awe as Tannis threw the plane about like a pro, she made 2 kills and saved many in her squadron.

'Eldridge, turn the bloody music down,' Ned rolled his eyes, then added, 'and throw her a curve ball while you're at it, get this over with.'

Upon command, she had one on her tail that she couldn't shake, she pulled up as hard as she could, struggling to breathe and stay conscious.

'She's gonna stall,' Ben spoke as a qualified pilot.

'That's usually her intention,' Ned tutted as he folded his arms across his chest and waited for the inevitable.

A small trickle of blood ran from her nose as the engine cut out and the plane went into free fall, her pursuer no doubt suffering the same fate, as the Messerschmitt also began to fall to the earth.

Tannis fought with the controls as the ground loomed ever closer. 'Come on, come on,' she breathed heavily, then with moments to spare, the engine restarted, and she pulled up out of the dive. Her assailant wasn't so lucky; her plane had heavy damage though, so she put it down quickly with no landing gear, back at what those watching assumed was the airfield that she took off from.

The simulation ended as she jumped out of the wrecked plane, wiping the blood from her nose and her head wound.

The wall behind her lit up, and she read the information it offered; mostly it was criticising her pushing the plane too hard when it was close to structural failure. Tannis stood hands on her hips, looking rather pissed off, 'Bullshit, you're too textbook, any half decent flyer knows the limits of their machine.'

Back in the dining room Ben had to agree, 'She's right,' he shook his head, 'and she's one hell of a pilot.'

The wall chastised her again, 'Yeah, well it works for me, then again, I'm one of the chosen few for your suicide squad, aren't I?'

The wall tried to rebuke her for her last comment, but this time she ignored it, 'You really are the epitome of talking to a fucking wall! Eldridge playlist track 14!' *Here I Go Again* by *Whitesnake* played loudly and Tannis raised her middle finger to the wall as she turned and left the room.

'Girl's got sass,' Hennessey didn't even try to hide the admiration in his voice, or in his expression for that matter, 'has she always been…'

Ned didn't need to let him finish his sentence, he knew what the Admiral was going to ask, it was standard as far as his sister was concerned, 'Oh yes, from the moment she could walk and talk, Tannis has been willful and defiant, but also dependable and loyal, she always followed her orders, and fought with the courage of a lion to protect us; and thank God she has a pure soul,' he looked from one man to the other now as he admitted. 'Tannis has the power that Phoenix wanted more than anything, they tried cloning and even natural conception to bring another like her into the world, but it always failed. Meg recovered a data stick one time on a mission, it seems that the Phoenix scientists believe that something happened to Tannis' father during the experiment, a possible DNA change, which when mixed with the DNA of Aunt Catherine, a fully-fledged Phoenix agent produced my baby sister.'

'She really is a force of nature,' Hennessey admitted.

Ned nodded, 'But that's all it is gentlemen, nature, Tannis is no different to any of us, maybe just a rung or two higher on the evolutionary ladder is all.'

'Good morning,' she smiled at them all as she entered the room and grabbed herself a mug of tea and some fruit, only then noticing the screen on the wall, 'For Christ's sake Ned!'

Her brother just shrugged, 'Had to explain the noise.'

'So, you can fly or drive anything?' Hennessey could see the potential of such a piece of equipment and thought it best to change the subject.

'Well, the capability is there, but we mostly just used it to learn evasive driving manoeuvres and how to control a few aircraft that we'd come up against, oh and the odd tank,' Ned admitted, 'but madam over there went full on fighter pilot during *The Battle of Britain*.'

Tannis, who was now seated in a recliner chair rolled her eyes as she cradled her mug of tea, 'Just helping out,' she replied whilst giving her brother the benefit of her sweetest smile.

'Wow, what else have you flown?' Ben was impressed.

'Lancaster's, Wellington's; a couple of Mustangs, a few helicopters too, you know this and that,' she replied honestly.

'Actually, there's one of your Apache's knocking around somewhere, that Tannis never returned,' Ned told the Admiral.

Tannis glared at her brother, 'And how was I supposed to do that? Oh, hi guys, I'm a time traveller, and I borrowed your attack helicopter to blow the crap out of some arseholes that were going to alter time, mission accomplished so you can have it back now, cheers!'

'Fair point.' Her brother acquiesced, then got back to reason for their guests' visit, 'talking of arseholes wanting to change time,' he gestured his hand toward the Admiral to give them the news.

Hennessey looked from his men to Tannis as he spoke, 'You will be pleased to know that we have managed to trace Jennings.'

'It seems our dear professor has decided to go back to the beginning to change things,' Ned told them. Tannis picked up her mug of tea and began to drink, *'how could she be so casual about it all?'* Jack thought to himself, they were discussing saving the world, and there she was curled up on a recliner drinking tea, it was surreal.

Ned continued, 'He's gone back to Bethlehem for the B.C./A.D. handover.'

'He wants to control religion?' Tannis mused, 'that's a new one.' 'How much power would that bring? Then he can leap forward and reap the benefits of whatever he set in motion,' Ned fiddled with his timepiece, 'we should be able to track him when we get there, Cole's timepiece will be leaking all over the place, it should give us a good trail to follow,' he paused to explain, 'we have equipment on board to monitor our timepieces should they get damaged, I've tweaked one up a bit to work long range, well up to a couple of miles at least, it's vital we get it back before he tries another leap, if it breaches the effects will be catastrophic.'

'What's our cover?' Tannis asked quietly.

'Three brothers, one wife off to register, you know, the Christmas story,' he looked at them all.

'Oh no, you're retired!' Tannis shook her head.

'Needs must dear sister.'

'No, we can't both go, it's too risky, besides Elea will kill you,' Tannis banged her mug down on the table spilling some of its contents.

'You need me out there, the Colonel and the Major may be good at their jobs, but they aren't trained in the culture and you being a woman won't be able to help them if you run into a problem,' he knew she couldn't argue with that.

So, after breakfast Tannis led them down to one of the holds, inside it was like a vast costume department, consisting of clothes, weapons and any other items they may need throughout history.

They chose the clothing appropriate for the day. The robes for the men were a dull light brown colour, nothing to make them stand out or look like a wealthy target. Tannis would dress similarly. Her outfit was brown with a cream coloured over shawl. She picked it up and grabbed a pair of leather sandals, then went to the weapons side of the room where she picked up an assortment of knives and daggers. She piled them on top of her clothes and left to change in her quarters.

Ned stood with Jack and Ben as they now selected their weapons, he saw them look over toward the firearms, 'Sorry gentlemen, if it comes down to it, we will have to fight hand to hand. Can't take the chance of a future dig finding a 2000-year-old bullet, can we?'

'Guess not,' Ben agreed reluctantly. Once Ned had given his approval to their choice of weapons, they went to their respective quarters to change and be ready in the forward hold to leave in 15 minutes.

Hennessey was waiting for them as they filed in a quarter of an hour later, Ned adjusted Tannis' shawl, she had to cover as much of her hair and face as possible. He then walked over to a grey metal locker that was fixed to the wall. It was opened by iris recognition as he looked into a small lit sensor on the door. Inside were timepieces designed for males and females, Hennessey peered in, 'I was only expecting to see four timepieces, Ned, there are dozens here?'

'When we get the opportunity to kill a Phoenix agent, we make sure and take the timepiece, if at all possible,' he looked at Hennessey now, 'it's not a trophy cabinet Admiral, it doesn't make us feel good when we open it and see them all. We can't afford to leave these things lying around. Just look at the mess we're in now,' he said dryly as he removed two of the timepieces before securing the door.

'Speak for yourself!' Tannis said under her breath, Jack and Ben standing either side of her said nothing, but they were impressed with the haul.

Ned came over now with the timepieces and gave one each to Jack and Ben, 'You really should have the training to use these, but needs must, Tannis and I will set them for you, just don't fiddle with them and keep them covered, remember watches haven't been invented yet where we're going.'

The four stood together now ready to go, Ned set Jack's timepiece for him, giving him a few last-minute tips as he did so.

Tannis turned to Ben, she held his wrist as she set his timepiece, 'You've done this before, so you know what to expect,' she kept her focus on the timepiece as she spoke. Ben was looking at her though, he couldn't stop himself, and as she finished, she looked up at him, he held her gaze. 'Thank you,' he said softly.

'Tannis?' Ned was uneasy about something she sensed as she looked across at him. 'We've never made a leap like this before, with so much residual energy knocking about, I'm not sure how the timepieces will react, we could overshoot or get separated. It may be for the best if you take us through,' he said as he powered down Jack's timepiece.

'Ok,' she agreed as Ben lifted his wrist for her, she made a small adjustment to the dial and his timepiece powered down too, but she didn't leave it at that, she made another change, 'If Ned and I don't make it, this will bring you back here, just grab Jack,' she whispered.

Ben looked at her again; a small frown furrowed his brow, 'We're all coming back, this is just the beginning,' he too lowered his voice.

'Ready?' Ned looked across to his sister now, the four of them stood facing the Admiral, who nodded proudly and said only, 'Good luck people!' He didn't need to tell them how much depended on the outcome of this mission.

Ned took a firm grip on Jack's arm, Tannis took Jack's hand in hers and held tight, then she slipped her other hand in Ben's holding tightly to him too, she felt him squeeze her hand, and she smiled a little, then took a breath and closed her eyes.

Next thing they knew they were standing in the burning heat of the desert; Ned released his grip on Jack and took the tracking device from his pack. Tannis let go of their hands and sat down slowly. 'She'll be ok in a minute,' Ned muttered as he tried to get a fix on the energy trail from the broken timepiece.

Jack and Ben looked around, there was nothing but sand, ahead in the distance was a rocky valley, but no one was in sight, they were safe for now; still Ben maintained a watch as Jack hunkered down in front of Tannis as she sat with her head in her hands, 'You ok love?' He touched her shoulder gently.

She looked surprised by his concern, 'I'll be fine in a minute, Jack, thanks.'

'He's about three miles ahead of us this way,' Ned motioned to the valley ahead.

'We should find some cover,' Ben pointed to their left. 'Sandstorm,' Tannis followed his gaze.

They moved as fast as they could towards the rocks hoping to find shelter from the coming storm, as the sun bore down on them, making it even more exhausting trudging through the burning sand.

The edge of the storm was on them before they reached the valley, it was fierce, the sharp sand whipped around them as they covered their faces with their scarves; it would soon be on them with its full force. Above in the rock face, were small pockets, not big enough to be caves, but they would afford them some protection. 'Climb!' Jack shouted above the noise of the ever-encroaching storm.

They were already tired from the race to get there and were now forced to scramble up the rocks; they were only halfway up when the storm hit with its full wrath. There seemed to be no air, and even though they had only been a few feet away from one another, they had now completely lost sight of the person they had been closest to. Ned took shelter in a small outcrop of rocks, it wasn't great, but at least he was a little sheltered and could breathe better. Ben, although oblivious to Ned's presence, took refuge nearby.

Jack, using mostly his sense of touch, now found his way around some rocks and into a small indentation where he found Tannis curled up. Space was tight, and he made to move on, but she grabbed him and pulled him into the shelter, wrapping her voluminous shawl over them, and holding it down with their hands and feet they huddled together in each other's arms more for reasons of space than affection; the noise was deafening now as Tannis rested her head on his shoulder, he held her tightly, they couldn't speak, their words would've been lost; all they could do was sit it out.

After what seemed like an eternity the storm moved on, and the team began to emerge from their shelter. Jack shook the sand from Tannis' shawl as they stepped out. 'Thanks for that love,' he said as he handed it back to her. She nodded and wrapped it back around herself as Ned and Ben joined them. 'We need to make up for lost time,' Ned said as he checked the tracking device.

They set off again at a quick pace, following the signal. Not stopping for food, just ate as they marched on, Jack was admiring Tannis' stamina as they continued in silence, Ben stole the occasional glance too; she was showing no outward signs of fatigue, just getting on with it; he wondered how strong she was, then thought about her powers and wondered how her father had felt when he found out about her mother's abilities. Although he had to ask himself with all they'd been through lately, what was normal?

It began to grow dark, and the temperature plummeted, but they continued for a while, wrapping themselves tightly in their garments and shivering involuntarily. Ned paused to check the professor's position, he appeared to have stopped, but he had made ground on them when they sheltered from the storm. They would not catch him for another day, and now they faced a freezing night in the desert. 'Looks like he's made camp,' Ned announced.

'We should too,' Jack said to them all, 'we need to get some rest.' He and Ned took the first watch, giving Tannis and Ben a chance to try and get some sleep, but it was so cold they just sat shivering; Ben, rubbing his hands together trying to keep them warm, neither spoke, they were both tired and hungry; Tannis tried to move her fingers; they were a little numb. 'You're freezing,' Ben whispered as he took her hands in his and began to rub them, she looked at him as he blew on her fingers, trying to warm them up, 'better?' He glanced up at her.

She nodded slowly but was startled as Jack called back to them in a loud whisper, 'We've got company.'

Ned walked over to them, 'Looks like Bedouins. Probably the Abbadi tribe in these parts,' he told them as he adjusted his sister's scarf over her head and face. He looked at Ben now, 'Tannis is your wife, she is submissive to you, she knows how to behave. You lead, and she will follow.'

'Do you speak their language?' Jack turned to Ned.

'We all do, Colonel, the timepieces are part of you. While you wear them, you will understand any language and in return be able to communicate in any language,' Ned quickly explained as the two riders came closer.

'Cool,' Jack looked at his timepiece, then covered it with his sleeve. When the riders reached them, Tannis took her place a few steps behind Ben, her eyes lowered.

They dismounted and approached cautiously, Tannis stayed back as the three men walked towards the strangers, Ned introduced themselves and gave their cover story. Tannis was not even mentioned until one of the riders asked if she was still Ird, meaning her honour intact and available for marriage, Ned told them she was Ben's wife, and that was an end to it, they were honourable people. They were then invited to join the Bedouin camp for the night and share their hospitality. Their Diyafa was never to be refused as it would be a great insult, so the decision was made for them. It was a short walk to the Abbadi camp where they were introduced properly.

Omar was their chief; he was in his forties, a good age for the time, he had two sons Baliek and Yousar, their wives were not introduced, they sat in a tent with the children away from the men. Tannis had joined them, summoned over by whom she guessed was Omar's first wife.

The men ate and drank and made polite conversation with their host, 'Would you men be looking for any more wives on your journey?' Omar asked them, 'I have many daughters ready for marriage,' he offered.

'We are poor merchants and can't afford wives yet,' Ned lied, 'our brother here only got his woman because her family owed us a debt and couldn't pay.'

'You took a woman as payment for a debt? she must be from good breeding stock, eh?' he gave a throaty laugh.

'Oh, her pedigree is exceptional' Ned looked from Omar to Jack, then Ben.

The meal ended, and it was time to get to their beds. Ned thanked their host for his hospitality and made him a gift of a small purse of gold to show his appreciation, then he and Jack were shown to the men's tent while Yousar put a hand on Ben's arm, 'You may collect your woman. Look, she waits for you, and your accommodation has been prepared,' he pointed to a small tent on the other side of the camp and left them. Ben looked at his companions unsure of what to do.

'Go and bed your wife, brother,' Ned slapped him on the back. Jack also made the same gesture, 'I don't need to say it, do I?'

Ben shook his head and walked away to where Tannis stood waiting for him, he remembered himself and carried on walking by, allowing her to follow him.

Once inside they stood in front of one another, aware that their silhouettes were visible, Ben removed her veil and slipped the shawl from her head, it fell to the ground, and she looked up at him as he reached over and turned out the lamp. The tent was in darkness now, but it didn't take long for their eyes to adjust, 'Um, I'll sleep over here, you can take the bed,' he said awkwardly.

'You'll freeze over there,' she whispered as she slipped out of her dress and, keeping her undergarment on, slid under the covers, 'besides the young women will bring us food in the morning.'

He looked at her lying there and hesitated, giving her the wrong impression again as she rolled over and turned her back on him. 'You only have to pretend to like me for the mission, Major,' she whispered.

Ben sat on the other side of the bed and undressed, keeping his underclothes on too. Then slid beneath the warm covers, aware of their proximity he could easily reach out and touch her, 'I don't have to pretend,' he replied, continuing their hushed tone as he lay on his back, his arms folded behind his head.

She turned to face him, 'I'm sorry Major, I get treated differently when people find out about me or see me fight, it's not appealing to come across as a ruthless killer, so I just…'

He turned to look at her, 'You just don't give anyone a chance?'

'It's safer that way,' she closed her eyes, 'goodnight, Major.'
'Goodnight, Ben,' he corrected her, 'you can call me by my name you know, after all, we are married,' he teased.

'Goodnight Ben,' she liked the way his name sounded on her tongue, but gave him a questioning look when she sensed his smile, 'what?'

'I like when you call me by my name, you know I don't think you're so tough after all.'

She rolled her eyes, 'Have it your way,' she sighed, the bed was warm and soft, and they soon fell asleep.

As morning came and the camp began to stir, Ben woke first. In sleep, they had drifted into each other's arms. Tannis' head lay on his chest, her arm across him; he had an arm around her shoulder and the other on her hand as it rested on him. He could feel her breasts pressing against him through her thin garment, he turned his head slightly to look at her as she began to wake up; she looked straight into his eyes and made to move but froze as a young girl came into the tent to bring them food and water, then quietly left.

Tannis moved away from him now, 'I'm so sorry, it must've happened in my sleep.'

'Hey, it's ok, don't apologise.'

'No, it's not. I'm sorry, I shouldn't have relaxed with you. It was wrong,' she jumped out of bed and dressed quickly. Ben lay there for a moment telling himself to let it go, that they had a job to do.

So, he dressed as well and then they shared their breakfast. When it was time to leave the tent, Tannis covered her head and secured her veil. He looked at her then, studying her eyes. They were a beautiful deep blue, almond shape.

'Ready?' he asked in a hushed tone. Tannis nodded, 'Ready.'

She followed him out into the sunshine and then waited as he joined Ned and Jack to say their farewells to their host. They left the camp feeling refreshed and grateful for the food and a good night's sleep.

Once safely out of sight Tannis removed her veil and let her shawl fall to her shoulders, she shook her hair and ruffled it gently with her fingers; Ned looked across at her, 'Ah the submissive peace will soon be shattered,' he teased.

'Get stuffed!' She walked on.

Jack grinned; her mother obviously taught her a few English rebuffs.

They walked on through the heat of the day until Ned confirmed they were close, 'Must be over the next couple of dunes,' he looked at the readings on the tracker. Jack and Ben went to check it out, they weren't gone for long though, and the news wasn't good. It turned out that the professor had hired some help, about twenty of them, they had a confirmed sighting of Jennings, but he was going in, and out of most of the seven tents, so it was impossible to be sure which one was his.

The plan was to go in that night, with less chance of being seen and only a small watch would be around.

They didn't have long to wait for the sun to begin to set, and as it did so, they opened their packs. Tannis unrolled her brown leather clothing and turned her back on the men as she began to undress. They too turned and got on with changing into black combat fatigues; they had known it was more than likely going to be a nighttime assault. 'You decent yet?' Ned asked over his shoulder.

'As close as it gets.' The three of them turned as Tannis was testing her wrist blade before she put her jacket on, she twisted her wrist slightly, and the blade extended, then twisted it a little the opposite way and the blade retracted.

'Gotta get me one of those,' Jack admired the weapon.

She pulled her jacket on now and smoothed the sleeves down.

'Is that all you're taking, just the one blade?' he frowned.

She didn't speak, just made as if she were folding her arms behind her head and pulled from beneath the leather two swords that had been crisscrossed and hidden behind her back. She swung them expertly in front of her, then as fast as she had produced them, she stowed them away again. But that wasn't all, her hands now rested on the laces of her basque as if she were going to undo them, instead she reached down a little in front of her breasts and once again hidden in the leather were two smaller and narrower, but no less lethal blades, which she quickly returned too.

'Nuff said,' Jack sniffed and picked up his arsenal from his pack.

They shivered with cold again as the four of them lay flat on their stomachs and looked down at the professor's camp below, the mercenaries had eaten their fill and were beginning to turn in for the night, but they would give them a while yet before going in. Jennings, they assumed, must've eaten in his tent and there he remained. That was going to make things bloody awkward; they would have to check each one to find him.

The camp was quiet now, most of its occupants asleep; Tannis lay between Ned and Jack. The latter looked across at her as she lay shivering in the cold. He had been impressed with her throughout, she had put up with all that desert had thrown at them and never complained once, but now he wondered, how would she handle herself if it came down to a fight, she seemed able, but he knew from experience that wasn't always enough. Still, she'd survived some intense battles by the sound of it.

He gave the signal for them to move out and they began to slide down the dune towards the sleeping camp, when they reached the bottom they split into twos, Ned was with Tannis, she searched the first tent as he kept watch. Jack and Ben did the same as they worked their way silently around. They hadn't had sight of the professor all night, when he appeared for his toilet break around the back of a tent, and walked straight into Jack as he stood watch. 'Assassins!' He yelled at the top of his lungs, Jack silenced him with a punch that floored him, but it was too late. Ben came running out of the tent as the camp erupted; from every opening, mercenaries poured out.

'Shit!' Jack cursed as he drew his sword, Ben was by his side weapon at the ready as a mob rushed toward them.

Ned and Tannis were already under attack, but they were both excellent fighters, swinging their swords killing each target they hit. Jack and Ben too were expert at what they did, dispatching their attackers swiftly. At one point during the fray, Tannis was confronted by a huge hulk of a brute, he towered above her, even his swords were longer than average, and it was all she could do to defend herself. She let him think he had knocked her to the ground and lay still waiting, as he stepped over her to make the kill. That was his downfall, as she kicked him hard straight between his legs and rolled out the way. He dropped to his knees, and she then stood in front of him and crossed her swords at his throat. With one swift, fluid movement, she took his head clean off then pushed the body to the ground with her booted foot.

Jack was impressed, he'd seen it all while keeping his attacker at bay, but Tannis only noticed Ben watching her out of the corner of her eye, she glanced over at him as he fought on.

Ned and Tannis were being surrounded now as her brother called out, 'Tannis, on me!' Like a well-rehearsed drill, they met in the middle of the circling killers and stood back-to-back, their swords twisting and turning waiting for the first comers.

They didn't have long to wait; the crowd soon rushed in. Jack and Ben had trouble of their own, they were fighting hard and couldn't get to the others to help, but Ned and Tannis had faced worse odds than this before, they fought bravely and soon trimmed the herd down to a manageable size, 'Get the timepiece!' Ned ordered her, confident he could handle the rest, she nodded and ran towards where Jennings lay. She stopped short though, Jack was in trouble, he had two on him; he knocked one back with his fist and then killed the other with his sword, but he'd shoved it in too far, it was stuck in the rib cage of the body, he pulled hard, but it wouldn't budge. He was defenceless now as the second man got up and raised his sword above his head, ready to bring it down on him, Ben was wrestling with one of his own and could do nothing. Jack pulled again at his weapon; it wouldn't budge, then his would be killer froze. Jack looked up to see a blade protruding from the man's mouth as he slid to his knees. Tannis stood behind him; she retracted her wrist blade as the dead man fell to the ground, she then picked up his redundant weapon and threw it to Jack. And she was gone, fighting her way towards Jennings again.

The professor was beginning to stir, he sat up and wiped the blood from his mouth when saw Tannis trying to make her way to him, there weren't many of his hired hands left standing now, he reached into his robes, pulled out a pistol and took aim at her; from a distance Ben saw what was happening and knew he wouldn't be able to get there in time, he quickly finished his assailant then reached down and grabbed the small knife he always kept in his boot, he threw it at Jennings yelling, 'Tannis look out!' as he did. It all happened at once, she spun around as the knife hit its mark, Jennings was already dead when he pulled the trigger and Ben looked on helplessly as the bullet hit and Tannis fell backwards.

'NO!' Ned yelled as he raced towards her. The fight was over now, with their paying employer dead, the mercenaries were no longer prepared to die for nothing. They lowered their weapons and walked away, taking what they could with them. Jack was closest to Jennings, he walked over and ripped the timepiece from the dead man's wrist, then grabbed the gun before he ran over to join the others where Tannis lay. Ned reached her first and looked down at her clutching her arm, 'You silly sod. You had me worried!' he chastised her gently as he maintained a watch, the mercenaries were looting as much as they could now; Jack too stood watch as Ben knelt and helped her to sit up, 'It's ok, just a graze,' she winced.

He slipped her jacket off her shoulders. Her left arm was red with blood that ran down to her fingertips. He gently turned it and looked at her wound, 'That's a bit more than a graze, it's a through and through,' he took a small field dressing kit from one of his pockets and cleaned the wound, she flinched as it stung, but let him dress it.

'Thank you, Major,' she said quietly, 'you saved my life.'

Ben smiled, 'Anytime.' When he was satisfied the dressing was secure, he helped her slip her jacket back on, 'You ok, you're trembling?' He lowered his voice so the others wouldn't hear.

'It's perfectly normal, a side effect of fear,' she tried to joke. He helped her to stand, and as they looked around the deserted camp, Ned picked up her weapons and went in search of the bullet, he was keen to get away.

'You, ok?' Jack's voice was full of concern.

'I'll be fine,' she gave him a small smile.

'That's another one I owe you,' he motioned to the body of the man she had killed to save him.

'Friends don't keep scores, Jack,' she dismissed.

'Look at you, three years out of action and the Major had to save your arse. You're getting slow, girl,' Ned teased as he held the blood covered bullet between his thumb and his forefinger.

'Well, if that's slow, you must be bloody awesome when you're on top form,' Jack grinned at her.

They fell silent, the campfires were almost out now, but something was lighting the place, and it wasn't the moon, that was nowhere near full. 'Look!' Ned pointed to the distant sky; they climbed the dune that they had slid down earlier. Tannis struggled

with one arm out of action, Ben took her good hand in his and helped
her up; they stood together at the top and looked ahead.

There in the distance was a star shining brightly in the sky,
'Bethlehem,' Ned said, 'the first Christmas.'

'Merry Christmas,' Jack smiled.

'Merry Christmas,' they all replied together.

Ben looked down, he still held Tannis' hand, he entwined his
fingers with hers as she looked up at him and smiled and they were
gone.

Back on The Eldridge, the Admiral welcomed them with the
news that time was running as it should be once more, the team were
exhausted and made their way back to their quarters to clean up.
Hennessey had requested a meeting in the dining room when they
were ready.

Ben had showered and changed now as he knocked on Tannis'
door, she opened it, standing in her PJs, her wet hair piled on her
head held in place with a clip.

'I bought you a clean dressing,' he held out the pack in his hand.

'It's fine now, but thank you,' she let her top slip from her
shoulder a little to reveal her arm as good as new, not even a scar.

'Wow,' was all he could say.

She lowered her head, 'We should go to the dining room and hear
what the Admiral has to say.'

Jack was coming out of his door, 'How's the arm love?' He did a
double take. She hadn't covered it yet, 'healed already? wish I
carried that gene, I'm gonna be sore for days.'

Ned was with them now, 'Tannis pj's? you know you've got to
take our friends home after we've spoken to the Admiral.'

'Yes, and then I shall go to bed and hide under the covers until I
can be bothered to surface. My boat, my rules!'

'Ship,' he corrected.

'Whatever!' she shot back over her shoulder as she walked on.

They all sat around the table in the dining room now.
'Congratulations on a job well done,' Hennessey praised them, then
he turned his attention to Ned and Tannis, 'have you had any more
thoughts on allowing the coalition to join with you, to work together

exploring new dimensions? who knows there could already be a cure for cancer out there,' he had brought the subject up with Ned the previous night when they worked together to trace Jennings.

Ned looked at his sister as he spoke, 'We're finished Admiral, we were forced onto the road, that aside, we did our job, and it killed all but two of us, Phoenix are gone.'

'Road?' Ben could see the hurt in Tannis' eyes.

'The road to come what may,' she looked directly at him.

'I don't expect an answer straight away. I know it's a big decision,' Hennessey conceded.

'And if we say no, what about Cole? will you take your ball home and not play anymore?' Ned looked directly at Hennessey.

'No, you have my word. Regardless of your decision, you will have our full cooperation with dating your brother's remains,' Hennessey was sincere, 'I would like to reiterate, however, that there could be more timepieces out there that could fall into the wrong hands. You said yourselves; there's only you left now. Could you cope with a new threat?'

'It's not just our decision, Admiral, If the coalition were to come here, the people of Atlantis would have to accept it too, they didn't have a lot of choice when The Eldridge showed up and took them out of sync with the world, and now they have to look at the bloody thing every day,' Ned said bluntly.

'How do you think I feel I have to live on it, rattling around on a big boat by myself?' Tannis fired back.

'Ship,' Ned corrected.

'Whatever!' she sighed.

'Well, you won't be alone if the coalition is on board, will you?' he chided, 'and there'll be no more treating the place like your own personal stereo system either.'

'You want my boat?' She sat up as she looked at Hennessey.

'Ship,' he corrected.

'Ugh,' Tannis rolled her eyes.

'It would make sense to have The Eldridge as a base to work from after all that was what it was designed for, and all the equipment is on board. Also, the people of Atlantis would hardly know we were here,' Hennessey explained.

'Well, I think I might notice a bit!' she grumbled.

'Admiral, if you would all like to stay another night on board, Tannis and I need to talk about this, you will have our answer tomorrow,' Ned said as he stood up, 'Tannis, walk with me.'

She got up and followed her brother, 'They want The Eldridge,' she whispered as she took his hand.

'You can always get a place in town,' he added unhelpfully.

'You too?' she snatched her hand from his, 'look, I know it's crap, but it's my home, Fucking Hell!' She marched on ahead of her brother and loudly called out, 'Eldridge play my *Go Fuck Yourself song number 1*, everywhere.'

As the two Atlanteans left the room *Think* by *Aretha Franklin* began to play throughout the ship.

When the song came to an end and the three men could finally hear themselves speak, Hennessey turned to his officers, 'Your thoughts gentlemen?'

'Big decision, sir, I wouldn't like it to be mine,' Jack piped up. Hennessey nodded his agreement, 'And you, Major Rhodes?'

'I've no idea, sir, they've been through so much. They thought it was over and then we showed up,' Ben replied honestly.

That night Tannis and Ned stayed up late talking, going through the pros and cons. They sat up on deck wrapped in blankets until the conversation started going around in circles and finally, they decided to call it a night. Ned kissed her on the cheek and made his way down the gangplank saying as he went, 'Not a word to Elea about the mission, remember.'

Tannis laughed, 'You're more afraid of her than anyone.' She yawned as she got up and went to her quarters, padding along the passage, it would be weird sharing with strangers she thought to herself as she opened the door marked number 7, she didn't even bother to turn the light on, just closed the door and climbed into bed and was soon asleep.

Morning came too quickly for Tannis' liking; she was tired and hated getting out of bed at the best of times and Ned banging on her door didn't help her mood in the slightest, 'Come on Tannis, get up, we're going to give our guests the guided tour of Atlantis!' he yelled.

She didn't answer, so he let himself in, 'Tannis, C'mon!'

'Ned, it's really early, and I will hurt you if you don't go away,' she mumbled from under the sheet.

'Up, now!' He pulled the covers off her, she sat up and rubbed her eyes. He was wearing white three-quarter trousers with a green silk floral blouse, 'C'mon, Tannis, what's up with you lately?'

'I don't want to come today. Please, you don't need me,' she begged, 'I just want to ride Jester,' she referred to her white mare.

'Ok, but you can walk with us as far as the stables?' he compromised.

'Deal,' she hugged him.

'You know if they do stay, you'll have to get used to being around the Major,' he whispered.

Her jaw dropped, but no words came out, 'You're my sister, I know you better than anyone,' he sat on the bed next to her now, 'he's a good guy.'

'Yeah, and if I was a normal girl, then maybe,' she sulked.

'Your mom and dad worked with it,' he said as he left the room.

Everyone was on deck when Tannis got there. She was dressed in a white bikini, covered only by a blue sarong tied at her waist. She walked barefoot, saying her good mornings to everyone as she headed for the gangplank with Ned, leaving the three men to follow.

Ben was trying his hardest not to stare, she had a fantastic body, not muscular, but toned and she had curves in all the right places, not like the so-called ideal woman of today, or tits on a stick as they were referred to back on the base. She was oblivious to the admiring glances she was getting, as they walked along the quayside; she had linked arms with her brother, and they wandered slowly toward the harbour.

'Are you self- sufficient?' Hennessey could see a market ahead. 'Not totally, but what the island can't provide, Tannis usually acquires for us, medicines and such,' Ned replied, 'but really life here hasn't changed that much since The Eldridge arrived. We tweaked things up a bit, but the locals are ok with that, we don't have a timeline to follow anymore.'

'How do you fund your activities?' Hennessey knew fine well the clothing and weaponry that they had cost money, and now Ned was talking about medication and other needs the islanders had.

'The folks sent back a huge gold reserve and tons of precious stones. We found a safe place to stash it on the island, couldn't bear looking at it in the holds,' Ned wrinkled his nose with distaste.

'Holds plural?' Jack couldn't keep the surprise out of his voice, he knew how cavernous the holds were.

Ned just shrugged, 'Yeah.'

Ben was impressed, clearly money meant nothing to them.

'This is where I leave you,' Tannis smiled at them, 'I'm taking Jester for a ride.' They were standing near a paddock where a beautiful white mare grazed, her long white mane hanging down as she ate.

'Jester, c'mon girl!' Tannis called, as she did the mare raised her head, whinnied and trotted towards the gate.

'Magnificent!' Hennessey gasped as he saw the horse.

'She's great, isn't she?' Tannis said proudly, 'see you later,' she called back as she walked on, the mare following loyally behind her towards a path that led to the hills.

'No saddle, nothing, I suppose you have to learn to ride all sorts in your game,' Jack mused.

'Great horse, do you breed them here?' Ben's eyes followed her as she went out of sight.

'We do, yes, but Jester was a gift from Wellington,' Ned told him.

'And a necklace, she must've made a good impression?' Jack noted.

Ben was thinking the same too, only with a tinge of jealousy. 'Tannis had a lot on during the Napoleonic wars, she fought for Wellington three times, he was a good general, he respected her and treated her well,' Ned smiled to himself, 'she wasn't very popular with the French though, but that's another story, shall we?' He gestured for them to continue their way.

Atlantis was like a time capsule, the market was as traditional as it could get, selling all sorts of food, drink, cloth, jewellery, anything a household could want; Ned introduced his three guests as they walked around the stalls, they were welcomed instantly, if they were friends of Ned and Tannis, then they would be welcome on Atlantis. The people were mostly dressed in traditional costume, some leaned a little more to the Greek way, some to the Roman style, but to the untrained eye, a robe was a robe.

Next Ned took them to a café where they sampled the local wine and met with the Elders responsible for all decisions made on Atlantis. He told them about the request that the Admiral had put forward and after a little wine and a lot of thought they decided that if Ned and Tannis thought it was a good idea, then they would offer their full support. It seemed that the people of Atlantis were grateful The Eldridge isolated them from the world outside, they enjoyed a peaceful existence with no foreign threats to worry about.

Then Ned took them out of the town; they headed up a grassy hill toward a small white wooden church, 'The crew from The Eldridge built this for themselves,' Ned told them as they drew closer. To one side of the churchyard were the graves of the four Eldridge crew members who were killed when Phoenix came to the island; their wives were also buried with them, 'Their wives fought and died alongside their men, my mother also,' Ned sighed as he touched the cross that marked his mother's grave. And across the other side, under the shade of a large weeping willow were four more graves 'Our sisters and brother,' Ned sighed as they read the names on the white crosses Will, Em, Charlie and Meg. 'Probably best Tannis didn't come.'

The next port of call was Ned's house for lunch. He had pre-warned his wife Elea. She was a dark-haired beauty, her accent almost Greek. A voluptuous woman with a good heart, she welcomed them to their home and asked them to make themselves comfortable as she nudged Ned to get some drinks.

Ned's place was built in the Roman style, with white walls and a red tiled roof, it wasn't pretentious, just homely. Naturally, it was larger than most; he had nine kids after all. They sat in the beautiful established garden that overlooked the harbour below; Ned had told his wife about the Admiral's proposition the night before when he had returned home. Elea was a woman who spoke her mind, 'So, you want to pick up where *DE-173* left off?'

'Sorry?' Jack wasn't familiar with the name.

'*The Eldridge Brats*, Colonel,' she explained, 'when the ship was sent back from the future, it contained written orders,' she nudged Ned, 'you did not tell them?' she rolled her eyes and continued, 'the orders were addressed to *DE-173* as a collective; they were named after the ship for God's sake and expected to fight and die to protect a world we no longer belonged to.'

'Dark times, sweetheart,' Ned put an arm around his wife, and she leaned into him, she looked at her three guests now. 'So now, you want to take over, and I say good luck to you, you're welcome, Ned and Tannis survived hell, they deserve to live their lives now, I need my husband and our children need their father, I'm not sure what Cole will think about it though if you manage to bring him back.'

'Who knows, the thought of death might change him,' Ned thought aloud.

'Change him how, exactly?' Hennessey sat forward now; nothing really had been mentioned about their late brother.

'He was a bastard,' Elea weighed straight in.

'He was in charge, my darling, had to make tough decisions,' her husband gently chastised her, then added, 'but yes he was a hard bastard, and only got worse as the war went on, to be honest he never was much like one of us, I suppose you have to maintain a certain distance when you're in charge eh Admiral?'

Elea served the food as the men talked about the endless possibilities of inter-dimensional travel. 'Is Tannis not joining us?' she asked.

'She's taken Jester out,' Ned reached for a fork.

'I know I saw her over in the hills earlier; she was riding hard, have you two fallen out again?' she raised an eyebrow.

'Not me this time, she's got things on her mind she needs to get straight.'

'Oh, a man at last I hope, she is always so lonely, she needs a man in her bed and a baby in her belly.'

'Bread, Colonel?' Ned offered a small basket to Jack, changing the subject, and the mood soon lightened now as their two-year-old twins came toddling in, hand in hand from their nap. Ned walked over to them, a boy and a girl, and scooped them up in his arms. 'Gentlemen, this is Em and Will,' he introduced. It didn't take a rocket scientist to work out that Elea would've been pregnant with the twins when Ned left for the final battle with Phoenix. *Nightmare* thought Jack.

The four men walked back to The Eldridge. It was mid-afternoon, and the sun was still hot as they strolled back through the narrow-cobbled streets, the locals calling out greetings to them by name.

Tannis was already back on board, lying on one of the wooden sun loungers she and Ned had used the night before. She had changed into shorts and a T-shirt now, the book she had been reading rested on the deck as she lay on her stomach with her eyes closed. Ned led the way to the door that would take them below, 'Give her a nudge, would you Major?' he asked as Ben was bringing up the rear.

'No problem,' Ben turned and walked over to where she lay and sat on the lounger next to her, she rolled over onto her back, then sat up.

'I'm sure he thinks I'm deaf.'

'Have a good day?' he asked her casually.

'Blew some of the cobwebs away thank you,' she looked at him 'and how about you? Ned didn't torture you too much, did he?'

Ben smiled and shook his head, 'This place is fantastic, the people are great, you must love it here.'

She warmed to him again now; she liked that he liked her home.

'Oh, it has its moments,' she smiled, standing up. Ben rose, too. 'C'mon, Major, it's time you all had your answer,' she sighed.

'Tannis, wait,' he held her hand gently, she didn't move to pull away, just looked into his eyes.

'For what it's worth, I'm not sure I'd like the idea of the coalition here if it were my home. So, if it comes to it when the three of us go back to the real world, well what I'm trying to say is, I guess I will keep messing with time, so you'll show up again.'

'You won't have to,' she said softly, they were very close now.

Realisation dawned on him, 'Really? That's great, hang on, don't you need to talk to Ned again first?'

'We made our minds up last night.'

'You're sure about this?'

'I think that's what we should be asking you, Major.'

Chapter Three

It was decided that Tannis would return to the real world with them while Hennessey made his report to the Coalition.

Jack and Ben had been ordered to report to the infirmary for a full medical; the doctors were keen to see the effects of time travel on the human body. The only records they had so far were the medical reports of the returning crew of The Eldridge back in 1943, and they did not make pleasant reading; it had also been requested that Tannis be present.

'But I'm not sick!' she protested as her two friends escorted her down the corridor.

'You don't have to be sick to have a medical,' Jack sighed at her latest excuse, 'it can help make sure you don't get sick.'

'I don't get sick.'

'Never?' He raised an eyebrow.

'Well in hindsight, I'd probably give licking a cane toad a swerve, but I was drunk,' she shook her head and turned to walk back the way she came, 'so, there's no need then.'

The two men grabbed an arm each and marched her to the infirmary. She was not pleased.

'Clothes off and lay on the bed,' the doctor's tone was unemotional.

'Buy me a drink first,' Tannis started with sarcasm. Both Jack and Ben guffawed.

'Hurry up, please' the doctor began to close the curtains around the bed. Tannis folded her arms, glared and stood firm.

'She doesn't have a weapon, does she?' Ben whispered to his superior.

Tannis was wearing jeans and a tight top, nowhere really to conceal anything. 'She is a weapon,' Jack whispered back as the doctor spoke again.

'There's nothing you have that I haven't seen before,' he droned.

'Then you won't need to see it now, will you!' She wasn't budging.

'Very well, we'll start with the blood tests,' he produced a syringe and made to grab her arm.

'You come any closer, and I'll stick it in your eye,' she hissed. 'And we're off,' Jack sighed.

This stopped the medic in his tracks, 'Perhaps you would prefer a nurse to perform the procedure,' he mumbled as he quickly left to find one.

Jack stood in front of her now, his arms folded across his chest, 'Are you going to behave?'

'I don't want any tests done, Jack,' she whispered, 'does everybody have to know I'm a freak?'

'You're not a freak,' Ben frowned.

Jack sat on the bed and patted the space next to him for her to sit on, 'Love, we're all different, why can Rembrandt paint a masterpiece and I can't even manage a stick man?' he took her hand in his, 'you've just got a talent for what you do!'

She'd never had it put that way before, 'Ok,' she agreed, 'but you two can wait on the other side of the curtains,' she looked nervously at the instruments laid out on a tray next to the bed.

Ben sensed her fear. 'There's something else isn't there?'

Tannis nodded 'Belsen 1942, my mark was a Nazi scientist taken by the Americans after the war for the space race. Phoenix killed him and altered time in favour of the Russians. I was sent back to save him, the scum of the earth and I had to save him,' she shuddered, 'he liked using scalpels and saws and needles just to inflict pain, sometimes for his so-called research,' she blinked hard and came back now, 'I'm fine with dentists, though,' she forced a smile. Jack put his arm around her shoulder, and she leaned into him before saying, 'go on then you two, get lost.'

A couple of hours later the three of them were back in the lab where it had all started. Dr Hodges was in charge now, he was chattering away to them about something, Tannis and Jack seemed to understand him well enough, but Ben was still none the wiser, he looked at the timepiece on his wrist, shook it and looked at it again.

Tannis stepped back a little and whispered in his ear, 'It only translates languages, not accents sorry.' Ben pursed his lips and stood in silence for the rest of the doctor's monologue.

He was asking Tannis for her help regarding the workings and maintenance of the timepieces when Jack and Ben were told to report back to the infirmary.

'We'll come back here for you, love,' Jack winked.

She knew that she had not been sent for because they were going to talk about her and this showed in her smile as she nodded, 'Ok.'

'This is out of order,' Jack muttered to Ben as they left her.

'We of all people shouldn't treat her like this sir,' Ben snapped. 'Don't worry, Major, it won't be allowed to happen again,' Jack said sharply.

'We have the test results back,' the doctor informed them as they walked into his office.

'And?' Jack sat first then Ben.

'And' the doctor shook his head, 'I've never seen anything like it. Her immune system is far superior to ours; I doubt she could either carry or contract a disease. Then there's her physical strength, stamina, and cardiovascular capability,' he removed his glasses, wiped them on his lab coat and continued, 'her metabolic rate is faster than ours, hence her healing capabilities.'

'We're alright then?' Jack frowned.

'What, oh yes, both you and the Major are fine, no adverse effects,' the doctor dismissed.

'Good to hear,' Ben added sarcastically.

'But gentlemen, you don't understand, I need Tannis back, I need to perform more tests,' he chatted excitedly.

'We understand better than you think, Doctor,' Ben said harshly. The medic looked at Jack to discipline his subordinate, but that was not on the cards.

'So, she's passed the medical?' Jack asked pointedly.

'With flying colours,' the doctor enthused, 'but I need to run more tests.'

'So, she's no different to us, just a bit more upgraded?' He fixed the doctor with his stare.

'Well, yes, except for the fact that we have 23 sets of 2 chromosomes, and she has 25 sets of 2, I need to test these for…' the medic didn't get the chance to finish.

'That's all we need to know. Thanks, Doc,' Jack said as he got up and left with Ben close behind him. A short way along the corridor the two men looked at one another, they both had the same uneasy feeling about the doctor. 'He won't be making the new crew list for The Eldridge,' Jack confided.

'Never thought we'd have to protect her from our own,' Ben's tone was harsh.

'Ants at every picnic,' Jack smiled, 'C'mon, let's see if Dr Hodges has made any progress.'

'I wouldn't know if he had,' Ben muttered to himself.

As they walked into the lab, they saw Dr Hodges tapping feverishly away at his keyboard thoroughly engrossed in whatever it was he was doing. Over by the far wall, Tannis stood chatting with a USAF Major; they were laughing together. Jack felt Ben's hackles rise the moment he saw them, *a perfect opportunity to wind him up a bit* he thought to himself, 'They look like they're having a good time.'

Ben snorted but said nothing, so Jack pushed further, 'You know I think it's good for Tannis, getting off the island and meeting blokes that she can spend some time with, you know, get to know them better,' he stifled a laugh as Ben strode off towards the happy pair.

'Hi,' she smiled, 'John was telling me about his days at the academy.'

'Really, well thanks, John, but we need to talk in private now, if you'll excuse us,' Ben's tone was blunt as he took Tannis by the arm and led her past Jack, who was grinning from ear to ear, and out of the lab, across the hall and into an empty office closing the door behind them.

Tannis pulled her arm free as they stood face to face now, 'What the hell was that all about? Who do you think you are? You were so rude!'

'The guy only wants to... well, he's just out for...' his words failed him now he had let jealousy take over.

'Sex!' She finished the sentence for him.

'Yeah,' he answered sulkily.

'I'm not a child, Ben,' her voice was calm, she had called him by his name, that had not gone unnoticed, he moved closer to her, they were almost touching now.

'I just don't want you to get hurt,' he stroked her cheek and gently ran his thumb across her lips. He leaned closer still but stopped at the last minute and pulled back; all the fights and battles he had been in, and his courage failed him now.

Tannis' eyes brimmed with tears as she took this as a sign of rejection, 'Then stop hurting me!' she choked as she left the room slamming the door behind her.

Two weeks had passed since the Coalition had given the green light for Admiral Hennessey to proceed with operations from The Eldridge. At first, a small unit of forty was sent through to set up a command centre. Tannis and Ned had stuck to their side of the bargain and cooperated fully, showing them how to use the equipment on board and the timepieces. The ops room, as the new arrivals called it, was easily explained and Ned was thrilled to be given his own office full of his beloved books, although he wasn't keen on the computer they had given him as he stood and poked the keyboard with one finger, his tongue sticking out of the corner of his mouth while he concentrated, only to shake his head, hit the delete button and pick up the manual again. Books were so much easier he thought to himself.

It hadn't been plain sailing for Tannis either. She had had to get used to sharing her home with a bunch of strangers who worked shift patterns; they had even fixed the tannoy system which they used with annoying regularity. Then there were the briefings to attend, reports to file literally every time she made a leap, no matter how small; she had also been banned from playing her music throughout the ship, which nettled her as she liked to dance her way to breakfast whilst tapping whatever tune she was singing along to with her drumsticks all along the passageways, although it soon became a moot point as the dining room was gone now too.

But it all came to a head one day when she was sitting in the sun in her favourite spot up on deck, a young Ensign came over and asked her to move as a new piece of equipment was going to be installed there for the comms system. She didn't bother venting her anger at him; it wasn't his fault after all he had to follow his orders. So, she just gathered her things and went below; she was almost at her quarters when she bumped into Jack, 'You alright? you don't look very happy, I thought you were up on deck?'

She opened the door and snapped, 'Not anymore,' as she went inside and threw her stuff on the bed, he followed her in, leaving the door open.

'Let's have it, then?'

'I'm sorry, Jack,' she sighed, 'it's just going to take some getting used to, all the people, all the noise and now I'm told I can't sit at the pointy bit anymore because some equipment has to go there.'

'Whoa, hang on a minute, say that again, the part about the pointy bit I mean,' he frowned at himself for not using the correct term. She told him what had happened, and that the Ensign was not to blame, he had been very nice about the whole thing. 'I just still see it as my boat and I shouldn't I suppose,' she shuffled awkwardly.

He walked over and hugged her 'Ship,' he whispered.

'Whatever,' her reply was muffled in his shirt.

He kissed the top of her head, 'Wait here. I'll be right back.'

She busied herself tidying her things away and true to his word Jack returned ten minutes later with the Admiral who apologised profoundly and told her the equipment would be moved elsewhere, and that part of the ship would be hers personally.

'Really? I don't know what to say,' she bit her lip.

'Tannis, it's us that should be thanking you. Think nothing of it,' Hennessey smiled, then excused himself, there never seemed to be enough hours in the day at the moment.

That night to blow off some steam and welcome a few more members of the crew, Ned threw a party, the music was loud, but as everyone in the local vicinity had been invited nobody minded. Besides these things were a common occurrence, Ned didn't need an excuse to party; he had insisted that the dress code be relaxed, and non-uniform was the order of the day. He and Elea were the perfect hosts, making sure that their guests had plenty to eat and drink and generally had a great time.

'No Tannis?' Jack asked as he sat down next to Ben and the Admiral.

'She's about somewhere,' Ned looked around, 'there she is, look!' He pointed through the crowd on the dance floor to the far side of the garden where she stood talking to Sarah, Ned's thirteen-year-old daughter.

Ben couldn't take his eyes off her; she looked stunning in the tight figure-hugging navy-blue dress she wore. He could feel the blood coursing through him, and it was all he could do to sit there and make polite conversation. Ned gestured to her to join them, and she smiled as she made her way over, saying hello to a few people on the way. The music changed before she reached them, and a huge cheer went up from the locals as *Turn Back Time* by *Cher* began. Tannis blushed and nodded, smiling awkwardly at the guests, then hurried head down over to Ned and the others.

Ned budged along the bench and put his arm around his sister, then he picked up his beer bottle and used it as a pretend microphone for the two of them to sing into. They both laughed at some of the words they sang. Jack, Ben and Hennessey had to appreciate the irony of the song too as they watched the adoptive brother and sister laughing together. When the song ended Tannis excused herself and went to get a drink.

The music had paused for a moment, indicating that it was going to slow down, Elea had her eyes on Major Harmon, he was a good-looking man, and Ned had told her about his relentless pursuit of Tannis, he was trying to extract himself from a group of local women who had all set their caps at him, but he was trying to make his way to Tannis. 'Major Rhodes, could I impose on you to be an officer and a gentleman and go and dance with Tannis, before she takes flight?'

Ben knew exactly what she meant, he had been watching her too, and Harmon for that matter, as soon as the music stopped Harmon tried to make his move, while Tannis started to look for an escape, as Harmon wasn't the only one eyeing her up for what they hoped was a grope on the dancefloor.

'My pleasure,' Ben acknowledged and got up as Elea made a beeline for Major Harmon and engaged him in conversation.

'She'd make a good general, that one,' Jack winked at Ned.

'A woman of many talents, my wife,' the three men raised their drinks in a toast to Elea.

When Ben got to where she was standing Tannis was already politely declining a few locals, he stood in front of her, 'Dance with me?'

She took his hand, and he led her to the dance floor just as *Never Tear Us Apart* by *INXS* began.

The words of the song were not lost on the pair of them as they moved slowly in each other's arms, never once breaking eye contact as Ben gently pulled her closer to him.

'Is this one of Elea's rescue missions?' Tannis swallowed and bit her lip as she looked up at him.

'Not from where I'm standing,' he struggled to keep a normal tone.

The song ended, and neither of them wanted to leave it there, 'Would you walk with me on the beach, I think I've had too much to drink, I just need to clear my head,' she asked, still looking up at him.

He didn't speak, just took her hand in his and led her away.

'Thank you Major,' she spoke clearer now they were out of anyone's earshot safely on the beach.

'You can at least call me by my name at a party,' he said softly as he stood by her side, thinking he wouldn't put it past Harmon to spike her drink.

Her hand went to her head, and she blinked slowly, 'The fresh air doesn't seem to be helping.'

'Here, sit down,' he helped her onto the sand and sat next to her. 'I think I have been foolish and let my guard down again,' she groaned.

'You shouldn't have to be on guard at your brother's house.'

'And here you are again to catch me when I fall,' she pulled her knees up under her chin and hugged her legs.

'Yep, and I'm the only one you won't trust.'

She looked into his eyes, 'It's me I don't trust, Ben,' she giggled, 'especially at the moment, I don't think it was just alcohol in my drink.'

He raised an eyebrow, 'Really?'

'Oh yes, really, I've never felt like this because of booze before.'
'Like what?' he was concerned now.

'Like agreeing to anything,' she said honestly, 'I should go home,' she tried to stand up; he helped her as she swayed a little and put his hands on her waist to steady her. She leaned into him, and he slid his arms around her, holding her to him, he could feel her breath on his neck. It took all his resolve to hold back.

'Major Harmon,' she whispered.

'Don't worry about him, I'll take care of that son of a bitch,' he hissed.

'No, you don't understand,' she was trying to piece the evening together, 'I picked his drink up earlier by mistake, and he stopped me from drinking it. He said it had a double vodka in it and I watched him pour me juice from the carton, it couldn't have been him,' she tried to clear her mind; as she nuzzled his neck, he stroked her hair, then she pulled away a little, 'Sarah spilt mine, then gave me her drink. One of the boys from the island brought it over. Ben, we must find her!'

He took her hand and led her back along the beach towards Ned's, 'Where would he take her?'

They heard muffled voices coming from the trees ahead of them followed by the sound of a slap, 'Get off me!' a young girl cried out.

'That's her!' Tannis tried to run toward the sound.

'Wait here. I'll take care of this,' Ben waded into the darkness, there was the sound of a very brief scuffle, and a few moments later he walked out of the trees with Sarah, she was safe and well if a little shaken.

'Please don't tell Daddy,' She begged them.

'Go back to the party Sarah and stay away from him in future. Tell your dad I've gone home, and I'll talk to you in the morning,' Tannis said as she turned and walked back along the beach.

'Thank you, Major Rhodes,' the young girl hugged him quickly and then ran back towards the house. He watched her safely inside then turned and walked after Tannis.

'Hey, wait up,' he fell in step beside her.

'I'm feeling better now thanks. You should go back to the party, enjoy yourself,' she looked across at him.

'I wouldn't enjoy myself if I were worried about you, now, would I?' She smiled and accepted his company, 'Do you have family, Major?'

'Ah now I know you're feeling better, we're back to Major again,' he teased, 'it was Ben earlier when you were doped.'

She stopped dead, 'I didn't say or do anything I shouldn't, did I?'

'You don't remember, Tannis, I feel so used.'

She narrowed her eyes at him, 'Very funny, actually I do remember now,' she said as they left the beach and walked along the tree-lined pathway.

'How much?' he teased again.

'This much,' she grabbed his hands, put them around her waist and looked up at him as she leaned in closer and nuzzled his neck, 'is this right?'

'Not quite,' he said huskily as he slid his arms around her and held her to him again.

She pulled away from him a little and looked into his eyes, 'Yes, I remember now,' she whispered as she put her hand on his chest, 'you were the perfect gentleman as usual where I am concerned.'

'It wasn't you back there, what did you expect me to do?' His frustration was burning into him, and he pulled back from her. 'C'mon, I'll take you home,' he said firmly as he walked away.

'Why, Ben, why do you treat me like this? If you dislike me so much why do…' She didn't finish, he had turned quickly back and marched the few steps towards her, and his lips were on hers, he held her head in his hands, she didn't resist him just wrapped her arms around his neck as he slid his hands down her body to her waist and pulled her into him. His kisses were deep and passionate, and she returned hers with the same feeling, he pulled slowly away and looked at her. 'This is going to be complicated,' his voice was thick with desire, and they kissed again.

Those of The Eldridge crew who had an early start the next morning had begun making their way back to the ship. Ben stepped away from her as they heard the voices getting closer, she gasped then vanished. He sighed and shoved his hands in his pockets. *This ain't gonna be easy,* he thought to himself as he joined the group heading back.

The next afternoon Jack and Ben were called to the new briefing room. It was what had previously been the dining room, but now much more modern in design. A large oval brushed steel table dominated the room with leather swivel chairs around it.

'Colonel, Major,' Hennessey acknowledged them as he sat at the head of the table and beckoned them to take their choice of seat, Jack sat to the Admiral's right while Ben sat on the opposite side but one seat down. It looked like someone already sat to the left of Hennessey, and they had left a metal case to mark their place. It was smaller than a suitcase but bigger and broader than a briefcase. It turned out Ned had claimed it as he walked in and sat down looking uncomfortably at the item in front of him.

'Ned has asked for this meeting,' Hennessey began, 'I understand you have some more Eldridge technology to share with us?' This was Ned's cue to begin; he paused to gather his thoughts.

'Actually, this is Phoenix tech,' he flipped it open to reveal a small screen and keyboard, resting on top were what looked like ECG sensor pads.

'Looks like a lie detector,' Ben leaned in for a closer look as Ned turned it for all to see.

'Not quite, Major. It's a memory detector, more thorough than torture. It can pick out a specific memory through word association and alter or implant a new fake one.'

'How did you get your hands on that?' Jack frowned at the innocent looking device.

'It was a prototype. Will brought it back from one of his missions. When the Admiral asked for a briefing on *DE-173*, I thought that instead of reading about us, you would get a better gist if you saw us in action, so to speak.'

Hennessey nodded, 'Very well, but you'll have to show us how to use it if you're going to be wired into it.'

Ned shook his head, 'No, it has to be controlled in silence, a single word uttered can affect the result, and once the memory is running, it must finish, it cannot be stopped otherwise the result would be catastrophic, I've asked Tannis to join us,' he looked at his watch, 'about now.' On cue, she appeared. She looked straight at Ben, they hadn't seen each other since last night, but the awkwardness of the situation went straight out of the window as her eyes alighted on the memory device.

'What the hell is that doing here?' She glared at her brother.

'I thought you could give us a demo and let them see *DE-173* in action. You know reading about it all in a file doesn't always tell the full story.'

'Bugger off! you're not plugging me into that thing, poking around in my head.'

'I promise I'll only look at the seven of us together, nothing personal.'

Tannis shook her head, 'Va te faire foutre je ne suis pas un singe performant,' she spoke French knowing Ned did and hoping the others did not.

'I take it you're cussing your brother out,' Hennessey was keen to see the machine in operation. 'Tannis, you have my word the procedure will not involve anything personal.'

'It would be easier than having to try and talk through a briefing,' Ned coaxed.

Tannis softened a little, 'Fine!' She sat down next to Jack and reclined the chair as Ned picked up the case, putting it on the table next to her and began attaching the pads to her temples.

'Thanks,' he whispered; in reply she just gave him a hard stare. 'Before I activate the machine, please remember, no talking, it will affect the result and is dangerous for Tannis.'

The three men nodded, and Ben gave her a concerned look; she managed a small smile.

'Ready?' Ned looked at his sister.

'Not really, no.'

'Eldridge, show memory device on screen,' Ned gave the command, switched the machine on, and instantly Tannis' head fell back and rested on the chair. She was unconscious; the screen was still blank. The room was in silence as requested; Ned opened his mouth to speak but the ship's tannoy system beat him to it. 'Attention all decks, final battle stations drill at 1600 hrs. Final battle stations drill at 1600 hrs.' A look of sheer horror washed over Ned's face as he looked at his sister, still unconscious as she gasped, and the screen came to life.

All six members of *DE-173* were standing in the hold of The Eldridge. Tannis was wearing her trademark leather, to her right stood Em, she was around the same height as Tannis, with the same colour blonde hair, however hers was curly. Next to her was Charlie, a fiery redhead, she was busy checking her weapons. Meg, the shortest of the bunch, but not by much was a brunette, her shoulder length hair was tied back in a ponytail. All the women team members were dressed the same.

Everyone present recognised Ned, who stood talking with his brother Will. Will was a well-built handsome young man with a shock of blonde wavy hair, a lot like his sister. Both men were dressed ready for modern day combat.

Will addressed them all now, 'Ok so this is our chance to wipe the bastards out once and for all, for the first time they're all together and we have the element of surprise, let's get it done and get out.' He walked over to where Tannis stood and taking her hand he led her away from the others, 'You ok?' he whispered, he could tell she wasn't.

'Will, I have a bad feeling about this, it's too easy, somethings wrong, maybe I should just go and check it out first?' She confided now as they were out of earshot of the others, she would never undermine him in front of them.

'Always the altruist,' he grinned, as he hugged her, but his expression soon changed when he realised that she was trembling.

'I'm frightened,' she whispered into his ear.

'It'll be alright baby girl,' he used the term of affection he'd always used for her since she was born, and he and Ned had watched out for her from the moment she took her first steps. They all knew that this was going to be their final battle with Phoenix, it had been discussed at length the night before, things were going to come to a head, and one way or another the time war would be settled.

'Come on Lionheart,' Will kissed the top of her head, 'you're the best of us, we need you out there.'

The image faded, as if in her unconscious state Tannis was fighting the memory, she even stirred in her seat. But the machine won, and another scene unfolded.

It wasn't clear where it took place as *DE-173* were already in the middle of a fierce fight, *The Final Battle with Phoenix* the trap had been made apparent, but as to how they had been betrayed no one knew. *DE-173* fought bravely, but Phoenix used their powers most cruelly. Em had killed three of them but the one left had mind powers and turned them on her with no mercy, she screamed as blood poured from her eyes and nose, then tried to fight, but could hardly move, she flailed for a moment then fell dead with a small whimper.

Will, stood now with dead agents at his feet looking over to his sister's killer. He aimed his gun and fired, but the woman was so fast she dodged them all and appeared behind him, running him through with a huge Sabre.

Charlie was relentless in her attack as she was fighting a female who could project multiple images of herself, so instead of one attacker she had six, but couldn't tell which one was real with the power to kill, she battled on but was decapitated from behind.

Tannis and Ned now fought back-to-back as they had done in the desert, their opponents were male twins who had the power to speed up time, so their attack was full on and hard to fend off, both were exhausted. Ned lost concentration for a moment and was sliced in the side by a sword, he fell to his knees and waited for death. But Tannis swung around and beheaded her brother's would-be killer, however in doing so failed to stop her own, who now seized the moment and drove his sword straight through her shoulder, pinning her to the tree behind them both.

The surviving Phoenix agents lined up in front of them now. It was over. 'Did you really believe you could win?' their attacker taunted, seemingly unaffected by the death of his twin.

He leaned closer to the brother and sister and whispered, 'We knew you were coming; you were betrayed by one of your own,' he laughed.

Tannis looked around at her fallen family, 'No!' She would not believe it, but clearly, they had been expected.

A very battered and bruised agent dragged a semi-conscious Meg over to the group by her hair; she had dispatched four agents, but they had been heavily outnumbered. Throwing her to her knees now to face her brother and sister, the triumphant twin sneered. '*DE-173* is finished, we will now rule as the Gods we are,' as he spoke, he lifted Meg's head and slit her throat. She collapsed to the ground choking on her own blood as her life ebbed away. Then the agent turned his attention towards Ned, and Tannis watched helplessly as he began to suffer the same fate as Em.

'No!' she screamed as she pulled herself agonisingly toward the end of the sword, where she snapped off the hilt, plunging it into the agent's neck, she forced herself free of the blade, as another stepped closer to her, this one wielding an axe.

'No, Tannis is to remain unharmed, she is mine,' a dark-haired agent spoke, his accent from the north of Ireland.

Tannis was filled with rage, she closed her eyes, and the sky turned black; thunder rumbled above them, and fear filled her assailant's eyes. 'No, it isn't possible, no one has such power,' but it was too late for words she thrust her hands out in front of her and a force of such power burst from them, there was a blinding flash, all that Tannis could hear were the words her beloved brother had spoken to her the night before when they stood alone on deck.

'It certainly can't be said that you lack courage, or that in the past you haven't been able to back up your words with actions. You are a warrior, and like a warrior you have confronted the enemy face to face, without looking for a way to escape from the battlefield. Some battles you have won, others you have lost, but you have always fought with the heart of a lion, you're the best of us Tannis.'

Then all was silent again as the sky cleared, Phoenix were gone. The screen went blank as Tannis collapsed.

Back on The Eldridge there was an eerie silence in the room Ned was rooted to the spot as tears ran down his face, Tannis was still unconscious. Ben stood and walked over to where she lay. He ran his eyes over the machine then looked at Jack, Hennessey sat forward and motioned to them to turn it off; Jack threw the switch.

Tannis' eyes flashed open, and she jumped out of her chair pulling at the sensors on her head, shaking uncontrollably as tears fell from her eyes. Ben stood in front of her, she stepped back shaking her head and made a leap.

Hennessey shepherded Ned back to his chair as Jack fetched some water from the cooler, and Ben took his seat next to him. 'I think next time we'll just stick to old-fashioned briefings,' Ned tried to joke, but his voice cracked.

'Ned, why don't you go home, take the rest of the day off?' Hennessey was unusually concerned. Ned just nodded, touched his timepiece and made the leap.

Ben was thinking of Tannis, where had she gone, was she ok? She shouldn't be alone, not after reliving that again. He was snapped back to the now by Hennessey, 'A very brave outfit, they gave their lives to save the world, and no one even knows they existed.'

A small blue flash announced the arrival of Tannis, she was in different clothes, and her manner was more composed, the three men looked puzzled at her calmness. 'I took a day,' she explained, 'the perks of time travel. Where's Ned?'

'Your brother has gone home,' Hennessey assured her.

She nodded then pointed to the memory machine, 'That thing should be binned.'

'It will be secured away, don't worry. Tannis, I must ask…' Hennessey gestured for her to sit down; she took her place next to Jack, opposite Ben, who could only give her a concerned glance. 'Tannis, are you able to generate that much power at will?'

'No, I told you before, I can only do it when I lose my temper, and that,' she pointed to the blank screen now, 'nearly killed me!'

'Would you be prepared to work with our people to try and control it?'

Tannis folded her arms on the table in front of her and rested face down with a deep sigh but not speaking.

'Very well, Colonel, Major, see Tannis back to her quarters,' Hennessey stood and left the room.

Jack rested his hand lightly on her back, and she slowly raised her head and looked at Ben. He gave her a small smile, she sat back in her chair and glared in the direction the Admiral had taken.

'You, ok?' Ben felt like he was in chains not being able to speak to her as he wanted.

'Are you?' she looked from one to the other, 'not very nice having to see the true side of the resident performing monkey.'

'We've been through this love, chromosomes, nothing more, you're no less human than any of us,' Jack always knew what to say.

'I'm not sure that's much of a compliment,' she laughed now as she looked him up and down.

'Cheeky mare,' he gave her a playful shove.

'I'd better go and look after Ned,' she stood.

'Won't Elea be there for him?' Ben frowned.

'Oh, he won't be home, he'll be in a bar getting hammered and looking for a fight.'

'We'll come with you,' Jack stood up, and Ben followed suit. 'Are you sure? It's not a pretty sight' she asked, although she would be glad of the company, Ned could tie one on when he was upset.

'Ok, then, thanks,' she took Jack's hand, and Ben's too when he moved around the table to join them. The two men blinked, and they were in the town outside a bar. It was dark now and judging from the raised voices coming from inside Ned was already causing trouble.

A couple of locals hurried outside, 'Oh, Tannis thank the Gods! we haven't seen him like this since you lost your brother and sisters.'

'I'm sorry, Elders, I'll take him home.'

She walked in to see her brother barely able to stand, leaning on the bar demanding more wine. A look of relief washed over the bartender's face when he saw Tannis. 'Come on Ned, let's save some wine for everyone else, shall we?' She took her brother's arm.

'Tannish,' he slurred, 'drink with me!' He noticed then that she had company, 'Colonel, Major, drinks all round!'

'Not while on duty, thanks,' Ben looked at the empty bottles on the bar as Ned knocked one over.

'Whoops, man down!' He motioned for the bartender to bring another.

'Let's try somewhere else, shall we, mate?' Jack steered Ned towards the door.

'Good idea,' he slurred again, 'I know a rowdy little dive near the quayside, not for the faint-hearted. Then again you three could never be accused of that, eh? Especially not you, my dear sis,' he draped himself on Tannis as they stepped outside, 'heart of a lion this one, always brought me home safe, I love you,' he planted a sloppy kiss on her cheek.

With Jack and Ben either side holding him up, they stumbled towards the water's edge, Ned monologuing all the way, 'I'd be dead if it weren't for her, you know, a hundred times over, Tannis come here,' he looked around for her, too drunk to notice she was standing in front of him.

'Ned, you're pissed, shut up!'

'I'm sorry,' he dropped his head.

'For what?' she soon found out as the two men held him up, he dropped his head and vomited all over her shoes, she closed her eyes and sighed heavily. After washing her feet in the sea, she leaped with them all to Ned's house, Tannis touched his face gently, he was fast asleep as she kissed him on the cheek, 'At least you'll sleep well tonight,' she choked a little on her words, then Elea opened the door,

Jack and Ben carried him inside as Tannis explained what had happened. After laying the drunken man on his bed, they returned to where the two women stood.

Elea thanked them for bringing her husband safely home, and as they were leaving, turned to Tannis, 'You shouldn't be alone tonight either.'

Tannis tried to shrug it off, 'How could I possibly be alone on a boat full of people.'

'Ship.' Elea corrected as she hugged her sister-in-law.

'Whatever,' Tannis stepped away and grabbed Jack and Ben by the arms and made the leap.

That night *Everybody Hurts* by *REM* could be heard coming from Tannis' quarters.

Ben paced up and down, it was eating him up, he knew that she was just a few steps away, but the ship was so busy, he couldn't even knock on her door without somebody probably writing a report about it, he should be with her, he knew that she would be crying.

The music stopped and suddenly he felt that he wasn't alone, he turned to see Tannis standing there, tears running unchecked from those beautiful eyes.

She was trembling when he held her to him, then she began sobbing, he moved her over to the bed and she lay with him as she cried herself to sleep. His heart was breaking for her, for what she'd had to relive. But he was also pleased, pleased that she had come to him for comfort. He wanted more but was happy to settle for this for now.

The ship's tannoy woke them at 0600 hrs, she was laying on his chest, just like she had on their first mission together, except this time when she woke up, she didn't flinch away from him, she just smiled. He rolled her off his chest now, so they lay facing each other as he stroked her face gently.

A loud knock on the door startled them both and ruined the moment, it was Jack, 'Major can I come in?'

They both jumped off the bed, 'Thank you for being you,' she whispered and was gone.

Ben sighed, he was right, this was going to be complicated, 'It's open sir,' he called out and Jack let himself in.

The first training sessions were scheduled for that morning, Tannis and Ned decided that they should be conducted outside in the open fields above Atlantis.

So along with Jack and Ben, another Major from the US Army, a Captain from the British Army and two Sergeants from the US Navy they made their way into the hills.

It was another beautiful sunny day. The military party were under Jack's command and wore combat greens and armed themselves with semi-automatic weapons, Ned was dressed similarly, although he wore makeup and drop earrings.

Tannis wore her own clothes: fashion cut combat trousers and a vest top in khaki, her hair piled on her head. Ned led the way nursing the mother of all hangovers, while Tannis was happy to be last, she was enjoying the peace; Jack dropped back and walked with her, they made idle chit chat for most of the way, until he turned to her. 'Tannis, the Admiral has asked me to put forward some names, you know, to make up three or four mission-ready teams,' he told her.

'And naturally you'll want the best for your team?' she teased. 'Perks of the job, love,' he grinned.

'How many in a team?'

'Three trained, four if we have to take a civilian along, you know eggheads and the like.'

Tannis laughed at his description of scientists, 'Choose carefully Jack I wouldn't like to work with anyone I didn't trust with my back.'

'Who do you trust apart from Ned?'

'Well, you and Major Rhodes of course, I've worked with you both.'

'And we both trust you,' he put a hand on her arm to stop her, 'Tannis, I've already asked for Rhodes to be assigned to my team.'

'Good, you work well together,' she frowned a little now, not sure what his point was.

'Tannis, love, I want the best on my team. That means I want you too!'

She was genuinely surprised, 'Me? Jack, I'm not military trained.'

That was what he admired about her; she was so unassuming, 'I think your track record speaks for itself.'

She put her hand on his, 'Thanks, Jack, that means a lot.'

'But?' He could feel one waiting in the wings.

'But' she smiled, 'your eggheads are working to see if they can adjust the timepieces so they can make interdimensional leaps. If they succeed, I'm finished.'

They walked on now as Jack thought for a moment, 'Nah, you're not the type to sit at home.'

'You reckon?' she smiled.

'I'll put your name down then,' he called over his shoulder as he picked up his pace to catch up with Captain Jackson. Tannis rolled her eyes. There was no point arguing with him that would have to wait until she made her decision.

She caught up with the group as they neared their destination.

Ned dumped his pack, satisfied the location would do.

Jack gave the order for the others to do likewise, 'Ok, listen up, you've all been briefed, today we're just making short leaps to orientate ourselves with the timepieces. Now, I know you have all made at least one leap to get to Atlantis, so you'll be aware of some of the brief side effects: nausea, dizziness, confusion and disorientation, and so on; but as the Major and I were told, it's just like getting your sea legs. Anyways, pay attention because what Ned and Tannis teach you today will probably save your life,' he nodded to Ned to take over.

'Right, before we start, does anyone have any questions?' He prayed for silence; his head was slamming.

'Sir?' It was one of the Sergeants.

'Yes, Sgt Naylor?' He read the surname on the front of his jacket. 'When The Eldridge reappeared in the Navy Yard back in 1943, some of the crew had fused with the ship. Do we face the same risk, I mean, is that why we're out here?'

'No, the timepieces won't allow you to materialise within another object. The best I can explain is they have a sort of built-in radar that guides you when you leap. The reason we're out here,' he addressed them all now, 'is because firstly grass is a bit softer for those awkward landings and secondly for safety reasons,' he looked at Tannis now, who smiled and looked at the ground as he went on to explain, 'I made my first leap when I was nineteen and didn't quite get the coordinates right and ended up at the Battle of Stirling Bridge. As I tried to make a hasty leap out of there two irate Highlanders jumped on me, and we all returned to The Eldridge,' he pulled a face of mock horror, 'bit of a rumpus ensued.'

Tannis put her hands on her hips and looked up, trying not to laugh. Ben stole a glance at her. She had a beautiful smile, and he thought about last night, it was frustrating as hell having to act like nothing had happened in front of everyone.

Jack, too, was watching her, but for different reasons. He was impressed by how she let Ned take the lead and followed his orders. Yes, he was the oldest, but Tannis could easily claim equal ranking with him, even higher with her powers. Yet she was happy to take orders from someone she trusted. He wanted her on his team, no matter what. She was damn good at her job and loyal too. He wanted the loyalty she showed her teammates of *DE-173*, where she would fight to the death for them, and she followed orders without question.

'Ma'am?' the other Sgt looked at Tannis, 'we've been told that the timepieces react with us at a molecular level, so that say we end up in France, we can understand the language and speak it, kinda like the matrix?'

'That's right, but that's all it will do for you, it won't turn you into Neo, although God knows that would've been useful in the past.'

'How long does the effect last when you take the timepiece off?' he asked.

'Once removed the effect wears off instantly,' she explained.

'How do you find it as a woman travelling back in time to when we were subjugated?' Major McGann gave Tannis a hard stare.

Jack rolled his eyes, he had no problem with women in the forces, most of them were an asset, but the odd few bra burners really got up his nose, and she was no exception.

Tannis looked at the woman who stood a little way down the line in front of her, 'I follow my orders, Major, and try to respect the culture and traditions of my surroundings. It's a mission and not what I'm about.'

'But you were forced to act as Major Rhodes' wife on your last mission,' she said bluntly.

'And he was forced to act as my husband. I think Ned will agree Major Rhodes drew the short straw there,' Tannis fired back, 'it's a fact that in some timelines I need the protection of a man. It's better to appear beholden to one than be used by as many as can get their hands on you, wouldn't you agree, Major McGann?'

'I guess so, ma'am, but some of us are born to lead, not follow. You must be so proud of your solo missions though, achieving all you did?'

Tannis shrugged the question off as was her way, 'We all had to work alone at some point.'

They began taking a couple at a time, making short leaps, no spatial distance, just time. It was difficult at first, and all of them except Jack and Ben threw up when they returned. Sgt Naylor almost passed out, and all the new recruits landed on their arse's a few times. 'They make you two look like a pair of pros,' Ned muttered to Jack and Ben.

'They'll get used to it,' Jack said as he watched them on their knees retching, 'not as gentle as leaping with Tannis though.'

She had been leaping with Jack and Ben together as lunchtime approached, testing their abilities, now it was time to take them solo, it was Jack's turn first, 'Ok, something a bit more challenging I think, I'll leave it to you.'

'Absolutely,' he grinned and grabbed her hand just in case.

'Jack, are we on a bloody roof?' Tannis hissed as they lay on their stomachs on corrugated tin, he edged himself forward a little, she followed gingerly, 'Is that what I think it is?'

'Oh yeah, Wembley 1966 World Cup final,' he was grinning from ear-to-ear, 'just kicked off too, I suppose we better get back,' he sighed.

But Tannis rolled over and closed her eyes, 'Wake me up when it's over.' He kissed her hand and settled down to watch the match. Returning them perfectly and within five minutes of leaving as had been arranged, although their clothes were dusty.

Ned gave Tannis a questioning look, 'Everything ok?'

'The Colonel's leaps are perfect,' she replied as she brushed down her clothes with her hands.

It was Ben's turn now; he took her hand in his, 'You can choose, Major,' she told him, then as an afterthought, 'you're not a sports fan by any chance?'

It was too late anyway, they had made the leap, and she smiled as she looked around, 'Kefalonia?'

'One year on,' he took both her hands in his now and pulled her closer, 'we need to talk.'

'It was wrong, Ben. I shouldn't have done what I did.'

'No, don't push me away,' he held on to her hands.

'You saw what I am in the briefing room; I can never lead a normal life. I shouldn't have thought I could, I'm sorry.'

'What's normal? A few weeks ago, I was in the desert in Iraq with the Colonel. Now I live on Atlantis and travel through time with the most beautiful woman I ever met.'

'No, Elea went through hell when Ned was away on missions, I won't.'

'Then come with us, the Colonel wants you on the team.'

'I know, he asked me this morning.'

He touched her face with his hand, 'At least give it some thought,' his voice was gentle.

'Ok I'll think about it, but we can only be friends. I won't allow myself to feel like this about you.'

'Like what?' his eyes searched hers as he gently pulled her towards him, she was trembling as their lips met.

She forced herself to pull back, 'Of all the things I've seen and done, being with you scares me the most.'

'I would never do anything to hurt you,' his voice was full of desire, 'I just want you to trust me Tannis.'

'You know I do.'

'Say it!' he breathed.

'I trust you, Ben.'

His lips were on hers now as he pulled her into him. She tugged at his T-shirt and slid her hands under it, feeling the muscles on his back, she ran her fingers down his spine, and he groaned with pleasure their kisses grew more and more passionate now as he too slid his hand gently under her top. He felt her tremble as his hand grazed under her breasts; then he led her to the shade of the trees where they lay and tormented one another with passionate kisses and caresses until Ben couldn't take it anymore. He sat up, 'We should stop, or I may not be able to act like a gentleman for much longer.'

Tannis sat up next to him and pulled her top off over her head. Then she did the same to him without saying a word. He lay her down, his passion rising as he felt her breasts on his chest, his kisses gently moved from her mouth to her throat, then down to take an erect nipple in his mouth. She arched her back and moaned softly. It was too much for both of them, they quickly undressed and lay naked in one another's arms.

Tannis looked a little hesitant, 'It's ok, we don't have to,' Ben reassured her.

'No, I want to, I really want to, but I just don't want to be a disappointment to you,' she said nervously.

Ben realised what she was trying to say, back when they first met, she'd told them that she could never see herself with anyone who she knew was going to die, or belonged in another time, he was going to be her first.

'You could never be a disappointment, this is perfect, we'll learn from each other.' Their lips met again, and Tannis reached down and took him in her hands. He thought he was going to explode there and then; he wanted to be inside her, the ache was that bad. He raised himself over her, 'Are you sure?' he breathed.

She couldn't speak, just nodded as she kissed him once more and guided him into her. They made love with the warm breeze blowing around them. He was gentle with her, but for saying that her passion for him burned they were insatiable, both reaching their climax together, they lay breathless in each other's arms.

Slowly coming out of their delirium for one another, Ben looked into her eyes as his fingers caressed her face, then he traced down her body and she smiled.

They couldn't stay there forever, although at that moment they wished they could, reluctantly they got dressed. 'Will they split us up?' Tannis chewed her lip, as he hugged her to him.

'I don't know,' he sighed, 'maybe for now we should keep it quiet.'

'But what if they do find out?' she began to fret.

He took her face in his hands, 'It's gonna take more than the coalition to keep me away from you,' he promised, she smiled then and kissed him again.

'Perfect leap?' Ned asked, none the wiser when they reappeared bang on time.

'Couldn't be better,' Tannis smiled as she released Ben's hand with a gentle squeeze.

After lunch, they all took turns to make solo leaps, nothing too much, same place, just a few minutes ahead in time, it was now the turn of Major McGann and Sgt Naylor again, 'Ok, let's shake things up a bit, 5 minutes from now and 4 miles due east, then back here,' Ned gave the command, and they set their timepieces and were gone. As the group waited for their return, Ned turned to Tannis, 'You still ok to babysit tonight?'

'What do you mean still ok, you never asked me in the first place!' she stared back at him in frustration.

'Didn't I? Oh well, go on, you can sit and watch movies and stuff your face with chocolates,' he coaxed.

She frowned for a moment, 'Oh, go on, gets me off the boat for a night I suppose' she was confined to her cabin of an evening now, didn't feel as though she had free run of the place anymore.

'Ship,' he corrected as he put his arm around her shoulder and gave her a quick hug.

'Whatever,' why did everyone always feel the need to correct her?

Ned caught Captain Jackson looking at them. He was a lean Afro English guy, very polite, Ned, like him, 'Something wrong Captain?' 'No sir, I just find it a little surreal sometimes, here we are learning to travel through time, being taught by people who saved the world on a regular basis and you're discussing this evening's childcare.'

Ned shrugged, 'Never really thought of it like that, but on the other hand, who could ask for a better babysitter, a fully qualified medic in case of emergency and a trained killer should the need arise all for the nominal fee of a box of chocolates and a movie.'
Tannis elbowed him in the ribs, 'Oi!' she glared at him. They stood in silence now and waited, Jack checked his watch 'They're overdue.'

Ned turned to his sister shaking his head, 'How hard can it be?'

Tannis put the toe of her training shoe under one of the semi-automatic weapons that lay neatly in a row on the grass, she flicked it up and caught it, knocking the safety catch off.

'Wait!' Jack stopped her as he picked up two more weapons, one of which he threw to Ben, 'just in case,' he cautioned. They made the leap, weapons at the ready, there was no threat, but there was a problem as Sgt Naylor stood alone, Major McGann was nowhere to be seen, 'Sgt, report,' Jack barked as Ben and Tannis scanned the horizon.

'Major McGann ordered me to wait here sir, I reminded her of our orders, but she said she'd have me on a charge of insubordination then she made a leap,' Naylor reported standing to attention.

'At ease, Sgt' Jack knew it wasn't his fault, 'I don't suppose she told you where she was going?'

Naylor shook his head, 'No, sorry, sir.'

'Course, not that would be too easy,' he muttered to himself, 'get back to the others,' Jack gave the order, and they were gone.

'What? Bloody hell!' Ned shouted in disbelief when he heard the news on their return, 'but she was checked, her record was clean!' Tannis laid the weapon that she had borrowed back down where she'd found it as did Jack and Ben then she moved away from the group a little, her stomach churning. Had they done the right thing allowing the coalition here? She didn't have time to let her thoughts wander further. Major McGann was back, and she wasn't alone. Two German SS officers were trying to force her to her knees holding an arm each, they were stunned by the leap and staggered slightly releasing their grip. Tannis was closest; she seized the opportunity while the men were still dazed and ran towards them dragging the Major out of the way. 'Time and place?' she demanded from her.

'What, err, Dachau March tenth, 1944,' the Major said groggily. 'Time of day?' Tannis yelled as she saw Jack and Ben race over.

'14.35 hrs.'

Jack called to the others to hold their fire as he and Ben reached the uninvited guests. They had overcome the side effects now, and one drew his weapon and took aim at Tannis. He pulled the trigger, but Jack kicked the gun out of his hand, and as the shot rang past her head she flinched and turned. Ben easily took care of his mark, and both men now stood in front of the SS officers aiming their weapons at them.

'Get behind me!' Tannis shouted, they did as she said. She closed her eyes and took a breath, the sky above darkened and a strong wind from nowhere blew around them, followed by a great pulse of energy as Tannis thrust her hands out at the SS men and they were gone. Then she dropped to her knees exhausted.

'See to Tannis,' Jack ordered Ben as he marched over to where Major McGann sat.

Ben knelt in front of her, 'You, ok?'

She closed her eyes and leaned into him, she was trembling, and he could feel her heart pounding. Ned had run over to them, 'Is she hit?'

'I'll be alright, Ned, you have to go,' she said weakly.

'I have to check for time discrepancies,' he apologised to her.

'I know, don't worry about me, I'll be fine,' her voice was muffled against Ben's chest.

Ben could see the look of frustration on Ned's face, he wanted to be there for his sister, but at the same time he had a job to do.

'Take care of her,' he looked at the man holding his sister.

'I'll stay with her,' Ben nodded.

Ned used his timepiece and made the leap back to the ship. Tannis' head was thumping as she leaned harder on Ben, he put a supportive arm around her but had to be careful, he was on duty, and they were not alone. In the background, they could hear Jack venting his wrath at the Major. 'What the bloody hell did you think you were trying to achieve?' he didn't give her the chance to answer, 'do you realise the damage you could've caused, not to mention the fact that you almost got Tannis shot!'

Ben held her tighter now.

'Get back down to The Eldridge!' Jack barked, 'This isn't over,' he glared at her as he ripped the timepiece from her wrist.

'I just wanted to prove myself Colonel,' McGann tried to explain.

'Prove yourself? All you've proved is that you can't be trusted,' Jack turned to Captain Jackson, 'see to it Major McGann waits for me outside the Admiral's office.'

'Yes, sir,' the Captain acknowledged his orders and led the team away across the field.

'You alright, love?' Jack knelt next to Tannis and touched her gently on the shoulder, his tone instantly different with her.

'I'll be alright in a minute or two, Jack,' she turned to look at him, 'it's harder to do when you have to aim for an exact time and place.'

'You stay here until you're ready,' Jack told her, then he looked at Ben; 'stay with her, Major, make sure she gets back to the ship safely.'

'Yes sir,' Ben nodded to his superior.

They watched Jack walk back across the field and disappear as he made the descent down the hill back towards The Eldridge.

Ben sat her down on the grass now and wrapped his arms around her as he had wanted to do all along.

'Told you it was dangerous,' she whispered.

'And we took care of each other as a team should,' he soothed.

She was feeling better now, he could tell as he leaned down a little and kissed her, but the moment was ruined as Ben's radio crackled and came to life. 'Major Rhodes, come in please?' Ben groaned as he reluctantly pulled away from her.

'Rhodes here, go ahead.'

'Sir, a message from Ned, he says everything's running smoothly and to remind Tannis that she's babysitting tonight,' the young man's voice rang out from the handset.

'Received. Rhodes out!' he raised an eyebrow, 'so, babysitting, eh?'

The next morning was another beautiful sunny one. Tannis was making her way through the streets of Atlantis; she had stayed the night at Ned's as she had been asleep when he and Elea returned. She hadn't seen Ben that night either, both he and Jack spent most of the evening with the Admiral or writing reports about the day's events. It had been a long night, and McGann was lucky to escape a court martial.

Tannis almost floated down the half-empty streets now, she was in such a good mood, still oblivious to the admiring looks she was getting as she passed by in a white summer dress, the bodice of which was tightly laced at the front, while the skirt flowed freely about her legs; her hair hung loosely around her shoulders. Both she and Ben had the day off, so they had arranged to meet at Jester's stable and walk into the hills together. He was there waiting for her when she arrived. 'Hey, you look great,' he said as he ran his eyes over her approvingly.

'Thank you, Major,' she bobbed a curtsey to tease him.

'Yeah, let's leave him here today, shall we?' he smiled as he picked his pack up.

'Oh, great food!' She grinned, 'Ned ate most of the chocolates he bought me, then offered me the leftovers from one of his experiments,' she pulled a face.

They walked into the hills leaving the harbour behind them. It cooled a little as they entered the wood, but the sun soon warmed them again when they came into a clearing which opened out to offer a breath-taking view of the ocean below. 'Wow, this place is fantastic,' Ben looked around as he put his pack down. Tannis knelt and opened it and took out a large blanket spreading it out on the grass, then she started to lay out the food, it was almost lunchtime, and they were both hungry from the climb, 'And no one to bother us either,' she added.

'Not so far,' he looked around.

'Not at all,' she told him, 'This is private property. No one ever comes up here.'

'Really, then how come we're here?' He sat next to her now.

'See that pile of bricks over there?' she pointed a little way off. 'Yeah.'

'Well, that was going to be a house. The owners bought the land but never built on it. Instead, they buggered off and left their daughter a boat to live on instead,' she wrinkled her nose.

'Ship,' he corrected as he realised what she was saying. 'Whatever,' she picked up a strawberry and bit into it, 'some catch, huh? a rust bucket and a pile of bricks,' she laughed, 'and in fact, I don't even own the rust bucket anymore.'

He smiled. She had given so much and begrudged nothing. They ate the food and talked about the past, but Ben's this time. He told her how he'd been raised by his grandmother when his mother skipped town a couple of days after he was born, his father long gone before that, and how she had refused to put him up for adoption. 'How did she feel about you joining the Marines?' Tannis asked as they ate.

'She told me it was the proudest day of her life,' he smiled at the memory, 'my grandfather was a marine too you see; he was killed in Korea.'

'Korea,' she shuddered.

'You were there, I know, I saw the photo in the Admirals file, 'how was it?'

She looked down at the grass, 'Cold,' she replied, 'and nothing to talk about on such a nice day,' she smiled at him, 'is your grandmother still in the real world?'

'No, she passed away two years ago.'

'She sounded like a strong woman,' Tannis said with a serious look on her face then reached down for another strawberry at the same time as Ben. They both looked into the bowl and saw there was only one left.

'Well, being an officer and a gentleman, I should let you have it,' he grinned.

'And being a lady, I should decline,' she teased.

'Ok,' he grabbed the piece of fruit and with an exaggerated movement made to eat it.

Tannis grabbed his wrist, 'You pig!' she laughed, and he dropped it as she relaxed her grip. He slid his hand into hers and their fingers entwined, with his other hand he moved a strand of hair that the wind had blown across her face and put his arm around her waist then pulled her to him. She trembled again, and this aroused him even more as he laid her down and kissed her. They made love and lay together wrapped in the blanket and stayed like that as long as they could until the sun started to set, and they forced themselves to return to The Eldridge.

Standing at the bottom of the gangplank, 'I guess this is where the Major comes back,' Ben said as he turned to face her, he squeezed her hand, they walked on board and went their separate ways.

Tannis was climbing into bed when there was a knock at the door. She opened it to find a young Corporal standing there, 'Pardon, ma'am, but Admiral Hennessey requests your presence in the briefing room immediately.'

'What's wrong?' She was on the alert.

'I'm sorry, ma'am, that was all the message I was asked to bring.' Ben was walking down the passage with Jack, heading for their quarters when they saw the Corporal at her door, then Tannis followed him quickly; barefoot in her pj's.

'Something up?' Jack asked the crewman who saluted them both. 'The Admiral asked me to bring Tannis to the briefing room a.s.a.p. sir.'

'Ok, Corporal, you go about your duties, Major Rhodes and I will see that she gets there.'

Tannis ran up the stairs in front of them, and they followed quickly behind her. She hurried along the passageway until she came to the door of the briefing room, then opening it, she went inside. Hennessey was alone. 'Where's Ned?' she demanded.

'I'm here,' he walked in from the door across the room that led to Hennessey's office.

She exhaled, 'You're, ok?'

'Better than ok,' he grinned.

She narrowed her eyes at him, 'I thought you were hurt, idiot, I didn't even get dressed, do you know how cold these bloody metal floors are!' she walked over to him and thumped him on the shoulder, 'give me your cardigan. I'm freezing.'

'I'm sorry you were worried Tannis, but Ned wanted to give you the news tonight,' Hennessey smiled. Tannis looked at her brother again who was grinning from ear-to-ear like a Cheshire cat; she smiled now too, 'You've got the results back, haven't you?'
Ned nodded, 'We can bring Cole home.'
Tannis yelped with delight and threw herself into her brother's arms. 'I gotta get changed, give me the date when I get back.'
'Hold your horses and sit down, the Admiral wants a word, if he can get one in,' he said as he shoved her to her seat.

'Colonel, Major, please be seated also,' Hennessey said, then looked at Tannis, 'the lab has been working on Cole's timepiece,' he raised his hand, 'not in the way you think, don't worry. They have however been able to extract information regarding the last leap he made, 16:47 hours May 12th 476 BC.'

'That's fantastic, Admiral, I don't know how to thank you,' Tannis beamed, then she looked at Ned, 'get the kettle on, we'll be back soon,' she said as she jumped up from her seat. Ben shot Jack frustrated glance which the Colonel picked up on straight away.

'Tannis love, slow down, you don't know what you're heading into out there if Cole was ambushed, you'd be in the thick of it too.'

Hennessey cleared his throat, 'Tannis, the whole point of the coalition coming here was so that you didn't have to face such things alone; you will go with a team for back up.'

'Really? I didn't think that would be allowed for personal stuff?' She sounded surprised as she sat back down.

'I think it's the least we can do,' Hennessey looked at her over the top of his glasses, 'and while we're on the subject of teams, I understand Colonel Marsters has asked you to join himself and Major Rhodes to make up our first team?'

'Yes, he did yesterday.'

'And have you made your decision yet?'

'I have Admiral, yes,' she said slowly but looked at Ned. Both Jack and Ben held their breath; they were both hoping for the same answer but for different reasons.

'Before you answer, Tannis, please let me say that I believe you would make a vital contribution to an already elite team.'

She blushed a little now and pulled her knees up into her brother's cardigan, 'I've taken my orders from Ned for the past three years, it just seems disloyal.'

'Tannis, I'm finished. I want to wake up in the morning and not say goodbye to Elea and the kids and wonder if I'll make it back that night,' he sighed, 'I'll tell you this though,' he looked from Jack to Ben now, 'if Tannis joins your team, you won't find a more loyal and trustworthy person to watch your back. God knows she's watched mine often enough and brought me home.'

Jack looked at her now, 'So, what's it to be? Will you trust me and follow my orders?'

'I will,' she replied, then stood up and hugged Ned, 'and you, you get to go home and grow old with Elea.'

'Excellent,' Hennessey looked like the cat that got the cream, which he had, 'the mission will be scheduled for tomorrow morning, all meet back here at 0700 hrs,' he ended the meeting as he stood and left the room.

'Welcome aboard,' Jack shook Tannis' hand. He and Ben had walked over to join them, Ben winked at her, and she smiled.

'You two take care of my sister,' Ned was serious now, 'I know she can be a pain in the arse at times, but I love her, and such good babysitters are hard to come by.'

'Git!' Tannis narrowed her eyes at him, 'you call me a pain, have you forgotten your stag night? I think you lot altered more time in one piss-up than Phoenix did in the whole war!'

'Well, we had had rather a lot to drink, and I don't think Jack and Ben want to hear about that now, you all need to get some rest,' he said quickly as he left the room.

Jack looked back at Tannis and raised an eyebrow, 'Tell all?' 'Maybe I'll let him save it for his memoirs,' she grinned.

'Can't wait to read that,' Ben smirked.
'Oh yeah, especially the part where Hitler woke up circumcised,' she called over her shoulder as she now too left the room.
'Jesus, I wish I could've known those guys back then,' Jack laughed.

Tannis found it impossible to sleep that night, she sat up in bed, her mind racing. It had undoubtedly been an eventful day. She had an idea; she bit her lip and made a leap. Ben jumped slightly as she appeared in his quarters, the lights were out, but he was still awake. She slipped out of her PJs as he lifted the covers and climbed in beside him. Neither spoke, he just held her in his arms as she laid her head on his chest. He ran his fingers gently up and down her arm and kissed the top of her head. She kissed his chest and slowly moved her kisses down to his stomach, he pulled her back up to his mouth and guided her on top of him, he was inside her again, she had never experienced anything so wonderful as when she was with him, he sat up and she wrapped her legs around him as they moved together, burying her head in his neck and trying to be as quiet as she could when she came, it was the same for him, knowing she was satisfied he lay her down and pushed inside her, his mouth was on hers as he flowed in her, trembling as he did. They slept together, only waking when the sunlight intruded through the porthole, then Tannis slipped into her night clothes and leaned over and kissed him. He touched her face lightly, and she was gone.

They all stood in the hold now, ready to leap. Jack and Ben wore their greens and Tannis her trademark leather.

'You're armed?' She looked at them as they checked their safety clips.

'We don't know what we're up against and in such a remote area, we can send in a containment crew to clean up later,' Jack informed her as Ben handed her a weapon of her own and gently squeezed her hand when no one was looking. Ned walked in now and marched straight over to Tannis, hugged and kissed her then wiped the lipstick off that he'd just deposited on her cheek.

'You watch her back,' he looked at her teammates, 'if it is Phoenix out there, they'll drop everything and go after her.'

'Well, when you're popular...' she shrugged.

Hennessey addressed them now, saying, 'Alpha team, good luck.' The three of them stood together, and they were gone.

They arrived at the cliff top an hour before Cole was due. It gave them a chance to check out and secure the area which they did so in the full heat of the day; much to their surprise there was nobody around and no sign that anybody had been there for a long time. So, they took position on the high ground that overlooked the run-up to the ledge and waited, still nothing.

'It's possible he could bring one through with him in a fight,' Tannis thought out loud as the time dragged on. Then he was there, dark-haired, dirty and bloodstained, Tannis made to get up, but Jack pulled her back down, 'Wait a minute,' they watched as Cole staggered forwards. Satisfied that it was all clear for the moment Jack sent Tannis to her brother while he and Ben watched her back. He turned when he heard her approach, it was an emotional sight as she hugged him, and they both fell to their knees. Cole raised his pistol, an army issue from the First World war which was the uniform he wore now, an ANZAC one, (his mission had been in Gallipoli 1915) as Jack and Ben approached.

'It's ok Cole, they're friends,' she choked as the tears ran down her face.

'Let's go,' Jack ordered.

'Tannis, what's going on?' Cole seemed dazed.

'C'mon, let's get back to The Eldridge,' Tannis took his hand, looked at Jack, he nodded, and they made the leap.

Ned had the biggest smile on his face as he rushed over to Cole and hugged him, 'Welcome back,' he fought to keep his voice steady. Cole looked around at all the crew and armed guards in the hold, 'Will somebody, please tell me what the hell is going on and where are the others?'

Tannis shot Ned a worried glance.

He sighed, 'Cole, we need to talk, you've been gone three years, mate, and as you can see a lot has happened.'

'What are you talking about three years, I've just completed my mission?' he looked at Tannis now, 'is this some joke?'

She just shook her head; she didn't know what to say.

Cole was shown to the briefing room where he was brought up to speed with the events of the past three years, but he struggled to accept what they were saying to him, 'So you're telling me that Phoenix are finished and Will, Em, Meg and Charlie are dead, killed in battle?'

'I'm sorry mate, but that's how it happened,' Ned told his brother.

'And yet the two of you survived?' his tone was harsh, 'how come?'

'We bloody well nearly didn't!' Ned snapped, 'look it's all documented, read it for yourself,' he dropped a file on the table in front of his brother. Cole read through it and sat brooding, 'They really are all gone.'

Tannis and Cole spent the night at Ned's catching up, they put it down to shock - the change in his personality - and hoped it would only be temporary. He drank himself into oblivion and passed out on the couch. Tannis covered him with a blanket and Ned led her out onto the patio. 'Something's not right,' Tannis couldn't put her finger on it.

Ned nodded, 'He always was a hard bastard, had to be, he was in charge.'

'I know I was mainly on the receiving end of his lack of charm,' she snapped.

'Tomorrow's another day,' Ned, ever the optimist. They watched over their brother that night, reminiscing; but Tannis couldn't shake off her feelings.

The new day did not bring the old Cole back. Instead, he demanded a meeting with Admiral Hennessey, and that was where they sat now. Hennessey, Ned, Alpha team, and of course Cole, who was straight to the point, 'I want the coalition off the island. I was not consulted, therefore, you,' he looked from Ned to Tannis 'had no right making that decision.'

'You weren't consulted because you were dead,' Ned pointed out bluntly, 'and if it weren't for the coalition, you still would be.'

'Well, I'm back now, and things are going to change, we can't trust these people; they could be Phoenix for all we know!'

'Phoenix are gone, Cole, besides, you know they can't make the leap here,' Why didn't he remember that? Tannis frowned a little.

'Yeah, well if a half breed like you can get through, maybe one day they will find a way too,' he sneered at his sister.

'Hey, FUCK YOU!' Ned stood now; he would not have his sister spoken to like that. Cole shoved his chair back as he walked over to face off with Ned. Both Jack and Ben rose too. Either one wouldn't mind a swing at this guy, but they had to keep the peace, so they placed themselves between the two would be opponents.

Tannis was shocked and confused, 'Why are you being like this Cole? What happened to you out there?'

'You want to know what happened to me? I'll tell you. I saw things for what they were! I realised that there was no point in this stupid time war, it didn't affect us, so why should we bother with it? Let Phoenix have their world, and we can live on Atlantis in peace,' he looked at them all as he walked around the room, 'the only fly in the ointment was you lot,' he pointed to Ned and Tannis, 'couldn't just stand by and let it happen could you, oh no!'

Ned was stunned, 'You saw the altered timelines, how they tortured people, set up extermination camps, of course, we couldn't just stand back and watch!'

'Well, it's all over now, and I'm in charge, you lot are to be gone by the end of the week!' he waved a hand towards the non-Atlanteans.

'That's not an option, Cole, I suggest you get some air and clear your head!' Hennessey spoke now.

'Maybe I will,' his eyes widened as if in a moment of realisation, he pulled his sleeve back, touched his timepiece and was gone.

'Would somebody like to tell me what the hell that was all about?' Jack sat back down.

'More to the point where's he gone?' Ben looked towards the spot Cole had just vacated.

'I told you there was something wrong!' Tannis looked fearful at Ned, 'this is more than guilt!'

'Guilt?' Ben looked across at her.

'When we went on a mission, it was usually to save someone Phoenix had decided to kill so they could change history for their gain,' she began to explain, 'but in the saving of that one life, sometimes we had to watch others die because that was what history dictated, it's hard. We had to tell ourselves that history killed all those people, not us, but it didn't always wash.'

'Must've been rough,' Jack gave her a sympathetic look.

Ned nodded his agreement, 'You're right, though, this is more than that!'

Cole returned later that same day and took up residence in his old quarters where he sat brooding now. The noises in his head got louder and louder; people screaming, always screaming! He stood and banged his head against the wall - anything to make them stop. The last thing he saw in his mind's eye before he blacked out from the pain was a vision of The Eldridge exploding then darkness and the peace of unconsciousness washed over him.

Tannis was in her quarters, too. It was late, but she was still wide awake, hardly surprising given the events of the past few days. She was confused by her brother's actions and hurt by his words; and she had barely spent any time with Ben since Cole's return except for on duty, which was torture for them both.

Wondering if he was awake, she made the leap to see. It was dark, and he looked like he was sleeping. She turned to leave, and it was her turn to jump this time as he reached out and grabbed her arm. He pulled her towards him, and she climbed into the bed, his body was warm and firm, he lay on his side and looked at her. She smiled up at him, 'I missed you,' she whispered.

He leaned down and kissed her, 'I missed you too. I'm sorry things aren't working out with Cole.'

'That's not the Cole I remember,' she frowned, but her face relaxed as she ran her fingers lightly across his stomach. He kissed her again and slid his hand under her top, caressing her breast, then he pulled at her pjs, 'Take them off.'

She did so willingly and lay down with him again, he kissed her all over until her skin was tingling. She let out a gasp as he raised himself over her and pushed inside. They made love with such wanting that it was hard to be silent. Afterwards, they lay breathless, their hearts pounding.

The sun's rays woke them the next morning, Tannis rolled onto his chest not wanting to get up, he held her for a moment, then tilted her chin up and kissed her. She was still half asleep as she nuzzled back into him, 'Tannis, c'mon Babe, you gotta get back to your quarters,' he whispered. She sat up awake now and reached for her pj's; he stroked her back as she put her top on then she lay down next to him again as she pulled on her bottoms.

'Can I come again tonight?' she asked, he traced her face with his finger.

'Tannis, I don't want you to think that this is all there is, coming to my room at night I mean.'

Her eyes saddened, 'You don't want me to come anymore?'

'God no, I can't get enough of you, what I mean is, I want you to know that I want more from our relationship than we have now,' he closed his eyes, getting frustrated with himself, 'what I'm trying to say is I love you Tannis, I've never felt this way before, I don't want to scare you off, but I need you to know how I feel.'

She smiled and pulled him down onto her mouth, he pulled away a little, 'I feel the same way too,' she whispered.

He kissed her again, 'Say it.'

'I love you, Ben,' she said honestly.

'You do?' he smiled.

'You have my heart and soul, Ben Rhodes.' They weren't touching for a moment, and that's when she made the leap.

Over the next few days Cole seemed to get better, he accepted the coalition, even liked the idea that none of the decisions rested on his shoulders anymore. He seemed to take an interest in the fact that Ned was still working for them, but purely as an advisor, he had made it perfectly clear that his mission days were over. 'So, the only one I have to worry about is Tannis,' he said to Ned over lunch one afternoon.

'Tannis is fine, Cole, she's part of the best team the coalition has, and as you know, she really can take care of herself.' The two men finished their meal together and headed back to the ship to meet her, and the three of them spent the rest of the day together, it was like old times again.

That night the rain came down like a monsoon, so loud it woke Tannis. She felt a bit groggy as she stood up and looked at her timepiece. It was 0300 hrs, how had she slept so long? She had only laid on her bed to wait until it was time to go to see Ben. Then it struck her. Apart from the rain falling there was no other sound, the crew tried their best to be quiet at night, but there was always some noise. She walked slowly to her door trying to shake off the foggy feeling in her head. Opening it slightly at first, then fully, stepping out into the passageway 'Oh Shit!'

In front of her and all around were red cables, to be more precise demolition fuse wires, and they led off everywhere. Tannis walked along the passage a little and saw a crew member lying motionless on the floor then another further along. She hurried to them and was relieved to find they had a pulse. Removing their sidearms, and making sure they were loaded, Tannis shoved one in the waistband of her pj's behind her and carrying the other, went on her way to the briefing room finding more and more crew unconscious but unharmed on her journey. The briefing room was empty as was the Admiral's office, then the tannoy crackled to life, it was Cole 'Would Tannis please report to the forward hold, Tannis to the forward hold please,' his tone was sarcastic.

Oh, Cole, what have you done? she thought to herself as she walked down the passage towards the stairs that led to the hold, stepping over more crew sleeping away their watch.

She stood in the doorway now, pistol in hand, to see her team, Ned and the Admiral on their knees, hands cuffed behind their backs lined up with Cole standing behind them. They were dripping with water. Cole looked from them to her, 'Sorry about the mess, I had to wake them up somehow,' he dropped the fire hose he had been holding to the floor with a clang, 'now, toss the gun into the passage and come in, notice we're all wet, so any of your tricks and they go too.'

She did as he said and stepped inside.

He gestured around him now to the fuse wires, 'Do you like what I've done with the place?'

'Cole, what the hell are you up to?'

'What I should've done years ago,' he moved over to a desk and picked up the detonator, 'you see with all of this gone there will never be another time war, because there will be only one side.'

'But we'll all be dead,' she looked at the hostages. They all seemed ok, just drenched.

'You should've been dead three years ago,' he grabbed Ned by the hair with his free hand, pulling his head back.

'I told you we were lucky to survive,' Ned gasped.

'I know, but you weren't supposed to, and you wouldn't have if it hadn't been for the half breed over there,' he glared at Tannis, 'you would've died when you were meant to!'

'I don't understand?' Ned croaked.

Tannis' eyes brimmed, 'You told Phoenix we were coming that day, that's why they were ready for us, you betrayed us,' her voice wobbled.

'Well done that, girl,' Cole released his grip on Ned, who turned his head slightly.

'You bastard, you killed them all! What, for a deal with Phoenix?' He tried to stand but Cole struck him on the head with the detonator in his hand, and he dropped to the floor dazed.

'Let me guess, they turned on you in Iraq, threw you over the cliff?' Tannis played for time.

'We'll never know what happened now, will we?' He raved, 'wake up, Ned, time to die!' He was borderline hysterical now, as Ned began to stir, 'you always said I was an emotionless bastard,' he leaned down to his brother. 'Well, guess what? I found the strongest emotion in the world-- HATE!' He quickly turned to Tannis now and saw the way she looked at Ben, 'Oh that's precious,' his smile showed malice as he saw the opportunity to make his sister suffer a little more before he killed them all. He moved across the line of his hostages and came to a stop behind Ben, 'Let's play a little game, shall we?' He laid the detonator down on the desk in front of Ben, then pulled out the knife he had belted to his thigh and held it to his prey's throat, 'If you can get the detonator before I slit the Major's throat, you get to save them all,' he glared at Tannis, 'well I doubt you'd make it in time to save the Major, but see how it goes,' he shrugged.

'Do it,' Ben spoke through gritted teeth as he looked at Tannis. 'Oh, how noble,' Cole made eye contact with Tannis, 'Ready?' In that instant he grabbed Ben's hair, pulling his head back, moving the blade swiftly for the kill.

Simultaneously Tannis pulled out her hidden weapon, took aim and pulled the trigger. Cole fell dead with a clean head shot.

She just stood staring at what she had done as Jack managed to get up and went over to the desk picking up the keys to the cuffs, he quickly unlocked his own then Ben's who hurried over to her. She'd lowered the weapon but still held on to it, he gently took it from her before handing it to the now freed Admiral who made it safe and laid it down on the nearby desk. She just stood emotionless through it all. Ben rested his hands on her shoulders. 'Tannis?' She just stared, then began to tremble uncontrollably as he pulled her into him. He led her out of the hold and took her back to her quarters where she just sobbed in his arms.

Jack came later to tell them that he had taken Ned home and explained it all to Elea. Tannis lay on the bed now where she had cried herself to sleep. 'The crew are waking up,' Jack said in a hushed tone as the two men stood by the door, 'looks like gas was put in the air conditioning to knock us all out while he did what he liked, I need to get a squad together to sort this bloody mess out,' Jack motioned to the fuse wires. 'You stay with Tannis, she's gonna be a wreck when she wakes up.'

Ben nodded and went back to the chair he had been sitting in by her bedside.

The sun was up, and the rain had stopped when Ned stood in the doorway of his sister's quarters, it was as if she knew he was there as she sat up in bed. Ben had dozed off but woke now as her hand slipped from his, she stood up and walked toward her brother, he hurried the rest of the way and grabbed her and hugged her tightly then the tears began again for both of them. Ben tactfully left, closing the door behind him, he made his way to the briefing room where he met up with Jack and the Admiral and explained about Ned showing up as he took his seat with the other men around the table. Hennessey sighed heavily, 'Dr O'Brian has performed an autopsy on Cole, and it would seem that the man was suffering from a malignant brain tumour in such a position as to affect his personality. This will go little towards helping Tannis in her grief, but perhaps one day she will understand the man she killed to save you, Major Rhodes and indeed us all was not her brother.' Jack had something to add, 'When we searched Cole's quarters, we found a suicide note in the pocket of his ANZAC uniform, during one of his more lucid moments he must've realised what he'd done and jumped off the cliff in Iraq, we didn't find it at the dig, it would've rotted away by then.' Ben just sat with his head in his hands, he wanted to be with her, she needed him, and he was useless to her, he needed to see her.

Two days later, Ned and Tannis followed Cole's coffin into the little white church. Hennessey, Jack and Ben attended in full dress uniform as a mark of respect for the side of the man they never met. Elea and her family were there too and a few of the locals. The service was of a mixed denomination, one of the Atlantean elders led it, he blessed Cole and thanked all their Gods for his presence in the world, then gave a speech about Cole as he remembered him as a child growing up on the island, then as the dedicated leader of *DE-173* and how much he would be missed. Tannis just stared at the coffin as more people got up and said kind words about him then it was time to lay him to rest.

Ned and three of the villagers carried the coffin outside and Tannis followed. She swallowed hard and fought back the tears as they all stood around the graveside. The Elder said a few words as the coffin was lowered into the ground then Tannis and Ned stepped forward carrying a red rose each which they dropped onto the casket.

Then, the crowd of mourners began to disperse and headed back to Ned's for the wake.

Ben followed Jack's gaze along the line of now five white crosses, then he stood and watched Tannis as she held her brother's hand and stood before the open grave. She had carried herself well throughout, but he knew she was screaming inside. It should be him standing there with her. It should be him comforting her; this was all wrong!

Soon everybody was back at Ned's house saying kind words about Cole. There had been no need to mention his actions to the people of Atlantis; it was better he should be remembered as he was before his illness took over him. Tannis stood talking with the Admiral and Ned;

they seemed to be deep in conversation. Jack and Ben observed from the other side of the room; Jack was distracted as the Elder who had led the ceremony engaged him in conversation, but Ben could see something was going on as Hennessey shook her hand before she hugged Ned tightly and went outside. He followed her out into the garden, 'Tannis, wait!' She stopped and turned, 'you're going away, aren't you?' He looked at her.

'I can't stay, Ben, I need to get away from here to think,' her voice trembled.

He took her hands in his and led her out of view of the house by some rose bushes, 'I'll help you through this,' he whispered.

'You're part of it,' tears ran down her face.

'I don't understand?' he wouldn't let go of her hands.

'Everyone I love leaves me or dies, Ben,' she sobbed, 'I can't be with you, the end will hurt too much.'

'I'm not the one doing the leaving,' he whispered as he pulled her into his arms, and she clung to him.

'We have to end it now, Ben.'

'No, I can't turn my feelings off like that and neither can you, I'm in love with you, Tannis, and I know you feel the same!'

Three of Ned's children too young to understand what was going on ran into the garden. Tannis stepped away from him, and she was gone.

'Damn it!' he cursed to himself, 'she's gone,' he sighed as Ned joined him now.

'And she'll be back, and when she is, give her some space, and she'll work it out,' Ned gave him a half smile.

'You think so?' Ben looked at him.

'I know so, she loves you, Ben, she needs to realise that life can be hard either way,' Ned said as they walked back to the house.

'Ned, who else knows?'

'I think the fewer, the better, for now, don't you?'

Chapter Four

Three weeks had passed since the funeral, and as proof that life goes on, things had returned to normal on The Eldridge from the outside looking in at least.

Ben went about his duties as was required of him, but his heart wasn't in it. Tannis was never far from his thoughts; where was she, how was she? It was eating him up inside, he lay awake at night wondering if wherever she was, was she thinking of him.

Ned had heard nothing from her either, but was annoyingly calm, he knew where she was and that she was safe, but he wouldn't tell Ben, he was waiting for her to come back on her own, not forced or dragged back, it had to be her choice. Well fine, but it didn't make him feel any better.

Jack too was worried about her. Sure, he wanted his chosen people for his team, but he liked Tannis, loved her like a sister, and of course, the place wasn't the same. The ship was too quiet without her chatting happily away to the crew as she walked along the passageways or hearing her laughter as she and Ned ribbed one another about something. She was the heart of The Eldridge, without her tearing around with her lust for life it was just a ship.

Jack smiled to himself now as in his mind he heard her voice as she called it her boat, or when she told them, she would be at the pointy bit. *Come back to us soon, Tannis, love.* he thought to himself as he made his way to the briefing room to meet up with Ben, Ned and the Admiral. Their first mission had been given the green light, and now they had to go over the final details.

As Tannis was still away, she had been replaced by Sgt Hicks from the Royal Navy, and they also had a scientist in tow too, a Dr Richardson; it was her research that had led to the mission in the first place.

She had found a power surge in some caves in Northern France, and it was the plan to travel back ten years to when the activity first registered on satellite imagery, she had a theory that it was another lost timepiece.

Not what Jack had in mind for their first mission as a team, but then again, he still didn't class it as their team yet, not without Tannis. He was sure Hicks was up to the job, but he had worked with Tannis and trusted her; she had proved herself. He walked into the briefing room and took his place at the table, Ned and Ben were already in their seats and a short while later Hicks and Richardson joined them. The red-headed Dr sat next to Jack; she smiled at him as she moved her chair forward. He could see that Ned and Ben were thinking the same thing as he was; she was sitting in Tannis' place.

Hennessey entered from his private doorway and sat down. The briefing wouldn't take long, it was mostly dotting the I's and crossing the T's. They were almost finished when Ned's cell phone began to vibrate on the table, he looked at the caller ID and smiled, 'Sorry Admiral, I have to take this,' he showed the phone to Hennessey who nodded, then turned to Jack.

'Bravo team is almost ready for their first mission, Colonel, Major Harmon and Sgt Barber have passed all their evaluations. They just need their third team member to become active.'

'Still no further ahead with that, sir?' Jack asked.

'Oh, I'd say that's imminent,' Hennessey looked smug.

Ned had finished his call, re-joined them once more and sat next to Ben, grinning.

'Good news was it?' as if Jack needed to ask.

'It seems we have two reasons to be cheerful,' Hennessey told them, 'Bravo team now has its third team member.'

'And the second?' Jack frowned.

Ned held up his cell phone, 'That was Tannis; she's in her quarters,' his relief was apparent.

'Yes!' Jack made a small drum roll on the table with his hands, 'So Sgt Hicks gets to join Bravo team then?'

'No, Colonel Tannis has been assigned to Bravo team for the foreseeable future,' Hennessey said calmly.

'But she's ours,' Jack forgot himself for a moment, 'sir' he added.

'Your team is prepped and ready to go. Tannis has been told to report to Major Harmon, whom she will serve under while you're away,' Hennessey stood now indicating the subject was closed.

Ned looked from Jack to Ben, 'She says she'll see you at dinner,' he held Ben with his gaze for a moment then continued with the mission briefing.

They all left the briefing room 15 minutes later, and Ben headed for the crew's quarters. Like hell was he waiting until dinner, he wanted to see her now and alone. He knocked softly on the door when he got there, his stomach in knots.

Tannis was expecting him. She opened the door and stood aside to let him in then closed it and turned to face him. He took her hands in his, 'I missed you,' he whispered.

'Ben, I can't do this, I …' her eyes brimmed.

He put his finger to her lips, 'It's ok. I'll give you all the space you need. I just want you to know my feelings for you haven't changed.'

'I'm so confused,' she blurted out, 'I just feel numb, every day, I go through the motions,' her voice cracked, 'I left because I didn't want to hurt, but I still hurt,' he pulled her into his arms; she didn't resist him, 'I shouldn't have come back,' she sobbed.

'You shouldn't have left,' he was gentle, not chastising.

As she looked up at him, he wiped her tears away with his finger, 'I'm here for you, just let me in.'

'It's shutting you out, that's the problem,' she sniffed, 'I tried so hard, but I can't.'

That was all he needed to hear, he took her face in his hands, and his lips were on hers, she clung to him as their kisses grew stronger, his tongue was in her mouth. The ship's tannoy intruded into their embrace, 'Bravo team to the briefing room, Bravo team to the briefing room,' but Tannis' quarters were empty.

In the heat of the moment, he didn't feel the leap, and it was only when he opened his eyes to look at her that he noticed their surroundings. They were in a bedroom now. Well, what was the point of having all that power if you couldn't use a little for yourself occasionally? He didn't care where they were so long as they were together, he knew they would be in a safe place.

Taking his time, he removed her clothes, savouring each part of her he took her in his arms and laid her down on the bed. Then quickly undressed and lay next to her, he leaned over and kissed her 'No more running away,' he said between kisses, 'this is for keeps, not just for tonight,' he looked into her eyes, 'say it,' his voice was husky.

'For keeps,' she said softly, 'I love you, Ben.'

His lips were on hers again, their desire for each other was too much, he wanted to be inside her now, and she felt the same, he thrust into her, and they both cried out, he was trembling as he fought to control himself while he looked at her, 'I love you Tannis,' he breathed. They made love with such passion, purely for the release of the past few weeks, and afterwards, they lay breathless holding each other, but it wasn't long before their desire retook them. Then for the first time in weeks, they both slept soundly only to be woken by the birds outside singing the dawn chorus. He stroked her hair as she rested her head on his chest, 'Where did you go?'

'I came here,' she said quietly.

He looked around them now, taking in their surroundings, Tudor four poster maybe, the décor kind of looked that way, but he was no historian, 'Where's here?'

'It's a secret,' she teased.

He rolled her off his chest and lay facing her, 'No secrets,' he said as he touched her face lightly.

'This is Avalon, only I can get here. It's a safe place to be when you need to think.'

'The Avalon, King Arthur and all?' He shouldn't be surprised, he thought.

She nodded, 'It's deserted now, no one can find it.'

'You mean like Atlantis?'

'Sort of yes, when I blasted Phoenix, Ned decided we should find somewhere to practice where I couldn't do too much damage. So, we went back a few thousand years and found this place, it was abandoned, so we used it,' she looked around the room, 'Ned built this house, I bring him and his family here for their holidays.'

'So how is it protected?'

'Ah, well,' she pulled a face, 'Ned was trying to make me lose my temper so it would happen again. He started waving a crossbow around when I was trying to concentrate, tripped over in his bloody heels and shot me in the leg.'

'Ouch!' he winced.

'Yeah, a bit more than ouch, like The Eldridge I changed something around here, but worse. You can't even get here with a timepiece now,' she kissed him slowly, 'we could stay here forever, and no one would be able to find us,' she slid her hand under the sheets and slowly moved her finger along his groyne, smiling at it having the desired effect. He pulled her hand out and rolled on top of her gently holding her wrists above her head as he kissed her. 'Neither of us will be fit for duty.'

They accepted the inevitable and got dressed ready to return to The Eldridge, he took her hands in his and sat down with her on the bed, 'Tannis, this is fantastic, more than I ever hoped, but we have kinda been playing Russian roulette.'

She understood, 'The kind where I get to carry the bullet around for nine months.'

'When we go back, we'll go and see the doc, sort out some birth control.'

She hugged him so hard he almost fell backwards, 'What was that for?' He laughed.

'For saying we,' she smiled.

'Can you get us back just after we left, I have a mission in the morning?' Ben rolled his eyes, not looking forward to it.

'I've got one tonight; didn't you hear them calling for Bravo team as we left?'

'Now you mention it, yeah, but I had my mind on other things,' he put his hands on her hips then frowned, 'Harmon.'

'Yes, Major Harmon, I saw him on the way to my quarters, he said he was looking forward to having me under him, suggestive git!' she tutted.

'What! who does he think he is, was that all he said?' Ben fumed. 'Apart from the bit where he asked me on a date.'

'Son of a bitch,' Ben was furious he paced the room, 'making a move on my girl.'

Tannis laughed, 'Ben Rhodes, I never had you down as the jealous type.'

He stopped pacing and smiled as he pulled her towards him. 'Sorry, but you're mine, and I can't stand the thought of you being anywhere near him.'

'Ben, you just said it. I'm yours, you have me, heart and soul remember,' she kissed him, 'c'mon, you ready?'

He nodded, and they were back in her quarters.

'Bravo team to the briefing room.' The tannoy echoed.

'I'll see you at dinner,' she kissed him and ran out into the passageway.

Jack was waiting for her as she hurried toward the briefing room, her face lit up when she saw him. 'Come here you,' he gave her a big hug, 'God it's good to see you again, this place has been too quiet,' he confided as he walked the last few paces with her.

'I missed you too, Jack,' she told him as they reached the door, then she pulled a face, 'gotta go.'

'I'll see you at dinner and just remember you're only on loan to Bravo team, you're Alpha and don't forget it,' he winked.

She gave him a grin and went inside.

About an hour later she walked into the Mess looking for them, they had saved her a seat, and she plonked herself down and picked up an apple from the plate of food they had ready for her.

'So, what's the gig?' Jack was referring to her mission with Bravo Team.

She sighed heavily, 'Ancient Rome, just babysitting, see how they blend in.'

'What's your cover?'

'I am Major Harmon's wife, he is a wealthy merchant, and Sgt Barber is our man at arms,' she waited for Ben's reaction, but it was Jack that surprised her.

'Hmm you just watch Harmon, wouldn't put it past him to try and cop a feel,' he said bluntly.

'Jack, I spent the night alone in a tent in the same bed as Ben, and he never tried to cop a feel,' she was gob smacked.

'Yeah, that's because he was brought up proper,' Jack winked at his officer.

She looked to Ben for support, but he raised his hands, 'Hey, I'm with the Colonel on this one.'

She laughed, 'Ok, I'll tell you what, any inappropriate behaviour and I'll just stab him, how's that?'

'Fine by me,' Ben approved.

'Me, too,' Jack grinned.

They ate their meal and enjoyed each other's company, as they were leaving Major Harmon met them in the passageway, he acknowledged the Colonel with a salute, then as he passed Ben he muttered, 'Hey Rhodes, Tannis told you about our toga party, can't wait to have her under me finally.' It was a red flag to a bull, Ben grabbed him and pinned him against the wall and with one swift punch in the gut Harmon was on his knees, 'You do not lay a finger on her,' he hissed as he walked away.

Jack had sensed a commotion and hurriedly led Tannis further along the passage; she tried to look back, but he put an arm around her shoulder. Ben caught up with them now saying nothing, Tannis wisely remained silent too, but Jack couldn't help himself, 'You'll have to excuse the Major, we didn't catch him young enough to tame him.'

They went up on deck to get some air, and Ned was waiting for them, she ran over and jumped into his arms, he swung her around and kissed her on the cheek, 'About time too, three weeks Tannis, what the hell did you find to do there?'

She just shrugged, 'Had a lot to think about.'

'Well, I'm glad you're back if you'd left it any longer. We were going to have to ask Jack or Ben to babysit,' he winked mischievously. They walked along the deck now to a quiet spot and leaned over the side looking at the bay.

'I should go and get changed,' she excused herself and vanished. 'I might just pop down and have a private chat with Major Harmon,' Ned straightened up, 'I think he has designs on my sister.'

'Oh, I think he's already got the message, Ned. Major Rhodes had a word with him just now,' Jack said tongue in cheek.

'Did you really Ben? Well done,' Ned slapped him on the back.

The three of them waited in the hold for Tannis to show up, Harmon and Barber were already there, Barber was ok they had to admit, but Harmon loved the part, as he strutted around in the finest robes, while Barber was practically dressed like a centurion. Tannis walked in now; she looked ethereal as her robes flowed with every step she took, her plaited hair was piled high on her head secured with a gold braid, a gold torque necklace hung around her throat, and a gold bangle coiled up her forearm to complete the outfit. She walked over to Alpha team and Ned.

Jack gave her the once-over, 'Are you armed?'

'Not much room in this, but' she lifted the skirt of her robe to reveal a small dagger strapped to her thigh, 'other than that I'll have to use harsh language,' she grumbled.

'Be careful.' Ned hugged her. She stepped back and nodded to Jack and Ben.

'Back soon,' she said and smiled then walked over to join Harmon and Barber.

Hennessey entered the room now, 'My dear, you look stunning,' he smiled at Tannis as she prepared for the leap, 'Bravo team, good luck.' That was their cue to leave.

'Sir,' Jack decided to push his luck with the Admiral about getting Tannis back on the team. Ben followed along. Bravo team wasn't due back until morning. Ned had wandered over to a Corporal who was standing near the latest piece of equipment that enabled them to detect peaks and dips in electrical energy, such as were used when making a leap. This handy piece of kit allowed them a brief warning that a team was returning. Just in case, as with Major McGann, they bought any unwanted guests with them at an unofficial time.

'About Tannis' temporary assignment to Bravo team,' Jack began.

'Colonel, I realise you requested Tannis for Alpha team and that she accepted, but your team is in place for tomorrow and will proceed as planned,' Hennessey was firm.

'Yes, sir,' Jack knew there was no point in pushing it further.

'However,' Hennessey called over his shoulder as he walked to the door, 'after Alpha and Bravo teams have completed their present missions, Tannis will be under your command once more.'

'Yes!' Jack clenched a fist, and Ben didn't bother to hide his smile either.

Hennessey was just about to leave the room when the Corporal called out, 'We got incoming!' No one was due back yet; the armed guards trained their weapons on the space Bravo team had vacated.

'Lower your weapons,' Jack ordered, it was Bravo team, but not as they were when they had left a few minutes earlier, 'Bloody hell!'

he gasped as he and Ben ran over to them, Tannis stood with Harmon and Barber on either side of her, they were unconscious on their knees as she held them by their wrists; her white dress clung to her breasts as it ran red with blood.

'Medic!' Hennessey yelled.

'You're hurt!' Ben reached her as she released her teammates into the hands of the medics, she was breathing hard, her lip was swollen, 'It's not my blood.'

'Tannis, report,' Hennessey strode over.

'They tried to stop a stoning,' she winced as she touched her swollen lip.

'My God, the first thing they were taught was not to interfere,' he snapped.

'Easier said than done sometimes, Admiral, she was a nine-year-old slave who had denied her master his sexual rights.'

'Are you injured?' He looked at the state of her.

'I'm fine.'

'Colonel Marsters, Major Rhodes, escort your teammate to the infirmary it won't hurt to have her checked out.'

'Yes, sir,' Jack nodded, she was theirs now.

The doctor was busy with Harmon and Barber, so Tannis was checked over by a nurse, and once she was satisfied the only injury was to her patient's lip, Tannis was allowed to shower and change into some borrowed medical scrubs while her teammates waited outside in the passage.

'She could've been killed out there,' Ben said as he glared through the window at Harmon lying unconscious on a bed, his face battered and bruised, 'as if it's not dangerous enough, they have to go and pull a stunt like that.'

'I agree with you, Major,' Jack tried to calm him down, 'but once again, it shows how good she is. They needed her out there a lot more than she needed them.'

The conversation went no further, Tannis walked out of the infirmary and stood in front of them, her lip almost healed, 'Does this mean I get to come with you tomorrow?' she asked.

'No,' Jack put his hands on her shoulders, 'this means you go to bed and rest tomorrow, where we know you're safe.'

'But I'm fit for duty, and…' she began.

'No buts Tannis, that's an order, now the Major will see you to your quarters, I need a word with the Admiral.'

Ben opened the door to her room, she walked in, and he followed, closing it behind him, she was in his arms in an instant, her face buried in his chest. 'My God when I saw you standing there covered in all that blood,' his voice shook.

She looked up at him, 'At least I'm back on the team now,' she smiled, 'ouch,' her lip hadn't entirely healed yet.

'I could've lost you,' he looked hard at her.

'It'll take more than the Roman Empire to stop me coming back to you,' she joked, then she saw the serious look on his face, 'Ben, this is what I do, it's what I've always done, we almost broke up because I couldn't handle the thought of you being out there, I had to accept it,' she stepped away from him a little, 'can you?'

'I guess I'll have to,' he conceded, 'but right now I have to get you into bed.'

'Yes, sir,' she teased.

'Alone, you know we can't right now.'

'Ok, I'll just get my pj's on then,' she undressed in front of him until she was naked and smiled coyly at him, 'could you pass them to me please, Major?' Ben bit his lip and nodded to himself; he'd asked for that one. He stepped over to the chair and picked up her clean folded night clothes and held them out to her. She reached for them, as he let them fall to the floor, grabbing her wrist and pulling her to him, she gasped as his mouth sought her breast and his hand slid down the flat of her stomach and settled between her legs. Something inside him needed to claim her again; he moved her back against the wall as she undid his belt. He picked her up, and she wrapped her legs around his waist.

She was soft and warm as he entered her, she was like an addiction, he couldn't get enough of her. She buried her head in his neck as she climaxed trying to be quiet, then it was his turn, he held her tightly as he thrust inside her then, oh, the release. They stood trembling and breathless. He kissed her gently so as not to hurt her lip, 'You are gonna get me kicked out of the military,' he sighed as they got dressed. Tannis climbed into bed, and he kissed her goodnight and left to find Jack.

Morning came, and it was her turn to see them off, and she liked it not one bit, they were dressed in their greens, and as they were only going back ten years, they were armed with modern day weapons which made her feel a little better. She stood by the door; her arms folded and watched them prepare for the leap. Both men looked over to her as Hennessey gave permission, she raised a hand in farewell, and they were gone.

At a loose end now she wandered down to Ned's office, he was shouting at his computer as usual, 'Come on you bastard, you know what fuck it, I'll just write it down!' he looked up and saw her standing in the doorway, 'bored without your new playmates?' he grinned.

'No, well just a bit worried, you know.'

'Oh, I should know, I go through it every time you leap my lovely,' he walked around the desk to where she stood and tucked her arm under his, 'c'mon let's go to *Antaeus' Café* and put the world to rights over tea and cake.'

She looked at the pile of papers on his desk, 'Don't you have work to do?'

'I'm having an attack of the fuck its today,' he announced, 'I walked in this morning and took one look at that lot and thought fuck it!' He grinned as they walked away.

Later that evening Tannis went to the hold to wait for her team to return. Ned and the Admiral were already there; it was hard for her to be casual about the wait. She was desperate to see him back safely and had worried herself sick all day. Ned picked up on her mood earlier at the café. She hadn't even raised an objection when he picked up the last cream cake, usually it was full on war who got it. 'He'll be fine Tannis, stop worrying,' he told her.

'I'm worried about both of them, actually,' she pointed out.

'Ah but you're not in love with Jack, are you?' he said as he sat back in his chair, 'I take it you're sleeping with him?'

'Bugger off!' she glared.

'Tannis, it's allowed, you know. You're both adults, and besides, I couldn't think of anyone better for my sister,' he gave her a genuine smile, 'you deserve to be happy.'

She frowned now, 'But is it allowed Ned? what if the coalition finds out, will they split us up?'

'Well, that's when you play the diva card isn't it?' He winked. 'What card?'

'Tannis, the boffins tried and failed to make the timepieces able to make interdimensional leaps. If they want to keep you, I'm sure they'll bend the rules a little, and technically you're not military, so you don't come under their regulations.'

Back in the hold, something was wrong; their return time had come and gone. Tannis looked nervously at her brother who gave her hand a little squeeze. 'Em was always late,' he reminded her, 'could be anything.'

'No,' she frowned, 'Jack and Ben are pros, they're the best of the lot for accuracy with their timepieces.'

'Deck officer, Alpha team's mission plan please,' Hennessey walked over to the desk, it would soon be time to think about sending in an extraction team in, Tannis was going to put herself forward to go after them but stopped short of making her request when she saw the Admiral's expression change from neutral to anger as he read the mission plan.

'What is it?' she asked instead as Ned stood behind her.

'This is not the mission plan I agreed to; it has been altered. They're not in France, they've gone to Turkey, it seems Dr Richardson has another agenda,' he fumed.

'But why, what's in a cave in Turkey?' Tannis looked at her brother.

'I think I might have an idea, come to my office,' Ned said as he hurried from the room. Hennessey and Tannis followed him along the passageways, all the way there her mind raced, she had to force herself to focus on the positive otherwise she was no good to them. Once inside Ned's office, he reached up to a high shelf that contained some of his most prized books and drew out a large leather-bound volume which he lay carefully on the desk. The binding creaked as he opened it up and thumbed through the pages to the section he was looking for, 'It's mediaeval,' he explained. 'Folktales, superstitions and the like.'

'What relevance does this have, Ned?' Hennessey was growing impatient.

'You'd be surprised how much fact is hidden in fiction, Admiral. Yes, through time stories are exaggerated and added to, but it all starts somewhere,' with that, he pointed to a drawing of the open mouth of a cave, 'prime grazing land around these parts and a large population of goat herds, but no one will use the land because the caves are cursed.'

Hennessey looked at Tannis who folded her arms defensively, 'Nothing to do with me.'

Ned continued, 'Apparently, a young goatherd boy lost one of his animals in the cave and fearing a beating from his father for the loss of the animal he went inside to find it. He returned to his village that night to discover his family were long dead and 150 years had passed. The boy told the tale of how after entering the cave he found he couldn't leave by the way he had come in, so wandered for hours getting lost deep inside until a woman found him and led him safely out, warning him to stay away because sometimes demons visited the cave.'

'A holding cell?' Tannis looked at her brother, 'I thought they stopped using them when time travel was outlawed?'

'It would appear one still exists,' then for the benefit of the Admiral he explained, 'there are natural weak spots where two dimensions rub together, sometimes they merge, and things come through. Well, the powers that be in the future found the worst of them and where possible they created holding cells to contain whatever came through until they could send it back.'

'How do you know this?' Hennessey looked at them both. 'Information sent back with The Eldridge,' Tannis answered.

'And you think this is where Alpha team has gone?' The Admiral knew Ned was probably right. He knew his stuff.

Ned nodded, 'Yes, they probably don't even know they're overdue.'

'Very good, well done,' Hennessey acknowledged, then turned to Tannis. 'Tannis, you will join Major Charles and Sgt Hancock for the extraction team, we will assemble in the briefing room immediately.'

Major Charles was British Army, Jack had spoken of him before, he was a good man and so was his Sgt, Charlie Team's other member, Captain Johnson was currently on sick leave, having been injured on their last mission. Oh well, at least they will approve of my teammates this time, she thought as she took her seat at the briefing room table next to the Major. He was a big guy, she thought, at least six feet tall, black and good looking to boot. Many of the women in the town had a crush on him and were always asking her to find out if he had anyone special. Hennessey outlined the problem to Major Charles and his Sgt, 'It should be straightforward getting in there, but the problem will be finding the way out.'

Ned hurried into the room now, 'There should be a control panel inside that will shut off the force field at the mouth of the cave, or at least allow a way out somewhere,' he still carried the large book with him, 'it says here that the boy left the cave from an opening deep inside.'

Major Charles read through the hastily cobbled together file in front of him, 'Ned, it says here that the caves are tidal if the protective field is in place, wouldn't the cave be full of water?'

'No, it allows inanimate objects to pass through freely, so the tide will rise and fall,' he gave them a concerned look now, 'from what I can gather about the technology of holding pens your weapons will be no use to you in there and neither will your timepieces. You may only be able to fire off a few rounds before they are rendered useless, but on the plus side it means that you can leap there close to Alpha team's arrival time as the residual energy will be taken away along with their power.'

'So, can't I just grab them and leap out?' Tannis frowned.

'I don't know, the holding pens are designed to hold life forms from other dimensions, so it may have the same effect on you, there's a good chance you'll be going in as a mere mortal like the rest of us.'

Tannis glared at her brother, 'I am mortal!'

'So, basically, what you're saying is when we're in there if we don't find a way out, we drown?' Sgt Hancock piped up.

'Basically, yeah,' Ned shuffled his papers, 'also remember, for that holding pen to activate after all this time something came through to our world.'

'No pressure then,' Tannis stared at her brother.

'People, due to the circumstances, I have to say that the mission will be undertaken on a voluntary basis now,' Hennessey looked at each one of them.

'Well, I'm going,' Tannis said straight away, 'my team is in trouble!'

'Me too, sir,' Major Charles added, 'I owe the Colonel from back in Iraq.'

'Me too, sir,' Hancock agreed.

Hennessey nodded, proud of them, 'Very well, you leave as soon as you're ready!'

It didn't take them long to prepare, Tannis went to her quarters to change into her leather combat gear then headed straight to the hold. Major Charles and Sgt Hancock joined her in the passageway, they were in their greens, once inside the hold they collected their weapons, although they knew they wouldn't have many shots if it came to it, and then they only had their knives to rely on.

Ned hugged Tannis, 'I suppose it's pointless to try and talk you out of it?'

She nodded and kissed him on the cheek, 'I've had worse odds than this.'

Ned stepped back and stood by Hennessey's side now as he gave them their permission to leave, 'Charlie Team, good luck!'

'Bugger!' Tannis looked down at her feet, Charlie team had made their leap outside the mouth of the cave not inside as Alpha had done, the tide was coming in, and they were already up to their knees in water. They didn't pause, no point, just walked straight inside. Once in, Major Charles tried to push his hand back out, but there was a solid wall of nothing blocking him, he then looked at his timepiece it had stopped. So, he led the way along the narrow cutting in the rock, and they waded on like this for a short distance.

'It's still light in here,' Charles turned to Tannis.

'Must be from the energy source, I suppose they needed to see what they'd trapped,' Tannis shrugged.

Ahead their narrow path began to open into a vast cavern. They approached it cautiously, then froze and pushed their backs against the wall as they heard what sounded like a weird animal half roar half screech followed by rapid gunfire. They peered inside and saw

Alpha team pinned down behind a large rock, being stalked by some creatures that appeared to be humanoid but could go against gravity and crawl along the walls and ceiling of the cave; they had no hair, just skin that seemed to be made up of green scales, and long nasty looking claws. There were three of them left. Jack and Ben had taken out one each before their weapons failed. They knelt now as they tried to find out what was wrong with their firearms. Hicks gave them cover fire, but his gun was soon rendered just as useless. They reached for their sidearms, which failed too as the three others stalked closer. One scuttled overhead and began to climb down the wall behind them, its long claws ready to attack.

Tannis whispered to Major Charles and Sgt Hancock, 'I can make the distance cover me; I'll take the one behind them.' Charles nodded as he and Hancock readied their weapons for what little firepower they would provide.

'Go!' Charles said in a loud whisper. Tannis ran down the slope towards the large rock her team were behind, she heard the predators call out to one another but kept running, as Charlie team opened fire, she felt a thud behind her when one fell dead from above. Then she ran up onto the rock her team sheltered behind. As Dr Richardson stood up, Tannis took aim, 'Stay down!' she yelled and opened fire; the creature fell dead inches away, it was over. The last remaining creature turned tail and ran.

Jack looked toward the entrance and saw Charlie team approaching, Ben gave Tannis a confused look as she smiled at him. 'Not that it isn't a pleasure, love, but what's going on?' Jack was still checking his weapon. Tannis jumped down and grabbed Richardson by the throat, shoving her back against the rock wall, she extended her wrist blade and aimed it at the Drs' head. 'You put my team in danger, that was a mistake.'

'Tannis, what the bloody hell has got into you? Stand down!' Jack barked. She retracted her blade and released her grip as the doctor gasped for air.

Stepping away, Tannis turned to Jack, 'She changed your orders, you're three hours late, and you're in the wrong place.'

'But we only just got here?' Ben was puzzled.

'And I checked the mission changes, Hennessey signed them off.' Jack frowned.

'She forged the lot,' Tannis pointed at the guilty looking doctor. Major Charles and Sgt Hancock joined them now, and Charles filled them in. Jack was furious with Richardson. He rounded on her, spitting out, 'You not only put us in danger but now another team has come through, why?'

'I knew Hennessey would get Ned involved and stop the mission. I've been monitoring this cave for months, it could help us find a way through to other dimensions instead of using Tannis,' the scientist said proudly, 'the technology will be invaluable, even she is powerless here,' Richardson glared at Tannis.

'Hmm, she'd still have kicked your arse if I hadn't stopped her, now I'm not so sure I should've called her off,' he said bluntly.

They all turned as water began to run into the cave. 'Everybody look for a way out, and stick with your partner,' Jack ordered, 'Major Rhodes with Tannis, Hicks, you're with me, You, too, Doc.'

They all spread out, and when they were out of earshot, Ben stood close to Tannis, 'You shouldn't have come. This could be a one-way mission,' he whispered.

'For keeps,' she touched his hand softly, 'we travel the road together now.'

'The road to come what may,' he remembered as he gave her hand a gentle squeeze.

'Anyway, we're babysitting tonight, so we can't die, Elea will be furious,' she joked.

He smiled now and shook his head, 'You're amazing; you know that?'

She winked at him then stopped. There was an opening behind the rock wall in front of them. They signalled to Jack and the others who came over to them through the steadily rising water.

'I'll take point,' Jack gave his orders, 'Major Charles, you and Hancock cover our rear.' Charles nodded as he and his Sgt stood to one side.

'Jack, if this is the only way out it also means big and ugly went this way,' Tannis put a hand on his arm.

'Well, we'll have to keep our eyes open then, won't we?' He patted her hand as he went through with Ben close behind, then Tannis with the others following. The walls of the cave were slimy and wet along this part, and the water was rising rapidly now. It was almost up to their waists, and it was cold. Again, the way ahead seemed to widen a little. Jack gave them the signal to wait as he and Ben went ahead to check it out, they soon returned. The group huddled closer as Jack whispered their findings, 'Whatever those things are, there's a nest of them in there hanging from the ceiling, it looks like they're asleep, we'll go through a few at a time slowly and quietly.'

He and Ben crossed the chamber first and stood guard at the entrance to the next passage; Jack signalled for Tannis and Richardson to pass next. The two women waded slowly through the cold water trying to make as little sound as possible. Tannis turned and looked back sensing that the doctor had stopped moving behind her, she was right. Richardson was looking up, one of the scaly beings was drooling in its sleep, and the thick saliva had run down onto her shoulder. Tannis motioned for her to keep moving, but she was frozen to the spot, so she walked back to her and took her arm to lead her on. The doctor was still looking up when a pair of eyes flashed open and stared at her, then the beast began to lower itself slowly in front of them. Richardson found her feet now and hid behind Tannis, shoving her towards the threat as she ran past Jack and Ben and on into the next tunnel. Tannis stepped back and extended her wrist blade. The others were waking up now from all the noise Richardson had made as she ran through, and they began to lower themselves down all around her.

'Get away from her you scaly gits!' Jack shouted, then the fight began. The one Tannis faced grabbed her and threw her across the chamber. She smashed into the wall and fell limply into the water below. Both teams attacked now. It was a vicious fight; the creatures tried to slash with their claws, their strength was immense. Ben was trying to fend off two as he looked for Tannis who still hadn't surfaced yet. He killed one with his knife, then as Jack finished his, he knifed Ben's second in the back.

'Find her!' Jack yelled as he waded back into the fray. Ben tried to make his way over to where she had fallen, but one of the beasts jumped out of the water in front of him and made a surprise attack. They wrestled together and fell below the surface, staying down for some time. He was close to running out of air but managed to break free for another lung full before it dragged him down again, and the struggle continued. Ben was trying desperately to wound the creature. He slashed with his knife and felt it go limp, but he was sure he hadn't made contact. Then in the blurred haze of the salt water, he saw he wasn't alone; he broke the surface at the same time she did. It was Tannis; she jumped back a little as the creature she had just killed bobbed up between them.

They both joined the frey again; there weren't that many left now. Jack was trying to fight his way toward Sgt Hancock who was in trouble but fighting bravely. Hancock killed one of his attackers but the second slashed his head taking part of his skull clean off. The Sgt dropped, Jack caught him as Major Charles finished the beast, slitting its throat from behind and letting it fall dead into the water. The one remaining creature Sgt Hicks took care of.

The chamber was quiet again now except for the sound of the water running in. Jack cradled the dying man in his arms as Hancock began to wander in his mind, the head wound was so severe, 'Lisa?' he called, 'Lisa, where are you?'

They all looked on helplessly, even Dr Richardson who had made her way back inside now.

'Lisa, darlin, where are you?' His voice was getting distressed as he called for her again.

'His fiancé.' Major Charles explained to them. Hancock called her name again, Tannis couldn't bear it.

'What's the Sgt's name?' she asked Ben.

'John,' he replied sadly.

She waded over to where Jack held the dying man and took his hand in hers, 'I'm here, John,' she soothed.

'Where've you been darlin'? I was getting worried,' his mind was so far gone, he didn't know it wasn't her, 'did you pick up your wedding dress?' He smiled as he asked, his blinded eyes staring blankly.

'Yes, Yes, I did,' she tried to keep her voice steady.

'I wish I could see it, what's it like?'

'You'll have to wait, you know it's bad luck,' her voice wavered a little bit.

'I can't wait. I love you, Lisa,' his voice slurred now.

'I love you too, John,' she whispered as his hand slipped from hers, he was gone.

'Thank you, ma'am, that was a kind thing to do,' Major Charles put a hand on her shoulder, 'now why don't you let us take care of him?' She couldn't speak for the moment, so she just nodded and turned away from them all and waded a little way across the chamber, standing with her hands on her hips looking up trying to compose herself. Jack looked at Ben; he could see he wanted to go to her but was pleased that his officer still knew his place on the mission, so he gestured his permission with a motion of his head.

Ben nodded his thanks and shoved past the floating bodies of the dead creatures as he made his way towards her. He put an arm around her shoulder, and she leaned into him, 'You really are an angel,' he whispered.

'Ben,' she looked up at him and half collapsed in his arms. He put his other hand on her waist to steady her, and as she flinched, he pulled his hand away, noticing it was covered in blood, he hurriedly helped her to the side of the chamber where a small ledge jutted out and raised her up to sit on it. It was just high enough to keep her out of the water and allow him to look at the wound. Jack made his way over to them; he could see something was wrong as Tannis leaned back against the wall wincing in pain.

'Major?' he questioned as he drew close.

'She's hurt,' Ben slowly moved the piece of torn leather to reveal a puncture wound in her side from which blood seeped as she breathed.

'She pushed you onto it when she ran,' Jack glared at the doctor as he remembered seeing Tannis flinch when it happened. Ben applied a waterproof dressing as best he could, then turned to Jack and said quietly, 'She can't heal, we have to get her out of here fast!' Jack nodded and turned to the others, Major Charles and Sgt Hicks had wrapped Hancock's body in his poncho. 'We're moving out Major Charles, Sgt Hicks, take point and keep your eyes open, God knows what else is in here,' Jack covered their rear walking behind Ben and Tannis, who was in a bad way, leaning heavily on her partner for support. The water had risen to their chests now.

Major Charles led them along another seemingly endless tunnel.

In the distance, they could see two twinkling lights floating up on the roof of the cave. Everyone paused and stared at the sight. The lights slowly got closer and closer until they danced in front of the teams. 'Now what?' Jack whispered as the lights moved between them all pausing at each person as if studying them.

'I think they're friendly,' Dr Richardson called back to Jack as one of the lights fluttered around her head. Ben pulled Tannis up a little, she had started to slip down, that was when both lights hovered around her and then in a flash they went back to their safe haven on the roof.

'Move out!' Jack called ahead to Major Charles, and they began to edge slowly forward. From their place above, one of the lights darted straight for them. It hit Tannis in the chest, knocking her and Ben backwards into the water. Ben surfaced seconds later holding her head up, she was out cold now. Jack waded to the other side of her and helped take some of the load from Ben, 'Did it go into her?'

'I'm not sure, I think so,' he tapped her face lightly, but she didn't respond.

Jack glared up at the other light safely out of reach on the roof. 'C'mon,' he helped Ben move her as they set off again. The tunnel opened into another chamber now, but this one was a dead end. 'The control panel must be in here somewhere, everybody start looking,' Jack ordered as he slipped his arm from around Tannis, but he didn't get far. She started convulsing, and the two men held on to her trying to keep her above the water. After a moment, she threw her head back, and as if in a concerted effort launched herself forward, as the little white light burst from her.

'Ew,' Tannis shuddered, 'that was weird!' The two men holding her up did a double take.

'You're healed?' Ben gave her a puzzled stare. 'Yeah, but it wasn't me' she grimaced.

Just then the two lights rushed at the teams once more. Major Charles ducked as they flew over his head and hit Dr Richardson and Sgt Hicks square in the chest this time, knocking them under water. They both surfaced quickly gasping for breath and conscious. Then they stared at each other, smiled and turned to the others. Richardson spoke, but it wasn't her voice, 'We are sorry if we startled you, but your female,' she looked at Tannis, 'was moments from death, and we knew we could help her.'

'Well, we're grateful for that, but there's nothing wrong with the two you're in now, so if you don't mind...' Jack's sentence was cut short by the doctor's guest.

'We are trapped here and wish to return to our dimension. We have been following you on your journey through the cave and heard you talking about the female Tannis. She has the ability to return us.' 'Is that why you saved her?' Ben didn't trust them; most things came with strings attached and where were they when Hancock was dying?

Hicks spoke now although it wasn't his voice either, 'We merely want to go home.' The water was rising fast.

'Ok, I'll help you if we can get out of here, but leave the Dr and the Sgt first,' Tannis said.

'I'm fine like this,' Richardson spoke with her own voice now, 'I am learning so much from Kira, I am free to think and do as I please.'

'Me, too sir,' Hicks addressed the Colonel, 'besides; they can't last too long in sunlight without a body to protect them.'

'If they're free to do as they please, how come I had to kick your arse out?' Tannis looked from one to the other.

Kira spoke through Richardson again, 'You do not trust easily, if you had allowed me to get close to your mind, we could've shared a lifetime of experiences.'

'Yeah, well I'm very picky about who I share what with,' Tannis fired back.

'But your memories, I could've re-lived them as if they were real.'

'She's not a fairground attraction for your entertainment!' Jack snapped.

'But I could feel the blood coursing through your veins when you ran through the ship as it was sinking, the ice-cold water, stabbing at your body,' Kira enthused.

'You have my memories?' Tannis glared.

'No unfortunately only that brief one as it flashed into your mind when we were both submerged.'

'Alright, that's enough,' Jack brought an end to the conversation. 'If you're staying put, and only for now, you can help look for the control panel.'

They all scoured the walls as the water rose around them, Jack kept Tannis between him and Ben, he didn't want Kira or the other one who hadn't given its name yet to have another go at her.

Tannis shivered, 'I don't trust them,' she whispered, 'they have access to all of Richardson and Hicks' memories.'

'Yeah, well it won't do them any good back in their dimension besides, you blocked them. They only got your memory of *The Lusitania*,' Jack reminded her.

'*Titanic*,' she corrected.

Both men looked at her as she stared at the wall in front of her not wanting to make eye contact.

'You were on it when it was sinking?' Jack couldn't believe it. 'When it sank,' she mumbled, 'I've never known water so cold, but this isn't great either, so let's find a way out shall we?'

The search was in vain. They found nothing and the water level was within feet of the roof now as they were all forced to tread water.

They had been taking turns to swim below and continue the search, Jack broke the surface from his try, he looked at his hand it was bleeding, 'No luck,' he gasped as he swam to join his team.

Tannis looked at his wound, 'These are puncture marks,' she showed Ben the three small holes in the palm of Jack's hand, 'how did that happen?'

'Dunno, I was running my hand along the wall, and it felt like something poked out and stuck in me,' he said, 'don't think it was the doorbell though.'

'Maybe it was,' Ben looked at Tannis, 'the powers that be built this place right, maybe they had to prove their DNA to get out. It makes sense, otherwise whatever came through might find the way out.'

'Well, if that's the case, we're one PTB down,' Jack looked at the roof of the cave. It wouldn't be much longer now. Ben shook his head. Jack wasn't following him, 'Yeah, but Tannis' folks went through to the future. If this stuff were left here, they'd know *DE-173* might need to get out, otherwise, why tell them about such places?'

'Worth a try,' Jack agreed, their heads touching the roof now, 'take your last breath and follow me down.' They did as he said and dived below the surface, Jack led Tannis to the right spot, she ran her hand down the wall, and they saw her flinch as the needles went into her hand followed by a small cloud of blood. They waited, but nothing happened, there was no more air up top, this was it.

Ben grabbed her jacket front with both hands and pulled her towards him, their lips met but only briefly as a force so powerful he couldn't stop it pulled her from his grip. The wall had opened, and they were being washed away down another tunnel with no way of stopping themselves; the surge was so strong, but at least they could breathe again. A thought hit Jack as they were hurled along, surely the PTB wouldn't just have a sheer drop at the end, would they?

As it happened no, they didn't. There was a small plateau overlooking the sea, but at the speed they were travelling they weren't going to stop when they hit it.

Sure enough, they were thrown clear of the plateau then found themselves falling towards the water below.

They all made it to the surface at about the same time, Alpha team immediately searched for one another, then treading water for a moment, they looked up at the great height they had fallen from. *What a ride*, Jack thought and grinned to himself.

It was a long swim to the beach, most of the area was a sheer cliff face, but eventually, they made it and slowly walked up the sand and sat down to catch their breath. Tannis lay between Jack and Ben, it seemed her usual spot to be between them, it was purely a subconscious act, but they all felt comfortable with it.

Jack lifted the piece of torn leather on her top, her wound was completely healed, no scar, but her hand was still bleeding. Her powers had not yet fully returned, he noted.

'Good job Ned was around,' she panted.

'You, too,' Jack pointed out, 'we'd never have made it out of there if you hadn't volunteered to come with the extraction team.'

She shrugged off his compliment, 'A fluke.'

'Fluke, fate, call it what you will, love, you were put in our way for a reason,' he winked at her and got up to help Major Charles drag Hancock's shrouded body ashore, leaving her alone with Ben.

'Nearly lost you back there,' he whispered.

'Back at ya, Major,' she smiled up at him. He had to agree she was right, didn't mean he liked it though, and maybe Jack was right too; she had been put in their way for a reason.

Jack re-joined them with Major Charles now; they were all aware that the doctor and Hicks had distanced themselves from the group. Jack looked at Tannis' hand, unlike his, it had healed, then a thought struck him, 'Hey back there with the beasties in the cave, you fought like you usually do, but you had no powers.'

'Yeah, that sucked a bit,' she admitted.

'But you still got on with it,' Major Charles added, 'and comforted a dying man with a hole in your side.'

'You all went through it, too,' she brushed it off again as she raised her head slightly and looked at the two hosts who stood by the water's edge deep in conversation.

'You ready to take our floaty friends back yet?' Jack asked her.

'Sorry, not yet' she shook her head as she rested it back on the sand, 'besides when I get there, I'll have at least a 24-hour wait before I have the strength to make it back.'

'It'll be more than 24 hours, you're not going alone, I don't trust them.'

'I agree sir, but they did save Tannis, so they must want to leave our dimension at least,' Charles added.

'Hmm,' Jack stared at Richardson and Hick's, 'I've got a bad feeling in my guts.'

'Oh, hold it in,' Tannis said quickly, screwing her face up.

Jack side eyed her for her sarcasm.

Their timepieces beeped now indicating they were functioning again. 'Major Charles get yourself back to The Eldridge and report to the Admiral. I want the Doc and Hicks contained when we return for a full medical,' Jack ordered and then on a more personal note, 'and thanks for coming after us, it must've been a tough choice.'

'No question, sir, none of us volunteered, we insisted,' and with that, the Major took hold of his fallen comrade, and made the leap. Tannis sat up now and pulled her knees under her chin and shivered, 'Oh, I can't wait to get back and have a nice hot bath full of bubbles.'

'You're easily pleased,' Jack still eyed the doctor and the Sgt as he spoke.

'I'm a woman of simple tastes,' she told him.

'So, I see,' he looked towards Ben and then winked at her as he got up and walked over to the other two. Ben and Tannis just looked at one another. Did he know? Was that what he was trying to tell them? Well, there was nothing they could do about it now, so they both shrugged and got up to join him.

'We've got a short wait while Tannis recharges her batteries, and then we'll take you back to your dimension,' Jack addressed the visitors.

Richardson spoke in her own voice now, 'That won't be necessary, thank you, Colonel. Kira and I are getting along quite nicely, and we can offer each other a lot more in this dimension, and I think you'll find Nyra and Sgt Hicks are of the same opinion, too.' Hicks stood by her side, 'You should feel the power they have, the power we can share.'

'You secure that crap, Sgt!' Jack ordered, 'both of you will leave your hosts as soon as you are returned to your dimension.'

Hicks un-holstered his sidearm, 'Sorry, Colonel, I liked you.' Richardson looked at Ben now as he and Tannis had joined their CO, 'And I really like you, Major. Join us, and we could share everything.'

'No thanks, I'm a one-woman man, and there's already two of you in there,' he grimaced.

Richardson turned to Hicks, 'Make sure you put a bullet in her head,' she sneered at Tannis, 'with you dead, no one will stand in our way.'

Hicks aimed at Jack first and without hesitation pulled the trigger. 'No!' Tannis yelled and thrust her hands out, time seemed to stand still in front of them. Hicks and Richardson were frozen, as the bullet hung in mid-air.

'I didn't know she could do that!' Jack gasped.

'I'm not sure how long she can hold it, sir.'

Jack got the message and moved out of the way of the bullet that was on target for his head with seconds to spare as Tannis fell to her knees and the bullet carried on its path into the sand behind them. Jack lunged for Hicks and Ben for Richardson, but too late, they were gone.

'Shit!' Jack cursed. Ben just looked at the empty space they had once occupied; they were going to be trouble.

Behind them Tannis lay on the sand, her eyes closed barely moving, the two men knelt either side of her. She had really been through the wringer today. She raised her arms and tried to focus on her timepiece, there was no way she was going home under her own power.

'Could I trouble one of you chaps for a lift home?' she asked sleepily as she let her arms fall either side of her limply.

Both men smiled, Ben set his timepiece and swept her up in his arms, Jack too set his, then with a quick glance around nodded to his teammate and they were gone.

Chapter Five

Ned and Tannis spent the next few weeks writing reports regarding their visits to other dimensions. This bored the living daylights out of her as most of them were just mirror images of their own with a few tweaks or quirks, but in typical military regulation, everything had to be documented. As her teammates came to Ned's office to meet them both and go to lunch, they could hear Tannis as they approached, 'God this is boring, c'mon let's go and sniff out a bit of trouble somewhere.'

'Those days are over for me; you know that. I actually enjoy the calm here, and I thought you would too. You know, no one trying to kill us every five minutes, besides this should only take another week or so.'

Tannis banged her head on the table as her teammates came to a stop in the doorway.

'Another week of this and I'll be begging for the hand of death to brush over me,' she groaned.

'Paperwork going well?' Jack grinned at her as she raised her head and looked at them both.

'I am stagnating here Jack; my mind is turning to custard.'

'Yeah, I heard, and no you won't go looking for trouble.'

Ned looked up from his notes, 'She doesn't have to, it usually finds her.'

'It'll find you in a minute,' she glared at her brother.

'Ok well, let's get some lunch, shall we?' Ben smiled at her and instantly diffused the situation. They left the room and walked on along the passage a short way in front of Jack and Ned who were deep in conversation.

'She's not just playing up you know, Jack. She's not wired the same as most people; she can't just sit and do nothing. Even when the Time War was over, she still made leaps to blow off steam.'

Jack nodded, 'I know the Major and I are getting a bit stale too just hanging about. I'll have a talk with the Admiral.'

True to his word, straight after lunch Jack went to see Hennessey and put the situation to him, 'As a matter of fact, I have been reading through some of their interdimensional reports and was thinking about Alpha team undertaking a recon mission. It seems dimension seven may have inhabitants that have a natural immunity to malaria.' Not exactly what he had in mind, Jack thought to himself, but beggars couldn't be choosers. 'I'll have Ned and the team report to the briefing room, sir,' Jack nodded to his superior.

'Better than a poke in the eye with a sharp stick,' Ned pointed out to his sister as she took her usual position at the table, a less than ecstatic look on her face. They went over the mission plan for the next couple of hours, and once it was agreed with the Admiral, the green light was given for it to take place the following morning.

It had been six months since the coalition had made Atlantis their home and quite a few of the crew had made the move from living on The Eldridge to living in and around the harbour. Now it was Jack's turn, he had taken an apartment on one of the rustic cobbled streets close to the quayside and with the help of his teammates he was decorating.

Tannis had introduced him to the best carpenter on the island who had gladly undertaken the construction of the furniture Jack had designed; it was piled in the centre of each room now as they painted around it. Tannis had helpfully made a few leaps to bring it all up to his self-named penthouse which was a Godsend as it never would've fit up the narrow staircase.

After a few hours of painting, Ned appeared with armfuls of food courtesy of Elea. They downed tools and ate their fill, Tannis still cautiously checking the lids for a black spot.

'You next, Ben?' Ned gestured to their surroundings, 'a place to call your own away from shift changes and tannoy announcements.'

'I hear that,' Ben sighed, 'no peace for the wicked-on board these days.'

'Used to be too quiet,' Tannis put in.

'Too quiet!' Ned almost choked on his food, 'you used to treat The Eldridge as your own personal stereo system.'

'It was,' she raised her head in defiance, as she stood up and walked out onto the balcony and looked over toward the ship.

'We better be getting back; we've got a mission in the morning.' Jack spoke as he too got up, Ben and Ned followed suit and began clearing away.

Tannis was still looking out over the harbour when Ned threw an empty plastic container at her to get her attention, but instead of hitting her on the back of her head, she spun around in an instant and caught it. 'Just checking,' he grinned at his sister, her teammates looked at one another, her reactions were amazing.

Next morning, Tannis' dreams were rudely disturbed by the ship's tannoy announcing the morning wake up, Ben pulled her back into him and kissed her. It was the norm now for them to spend their nights together. 'You know, Ned's got a point, we should get a place in town,' he sighed, that woke her up.

'We?' She turned to face him.

'Of course, we I mean, if you want to?' His eyes searched hers, although they had been discreet about their relationship and always maintained a professional stance when on duty, it was common knowledge they were together, and for all their worries, the coalition had no problem with it, Ned had been right. Tannis was too valuable a commodity to lose.

Her eyes lit up, 'You want to live with me, I mean properly?'

Ben smiled, 'Yeah, properly, I'm tired of this sneaking around. I want us to have a place of our own where we can be together.'

She kissed him, 'Oh, yes, please,' she jumped out of bed now and pulled on her pj's, then jumped back into his arms and kissed him again, 'I love you,' she smiled.

'I love you, too,' he held her to him for a moment, and then they climbed off the bed again, and she made the leap.

They discussed their plans with Jack over breakfast, 'About time, too,' he gave his approval then frowned, 'Ugh, more decorating.'

In the briefing room Tannis was still less than enamoured with the mission, but now it was more because she wanted it out of the way she and Ben had places to go, people to see and things to do. She sat patiently and listened to the brief along with the others, then went to change and meet in the hold. As it was an almost mirror image dimension, the men were dressed in civilian clothes and Tannis in her leather. Ned joined them as Hennessey went through the mission plan once more with the officer of the day in the hold. 'Nice quiet one for you,' he kissed his sister on the cheek, 'so far so good,' he approved.

'So far so what,' Tannis muttered under her breath.

'Behave, we're on the clock now,' Jack leaned closer to her so as not to let anyone else hear.

She took their hands firmly in hers and prepared to leap as Hennessey said, 'Alpha team good luck.'

Blink and their surroundings had changed, although not exactly to what they had in mind. 'Well, that was a slap and a tickle' Jack said sarcastically, as in front of them The Eldridge was moored happily in Atlantis. He gave Tannis a raised eyebrow look for her to explain. Ben was confused, too, they were supposed to be just outside a small town in a parallel Belgium in a barn. She staggered back, and they held her up, a sure indication she had drained her power 'So this isn't our Atlantis?' Ben helped her to sit, and she shook her head. 'Something went wrong, there was someone else there when I made the leap they pulled me here, I couldn't stop it I had to hang on to the two of you.'

'Someone else?' Jack scanned the area.

'That's how it felt. It's never happened before, whoever it was, isn't around now,' she reassured.

Although there was no time to relax, 'On your knees, hands on your heads,' three armed men walked towards them in army greens. 'Major Charles?' Tannis recognised the man, as she knelt one of his subordinates quickly stood behind her and shoved his gun barrel painfully into the back of her head, 'Should I finish her now sir?' he asked his CO.

'Wait!' Jack looked at the alternative Charles, 'we're not from this dimension, if you're from The Eldridge you'll know that's possible.'

Tannis turned her head slightly to him, her eyes flashed; she was ready to strike but waited for his permission, which he didn't give, with an almost imperceptible shake of his head obeying her orders she faced forward head down once more.

The trigger-happy Sgt asked his CO again, 'Sir, she can turn at any minute and use her mind against us?' He was hungry for blood.

'If she had these so-called mind powers, don't you think you'd be dead already?' Ben noticed this Charles was a Colonel not a Major. A Colonel who didn't seem so keen to kill without reason as he stepped closer and stared at Tannis.

'This one's hair is blonde, not white,' he frowned then addressed Tannis, 'and up close you don't look like her, but there is something…' He motioned with his head for his Sgt to stand down, who did so reluctantly and went to stand at his Colonel's side.

Alpha team were cuffed and marched at gunpoint to The Eldridge, where they were taken to the briefing room which didn't look modern or military at all, more like something from 18th century France. Tannis looked around and turned her nose up.

As the door opened across the room, the team almost looked forward to the arrival of either a new Ned or a new Hennessey. As it happened, they were treated to both although Ned, as he was still called, looked like a poor imitation of theirs, his taste in clothes was not the same either. And as for the Admiral, she was British and carried the presence of a right bitch, Jack thought to himself.

She sat at the head of the table but did not extend the courtesy to them. Ben watched as Ned sat to the Admiral's left. She stared at them for a moment then clicked on a plasma screen at the foot of the table on the wall. Both Jack's and Ben's military records and photos showed on the screen. Again, they looked like poor copies. 'Our Colonel Marsters died while on leave in 2005 and Major Rhodes was killed in Iraq in 2007 by a sniper,' her voice was harsh and her manner abrupt, 'and,' she changed the screen image now to one of a platinum blonde would-be Tannis, 'our Tannis is wanted for crimes against the coalition. It seems she has more powers than you,' she gave Tannis a dirty look.

'So, if you believe we are who we say we are, can the cuffs come off?' Jack matched the Admiral's hard stare.

'Very well,' she agreed and motioned for Charles to remove their restraints. Before he could reach for his keys, Alpha team placed their cuffs on the table, they had been free for some time.

'Thank you, Admiral,' Jack was proud of his team. They were allowed to sit now, Jack and Tannis took their usual seats, but Ben took the chair next to Tannis, he didn't feel comfortable with the other Ned.

'I'm guessing your reality is different to ours,' the Admiral continued, 'so I shall go first,' the world she described couldn't have been more polar opposite. It seemed that even before *DE-173* had been formed Tannis had rebelled against her parent's tough love and left Atlantis only to be raised by Phoenix. Her powers only differed from Alpha team's Tannis in the fact that she could kill with her mind powers, but not freeze time around her. *The Time War* still happened, and *DE-173* couldn't cope, so asked for the help of the coalition.

The outcome was victory over Phoenix, and still, only Ned and Tannis survived but on opposite sides. Jack then retold their version of events, the Admiral continually glanced at Tannis making her feel uncomfortable.

When the unscheduled meeting was over Alpha team were offered quarters on board. 'I understand it takes a day before you can leap back to your dimension, so please make yourselves comfortable,' the Admiral told them.

They thanked her for her hospitality and headed off toward the crew's quarters with an escort who was, of course, Colonel Charles.

He opened the door to what looked like a stateroom and followed them inside. 'Dinner is at 1800 hrs, I suggest you stay together and leave as soon as possible,' he said in a hushed tone so their conversation could go no further.

The Admiral walked through the door just as the ship's alarm sounded and there in the corner of the room was this dimension's Tannis, who sent a power surge from her hands at the Admiral and Colonel Charles, sending them crashing into the wall behind them, where they fell unconscious to the floor.

Tannis and Tannis now stood face to face. Jack frowned, 'Err shouldn't we have a paradox right now?'
The two women looked at one another, 'We're not the same,' they said together.

'She's more Phoenix than me,' Alpha Tannis said.

'She's more human than me,' the other added, 'we're more like cousins.'

'Why did you bring us here?' Jack guessed it had to have been her.

The alternate Tannis didn't take her gaze from her counterpart 'We were leaping at the same time, and I sensed your powers as you sensed mine. It was meant to be. A gift from the Phoenix God's, you were sent to help me finish the fight!'

'So, they have a God complex here too,' the Alpha team's Tannis sighed, 'look, this isn't my world, and I'm damn sure it isn't my fight. Your Time War and mine are over. Your Phoenix are dead, and mine are dead too or banished to another dimension, if you don't like it here, go and find a more peaceful world to live in.'

Alternate Tannis was stunned at the response she had got, 'How can you say that after all that's happened here?' she pointed to the now stirring Admiral and Colonel, 'they wiped out almost everyone on Atlantis when they came here and decided to change history for their own gains.'

'You weren't the ones changing time for yourselves?' Ben asked as he walked over to the nearest porthole and looked out, Atlantis was deserted, and as he looked closer, he could see shell damage to some of the buildings. Jack looked to his officer for confirmation. 'Well, whoever happened out there, it was bad. I don't see any movement and a lot of the buildings have been destroyed,' he confirmed.

'I don't understand,' alternate Tannis looked more confused now. 'How is your dimension so different yet your Phoenix are gone too?'

'Everything's different,' Jack tried to explain, 'but I think we should get out of here...' his sentence was drowned out by a shot.

Colonel Charles had regained his wits and fired at his Tannis. The bullet hit her in the arm, and she vanished.

The Admiral stood, 'What did she say to you?' she barked.

'She just gave us her version of events,' Jack showed no respect.

'So, we control the Earth from here, so what? It's a fact that too much free choice is the undoing of society. If we didn't control all life on this planet, there would be constant wars and struggle. Now it is just run as one big corporation. We say who lives and who dies. The world could not sustain itself, so some countries were cleansed of their populations to enable us to grow enough food for the more deserving,' she said proudly.

'And who decides who the deserving are?' Ben sneered.

'The President of Corporation Earth, of course,' she looked at him as if he was stupid, 'and now, with your help,' she looked at Tannis, 'we will be able to go to your Atlantis too and expand our corporate needs.'

Tannis folded her arms, 'And just how do you expect that to happen?'

'Oh, we have an excellent team of medics who can be very, shall we say, persuasive,' she gave a mirthless thin-lipped smile.

'Ha!' Tannis raised her head defiantly, 'I'd like to see you try!'

'Ned!' The Admiral shouted beyond the closed door, and in he walked carrying a syringe.

'Just a little something to stop you leaping,' he raised the needle as he drew closer to her. Jack and Ben were stopped in their tracks by armed guards following through the door. Tannis extended her wrist blade and put it between her and her alternate brother. 'Now don't be silly, dear sister,' his tone was confident, 'you wouldn't kill your brother,' he smiled.

Tannis took a deep breath and glared at him, 'It wouldn't be the first time, and you're not my brother,' she hissed as she shoved her blade through him, then stepped back to be with her team, she grabbed their hands and leaped with them before the first shot was fired.

They were in a cave now, 'Will you stop doing that!' Tannis growled as she let go of her teammate's hands.

'Your cousin again?' Jack was being rhetorical.

'You were only moving to safety, I just helped you find somewhere,' she stepped into the light. 'Do you know what's happening out there in my real world? Death camps for the undeserving!'

'Look, even if we could help, without access to the time screens we wouldn't know when and where your past was changed,' Jack placated.

'I already know. I went on board The Eldridge before you showed up and checked it out. That's not the problem; the problem is that when I go back and fix the past…'

'They just keep changing it back,' Ben finished for her.

'Exactly, that's why I need your help. I have no problem fixing time, but when I do, I need you to take care of The Eldridge, all timepieces will be on board, and once it's destroyed no one can ever return to or leave Atlantis, the real world will be safe.'

'And with The Eldridge destroyed there can be no time war,' Tannis recalled another conversation like this.

'So, you'll do it then?' alternate Tannis enthused.

'That's Jack's call, not mine,' she looked at her teammates; clearly, they remembered Cole's speech too.

Alternate Tannis was surprised, 'But you rule time, why do you take orders from anyone?'

'I don't rule anything, and I need Jack, he's my commanding officer. None of the decisions are mine anymore, and I like it that way. I trust him; he knows when to rein me in, believe me, he's a lot wiser than he looks,' Tannis said honestly.

'Well, that was almost flattering for a moment,' Jack folded his arms.

Ben moved around the cave checking it out. There seemed to be some food and fuel supplies stored there. He knew Tannis wouldn't be ready to get them home until morning at least and the temperature was dropping now, 'Is it safe to light a fire?'

Alternate Tannis nodded, 'They won't find us here, don't worry.'

'I'll get some wood,' Ben walked out of the mouth of the cave cautiously. Jack followed, there was plenty of driftwood close by so it wouldn't take long.

Back inside, alternate Tannis faced her cousin, 'We could do this together. I know you're not strong enough yet, but I could send them back to your dimension, I know where it is, I saw you come through. Then we could take on the coalition together.'

'No, you don't touch them,' Tannis was firm, 'and stay out of my head, I feel you poking around.'

'So, it's your commanding officer I must appeal to? There's no moving you?' she conceded as the two men walked back inside, she didn't doubt they had heard everything, 'well, if we're going to be spending the night together, you're all going to have to call me Cousin, otherwise, it's going to get confusing.'

Dinner was prepared as the night closed in, nothing fancy, just army rations, but better than nothing. As they lay around the fire, now the conversation turned once again to helping put things right in the dimension's real world.

No one could deny she put across a strong argument, but it wasn't their war. But was that any reason to allow the mass genocide of innocent people when you could make it right? These thoughts bounced around Jack's head all evening, and he knew it was eating at his teammates too. His brief was that when he was off world, he was in charge. The coalition gave him the final word. They all had faith in him to do the right thing, but also not to interfere in a true timeline. But this wasn't a true timeline, and after all, this wasn't the mission he had been given orders for, was it? He turned to his teammates; he didn't have to ask. He knew them well enough to know they wanted to go in and the look on their faces confirmed it. 'So, what's your plan, Cousin?'

The sun hadn't risen as Alpha team swam silently around The Eldridge gently planting the explosives at strategic points. They were running to a strict deadline as Cousin had made the leap to the past in her real world to make the true timeline run as it should. They had seven minutes now to get as far away from The Eldridge as they could before Cousin returned and they blew the charges.

Alpha team sat a safe distance from the blast zone and waited, on cue, Cousin appeared grinning from ear-to-ear. Her mission had been a great success. Jack handed her the remote detonator. 'Your privilege, I think.'

'Thank you, Colonel,' she took the device and pressed the button. Nothing happened. She pressed it again and again, 'I don't understand?' She looked to Jack for an answer, but it didn't come from him.

'The President of the World managed to get part of a distress call out as his timeline began to change,' Colonel Charles approached with his team, their weapons primed and ready.

'No,' Cousin shook her head helplessly.

'It's over, now move,' he gestured toward The Eldridge and snatched the detonator from her hand. 'You won't need this; The Eldridge is blocking the signal.'

As they were marched through the woods Cousin slowed and dragged her feet. 'It doesn't matter how much time you waste when we return to The Eldridge, my team and I will put right the damage you did in the past,' Charles said bluntly.

'Just what we needed to know,' Jack made a grab for the nearest man to him, a Sgt, and he quickly twisted his head and broke his neck. Ben did the same with his target, a Captain if the uniform was correct. That just left Colonel Charles and Cousin dispatched him with the knife she kept in her boot.

'They haven't made the leap yet; we can still blow the ship!' she called as she ran ahead and as if to hurry them on their way bullets sprayed the trees close by, Charles had brought back up.

They became separated in the densely wooded area, Jack and Ben met up as they crossed a shallow stream, and suddenly bullets hit the ground at their feet. They stopped running and turned to face their executioners, Tannis stood breathless on an outcrop of rock above, and watched as the men drew closer.

She waited until they were halfway across the stream then made her move, she jumped down landing in front of her team and dropped to one knee. Touching the water's edge, she sent a surge of electrical charge into it. The men were killed instantly. 'That's it!' Cousin joined them, 'I can send an electrical pulse to The Eldridge and trigger the charges!' But Tannis shook her head, 'You can't do that.'

'It's the only way; if we don't blow it soon, they'll send another team through,' Cousin turned to them, 'thank you all, you saved my world' she had tears in her eyes, 'here,' she handed a small memory stick to Tannis, 'this is for you, I should've trusted you. I'm sorry.' And with that, she was gone.

'No!' Tannis called after her, but it was too late, she grabbed her teammates and leaped as close to The Eldridge as she dared, just in time to see Cousin wade into the water. 'The water's too deep, she'll have to use too much power, she'll kill herself,' Tannis made to run to Cousin, but Ben held her back, it was too late. Cousin summoned all her strength and sent a power surge so strong it knocked them off their feet. Ben covered Tannis with his body as the charges on The Eldridge blew, by the time the dust had settled there was nothing left but twisted metal.

There were no bodies to search for when they moved closer, the heat and power had been so intense nothing could remain.

While they waited for Tannis to regain her strength fully, the team walked into the town. It was deserted and had been for some years. The walls of the quayside were riddled with bullet holes, the scene of a mass execution. Tannis shuddered, and Ben put an arm around her.

'Let's get out of here,' she took their hands, and they were gone.

Back in their dimension and back on their own Eldridge Alpha team sat in the briefing room and gave their report. 'There but for the grace of God,' Hennessey quoted.

'I can't believe Phoenix were the good guys,' Ned shook his head in disbelief, 'Did you tell her what arseholes they were in our dimension?'

Her face dropped as she heard Cousin's last words to her, 'This is for you. I should've trusted you. I'm sorry,' Tannis spoke them aloud and she looked at her team as realisation dawned, 'I told her they had been banished in our dimension, not killed.'

'The USB,' Ben remembered. Tannis handed it to Ned, he put it in his laptop, and there was Cousin. 'She doesn't look like you,' Ned frowned, 'Eldridge laptop on screen' he commanded.

'Ned didn't look like you, either' Tannis pointed to her report on the table.

'Hi alternative Earth,' she was filming as she walked towards a nondescript tent, 'I searched your mind while you were sleeping Tannis and guess what? I found out where you sent Phoenix. Let me explain. This is an insurance policy. If you change your mind in the morning and make the leap home, you won't have this USB, and these guys will be free once more,' she opened the flap of the tent and panned the camera inside. 'It's ok; they're all out cold, I found them in a very weakened state in that nasty world you sent them to, and to make sure I gave them a little something to help them sleep.' She zoomed in on five used syringes and five empty morphine vials. 'I'll give you the coordinates when the mission is over, oh, and as a thank you, there's this too, but that's a surprise,' she held up another memory stick and laid it down next to the vials and syringes, the film ended.

'And she died before she could give you the coordinates,' Hennessey sighed as he sat back in his seat.

Ned threw his sister a knowing look, 'Time for some introductions, I suppose,' he moved the image back a few frames and zoomed in on the first sleeping Phoenix agent.

'Jefferson,' Tannis sneered, 'piece of shit.'

'Ned, perhaps you can expand on Tannis' description?' Hennessey turned to his assistant. Ned looked at the man on the screen. A short, fat and balding middle-aged man. 'He will probably take the lead with this lot. He's a sadistic coward, likes to change the past to run the world as a dictator, makes Hitler look like a nun. His powers are mind control, he can't kill with them, but he can control his victims and usually ends up making them kill themselves in any number of hideous ways.'

He moved on to the next image, a woman who they all recognised as Charlie's killer, the redhead who could make multiple images of herself. 'Kaitlin,' Ned confirmed.

The third was another woman, blonde hair, not stunningly beautiful, but not unattractive either and she seemed familiar.

'Have we seen her before?' Ben tried to place her.

'A bit maybe,' Tannis looked directly at him, 'she's my Aunt Elsa.'

'Wow,' was all he could say.

'What about her powers?' Jack stared at the image.

'The usual mind control, but she can kill with hers and she can generate a force but nowhere near as powerful as Tannis,' Ned informed, as he moved the image to that of the dark-haired Irishman, everyone recognised from the final battle.

'Ah,' he looked at his sister again and continued, 'this is Rafe, his powers are mind control, and he can heal almost as well as Tannis.'

Jack turned to her, 'there's more to this I'm guessing?'
She just sat back in her seat and folded her arms across her chest. 'He wants me to breed with me. He believes our children would be the ultimate in genetics.'
'Does he have a soft spot for you, one that we could exploit?' Hennessey leaned forward.

'Oh, I found his soft spot once and stuck a blade in it, obviously not deep enough though,' she glared at the image on the screen, 'he won't kill me, you saw that in the final battle, and he also saved me from being gang-raped by other Phoenix agents my first mission out.

He killed them instead of me,' she admitted grudgingly, 'he knew who I was and wanted to save me for himself, but not until I was older. He may be a lot of things, but he's not a paedophile or a rapist,' she looked at her team and the Admiral, 'I will kill him, he's Phoenix scum.'

'No competition there then,' Jack grimaced at Ben.

The final image was another male, blonde hair and very lithe looking.

'This Aryan looking chap is Gunther, he's obsessed with genetics too, but on a more sinister level, he likes to experiment, specialises in cloning. His powers are mind control, comes as standard with these bastards; but he can touch you and home in on any part of the body and look what's inside and destroy it. He would use his powers on pregnant Phoenix women. If the foetus showed no powers, he would abort it there and then,' Ned turned the screen off. 'At least there's only five,' he sighed, 'just make sure they can't come back this time,' he made eye contact with Tannis who quickly raised both eyebrows then looked away.

'People, we must prepare….' Hennessey began to speak but was silenced by Ned shaking his head as he looked down at his hands 'You can have no idea what you're going to be up against.'

In a literal flash, Tannis disappeared, then reappeared, placing the memory device on the table in front of her, 'Then we will show them,' she said firmly as she raised her head and looked directly at her brother.

Ned rallied himself, stood and walked over to where his sister sat and began to attach her to the machine 'Lion heart' he whispered, but before he threw the switch, he had an idea, 'Eldridge, Tannis' playlist number 25. Tannis gave Ben a half smile as Ned informed them all the music would drown out any outside noise, and the song, well, it was their unofficial anthem for *DE-173*. He flicked the switch and Tannis fell back unconscious, just as *Welcome to the Black Parade* by *My Chemical Romance* began to play.

Those present were treated to a five-minute sensory overload as Tannis' memories flashed on the screen, they witnessed her fighting Phoenix agents, alongside her brother's and sister's and bore witness to all the horrors the agents could visit on a body.

DE-173 were seen fighting against Roman Legions, Vikings, Norman Knights, they were involved in cavalry charges, dog fights, trench warfare, they had seen and done it all. Even Cole was there at his best, before his illness took him.

Their courage and determination were apparent, the three non-members of *DE-173* watched in awe.

The song ended and Ned turned the machine off, Tannis came round in an instant, she was bathed in sweat and breathing heavily as Ned removed the pads from her head.

She stood up, fists clenched, they all had an idea what was coming, she was so pumped with adrenaline, backing away from the table, she was going to make a leap to vent her rage in a battle somewhere. 'Tannis, please retake your seat,' Hennessey tried to take command of the situation, but Tannis extended her wrist blade.

Jack leapt out of his chair, pinning her to the wall, his forearm across her throat, 'Stand down, that's an order!' He growled, his body was pressed against hers, they were nose to nose.

Hennessey looked on with interest, a good test of loyalty and leadership.

Tannis retracted her wrist blade and Jack moved away from her a little, neither breaking eye contact, then he whispered to her, 'Look at him not me,' he was aware that Ben was standing close by.

Tannis looked over slightly at Ben, that was when Jack let her go completely as he felt her relax.

Hennessey was impressed, his officer knew his teammate well, and she followed his command even under duress.

'Tannis, with your permission, I'd like to have the other team's watch what you have just shown us?' the Admiral asked.

Tannis just nodded.

'Very well dismissed,' Hennessey stood.

Ben took Tannis by the hand and, in a flash, they were gone.

That was when Hennessey showed a different side to himself, 'Bloody Hell Jack, what do you do in your spare time, wrestle bear's or tame lion's?' He chuckled.

'You've certainly got a set,' Ned agreed.

'I just know my teammates sir,' Jack smiled, 'she may fight like a lion, but she also knows what pride she belongs to.'

Chapter Six

It was a beautiful sunny morning, Tannis stood on deck looking into town, she was still in her pj's, crop top and loose-fitting bottoms. As she leaned on the railings with a mug of tea in her hand, she was as always oblivious to the glances she was getting from the crew as they went about their duties. One person very aware was Jack as he walked out on deck glaring at his subordinates; they instantly got the message. Standing next to her now he leaned on to the rail and reached across for the mug of tea she held, taking a couple of drinks, he handed it back to her; the two of them had bonded well together, they had a closeness and ease in each other's company much as she shared with Ned.

Ben joined them and now standing on the other side of Tannis he looked across, 'Ugh, how do you drink that stuff?' He grimaced at her mug of tea.

'Better than that sludge you call coffee!' Jack joined in.

'Hey, the guys in Boston found the right place for tea,' he retaliated,

'And we all know how that one turned out,' Tannis shook her head.

Simultaneously: their cell phones rang, they were wanted in the briefing room, Jack rolled his eyes 'Back down all those bleedin stairs again, I only just got here.' Tannis gave him her mug to hold, then grabbed both their hands and blink they were outside the door.

'You could've stopped for me on the way,' Ned panted as he hurried past them. Inside they took their usual places as Ned caught his breath and they waited for the Admiral to come through from his office. As soon as he had done so he nodded for Ned to begin.

'Ok well it's started, someone has been messing with time as I'm sure you gathered, Eldridge on screen.'

The screen came to life, showing newspaper cuttings from 1997 and 1998. 'The DOE contract IBM to build a ten trillion operation a second computer system so that it can calculate the effects of weapons in the nation's stockpile without detonating real nukes,' he swiped the tablet in front of him to the next clipping, 'earth drags space and time' swipe, 'solar system snapshot GRB971214 was observed using NASA satellites, the most violent explosion in the cosmos, first solar image!' he turned to them all now, 'but no sheep!' the room was silent 'ah I knew you'd be shocked!' Ned grinned at them.

Jack leaned his head slightly to Tannis, 'Just when you think you've got life sussed eh?'

'Welcome to my world,' she whispered back, then looked at Ben as he mouthed 'What?'

She just shrugged and made the crazy sign with her index finger circling her temple.

'No sheep?' Hennessey frowned.

'No, not a mention of Dolly or Bonnie for that matter,' Ned nodded.

'Oh, the clones,' Jack sat up in realisation.

'Exactly,' Ned folded his arms, he was the best if not a little eccentric at times, so the Admiral stayed with it, 'Ned I'm going to need a little more than sheep rustling to go on.'

'Yes, of course, sorry, in 1997 Dolly the sheep was the first mammal to be successfully cloned from an adult cell, and then on 14th April 1998 Dolly gave birth to Bonnie, a healthy lamb at The Roslin Institute in Edinburgh, sparking controversy,' he explained.

'Didn't Dolly have to be destroyed because of premature arthritis and lung disease?' Ben noticed everybody looking at him now, 'I read newspapers too,' he added sulkily.

'Really?' Ned continued, 'well it would appear that not only did the sheep not make the news but also The Roslin Institute was never founded in 1993 a private sector company now owns the site conducting medical research and the like.'

'So, they changed history in 1993?' Hennessey needed hard evidence to give a time change order. 'Well yes, but only by making a higher bid and offering their services to the government,' Ned looked uncomfortable, he knew this wasn't enough he sighed, 'I don't know how they did it, but they can't be allowed to continue, Dr Alan Harkman is their chief of research, he was at Montauk, believe me, he'll be churning out Phoenix clones on a conveyor belt and making new agents as we speak with all that modern technology.'

'Your theory is sound, Ned, but if I am to issue a time change order, I am going to need more evidence. How could a scientist just living through the natural course of time know how to make such strategic moves?' the Admiral steepled his fingers.

'Well, couldn't the five that returned have gone back and helped him?' Ben asked.

'No, they wouldn't help Harkman. They don't like each other very much, but they really hated him, he was experimenting with a drug that when given he could control them all, so they wouldn't trust him,' Tannis frowned.

'God, I wish this job came with a rule book,' Jack groaned.

Ned sat bolt upright, 'Colonel; you're a genius!'

'Of course, I am, what did I say?'

'Samuel Madden,' Ned said and looked at his sister.

'I thought you read it and said it was total fiction,' Tannis returned his stare.

'Maybe not the suppressed version,' he fired back.

'Err should we come back later?' Jack's tone was dry.

'Well?' Tannis looked at her brother, who gestured for her to continue as he sat back in his chair and closed his eyes to listen as a schoolteacher might test a pupil. Tannis rolled her eyes. 'In 1733 an Irishman named Reverend Samuel Madden wrote a book which some regard as the first science fiction novel, it was called Memoirs of the Twentieth Century,' Tannis could see she had their attention now, 'the story was a narrative in which a man describes how his guardian angel travelled back in time to give him documents from British Ambassadors and the like telling him what life was like in 1997 and 1998,' she paused as Hennessey leaned forward his interest piqued, 'Please continue.'

'Well, Robert Walpole, I suppose you could call him the first Prime Minister for reasons known only to himself, suppressed the publication of the book,' she shrugged, 'a few were still printed, but it was just fiction.'

'The original disappeared,' Ned cut in, 'some say that Walpole had it confiscated and then it was just lost in time.'

'I bet I know who found it,' Jack looked at the Admiral who thought for a moment before saying, 'There's still not enough evidence of intent for 1993, how could Harkman have known where to find the book?'

'That's easily done, a small transmitter hidden in the binding, they've done it before in the early days of Phoenix. If their timepieces got damaged, they could send out an S.O.S, so they'd still be listening out for them,' Tannis tried to help her brother's case.

'I can't go for 1993,' Hennessey told them.

'But…' Ned began.

'But' the Admiral raised a calming hand, 'nothing is stopping you going back to 1733 and checking out the book.'

'1733 it is then,' Jack looked at his team then to Ned, 'we'll need a cover and a good one too to get us access to Walpole's house.'

'Not a problem, we'll just sell my sister,' Ned picked up his paperwork.

'Beg pardon?' Tannis folded her arms across her chest defensively.

Her brother rolled his eyes, 'I mean you will be staying in London for the season, a wealthy cotton merchant from the colonies,' he looked at Jack, 'and his servant,' he looked at Ben now who frowned, 'and his sister for whom he is looking to make a good match,' his gaze rested on Tannis.

'Is that the best you can do?' She raised an eyebrow.

'If Jack splashes enough cash around and you play your part well the suitors will soon come calling, and you'll find yourselves invited to the best houses in town, Walpole's included. Let's face it, you don't scrub up too bad,' he winked at her.

They met an hour later in the hold, Jack and Ben were dressed in period costume, Jack's was made of the finest cloth, Ben's, however, was cut from a coarser material as befitted his servant status. The privilege of rank, he thought to himself as Jack mockingly flapped a lace hanky in his direction.

Tannis seemed to float into the room in a dazzling yellow silk gown pulled in tightly at the waist. Her breasts, barely covered by her bodice rose and fell as she breathed, and her hair had been piled on her head in ringlets.

'You are breath-taking, my dear,' Hennessey bowed as she lowered herself into a curtsey.

Jack walked over and took her hand as she rose, 'I can see we'll be beating them off with a stick when your suitors come to call; you're gorgeous,' he kissed her hand then walked away with the Admiral for a last-minute word or two. So, she made her way over to stand with Ben ready for the leap. She took his breath away, and he narrowed his eyes in jest, 'just remember you're spoken for,' she smiled at him as Jack joined them now.

'You know one thing that's weird about this era, it's shocking for a woman to show her ankles, but it's perfectly acceptable to have the shutters up on the shop front!'

Tannis looked self-consciously down at her chest, 'Thanks for that.'

Ned hurried into the hold and headed straight for her, 'Oh, that dress is fab!' he twirled her around thinking he could add a few panels to it and let it out for himself to wear after the mission, 'don't kill anybody in it, blood's hell to shift.'

'I'll try,' she pursed her lips.

Then he hugged her, 'Be careful,' he said as he let her go and stepped back, 'I don't know what I'm worried about,' he put his hands around her waist, 'you must be bulletproof in that stuff.'

He stepped away and joined Hennessey who gave the order, 'Alpha team, good luck!'

They took the best house in Richmond not far from Walpole's. London 1733 was a busy, noisy and somewhat dirty place. They took a carriage everywhere and hired more servants than they possibly needed, although Ben was pleased because it meant he could let them do all the work. The first week there they attended the opera and the ballet and a music recital. The well-to-do ladies took Tannis under their wings. She was a fresh face and beautiful, they saw it as their duty to find her a good match, so they were invited to take tea at their many houses and with Ben dispatched below stairs, Jack and Tannis were forced to endure hours of idle chit-chat about possible suitors and of course the local gossip and scandals. So, it soon came that they began to receive invites to parties and social evenings. A long week turned into a tedious fortnight, and Jack had calling cards from would-be suitors shoved at him from all directions. All too soon they started to call at the house to take tea with them.

One such hot and sunny afternoon there seemed to be no air in the walled garden as they sat outside with a chinless milksop who had come to call. Ben stood dutifully by as they passed the time of day with yet more idle chit-chat. After the conversation had exhausted the would-be beau invited Tannis to take a turn around the garden with him. Her teammates kept a keen eye on the two of them; they had agreed a prearranged signal which she gave now as Jack saw the man leering closer towards her. She pretended to swoon a little, and Jack hurried over to her, 'I think the heat is a little too much for my sister,' he said as politely as he could. With that, the odious letch told her that he hoped she felt better soon and that he would call again later in the week, but not before wishing her flights of angels sing her to her rest, he then bowed before flouncing his way back to the house.

'Tit,' Jack muttered under his breath.

Once he had been shown out by one of the servants and the coast was clear, Tannis began to pace up, and down the lawn, her chest rising and falling as she became more and more frustrated. 'You'll be out of that if you don't calm down!' Jack pointed to her bodice, she turned and stormed off towards the house. 'Where are you off to?' He called after her. Ben had joined him now, and the two men stood together as she spun around and marched straight towards them.

'I am going inside to get this bloody body armour off, it's too hot, I can't breathe, and if I must make small talk with one more hanky flapper I am going to scream! how the hell women of this day fall for that is beyond me,' she raised a finger, and they both flinched, 'I do know actually, they have no choice. Sold off like cattle! In fact, not even sold off, you must pay them to take me off your hands!' and with that, she stormed off into the house.

The two men both exhaled slowly at the same time; Jack looked at his friend 'You two had your first row yet?'

Ben just shook his head. 'Good luck,' his CO laughed as he walked back to the table.

Later that afternoon Jack took a tray of food to her room. She hadn't been downstairs since her outburst and now lay naked wrapped in a bed sheet with all the windows open allowing the cool breeze to drift in. She sat up gratefully and ate and drank. 'Cook tells Ben that I'm too soft on you and you should be whipped, apparently, her last master had his daughter regularly thrashed to keep her in her place, even showed her future husband how to go about it.' 'Bastards,' she mumbled, her mouth half full of cake.

'So, are you going to tell me what our guest did this afternoon to upset you so much?'

She put her food down and looked at her CO, 'Sorry Jack, I know I lost it a bit with the two of you, I've been spoken to worse than that before but...'

'Worse than what?' he frowned.

'You know,' she looked down uncomfortably, 'stuff he wanted me to do to him and stuff he wanted to do to me.'

'I thought these were supposed to be gentlemen callers, are they all like that?' It was his turn to pace up and down now.

'No, not all of them, mostly they behave as they should. It was just, well, he tried to make me touch him, it just made me feel like a....'

'Oh no,' Jack sat beside her now and put an arm around her shoulder, and she leaned into him, 'don't you dare go feeling like that! you're a lady, you've got the highest set of morals I've ever known in anyone,' he was furious, 'from now on if you walk with any of them either me or Ben will go with you.'

She nodded and picked up some food and began to eat again.

'Now, we have a party to attend, dear sister,' he said as he stood up, 'and the Walpole's will be in attendance, so we need to be our most charming to get invited to theirs.'

'It would be much easier if we could just break in,' she sighed. 'We've been through that, security is too tight, and if we didn't find it first off, he would be on to us and move it,' he grinned at her, 'now get dressed, Catherine, or I may take the cook's advice!' He used her cover name. Tannis reached over, grabbed a pillow and threw it at him; it hit the door as he ducked out.

The party that night was a dazzling affair. No expense had been spared on their costumes; they danced and socialised, while down in the servant's hall Ben made the acquaintance of Tom and Amy who worked for the Walpole's, he found it easy to get them to talk about their employer. All he had to do was sound impressed by their position with a most influential man. Amy even told him of the extensive library he had both in his townhouse and his country manor. He didn't push any further with his questions; he knew that to build their trust would take time. He wondered how it was going upstairs. This mission sucked. He hadn't seen Tannis alone for over two weeks now and was forced to bear witness to her being courted by countless assholes he would love to punch out. He knew he shouldn't let it get to him, but it was keeping him awake at night. Sure, he knew it wasn't real, but if only he could be with her, talk to her, it was the separation that got to him.

They returned home later that night; it was raining and had turned cooler. The servants had all turned in early as Jack had instructed, he wanted Ben to be able to join them both without questions being asked. Jack sat in the window seat watching the rain run down the panes of glass, thankful for the coolness.

Ben sat in the armchair by the fireside, Tannis on the rug at his feet, both staring into the empty grate saying nothing. All three of them had had enough of this mission; it was not what any of them were used to. Jack looked down into the street below. It was deserted now except for the odd carriage taking its privileged occupant's home. He turned his gaze to Ben and Tannis; he could tell that something wasn't right between them but was impressed that they had both performed their duties without question.

He thought of the cook's advice on how to make women submissive to their men with a beating. He would like to see anyone try that with Tannis, she was the most independent, strong-minded and yes, he had to admit it, willful person he knew, she would never submit to force and yet here she was sitting at Ben's feet, resting her head on his leg, she was devoted to him.

His heart ached for the love that was lost to him, as he watched them his mind went back to her, his beloved Caroline; he closed his eyes tightly to blot out the image of her that came to him, he couldn't allow himself to feel like this now. He stood up quickly, 'I'm going downstairs to get some grub,' he announced as he headed for the door, closing it softly behind him.

Finally, Ben and Tannis were alone together. He looked at her as she sat with her back to him, and gently ran his finger along her shoulder, she reached her hand across and entwined their fingers; 'It's not real, Ben,' she knew exactly how he was feeling.

'I know,' he sighed, 'I just hate the way they look at you' he squeezed her hand, 'like you're a piece of meat,' his frustration grew now, 'and I have to listen to the servants bragging about what their masters say about you, what they want to do to you!'

She turned to face him on her knees, 'I'd like to see them try, Ben, you and me are the only thing that's real.'

'And I just have to sit back and take it?' he snapped.

'It's only words, Ben,' she tried to soothe him, but he pulled his hand away from her, Tannis stood up and rounded on him, 'well, you may have to listen to it, but I'm the one who has to be paraded around like a whore,' she fired back as a tear ran down her cheek. Jack opened the door carrying a tray full of food and drink as Tannis hurried past him, 'I'm not hungry, thank you. I'll see you in the morning.'

He laid the tray down on the table and poured two drinks then walked over to where his teammate sat now rigid with temper.

Ben took the drink his CO offered him but said nothing as he sat in the chair opposite. Jack was a man wise beyond his years sometimes, he sat in silence with his friend allowing him to calm down before he spoke, 'Can you imagine what she's going through? a fine lady like that having to act submissive and attentive to pillocks not fit to lick her boots, I'm only going to have this conversation with you once Ben; you two have got something most people will never have, neither of you has to prove a damn thing to each other, one needs the other knows and is there, you'd go through hell and high water to save that girl, and she'd do the same. Bloody hell, Ben, she killed her own brother to save you,' he knew he'd hit a nerve as Ben glared but he continued, 'I don't like this circus either, but that's all it is, and at the end of the day you'll be the one taking her home not them,' he leaned over and took the glass from his officer, 'now go and sort it.'

Ben looked at his CO and friend and knew he was right, he had been so stupid 'Thanks,' he said as he left the room.

Jack poured Ben's untouched whiskey into his glass and settled back into his chair.

Tannis was in her long flowing nightgown, she had unpinned her hair, and brushed it straight and looked at herself in the mirror, she was Tannis again, she turned quickly as the door opened and watched Ben step inside then looked away and closed the open drawer in her dresser not wanting to see him. He knew this as he walked across the room and put his hands on her shoulders turning her to face him, her eyes were full of tears as she looked up at him 'I'm sorry, I'm an idiot,' he whispered, 'I just get a knot in my guts when I see them looking at you the way they do.'

'I'm just a business transaction,' she said sulkily.

'No,' he pulled her closer, 'you're mine,' he kissed her as he unlaced the front of her nightgown and let it fall to the floor. His lips moved down her neck now, and she threw back her head and gasped, their lips met again, and his tongue was in her mouth she returned the passion of his kisses as he picked her up and carried her over to the bed. He lay her down, undressed and climbed on top of her running his hand down her naked thigh then between her legs. Tannis slid her hand down and felt his desire as she took it in her hand, he raised himself over her and pushed hard inside her. She gasped at his need as he took both her hands now and held them above her head, he was claiming her as his own.

'I'm yours, Ben,' she whispered, her words soothed him, and his hands slid down her arms as he took her face in his hands and kissed her gently this time, then he rolled her over on top of him.

'We shouldn't have done that,' Tannis said in a hushed tone as they lay under the covers holding each other.

'Oh, yes, we should, and I think we should do it again,' he smiled lazily as he kissed her.

'Ben, we're on a mission.'

'I know,' he sighed, 'I just needed to…'

'Claim your property,' she finished for him.

'I guess I'm just a caveman at heart,' he grinned.

'Well, it's time you went back to your cave before the servants catch us.'

'I bet we're not the only ones,' he pulled her warm naked body closer then sighed, 'ok, I'm going,' he kissed her, 'back to my cold empty bed,' he kissed her again.

'And no more green-eyed monsters?' She touched his face lightly. 'Scouts honour,' he smiled as he jumped out of bed and got dressed, 'in fact, I've even decided who your future husband is going to be.'

She frowned, 'Who?'

He leaned over and kissed her again before opening the door slightly and checking the coast was clear, 'Me!' he whispered and was gone. She sat up in bed, had she heard him, right? she was sure she had, Tannis smiled to herself, and snuggled down under the warm covers.

Jack was relieved the next morning to see normal service had been resumed. The doorbell rang as the two of them ate breakfast together, and a few moments later Ben brought a letter up, there were only the three of them in the room, so he took a piece of toast and began eating it as Jack read the mail. 'Well, it seems you worked your charm on old Lady Walpole last night,' he passed the letter to Ben to read, 'we've been invited to their country pile for the weekend, seems Lady Walpole thinks a rest from the London social scene and some country air will do you good,' Jack filled her in.

'A ball will be held on Saturday night for local gentry only,' Ben read.

'Ah, a weekend away,' she relaxed back in her chair.

The country manor was more like a stately home, 'They've got a ballroom I could play baseball in,' Ben told Jack as he helped him unpack.

'I'm going riding,' Tannis burst through the door wearing a black riding habit with a matching hat and a fishnet veil.

'With whom, Catherine?' Jack knew the score she had left the door open to tell him someone was out there, clever girl.

'Lady Armatage invited me, her footman will escort us with your permission?' Her eyes begged him, she loved riding, and she deserved a break too.

'Very well, I'll see you at dinner,' he agreed. She kissed him on the cheek like a dutiful sister and winked at Ben as she swirled out of the room Ben held the door for her and saw Lord Armatadge loitering nearby watching her as she left.

Lord Armatadge was an obese odious red-faced man, full of his own self–importance who blustered along the landing now towards his rooms. 'Dirty old man,' Ben hissed as he closed the door.

'Who was it?' Jack whispered.

'Lord Armatage,' Ben sneered; he hated the way the upper classes of this society thought they could get away with anything.

They both moved over to the window now as they heard the clatter of horse's hooves on the cobbled courtyard, Tannis and her two companions were leaving for their ride. 'Very elegant,' Jack commented as Tannis rode side saddle. They watched as they took their horses at a gentle pace into the nearby field. Ben smiled as he saw her let the horse have its head then and rode hard into the distance, 'Do her good,' Jack nodded as he turned back to his trunk.

Ben watched her for a while longer until she disappeared from view. This weekend would be good for them all; maybe they would strike lucky and find the book then they could get the hell out of there. But even if they didn't, all the so-called eligible bachelors had stayed in town so Tannis could relax and so could he.

That evening as Ben ate his meal with the other servants he got to chat with Tom and Amy once more. Amy was happy to tell him about Lord Walpole's library as she was the only one allowed to clean it for him and the one in his London house too. But there was no mention of a special book or where he might keep such a thing.

Jack and Tannis had dinner with the other guests who all turned in early, tired from the journey and wanting to be fresh for the ball the following night.

Morning came clear and bright, Jack had mentioned his love of books to Walpole the previous night, so he had been invited to join him in his library after breakfast, he wouldn't be able to dig too deep, but it would give him the chance to give the place the once over.

So, while Jack rubbed shoulders with once one of the most powerful men in the land, Tannis took a turn around the grounds, escorted by their footman, of course. Ben was forced to keep a respectable distance from her as they walked, but it was enough for them to be together. They wandered along the edge of the woods then followed the path inside. They hadn't gone too far when there was a noise from the bushes, someone was watching them.

Tannis froze and looked at Ben. They must be cautious not to blow their cover, so she must remain Catherine, until the threat was identified. Ben walked a short way into the undergrowth and stopped in his tracks, Tannis hurried over, 'What is it?' It was not what either of them expected to find, for there hiding in the brambles was a young boy of around twelve and a black slave.

'I take full responsibility,' the boy stood before them carrying a small cloth bag, probably food.

'You're helping him escape?' Ben looked from the boy to the slave who also stood now.

'I am, you are a servant, yet you are given a wage and treated fairly, why should this man be treated any differently just because of the colour of his skin?' The child was defiant, 'I may take a beating for this, but I will stand by what I believe.'

They could hear men's voices getting closer, obviously searching for the slave. 'You may take a beating, but that won't save this man's life,' Ben grabbed the bag of food and threw it as far as he could, but there was nowhere to run, and the men were getting closer.

'What's your name?' Tannis asked the slave.

'Jacob, ma'am,' he said slowly as he still struggled with the English tongue.

Tannis looked around and lifted her skirts, 'Hurry, I could hide a small army under here.'

'Ma'am, I couldn't,' he looked shocked.

'Jacob, if you don't, if you're lucky they'll hang you. If you're not, it will be much worse.' He quickly ducked under her skirts, and she spread them out smoothly then turned to the young boy.

'And you sir, what is your name?'

'Charles Middleton, ma'am,' he bowed graciously. Ben noticed a flicker of realisation on her face, but that would have to wait, the crowd of thugs were on them now. Charles took her arm as they approached.

'Your pardon, my lady,' one of them touched the brim of his hat, 'we're looking for an escaped slave, might you have seen anything on your walk?'

'I fear I should faint, sir if I saw anything of the sort,' she held Charles' arm for mock support. The leader apologised for frightening her and suggested that they return home for safety's sake and went on their way.

Once the mob was safely out of sight Tannis lifted her skirt a little and Jacob, eyes still tightly shut, stood up slowly and opened them one at a time, 'I kept them closed tight ma'am,' he told her, head down.

'Don't worry there are so many layers,' she smiled.

'Do you have a route planned?' Ben asked Jacob.

'Yes, sir, I am to be met at the edge of the woods and taken by cart to safety,' he trembled as he spoke. Ben looked at Tannis, this wasn't part of the mission but what could they do? She knew what he was thinking and nodded.

'We'll see you to your meeting,' Ben looked from Jacob to Charles.

'Thank you, sir, ma'am,' Jacob smiled for the first time. They hurried as fast as they could and as they approached the lane that ran by the tree line, they saw the cart waiting, Charles stepped out into the road and spoke with the driver then summoned the others all was well and they hurried over, Jacob was helped under a cover by the carter's wife.

She smiled at Tannis, 'Don't worry my lady, we'll take good care of him, our church has helped over fifty of these poor souls.'

The cart moved away, and the three conspirators went back into the shelter of the woods, they walked a short distance together when Charles turned to them, 'This is where I must leave you, my family are guests in the house Jacob has just escaped from so I should get back and appear innocent,' he shook Ben's hand and bowed to Tannis, 'it's been an honour, I just wish more people were like you. I thank you.'

Tannis curtseyed to him.

'You'd be surprised how many people feel the same, just have faith,' Ben had a feeling about this kid.

Alone again, they headed back to the house, Ben had the biggest grin on his face.

'Not all so bad, is it?' Tannis returned his smile.

'You recognised his name,' Ben remembered their meeting.

'Oh yes, Charles Middleton will be hugely important to the abolition of slavery in Great Britain, he will pass the baton on to a chap you may have heard of: William Wilberforce.'

He was stunned, 'Oh, my God, really? The William Wilberforce?'

'Yup,' she grinned.

He looked around, they were completely alone as he took her hands in his and kissed her, 'This is why you do it isn't it? it sort of cancels out the bad stuff?'

'It does make it all worthwhile sometimes,' she looked back the way Charles had run, 'it puts my faith back in mankind, people like this are true heroes.'

'Hey, let's not forget *DE-173*, you guys were a special bunch too,' It always amazed him how she never thought of herself as a hero.

'Nah, we could just get out of it, these guys are trapped in their timeline, constant in their courage, that's special,' she squeezed his hand and kissed him quickly, 'now come along my good man, I have a ball to attend,' she teased as she walked on ahead of him.

'You'll keep,' he taunted, as they went on their way.

That night at the ball Tannis played her part well. She danced and socialised, it was a grand affair just as they had expected. At the pre-arranged time, Jack gave her the nod, and she joined him and the group of gentlemen he had been talking with, 'John,' she called him by his cover name, 'I'm sorry, I have danced so much I need some air, would you take me out into the garden?'

Jack excused himself, and she took his arm as they left through the French doors and out onto the lawn, they wandered a little until they were out of sight then hurried along to the library window where Jack easily picked the lock while Tannis kept watch. Then she reached down into her bodice and pulled out a small electrical device that Ned had knocked together for them to home in on the transmitter with if the book was in the room. He went inside and pulled the doors shut making his sweep, he found nothing. Between the three of them they had scanned the whole house; now they would have to search the London residence. He was making his way back to the French doors when voices outside alerted him. One was Tannis the other, Oh Christ; it was Lord Armatadge.

'Ah there you are, my dear, come let me show you the gardens,' he barked.

'Oh, thank you sir, but my brother will be along shortly, and he will worry if I am not here.'

'Nonsense, a fine young Filly like you shouldn't be left alone in the first place,' he grabbed her by the arm and half dragged her across the lawn, 'a firm hand that's what women of today need.'

Jack had made it to the doors now but was forced to hide behind the desk as the key turned in the lock of the door leading from the hallway, it opened and in came Lady Armatage and their footman. She closed the door, and they were in each other's arms then hurriedly undressing each other. Jack grimaced at the sight, she was just as obese as her husband with bad breath from her rotten teeth and always stank of sweat. He waited until they were completely occupied with one another then crawled on his stomach to the French doors and silently made his escape.

He ran around the walls of the great house trying to find Tannis; if the dirty old man went too far, she would be forced to defend herself. He just hoped she would do it as befitted her delicate female cover; they still had the London house to get in now. He caught up with them as he saw her being dragged into the stable block, protesting desperately as they went, Jack raced around the corner only to bump into Walpole himself, he too had seen Tannis being pulled along by the predator and intervened, 'Henry, how good of you to show Miss Catherine the way back to the house,' he said, ever the diplomat, 'but look, here's her brother now,' he gestured towards Jack as he took Tannis from the old letch and placed her trembling hand in his.

'Thank you, my Lord,' Jack acknowledged Armatadge, who Walpole then led back to the house, nodding his appreciation to Jack as he went.

Tannis had fingermark bruising on her arm, 'He hurt you,' Jack sneered at the fat pig as he waddled on with Walpole.

'Just give me a minute, they'll fade,' her voice trembled a little. 'Here, sit down,' he led her to a nearby bench and sat next to her, 'I'm sorry, love, I couldn't get out of the library, Lady Armatage came in with the footman.'

Tannis gagged.

'Yeah, I know what you mean,' Jack laughed.

'I guess you didn't find it then?' She looked at him as he shook his head and put an arm around her shoulder.

'Bugger,' she leaned into him.

'Yeah, bugger' he sighed, a deafening rumble of thunder sounded above them; they both jumped, Jack turned to her.

'Don't look at me,' she said defensively, they laughed together and hurried inside, the weather was turning.

The storm raged as they worked their way through the many dinner courses, then it was time for the gentlemen to retire for their brandy and cigars. Only five young single women were staying at the house. Old Lady Walpole was ready to retire, and no one knew where Lady Armatage had gone, so the young women gathered in one bedroom in their nightgowns and gossiped about their wishes for the future. Tannis was with them, and as she listened to their hopes and dreams, she couldn't help but feel sorry for them when she thought about what they would have to settle for.

It was late when Lady Walpole's maid put her head around the door and told them that Her Ladyship had asked her to remind the young ladies of the time and perhaps, they should retire for the night. They did as they were bid, all lighting their candles from the ones that already burned in the room.

It was freezing in the hallway and creepy too as the thunder crashed and the wind whistled through the cracks in the windows like an episode of Scooby Doo, Tannis thought to herself as she made her way slowly.

Upstairs in the servant's quarters Ben lay fully clothed on his bed, he had hoped that Jack had found the book and they would be on their way home, or not it seemed. His hopes soared when there was a knock at the door, maybe they had found it, he jumped off the bed and opened it, but it wasn't his team that stood there. It was Amy, and she was shuffling nervously, 'Amy, what's wrong?'

She wrung her hands now, 'Oh Ben, I don't know what to do, Miss Catherine is such a lovely lady…'

Ben was on the alert straight away, 'Miss Catherine? what happened?'

'Nothing yet, she's still with the young ladies in Miss Annabelle's room,' she was too scared to say more.

'Amy, it's ok, you can trust me I won't tell anyone you said anything.'

'Lord Armatadge is waiting for her in her bed. I saw him go in there just now as I was taking a drink to one of the guests, he'll hurt her, Ben, you know what these toffs are like, he's got his riding crop with him too. I know he's only done it to his servants before, but I think he means to do it to Miss Catherine now.'

Ben leaned forward and kissed her on the forehead, 'I'll take care of this Amy, you go to bed and think no more of it. You did the right thing, thank you.'

She smiled at him then turned and hurried away to her quarters, her conscience was clear, and she'd had a kiss from a handsome man. Tom was the only one for her, but Ben was very handsome.

Tannis was still making her way cautiously along the landing, she froze as the thunder crashed again, for goodness sake, you've faced worse than this she mentally chastised herself. As she passed the staircase which led up to the next floor to yet more rooms, a door within it opened. It was a cupboard used by the servants for storing cleaning equipment, 'Hey!' Ben whispered loudly.

Tannis almost jumped out of her skin as she turned around and hurried over to him, he pulled her inside quickly and closed the door blowing her candle out as he did so, someone wasn't far behind her. It was another servant catering to the whims of their masters carrying a silver tray with a bottle of brandy and two glasses on it; satisfied the coast was clear Ben whispered to her, 'Armatage is waiting for you in your bed.'

'Jesus Christ doesn't that man ever give up?' she shut her eyes when she realised what she'd said.

'What's that supposed to mean?'

'He tried to drag me into the stables earlier this evening, nothing happened Jack was there for me,' she waited for his reaction.

'You shouldn't be so desirable,' he murmured and then pressed her against the wall and kissed her, she was shivering with cold as he held her to him, trying to keep her warm. 'We can't stay here all night, you'll have to sleep with Jack,' he whispered, and she shot him a questioning look, 'well, I'm in the servant's quarters, and he's supposed to be your brother. Just say the storm spooked you, so you crashed with him, only in 18th-century talk.'

She stifled a laugh, 'I love you,' she kissed him.

'Go on; you're freezing, go stay with Jack,' he rubbed her arms to try and keep her warm. She didn't say anything, just looked at him. 'Hey, I trust the guy with my life, and he's the only guy I trust with my girl, c'mon' he led her out and watched as she opened Jack's door and went inside, then he made his way back to the servant's quarters.

'Jack,' she whispered as she walked in.

'What's up?' He sat up in bed bare-chested, she turned her back on him not knowing if he was naked.

'Lord Armatage is waiting for me in my bed,' she shivered with cold, 'can I sleep with you tonight?'

'I'm decent,' he said, 'how do you know about Armatage?'

'Ben told me; he was outside just now,' she turned to face him again as he moved to the far side of the bed and pulled the covers back for her to get in on the other side, she saw he was still wearing his breeches.

'Couldn't bring myself to wear a nightie,' he confided as she climbed in beside him still shivering; he touched her shoulder, 'You're frozen. Come here,' he held her in his arms, and she leaned against him.

'Night, Jack,' she yawned.

'Night, love,' he whispered back.

The sun shone through a gap in the curtains; it was only 0500 hrs according to the carriage clock at the bedside. Tannis rolled over and looked at Jack as he slept. She had never seen him half-naked before and noticed there were two scars on his chest and one on his shoulder. She'd seen injuries like this before on her brothers. Ben also had one on his thigh, Jack had been shot. She closed her eyes and tried to drift off once more, but in his sleep, he stirred and pulled her into his arms, her hand went to his chest to gently push him away, but as she did her fingers grazed over his scars. She saw a glimpse of a beautiful woman and two children, a boy and girl all laughing and calling for him, then she felt pain in her shoulder and chest so bad it took her breath away and she was left with such a feeling of loss and heartache, she hadn't inherited all her mother's powers but sometimes when she was close to someone, not physically close, but spiritually, she would have flashes of their intense emotions; but never anything like this before, what had happened to him? she rolled away in agony and closed her eyes, she would ask Ben when they had a moment alone.

Jack was up and dressed when Ben brought them their tea. Tannis was still asleep, so the two men sat by the fire. Jack told him the book was a no-go so it would have to be the London house.

'At least Armatage won't be in London, his servants say they're going further south for the week,' Ben said as he shook his head, 'it's the wife I feel sorry for.'

'Don't pity her, she was at it in the library with the footman last night, right pair of bleedin' swingers,' Jack grimaced.

'Pity the footman,' Ben changed his plea.

Tannis woke, and sat up, 'Can I go back to my room yet?' she yawned.

'I heard him leave about half an hour ago,' Jack nodded.

'I'll send a maid to help you dress,' Ben smiled at her as he left the room. She got out of bed and stood by the fire as Jack passed her a cup of tea.

'I don't want you out of my sight today, that dirty old sod is determined to have you.'

She put her cup down on the mantle and hugged him, 'You're a good man, Jack,' as she stepped back, her nightgown slipped a little from her shoulder showing a nasty bruise.

'I thought he didn't touch you last night?' Jack frowned.

Tannis bit her lip and pulled her nightgown down a little more to show the other two bruises just above her breasts. All three exactly matched his, and he knew it as his hand went to his chest.

'It wasn't him; it was you, Jack' she said softly.

'How?' he stared at her.

'I don't know, it's never happened like this before, only years ago with Ned or Will, someone I was close to, but that was just feeling mild emotions,' she shook her head.

'And Ben?' He pulled her nightgown back to cover the marks. 'Ben hasn't had such pain.'

'He's been shot!' He turned and looked out of the window, his guts in a knot.

'So have I, Jack, and it hurts, but it doesn't break your heart,' she touched his shoulder gently, and he turned to face her again, having regained his composure.

'It was a long time ago, and I've moved on, so just forget it ok?' She nodded as she turned and left the room, like hell have you moved on, she thought to herself.

They left the country manor that afternoon and headed back to Richmond with an invitation to the Walpole's townhouse for that Friday to attend yet another party. This time a masked ball. Tannis never mentioned anything to Jack again about his pain, but it prayed on her mind she would get to the bottom of this when the mission was over.

Ben managed to sneak into her room one night, and they grabbed a few hours together, she told him about what had happened and what he'd told her 'Babe if he says leave it, you have to respect his wishes. Maybe he has moved on, and if this has never happened to you before maybe you saw it wrong, you know if he's divorced that's his business.'

'I guess so,' she stroked his chest as they lay in bed, 'I just want him to be as happy as I am.'

'You can't save 'em all, Hasselhoff,' he grinned as he pulled the sheets over them and made love to her again.

At last, the big night arrived. Jack and Tannis were once more dressed in the best clothes money could buy, even Ben was dressed in his finest servant outfit. The carriage arrived and took them to Walpole's townhouse. As they approached Tannis, put her jewelled mask over her eyes and helped Jack with his, while he complained, 'Feel like a bleedin highwayman.'

'Well, we are planning a heist of sorts,' she reminded him.

Ben helped them alight, thinking how dazzling Tannis looked and what a lucky guy he was as he made his way around to the stable yard with the carriage to wait until it was time for him to make his move.

Inside Tannis danced with a few of her suitors while Jack mingled with the other guests. It was a pleasant enough evening; he thought to himself as he saw Tannis float by in the arms of yet another man desperately trying to win her affections, good job Ben can't see this, he thought and then pulled himself up. Ben was doing fine, he was a pro and played his part well he thought as he checked his watch and gave Tannis the signal, she made her way over to Lady Walpole and swooned a little, and he watched as the ladies helped her out of the room. Sure enough, within a few minutes, he was sent for, she had been taken upstairs to lay down and had called for her brother. Good location he thought as he was taken to her, directly above the library. Lady Walpole was with her as he entered the room, 'Your sister swooned a little in the heat, sir.'

'I thank you, your Ladyship, please don't let us keep you from your guests, I shall take care of her now,' he bowed politely.

'Very well,' she rose and patted Tannis' hand, 'return as soon as you can my dear, you are the belle of the ball.' And with that, she left them alone. Jack held the door for her then locked it quickly and hurried over to the bed. As Tannis got up, he stood behind her and quickly unlaced her gown, she stepped out of it already wearing breeches underneath. Then he moved in front of her and helped her step into a harness which had also been hidden under her voluminous skirts.

He secured the straps and attached a rope, taking up the slack he walked over to the window with her, she opened it and, looking out; they could see Ben on the roof of the stable block, with a small lantern in his hand he signalled to them it was good to go. He could get no closer as Walpole had security all over and servants of guests were not allowed anywhere near the grounds. Tannis climbed carefully out of the window. The wall was practically smooth brick with a very narrow ledge running across, she gripped on as well as she could and inched her way down towards the library as Jack took the strain. It was a difficult climb for her; she was almost above the target window when Ben signalled they were going to have company. Tannis froze, looking below she saw a young couple walking together, they paused for a moment right beneath her. She looked up at Jack, her fingers were losing their grip, he could see that she couldn't hold on much longer and even though he had a good hold on her, if she let go, she would be swinging in the air above them, sure to catch their attention.

Not before time, the couple moved away, and Ben gave them the all clear. She was close enough, Jack determined, so he nodded to her and slowly lowered her down. She swiftly disconnected the rope and slid the huge sash window up and went inside. Her search was quicker than expected, too quick, thought Jack as he took up the slack once more and helped her with her climb back into the room. Once she was safely inside Jack closed the window and Ben climbed down from the roof and went back to the carriage, he too thought something was not right.

'It's gone,' she panted a little from the hurried climb, Jack helped her to dress and pulled tightly on the laces of her corset, 'So, it was there?'

'Yes, I got a trace. It has been there and very recently too, someone has turned the library over, Jack.'

'If not Phoenix then who?' he asked as he fixed her mask back on.

'I found these on the floor,' she said and held up two red feathers. 'There's a woman downstairs with these on her mask,' he remembered, 'you ready?'

Tannis put her hand to her chest to try and calm her breathing, she had been forced back into the constraints of her costume before she could get her breath back properly. He looked at her as she nodded, then took her hand and led her to the door muttering, 'No wonder they swoon all the time, how do you breathe in that stuff?'

'Not well,' she informed him.

Downstairs it was not difficult to find the woman with the red feather mask, she was just leaving. Jack hurriedly made their apologies, blaming Tannis' health, and called for their carriage. Ben anticipated the call, so they didn't wait long, and they had paid handsomely for a no questions asked driver. Jack gave him his instructions as Tannis climbed inside, Ben was already there hidden in the shadows.

Jack jumped in, and they raced off, following the carriage ahead of them, they filled Ben in while being bounced around as the driver hurried through the streets. Eventually, the horses slowed down and came to a stop, ahead of them the carriage they had been following had allowed its passenger to alight then moved on to the stable yard behind the building. As arranged their driver had completed his part of the bargain so climbed down and walked away counting his very ample payoff.

Tannis had removed her mask and now looked out of the window, 'Oh God!' she sank back into her seat.

'You know her?' Ben tried to get a look but could only see the back of the woman as she went inside.

'I know of her, that's Lady Olivia Fenton.'

'Really?' Jack smirked.

'Wanna share?' Ben looked at them both, and it was Jack's turn to show his historical knowledge now, 'Lady Olivia Fenton, proprietor of *The Hellfire Club*, it's a private members club for the upper classes where if you can afford it, you can do it.'

'What would she want with the book?' Ben frowned, 'how could she know what it is?'

'Leverage maybe?' Jack mused, 'wasn't Walpole for shutting this place down?'

Tannis nodded, 'Yes he was.'

'Well, whatever the reason we have to get in there,' Jack chewed his lip, you'll have to sit this one out,' he said as he looked at Tannis. She shook her head, 'You're not a member, and you're a known associate of Walpole's, you'll never get over the threshold, if you're going in, it won't be through the front door, and you'll need both of us with you.'

'And since when did you give the orders?' Jack raised an eyebrow.

'I don't, that's your job, I merely offer good advice,' she smiled sweetly and turned for one of them to help with her gown. Jack nodded, and Ben began to unlace her; she looked hot in a corset top and breeches especially when she pulled on the thigh length black leather boots she had stashed under the seat.

'Could get you a job inside looking like that,' Jack pulled a face. She stuck her tongue out as they reached under their seats again, this time pulling out a cache of weapons. Once armed they all climbed out of the carriage, Tannis took Ben's hat and cloak as they walked around the back of the building and scaled the walls of the stable yard, dropping silently onto the cobbles below.

Hiding in the shadows, they saw a couple of working girls coming outside for a break, they walked across the yard and stood with their backs to the house smoking clay pipes.

Alpha team crept inside undetected. Tannis removed her cloak and hat; Jack slipped off his jacket too as they came to a set of back stairs. 'You two keep looking down here. I'll try upstairs,' he instructed.

As they walked along the hall past the downstairs bedrooms, the noises they heard were disturbing and not what you would associate with pleasure. Ahead there was a door slightly ajar, and Ben looked inside, it was just an empty bedroom decorated in gaudy red with a range of whips and bondage equipment hanging on the wall ready for use. He grimaced as that kind of pleasure-seeking was not to his taste.

Someone was coming down the hall now, one of the girls and a client looking for a room. Ben grabbed Tannis and pulled her inside; she stared open-mouthed at the array of whips and chains and even scalpels as he closed the door, 'People like to be hurt?' she whispered.

'Each to his own,' he shrugged, 'so long as both parties are willing.' She looked at the wall again and then back to him, he smiled, 'Babe, we're perfect the way we are, although you're really doing it for me in that outfit,' he looked her up and down, and she smiled at him now. Outside the door, they heard the couple stop. They weren't going to pass by the handle began to turn, and Ben pushed Tannis on the bed and lay on top of her. She pulled his mouth down on hers and wrapped her legs around him.

'Oh, sorry, Love,' the girl giggled as she closed the door and carried on down the hall with her client in tow.

Upstairs Jack had found what he had been looking for, Lady Fenton's office was empty, so he let himself in and hurried over to the desk. Bingo! It was in the top drawer, shoving the book in his waistband, he made to leave the room when Lady Fenton and a rather large man servant walked in, their pistols aimed in his direction.

'I knew I was followed,' she kept her eyes and her aim on Jack as she spoke, 'get the book and take him outside.' Jack was marched at gunpoint back the way he had come. The smoking girls were ordered back inside as he was shoved into stables. 'So, Walpole sent you to retrieve his precious book, didn't he? Well, I'm sorry you wasted your life for that. I have a buyer who has already paid me more than I could ever spend.'

'Let me guess,' Jack stalled for time, 'you received a large down payment from a client with instructions of when and where to find the book, and once you've deposited it at a bank or solicitors, they give you the balance?'

'Something like that,' she was a bit surprised by his knowledge, 'little matter as you will be long gone by then,' she smirked.

'Just not in the way you think,' Ben stepped from the shadows. Lady Fenton spun around to see him holding a pistol on them, she gave him a dismissive look and turned her weapon back on Jack.

'You have one shot, we have two. The odds are against you.'

Tannis stepped silently out of the darkness now, put a hand over the man servant's mouth from behind and thrust a small blade up into the base of his skull, he fell dead as she removed the pistol from his hand and threw it to Jack, 'I'd say the odds have just changed, wouldn't you?' he said as he took aim.

Ben took her weapon and disarmed it; gunfire was to be avoided at all costs; they didn't need the attention it would bring.

Lady Fenton looked at Tannis, 'I could use a girl like you, you'd be rich, never want for anything.'

'She's not for using,' Jack said as he tied her up, Tannis ignored her as she picked up the book and read through it. Ben put a gag in their captive's mouth now, and the two men stood either side of Tannis and read over her shoulder. They all saw that Ned had been right, this was accurate material, and yes, Dolly and Bonnie were well documented.

Safely back at the townhouse with the servants already paid off and dismissed, they made a final sweep, the place was clean with nothing left. It was as if they had never existed, Ben lit a fire in the grate and placed the book on top, the three of them watched as the problem burned away to ash and the future was saved.

They made ready to leap when outside there was a creak on the landing. The door opened slowly and to their surprise there stood Walpole, 'Don't be alarmed,' he spoke quietly as he came into the room, 'I knew this day would come,' he offered Jack a letter.

'Although I only knew it was you when my men watching *The Hellfire Club* reported your actions.'
Jack took the letter and read it aloud.

'Hello, my brother or sister,
if you've come to find the book, then it must've been used against us somehow. I met Madden when he was writing it and thought it might be trouble. I took care of the agent responsible and asked my friend Robert to suppress it for reasons of national security, knowing him, he would've kept the original, so do us all a favour and destroy the bloody thing.
See you later,
Will.'

Jack passed the letter to Tannis, she sighed and reread it.
'Your brother saved my life some years ago, now,' Walpole looked at Jack who shook his head, 'Her brother.'
'Well, my part of the bargain is complete,' he nodded curtly, 'and as promised this shall go to my grave with me.'
He turned to leave, 'I do not pretend to understand who you people are, but I believe you are owed a great debt,' he gave them a respectful nod and closed the door behind him.
'Good old Will,' Tannis folded the letter and put it in her pocket. 'Saving the future as well as the past,' Ben smiled at her.
They set their timepieces. 'Let's go home,' Jack took one last look at the 18th century, and they were gone.

Chapter Seven

Tannis sat up in bed working on her laptop, she looked up and smiled as Ben entered the room. 'What are you up to?' He climbed into bed beside her and tried to look at the screen, but she closed it and put it to one side before he could see anything.

'Just sorting out Jack's birthday present,' she leaned over and turned the lamp out; moonlight flooded the room as she lay down beside him. They had just moved into their new home together, and unopened boxes were all around the room as they had only just brought Ben's things from the real world. It wasn't a huge place, but it was just right for the two of them. Jack and Ned had helped with the move earlier that day, but now, at last, they were alone.

'You cleared it with the Admiral to be off duty, tomorrow, right?' He looked at her.

'I'm all yours,' she smiled.

'I like the sound of that,' he wrapped his arms around her, she pulled him down to her mouth and sighed with pleasure as he moved his kisses down her neck.

'Ah, no coalition, no regulations and no boat.'

'Ship,' he whispered as his kisses fluttered down her stomach. She arched her back and grabbed the metal frame of the headboard as his tongue caressed her.

'Whatever,' she breathed.

Ben was woken by the morning sun dancing in his eyes as the curtains billowed in the breeze; they were still in each other's arms, he smiled to himself as he watched her sleep; This was how it was going to be from now on, and he couldn't wait to take the next step. He'd been thinking about it for some time now, he even let it slip that night back in 1733, but it had never been mentioned again. He knew Tannis would never bring it up; she wasn't like that, she stirred and nuzzled his neck pressing her body close to his, her arm across his chest. He moved away a little to look at her, she half opened her eyes then smiled as she closed them again, 'Hi.'

'Hi back,' he kissed her gently, 'Happy?'

'Couldn't be happier,' she whispered as she opened her eyes and looked at him now.

'I could,' he gazed deeply at her.

She smiled again, 'Your wish is my command,' and began to slide her hand down his stomach.

He put a hand on hers to stop her, 'Not that, well yes that but, tell me, tell me you love me.'

She was concerned now, 'I love you, Ben.'

He stroked her face, 'Marry me?'

Her face lit up, 'Really? You want me? I mean that's forever, you know?'

'I know, I want forever, I love you, Tannis.'

She threw her arms around him, 'We're getting married.'

'Not until you say yes.'

'What? Oh yes, yes, yes!'

The ring he gave her had belonged to his grandmother, a beautiful solitaire diamond which she now wore as they made their way to Ned's house for lunch. Jack would be there too so it would be the perfect place to make their announcement.

Jack greeted them as they walked around to the back garden. 'Sorted all your junk yet?' He referred to the boxes they still had to unpack when he and Ned left them last night.

They didn't get the chance to reply because Elea came out to welcome them now, Ned close behind her with a tray of drinks which he almost dropped when his wife half screamed as she grabbed Tannis' hand and stared at the ring. 'Ned, look!' She dragged the poor woman towards her brother with the ring in full view.

Jack shook Ben's hand and slapped him on the back 'Congratulations mate, and about time, too! You really have got one in a million there, take care of her.'

Ned was hugging Tannis as Elea ran over to Ben and hugged him too.

'Are you sure you know what you are letting yourself in for?' Ned called over to Ben.

Jack hugged Tannis and kissed her on the cheek, 'Congratulations love, you deserve to be happy.'

'So do you,' she smiled up at him.

'I'm fine as I am,' he joked as he held her at arm's length and looked at her. Her shoulder and chest began to throb in the same place as before, but she didn't show it this time, she just smiled.

Back on The Eldridge the next day Hennessey offered the couple his sincere congratulations when they told him the news, 'Set a date yet?' he asked jovially.

'Not yet, sir,' Ben replied, 'but soon.'

The two men walked down to the hold together to meet the inbound team due to return while Tannis made the excuse that she was waiting for Ned and hung around outside his office opposite Hennessey's. But that wasn't her plan at all, when Ben and Hennessey were out of sight she darted back into the Admiral's office and opened his filing cabinet; she only had a few moments before Barbara, his Rottweiler of a secretary, would show up for work, so she had to be quick.

She fingered her way through the personnel records hurrying to the letter M. 'Marsters,' she whispered as she pulled out Jack's file and read through it, once she had found the information, she needed she returned the file and hurried over to Ned's office just as Barbara stalked her way along the passage. Tannis didn't like Barbara, she was a stick thin crone who was always brusque, never pleasant. Still, at least she wasn't biassed, she treated everyone with contempt.

Ned wandered into his office a short while later and sat in the chair opposite his desk. Tannis didn't look up; she just carried on busily tapping at the keyboard. 'Oh, don't mind me, it's only my office after all,' he grumbled.

'Be done in a minute,' she still didn't look up, so he leaned closer, 'What are you up to?'

'Jack's birthday present,' she muttered.

'That's tomorrow, haven't you got him anything yet?'

She switched the computer off and stood up, 'I have now,' she walked over to Ned and hugged him tightly, 'love you big brother.'

'Love you too, Tannis,' he said cautiously, 'what are you up to?' 'Gotta go. See you later,' and with that, she darted out of the room.

Not having her own quarters on board now since she and Ben had moved in together Tannis headed for the locker room where the teams showered and changed before and after missions, she slipped into her leather trousers and top, but no jacket and she remained barefoot. Then attaching her wrist blade, went looking for Ben.

She found him coming out of the Mess with Jack, he frowned, 'Why are you dressed like that?'

'There's something I have to take care of, I'll be back soon,' she took the hand of each one of them and gave them a squeeze, Ben shook his head as she let go of them, 'No, something's wrong.'

Ned came racing towards them, 'Tannis, wait.'

Jack smelled trouble, 'What's going on?'

Tannis looked at her team 'Just trust me ok, if I can't do this then what's the point of it all?'

Ben made to speak but she was gone, so he turned to Ned who had joined them now, 'What's she up to?' Ned looked awkwardly at Jack who just shrugged, 'Out with it.'

'It would be easier if I showed you, come to my office,' he said nervously.

They followed him and stood in front of his desk now as he turned the computer on.

'She said she was looking for your birthday present,' Ned looked at Jack, 'but she wouldn't say what it was, I could tell it was a bit more than a book token so when she left, I searched through the history,' he clicked the mouse and a picture of a medium size cruise liner appeared on the screen on the wall behind him with full schematics alongside it.

'Jesus Christ, it's *The Wind Dancer*,' Jack whispered as he sat down hard on a nearby chair, 'how could she know?'

'Know what?' Ben had no clue what was happening.

'She read your file,' Hennessey stood in the doorway. Ned pulled another file now with a newspaper headline dated 8th August 2005, it described how Pirates had hijacked *The Wind Dancer*, but something went wrong, and all aboard were killed when there was an explosion. The ship went down, and a sole survivor was found floating in a lifeboat by the coast guard, close to death having suffered three bullet wounds. Ben and Ned looked at one another, their faces awash with disbelief.

'I never mentioned it because I tried to put it behind me,' he sighed, 'she saw the scars on me that night in 1733 when she stayed in my room, I should've known she wouldn't let it lie.'

'The woman and children Tannis saw?' Ben gave his CO a look of genuine pity.

'My wife and kids,' Jack closed his eyes.

Ned lowered his head, 'You have the power to travel through time, but you couldn't cross your own timeline to save them.'

'Not to mention it's against regulations to change time for personal gain,' Hennessey was proud of Jack for never once asking for help in this matter, the coalition had been clear on the issue, after all, that's what *DE-173* had been all about keeping time true.

'And now she's risking her neck,' Jack rubbed his hands over his face.

'My sister has been doing this since she was fifteen, she's not stupid. She researches her marks well, have faith,' Ned switched the screen off, 'she's a pro,' he held up her timepiece, she'd left it on his desk in case she was caught.

Hennessey pulled an act of pure genius. He leaped back to 2005 and arranged for military satellites to record the events on *The Wind Dancer* with strict instructions not to interfere. Then he had the recordings sent to him now on The Eldridge, 'They were given a picture of Tannis and told to track her on board,' the Admiral explained as he put the disc into the machine, then they sat in the briefing room and watched as the satellite homed in on its target at the allotted time and place.

The pirates had already boarded, their ship was moored alongside. It didn't take long to home in on Tannis; she was hiding by a lifeboat station watching as the pirates had all the men lined up on one side of the ship, the women and children on the other, they were all dressed for dinner. She saw Jack, he had no jacket on, and his bow tie hung loosely around the open collar of his white shirt. Tannis flinched as, without warning, the pirates opened fire on the unarmed men, sending the dead and dying into the sea. She looked over the side for her CO, but somehow, he was heading to the bottom like the rest of them.

'Come on Jack, you were found in a life raft, where's the yellow life raft?' She patted her hand nervously as she waited then looked down and noticed it was resting on a yellow life raft, 'Oh shit!' she gasped in realisation as she grabbed it and threw it into the water then dived in after it. No one heard the splash above the screams of the women and children, she dived down, pulling the bodies of the dead out of her way until she found him; he was bleeding and unconscious, she pinched his nose and breathed her lungful of air into him then held on tight as she kicked as hard as she could for the surface. Not realising how far down she had gone, it seemed like it was beyond reach but she struggled on, kicking harder until they broke the surface, gasping for air Tannis floated Jack on his back, he wasn't breathing, but she found a faint pulse and treading water now forced more air into his lungs and then began to swim towards the life raft that had inflated on impact. She dragged him into it and carried on breathing life into him. Finally, he choked and started to breathe for himself, he was still unconscious though, so she put him in the recovery position. 'See you in three years,' she squeezed his hand and lowered herself back into the water once more.

Climbing the anchor chain Tannis slipped back on board undetected, the women and children had been forced inside again now. She heard footsteps approaching, one of the pirates on watch stood before her suddenly, but before he even took aim, she kicked out and knocked the weapon from his hand then grabbed his neck and twisted. She dumped the body over the side and picked up his weapon which was a handgun with a silencer attached. She threw his AK47 overboard and carried on inside. A short distance down the passage a door opened, and another target walked out, he didn't even see her when she took the shot and sent one bullet straight into his head. The door closed quietly as she hid the body back where he had come from.

Looking up, Tannis spied the air conditioning vent which would be her access throughout the ship, she moved the mesh screen and raised herself inside, covering her tracks as she went, making her way silently along the narrow metal tunnel until she was above the ballroom and looking down at the awful scene below. All the women and children were being held there at gunpoint while one of their captors read out their names from the passenger list, as the names were called the innocent stepped forward and were taken to their staterooms where they would be forced to open the safes and hand over their valuables, no doubt then being murdered once they had outlived their usefulness.

'Caroline Marsters, travelling with daughter Katie and son James,' the emotionless toad called out.

Back on The Eldridge Jack's hand went to his mouth as he saw his family alive for the first time in three years, his heart breaking all over again. There was his beautiful wife, fair-haired like him and still retaining her slim figure after two pregnancies, and his beloved children, Katie, the image of her mother, nine years old going on thirty, and little James, five and that all important half as he always added, he was more like his father.

Tannis knew where Jack's stateroom was, she had already checked so she made her way there as quietly as she could.

Caroline and her children were dragged by a sweaty hulk of a man along the passageway to their stateroom, and once inside he ordered her to open the safe as he turned his gun on the children who cowered in fear by the door, she did as she was told and handed over their jewellery and cash. Her captor waved for her to stand over by the children as he shoved his ill-gotten gains into a pillowcase he produced from his pocket.

Then his attention turned to Caroline as she stood there now, looking stunning in her floor-length evening gown, 'Strip!' He leered at her, but Caroline shook her head and stepped back against the wall, 'you or the girl, you choose,' he started to loosen his belt.

'She's only nine,' Caroline gasped. He moved towards Katie. 'No!' Caroline cried, 'I'll do it,' she stepped over to the bed and looked at her children. 'Close your eyes and don't open them until Mummy tells you, ok?' She tried to smile. The children nodded in mute terror and held on to one another, their eyes tight shut. Caroline was visibly shaking now as she slipped one of the dress straps from her shoulder.

'Damn it, Tannis, move!' Jack yelled at the screen, as if following his order, she kicked open the vent in the ceiling at that moment and shot the piece of filth between the eyes. She then lowered herself down into the room and covered the body with the counterpane from the bed. Caroline froze for a second then ran to her children and held them tightly.

'You can open your eyes now,' her voice shook.

Tannis picked up her latest kill's weapon and shoved it in her waistband.

'Thank you,' Caroline struggled to keep her voice steady, 'who are you?'

'My name is Tannis, your husband is my commanding officer.'

'Jack's… I saw them…' she broke down and hugged her sobbing children.

Tannis crouched down in front of them, 'Hey, your Daddy's going to be fine, he's just wounded,' she smiled at them.

'Really?' Caroline sniffed.

'Hand on heart,' she made the gesture as James plucked up the courage to step forward, 'You work with Daddy?'

Tannis gently touched the brave little chap's cheek, 'We travel together from time to time,' then she jerked her head quickly, someone was turning the door handle, 'get behind me!' Tannis ordered. As they did so, the door burst open and two armed men raised their weapons as they saw their dead colleague half covered on the floor, 'Yes, this one fight's back,' she sneered and thrust her hands forward, and they were gone. She hurried to close the door.

'What the hell are you?' Caroline pushed her children behind her now.

'Complicated,' her words hurt Tannis, 'we have to get out of here, this boat is going to sink.'

Caroline didn't budge, 'Ship - and it seems fine to me.'

As if right on cue, there was a huge explosion, and the ship listed violently. The children screamed as water began flooding in under the door. Tannis took the little one's hands in hers and held them tightly, 'You have to hang on to me!' she shouted now as the rush of water was getting louder.

'What good will that do?' Caroline tried to pull the children from her.

'You've just seen me get rid of those guys, I can get us out of here, hang on to me!' The water was so deep now Tannis had picked James up to stop him from drowning, Katie was struggling, too.

'Daddy wouldn't be her boss if he didn't trust her,' the little girl cried.

Back in the briefing room, the picture faded. The ship had sunk and was out of range for the satellite. Everyone raced to the hold; they burst in to find it empty except for the usual crew.

'Come on, Tannis come on girl,' Jack spoke through gritted teeth. 'Come on, baby, come back to me,' Ben whispered to himself.

Crash! She'd done it, they were on their knees coughing and gasping for air. Jack ran over to them and fell to his knees too and pulled his family into his arms as tears of joy ran down his face, Caroline clung to him, 'You're alive, how?' she looked around them, 'where are we, Jack?'

'You're home now, love,' he never thought that he would hold them again. Ben had rushed over to Tannis, she had shoved herself away from the group and was flat on her back, tired and gasping for breath, he sat her up in his arms as she began to breathe normally again.

'Are you mad at me?' She looked up at him.

'I know why you did it, and I know why you couldn't tell us, but no more, Babe, I don't care how much trouble I'd get in; you don't risk yourself alone again,' he kissed the top of her head then looked up as Hennessey marched towards them, 'I think I know someone who is mad at you though.'

'Tannis, my office, please!' The Admiral was abrupt as he turned and marched out of the hold. Ben helped her to stand now and slipped an arm around her, they walked to the door, and she leaned into him as they came to a stop in front of Ned who stood, arms folded across his chest, with a stern look on his face, but he soon smiled and winked at his sister as he handed her timepiece back to her.

The medical team were giving Jack's family the once over, 'Be right back,' he squeezed his wife's hand and went to catch up with his teammates which he did as Tannis was handing over her weapons to the deck officer. He put his hand around the back of her head and pulled her towards him; their foreheads pressed together. 'Thank you, you saved my life and my soul,' he kissed her on the top of her head. Tannis smiled, 'Happy Birthday, Jack.'

Hennessey closed the door as Ben and Ned joined them, 'What the hell am I going to do with you, Tannis? You of all people know that you cannot manipulate time for personal reasons! Do you know how many coalition members have lost loved ones and can't cross their timeline to bring them back?'

'Yeah, me and Ned for a start,' she folded her arms across her chest, 'I am aware I can't change the past if it alters the future, but in this case, no bodies were ever recovered so to the real world nothing has changed. They just have to stay on Atlantis,' she countered.

'It was the fact you undertook the mission without orders or even permission for that matter!'

'You wouldn't have agreed to it,' she fired back.

'Tannis,' he sighed, 'you know I couldn't have given permission,' he sat down deep in thought.

Ned interceded on his sister's behalf, 'Admiral, Tannis going back to *The Wind Dancer* is a fixed point in time.'

'How so?' Hennessey frowned.

'Because she had already gone back to save Jack in 2005 otherwise, she would never have met him in 2008. One cannot happen without the other.'

Hennessey took a moment; how could he argue with that? 'Very well, Colonel Marsters will be on compassionate leave for the next two weeks, so Alpha team is stood down from operations, Major Rhodes, you will report to Ned and assist him in bringing the recruits up to speed.'

'Yes, sir,' Ben acknowledged.

'You too, Tannis,' he dismissed them.

'Well, that went well,' Ben commented when they were safely out of earshot from Barbara.

Both Tannis and her brother gaped at him, 'What did I say?'

'It's historical etiquette and 18th-century dancing,' Tannis pulled a face.

'No weapons training or unarmed combat?' his eyes pleaded to Ned, who shrugged, 'Sorry mate, it's hanky flapping bullshit for the next couple of weeks.'

It had been three days since Tannis had brought Jack's family back to him and his teammates hadn't seen him since. He had been busy finding a suitable house and moving out of his flat. The chosen abode was just along the pathway from Ned's, it would take some adjustments for all of them to get used to the status quo. Ben and Tannis had discussed it with Ned at length, and they had all agreed to let them have some space.

So now, after 12 hours of sheer bliss in the coalition's new training facility which had been discreetly built in a wooded area overlooking the harbour, Ben and Tannis emerged from the tree-lined pathway and headed down the hill towards The Eldridge, they were off the clock now, as he slipped his arm around her, and she leaned into him. Barbara stalked past them on her way up the hill to her Pilates class, glaring at Tannis as she bid Ben a good evening.

'That woman is a total cow!' Tannis fumed.

'I can hear you!' Barbara's throaty voice rasped.

'I said it loud enough!'

'Oh, don't worry about her, she's just pissed off because a house fell on her sister,' Jack stood at the bend in the path.

'What are you doing here?' Tannis hugged him. 'You should be with your family.'

He squeezed her tightly, 'Came to invite you to dinner didn't I,' he grinned.

'Great, I'm starving,' Ben smiled, 'this punishment detail is worse than Iraq.'

'Hennessey giving you a hard time?' Jack asked awkwardly.

'No, we just got stuck with this crap,' she gestured back up the hill, 'more of a punishment for you, really,' she looked sheepishly at Ben.

Jack's house was spacious, again in the Roman style like Ned's, but not as huge and very homely. Caroline and the children were at the door to welcome them. The children were very well behaved and polite as they shook hands with Ben and were properly introduced to Tannis this time. After drinks in the garden, the children were put to bed but not before they asked Tannis to take them to different times in history.

'I thought I told you two to mind your manners,' Jack gently chastised them. But they begged their father and gave a wide-eyed look that would weaken any resolve more so as he'd just got them back, 'Ok,' he buckled, and they jumped up and down excitedly, he raised a finger to calm them, 'maybe if we ask Tannis nicely, she might take us to the gangplank of The Eldridge and back, that's it.' Instantly they turned their pleading faces to Tannis.

'How could I say no?' She smiled as Jack took his kid's hands, Tannis followed suit, and they stood in a circle. Ben gave Tannis a knowing look and stepped back with Caroline, a little blue flash, and they were gone. Caroline turned to Ben, but before she could speak, they could hear giggling coming from the bedroom, Tannis had left Jack to put the kids to bed and walked back out into the garden.

'That's going to take some getting used to,' Caroline sighed, 'the children seem to just take it in their stride,' she was amazed.

'I imagine the whole place is taking some adjustment,' he remembered his first trip. Jack joined them now, and Tannis went to help Caroline in the kitchen as the two men sat outside talking shop.

'Tannis, I want to apologise to you,' Caroline began.

'For what?'

'For asking what you were back on the ship,' she said sheepishly. 'I would ask the same question in that situation, forget about it.' 'Thank you,' the woman smiled at her now.

'So, how're you settling in? It must be weird trying to get your head around stuff?' Tannis changed the subject.

'I love it here; I don't think I'd ever want to leave. You have given my children and me a second chance to grow up in a safe environment; I owe you everything,' she touched Tannis' arm lightly. 'You don't owe me a thing, although dinner would be great, I'm starving,' the two women laughed together.
'Sounds like they're getting on,' Jack relaxed back in his seat, 'keep hold of her Ben.'

'I intend to, don't worry about that,' his friend replied, looking across the lawn as Tannis and Caroline joined them now, and they sat down to eat.

'Ben and Tannis make a great couple,' Caroline thought aloud as she climbed into bed and Jack walked out of their bathroom.

'Yeah, it hasn't been easy for them, but they got there in the end,' he lay on the bed next to her and kissed her softly, she smiled at him, but there was sadness in her eyes.

'What's wrong?' He touched her face gently.

'I keep seeing them shoot you,' her eyes filled with tears, 'I thought you were dead.'

He held her to him, 'It's over now, don't think about it,' he kissed her again, and she clung to him as he lay her down. Their kisses grew more passionate as he ran his hand down her stomach, she moaned softly as he slid his hand between her legs and stroked her with his fingers, she trembled as she climaxed then he was inside her, there had never been anyone else, not even when she was lost to him. Their rhythm grew stronger as he slid his hand under her back and lifted her closer to him, his lips were on hers then he gasped as he flowed into her, the only thought on his mind was he wanted to make her pregnant again.

The two weeks flew by for Jack, and before he knew it, he was kissing Caroline and the children goodbye and making his way to The Eldridge. Caroline knew better than to ask about missions, but having just been through what they had, she was more worried than usual about him being mission ready again, so last night he had invited his teammates over for dinner to try and lay her fears to rest.

'Are you leaving?' Tannis asked Jack during a moment alone; he was taken aback for a second, 'Is that why you two think you're here tonight?'

She shrugged, 'We just thought, you know, well, maybe you see things a bit differently now like Ned.'

He hugged her to him, 'I've got the best team I could wish for watching my back doing the best job in the world, I'm not going anywhere,' he dug her in the ribs now, 'besides who else can handle you when you're off the chain?'

She glared at him then shrugged, 'Fair point.'

The rest of the evening was spent putting Caroline's mind to rest, telling her that it was all just observation and recon work, they explained about the different medical advances other dimensions might have and could share. There was no mention of Phoenix or Kira and Nyra.

The locals had been only too happy to tell Caroline all about *DE-173* and their exploits, but she'd been careful not to mention them too much so as not to dampen the mood of the evening. 'So, if you time travelled in our world during training what was the best moment?' She asked Ben first.

'Helping one of the founders of the abolition of slavery get a man to freedom.'

It was Jack's turn now, but before he could answer Caroline looked at him and smiled. '1966 by any chance?' she laughed, he smiled back at her, she knew him so well, 'Oh yeah, Wembley 1966 world cup final, had a bird's eye view too up on the roof,' he winked at Tannis who then turned to Ben, 'Your first training leaps.'

'Oh, so that's why you were covered in dirt when you got back.'

The two couples enjoyed each other's company until late into the night, and as they walked home together, Ben and Tannis were relieved their CO was staying with them. It would've been the end of Alpha Team as neither of them could ever serve under anyone else, the three of them knew what each other's thoughts and actions would be before they were made and the trust, they had in one another could never be the same with an outsider.

Next afternoon as Alpha team and Ned walked down the gangplank, Caroline and the children were there to meet them. The children were very excited, they had been to see their new school and couldn't wait to start the following day. They told their father about the funny white robes their headmaster Mr. Archimedes wore. Jack stopped in his tracks and looked at Tannis 'Mr. Archimedes? Have you been time shopping again?' He frowned.

'Oh no, you can't pin this one on me,' with the children present Tannis had to mind what she said, 'I was nursing a boo boo from the Crimea,' the thought of more etiquette and dancing loomed over her, 'this one was down to Will, he couldn't stand the thought of such a brilliant man being killed in a case of mistaken identity, so he switched him for a Phoenix agent.'

'I thought it was France 1801?' Ned frowned.

'No, that boo boo was the mission before,' she rubbed her shoulder at the painful memory.

'Any more little trips we should know about?' Ben looked at the brother and sister who both shuffled awkwardly.

Caroline tactfully walked on ahead with the children as Jack turned to Ned and Tannis now and folded his arms, 'Continue.'

'Well, it's not people so much as stuff really,' Tannis told him. 'Stuff?' Ben was intrigued.

'Well, there're a couple of cars, planes and motorbikes we may have been forced to bring back with us when we've had to make a hasty exit, like the Apache I told you about, the coalition can take them away if they want, oh, except for Tannis' Spitfire and her Aston Martins,' Ned shrugged.

'Ned, you Massive Twat!' she hissed through gritted teeth.

A look of guilt washed over his face as he turned to Jack and Ben, 'Sorry ruined your Christmas surprises.'

'You have a genuine Spitfire?' Ben was stunned, it had been a life-long ambition to fly one ever since he was a kid, but the closest he'd got so far was the Sim onboard The Eldridge, which was totally amazing, but not the real thing, 'can I see it?' he looked eagerly at his fiancée who wrinkled her nose, 'Well, it needs a bit of work. I had to land it in a hurry,' she glared at Ned, 'I was going to get it fixed up, but I suppose so now the surprise is ruined,' she pouted. He took her hand ready for the leap.

'Hold your horses,' Jack tilted his head to one side coyly, 'Aston Martin?' he smiled.

'DB5,' she returned his expression, and he grabbed her other hand then looked guiltily toward Caroline and the children. 'Don't worry, they won't even notice we're gone,' Tannis grinned.

Chapter Eight

The cool summer breeze blew gently around them as Tannis and Ben lay sleeping in one another's arms, the bedside clock read 03.30 hrs.

Across town, Jack held Caroline as they slept, their children, safe in their beds.

Over at Ned's house, it was situation normal, he and Elea slept precariously balanced on opposite sides of the bed as their three youngest had at different intervals during the night, crept in to be with their parents.

All at once, their mobiles sounded general quarters.

Tannis pulled the covers over her head to ignore the offending item, as Ben reached over and picked it up, opening one eye to reply *message received.*

Caroline picked Jack's up and nudged him awake, he slept so soundly when he was at home.

Half asleep, Ned reached over for his, and fell on the floor; there was no bed left.

Ben jumped out of bed and hurriedly got dressed as did Tannis, then, as had been previously arranged for such emergencies she leaped them both to collect Jack, and then Ned and onto The Eldridge. They appeared in the briefing room just as the Admiral was seating himself. Jack helped Tannis to her seat; she was a little weary from making so many leaps before she was fully awake.

'Thank you for being so prompt,' Hennessey looked serious. He came straight to the point, 'Washington received a transmission from Phoenix almost fifteen minutes ago. They are having a problem.'

'Nothing trivial, I hope,' Ned sneered.

The Admiral let Ned's comment slide, 'It seems the past is changing, Washington only managed to send part of the transmission before they ceased to exist,' he passed a file to each one of them.

Ned read it aloud, 'The unspoken truce has been broken by neither side, others are to blame, you will be next,' he looked at Tannis and rolled his eyes, 'Jefferson, he always was a bit cloak and dagger.'

'Someone's messing with *The Philadelphia Experiment*?' Ben frowned; it didn't make sense.

Hennessey rested his gaze on Tannis, 'I need my best team on this one, and it won't be easy, there's a good chance you'll run into your father and Ned's, can you handle it?'

Ned felt for her. 'It'll be rough little sister, seeing them again and them not knowing you yet, you can't tell them anything, otherwise, we won't exist. Jack and his family will die on *The Wind Dancer*, and if you don't exist, you'll never meet Ben.'

Tannis was furious, 'Really, gosh thanks for telling me, I had no fucking idea,' she glared at her brother, 'I have never changed history at the expense of others, you know that! I followed my orders even when we didn't know if it would make a difference or not that night!' She stood up now and looked at the Admiral, 'I will follow Jack's orders as I always do!'

'That's good enough for me,' Hennessey looked directly at her then addressed them all, 'you will report back in one hour for a full mission briefing.'

Tannis had already left the room when the Admiral rose from his seat.

'What night?' Jack asked Ned, 'she said she followed her orders even when you didn't know if it would make a difference or not.' The other two men stopped to listen too as Ned hung his head.

'Phoenix used to play mind games with us to try and break us,' he sighed, 'Will and I were not told about the mission until she had left, otherwise believe me we wouldn't have allowed it to happen,' he glared at the memory as he continued, 'Phoenix had steered the Titanic away from the iceberg and let it successfully dock in New York. Cole had no way of knowing with so many survivors if all or any of them would affect the future, you know some people just plod on through life not affecting anything. But he couldn't take the chance, it could take forever to trace faults back to someone who maybe wasn't even registered; they could've stowed away or stolen tickets. Anyway, he sent Tannis back to make sure history ran its true course,' he rubbed his hands over his face and stared up at the ceiling, 'she blamed herself for killing over 1500 men women and children that night; and stayed on board until the very end, she was half frozen when she came back to us and would never speak of it.'

Jack closed his eyes to control his anger, 'How old was she?'

'We had a job to do, remember she was 15 when she killed her first agent.'

'The Titanic, Ned, how old was she when Cole sent her to do his dirty work?' Ben fixed him with a stare.

'Sixteen,' Ned sighed, 'they were dark times, Tannis was the best trained of us all I guess that's why he used her the way he did.'

Ben looked away in disgust, 'She was just a kid.'

'Tannis was raised with a strong sense of duty and discipline. You know that you've worked with her,' Ned looked from Ben to Jack.

'Didn't you ever question him?' Jack couldn't believe what he was hearing.

'Oh, Will and I often came to blows with him over the way he treated her, but at the end of the day our folks made him the CO,' he shrugged helplessly and made his way to his office to work out their cover details for the impending mission.

Hennessey shook his head as he too left the room, 'Un fuckin believable.'

Jack joined Ben as he went to look for Tannis. 'She ever talk to you about this stuff?' he asked as they made their way up on deck.

'Some of it, yeah, I knew about Titanic, she told me about it when we got back from the cave in Turkey, but I didn't know how old she was, it's not easy for her, she tries to be loyal to Cole, but since working with us, she sees things differently.'

They found her on deck looking over the side towards Atlantis where the sun was coming up now.

'Just give me a minute, mate,' Jack spoke to Ben as a friend now, not a senior officer, so he stayed put as Jack walked over to where she stood and leaned on the rail next to her. 'You know I never doubted you,' he looked across at her as she smiled.

'Lost it a bit, didn't I?'

'Long overdue, I'd say,' he put his hand on hers, 'listen if there's ever anything you want to talk about or get off your chest, you know I'm always here for you.'

'Ned told you about Titanic?'

'Oh yeah,' he said bitterly.

'Killed a lot of innocent people that night Jack,' she whispered sadly.

'History killed a lot of innocent people that night, love, not you.' She looked at him again, 'Could I tell you everything, Jack? Would you see me differently?'

'I don't know everything you went through, but I do know you're a good person Tannis, I would never judge you, you might tell me things that would shock me, but it wouldn't be your part in it that shocked me.'

She smiled now leaning towards him and nudged him, 'Thanks, Jack.'

'I'll see you at the briefing,' he said as he left, nodding his thanks to Ben as he passed him on his way back inside. He turned back to see her in Ben's arms, a no-no on board, bugger it; he thought as he closed the hatch behind him.

Ned caught up with Tannis a short while later and cleared the air. They walked into the briefing room together now and sat in their places. Their cover was simple enough. Jack would be a Royal Navy Commander on secondment to the US Navy, they had all the relevant security to allow anonymity; his job would be classified with the highest clearance so he could come and go as he pleased. Ben would be his US Navy liaison officer with the rank of Captain and Tannis would be a US Navy nurse with the automatic rank of Lieutenant and therefore access to the Navy Yard, too. Also, they would have their own secure lodgings.

The only conclusion Ned could draw was that someone had got to Reno at some point. Reno, being Dr Reinhart, the mind behind The Philadelphia Experiment and later, the early days of Phoenix, so he was to be their mark for the next few days leading up to the 28th. As for those responsible, that was anybody's guess, they thought maybe a possible renegade from Phoenix, after all, Tannis' mom had tried to get back there to put a stop to it but wound up on Atlantis instead.

Tannis was in the locker room getting changed, she was looking at herself in the mirror when Ben stood in the open doorway and whistled, 'Wow, you look great!' He took her in his arms as they were alone, her uniform was the bright white blouse and skirt of a 1940's US Navy nurse; her hair was in a bun with her hat secured in place. Ben wore a beige Navy uniform that depicted his rank of Captain.

'Oh, I'm sorry, I'm engaged to a Major,' she teased.

He pulled her into him and kissed her, as she wrapped her arms around his neck, he slid his hands down her slender waist to her thighs, then pulled away and looked at her, 'Oh my God stockings!' His lips were on hers again.

'Alpha team to the hold, Alpha team to the hold,' the tannoy announced, they both sighed and moved away from each other; he touched her face gently, 'C'mon,' he took her hand and led her to the door.

They met Jack, Ned and Hennessey in the hold. Jack looked great in his black uniform as he adjusted his sleeves and put his hat on, the three of them stood in a line now, as Hennessey inspected them, Ned winked at his sister, 'Remember, American salute on this one,' she nodded, Hennessey saluted them, which they returned and were gone.

It was October 26th, two days to go, Jack and Ben had managed to get a room each near to the Navy Yard, Tannis was ten minutes away. She had an apartment that they used more than the rooms they had rented. Using the forged documents Ben had managed to secure an office in the Navy Yard for the two men to use. It suited their purpose well, giving them a clear view of Reno's office across the way. For the first day, they kept watch as nothing happened. Reno spent most of his time either in his office or on board The Eldridge, which they could also see from the other side of their room. It was a hive of activity; the hull was wrapped in wire; it was just as the photographs depicted.

Tannis, posing as Ben's girlfriend, joined them for lunch. She walked over to the window and looked out, 'Messing with my boat,' she muttered under her breath.

'Ship,' Jack startled her as he stood at her shoulder.

'Whatever,' she made a mental note to look up the difference when they got back.

Reno went back to his office for his lunch break now, Tannis watched him with no sign of emotion on her face as he collected his hat and coat and left. That was their cue to follow, Tannis and Ben tailed him to the local café and sat close enough to keep an eye on him. Ben ordered for them; he could see her mind was elsewhere as she looked out of the window, 'Hey,' he whispered, 'you only have to pretend to like me for the mission.'

She pushed her thoughts to one side and smiled at him, 'I don't have to pretend,' she took his hands in hers. They ate their lunch and ordered something to go for Jack then followed Reno back to his office for a rather uneventful afternoon's observation. It seemed Reno was a creature of habit and not very interesting habits at that.

Tannis, on the other hand, was very busy in the Navy Yard's small infirmary. A new face, especially a pretty one, warranted a visit, so they were inundated with some of the most minor injuries imaginable. 'Please tell me you're spoken for honey?' Sally, a large friendly nurse, looked pleadingly at Tannis who smiled and told her about Ben. 'Thank goodness, the last one we had was single, we didn't have a minute's peace for a week. He picking you up later, Lucy?'

'Yes, he is,' Lucy was her cover for the mission.

'Good. That should sort it,' Sally grinned and picked up a large syringe from the tray she was carrying, 'now all these cut fingers are gonna need a shot,' she winked at Tannis as the room quickly began to empty.

The afternoon plodded on. Sally showed Tannis around; there wasn't much to see really. 'I would say that nothing happens here, but that's what they said at Pearl Harbour.'

Tannis nodded her head in understanding, *you'll see your share in a few days too*, she thought. The two women decided to roll some bandages to pass the time and sat chatting when suddenly they heard the screech of brakes as a vehicle struggled to stop followed by a crash. Their door burst open, an M.P. from the gatehouse rushed in.

'One of our men is trapped under the wheels of a truck!' He yelled. Tannis grabbed her kit and turned to Sally. 'You find a doctor; I don't know where to look.'

Sally nodded and was gone. The M.P. took Tannis' bag from her as she ran behind him to the scene of the accident; it looked like the lorry had lost control and swerved to miss the gatehouse but hadn't quite made it. The vehicle was wedged in the brick of the building with a man trapped underneath; the structure creaked ready to collapse at any time.

Reno had come outside to see what the commotion was about, and Jack and Ben had followed, they saw Tannis as she rushed towards the wreckage, the injured man's legs the only part of him visible from under the lorry, without hesitation, she got down on her hands and knees to check the casualty. His arm was trapped under one of the two wheels that made up the rear nearside of the lorry. He was unconscious from a head wound too. The structure of the gatehouse began to creak again as Tannis made a quick check of his injuries. She crawled back out, her teammates were close by now, still maintaining a watch on their mark.

Sally came running along with the doctor, 'Your assessment, nurse?' He was blunt.

'His arm is trapped under the inside wheel of the rear two, Doctor, he also has a minor head injury; he's unconscious but stable,' she reported.

The doctor looked at the position of the lorry and the precarious condition of the gatehouse wall. The truck wasn't going anywhere for some time. 'We'll have to amputate,' the doctor announced as he opened his case and took out a large scalpel, his hand was shaking. He was very young and scared looking. This must've been his first posting, she thought.

Tannis stepped closer and whispered in his ear, then she stepped back as he crawled under the lorry for a closer look, the scalpel still in his hand. There was a hiss of escaping air followed by the young doctor crawling back out dragging the injured man with him. Two orderlies placed the unconscious casualty on to a stretcher and hurried him away to the infirmary, Tannis and Sally followed.

The M.P. turned to the doctor, 'How'd you get him out, Doc?'

'His arm was trapped under the inside wheel, so if I burst it, the outer wheel would support the weight, and I could pull him free,' he said a little nervously. 'You're a hero, Doc; you saved his arm!' The M.P. shook his hand.

'I must go to my patient now,' the medic stammered as he left.

Jack looked at Ben, 'It's a good job she doesn't care about stuff like that,' he muttered as they made their way back to the office to keep their watch.

After work, Ben waited outside the infirmary for Tannis. She smiled when she saw him and took his arm as they walked to the gatehouse together. The lorry had been moved now, and work had already begun on the rebuilding.

'Saw what you did today,' he said as they walked out onto the street, 'how's the patient?'

'He's going to be sore for a while but other than that he'll be fine,' she was pleased it'd turned out so well, 'anything interesting happen with you two?'

He shook his head, 'Just watching you save a man's arm.'

'The doctor did that, not me,' she dismissed as she usually did.

'You mean he got the credit for it,' he gave her a sideways glance. She stopped now to look in the window of a hat shop, 'It's the outcome that's important,' she kissed him on the cheek, 'Ned would love that hat.'

He turned her to face him, 'Well, I'm proud of you,' he kissed her slowly.

She smiled up at him, 'As I am of you, although I almost had to beat the other nurses off with a broom to get to the door before them. I can see I'm going to have to keep my eye on you, sir!' They laughed together as they walked on.

Jack was taking the first night's watch outside Reno's apartment, and he'd told Ben to stay with Tannis. He didn't like the idea of her being alone when they still had no idea who or what they were up against, although she had protested and rightly so that she could take care of herself. She was more worried about Jack being on his own, but his orders were final, and he had told them he wouldn't make a move without calling them on the radio first.

Ben closed the apartment door behind them and threw his hat on the table, they had been out to dinner, but Tannis had not been herself again, he knew she was looking for her father all the time. He would do the same, he guessed.

She dropped her hat next to his and went into the small kitchenette to make some coffee; there was no chance of any tea on this mission. Ben followed her in and wrapped his arms around her waist as she stood at the counter, 'Come back to me,' he whispered.

She put the coffee pot down and turned to face him, 'I just keep looking for him, and it's stupid I know, I mean what would I say to him if he did speak to me?'

He rested his arms on her shoulders, 'The right thing,' he said softly. She leaned into him, her head on his chest, he held her close and kissed the top of her head. She pulled herself round and looked up at him as she reached for the coffee pot once more, 'Want some?'

'Oh yeah,' he said suggestively and began to unbutton her blouse, 'now about those stockings,' he kissed her as he opened her blouse then picked her up and sat her on the counter.

'Captain,' she said coyly.

'Lieutenant,' he breathed as their kisses grew more intense and she wrapped her legs around him. He picked her up and carried her to the bedroom, shoving the door open with his elbow, he carried her over to the bed. She undressed in front of him, then gently pushed him down on the bed and lay on top of him, he ran his hands down to her stocking tops and smiled as he flipped her over onto her back, he was on top now, 'Well I do outrank you, Lieutenant,' he kissed her neck and moved down to her stomach.

'Oh, yes sir,' she gasped.

Ben left Tannis at the apartment the next morning as he went to relieve Jack, she wasn't on duty today. As he opened the door, Jack could smell the delicious aroma of a fry up, Tannis smiled as she put a plateful on the table for him, he sat down quickly, 'You're a star,' he grinned as he cut into the thick bacon.

The plate was empty when he pushed it away from him and yawned, 'Right, I'm off for a bit of kip, I told Ben I'd be back at the office at one, what are you up to?'

Tannis gave him a puzzled look, 'Watching your back,' she said as she put his plate in the sink, 'like you said last night we don't know what we're up against and you need some proper sleep, not one where you listen out for the slightest noise, so I shall stay here.'

He stood up, 'Thanks.'

'No need for thanks, we're a team, it's what we do,' she picked up a newspaper and sat down on the sofa tucking her feet under her.

Five hours later she knocked on the bedroom door, 'Jack, it's twelve,' she called in a lowered tone.

'Thanks, love, I'm up,' he replied. A short time later he joined her in the lounge, he was washed and dressed and, in his uniform, once more.

'You sleep, ok?' she asked as she passed him a cup of sludgy coffee. They both grimaced as they forced their drinks down.

'Out like a light, nice to have your own bodyguard.'

She picked up her hat and coat, 'I'll go first. I'll see you at the office when I meet Ben for lunch.'

'Don't worry, I wasn't seen coming in, I'll be the same on the way out,' he told her.

'Good, that doctors already got it in for me, the last thing I need is the reputation of a slut,' she laughed.

'The doctor from yesterday?' he eyed her cautiously, 'what's up? didn't you make him look good enough?'

'It's nothing I can't handle; besides I think when Ben met me yesterday it helped for him to know I have a boyfriend who could pummel him,' she winked and went out the door.

They all met at the office later at respectable intervals. Nothing had happened so far, but there was a dance that night for officers only and Jack had found out Reno was going to be attending, it would be the prime time for someone to make a move.

They picked Tannis up from the apartment later; Jack waited in the car while Ben went to collect her. She opened the door to let him in 'Just a second...' She did a double take, he was in his Navy white dress uniform and looked stunning, 'hello sailor,' she said with a wicked glint in her eye. He was feeling the same way about her too, she was out of uniform wearing a red tight-fitting dress, and oh boy, she had some curves.

'You look fantastic,' he kissed her, 'c'mon, we gotta go!'

Jack was in his dress uniform too. He was a good-looking guy Tannis thought to herself, as she noticed all the admiring glances the men in her team were getting as they walked into the dance hall.

They managed to get a table near Reno's, and it wasn't long before Jack had a couple of attractive ladies asking him to dance, he was trying to think of an excuse not to when Tannis kicked him under the table, 'He'd love to,' she smiled at the latest brave soul to pluck up the courage to ask. He narrowed his eyes before he stood up, but she just whispered something to him, his expression immediately changed as he shrugged in defeat and led the woman to the dance floor.

'What did you say to make him take it so well?' Ben was puzzled. Tannis smiled as she sat back and leaned closer to him '1733.' Ben looked at her. 'Ah, revenge,' he grinned as they watched their CO dance with a string of women while keeping watch on Reno and the men on his table. There was no one new sitting there, the CO of The Eldridge, two other scientists and an Admiral down to observe the test tomorrow. Jack sat back down with them now, having managed to ditch his entourage just as Reno came over to their table. 'Gentlemen, ma'am, I wonder if I might intrude on your party for a moment or two, my table is getting a little rowdy?' he motioned behind him. Four women had joined his group now, and they were getting a little noisy.

Jack had no choice really, and besides, it did make their job a lot easier, 'Of course, won't you join us?' He made the introductions and looked over to Tannis; she seemed to be handling it ok. Yes, Reno was the one who started the whole thing, but he wasn't responsible for the evils of Phoenix. Reno ordered a bottle of champagne and chatted with Jack about the war in Europe but nothing anyone in the street wouldn't talk about.

Tannis slipped her hand into Ben's under the table. 'Dance?' he asked, he knew her so well she thought as he led her to the dance floor. He held her close and felt her relax in his arms, it seemed surreal to him that he was in 1943, right in the middle of World War Two, dancing with the woman he loved to Glenn Miller's Moonlight Serenade. This was a moment in history that touched him, he was in his country with his people at a time when no one knew what was going to happen, or who was going to win the war, but the bravery of these people shone through even at the darkest of times this moment would stay with him forever, she looked up at him as if sensing what he was thinking, 'It's because of the way they are that they never surrender, you're right to be proud of them.'

He held her to him and whispered in her ear, 'I want to marry you as soon as we get back, I don't want to wait, I know what I want more than ever.'

She rested her head on his shoulder and smiled 'Yes.'

The mood soon changed as he felt her stiffen, 'What's wrong?' 'I've just seen Ned's father,' she said as she scanned the room behind him.

He turned her as they danced so he could get a better look, 'I don't see your dad, maybe he couldn't make it.'

She shook her head, 'Those two were practically joined at the hip.'

'So, I see,' he said as he recognised her father from the photograph on file. Tannis looked up at him wide-eyed now, 'You sure?' he asked as she tried to turn and look, she nodded, and he turned them again as they danced. Hearing her gasp when she saw him, he pulled her back into him to stop her from staring.

'I'm sorry,' she remembered herself.

'Hey, that's what I'm here for,' he smiled trying to imagine what she must be feeling.

The song finished and they made their way back to the table and sat down. Tannis' mouth was dry, so she took a large swig of champagne. Jack, as always, noticed everything. He shot Ben a questioning look who in turn motioned to where Tannis and Ned's fathers stood. Reno too saw them leaning against a nearby pillar, he had been working with the two officers a great deal on board lately and got on well with them, so he motioned for them to join him, 'You don't mind, do you? They're good guys, I've been working with them a lot,' he asked Jack who, once again, couldn't say no.

Reno made the introductions and so Captain James Weatherly, dark-haired and well-toned, and Captain Edward Franks, a little shorter and not so in shape, joined the small group. Jack was proud of Tannis; she didn't miss a beat as she shook her father's hand when he offered it. 'Have we met before?' he asked as he took in her features.

'I work in the infirmary; you've probably seen me around the Navy Yard,' she smiled. They ordered more champagne and toasted the allies, and then it happened, her father asked her to dance.

'Do you mind, Captain?' he asked Ben politely, once again an impossible situation.

'Sure, go ahead,' he gave Tannis a half-apologetic look as her father took her arm and led her away.

'Don't worry Captain, he's a decent guy,' Ned's dad said to Ben who just nodded as he poured more drinks for them all.

'Are you sure we haven't met, there's something very familiar about you?' James asked as they danced.

'I must just have one of those faces,' she smiled.

'Well, it's a very beautiful one,' he felt her tense as he told her, 'It's ok Lucy, I'm not trying to come on to you, anyone can see you and your Captain are head over heels with each other.'

She relaxed again, 'Do you have someone special?'

'No, I'm too busy with the Navy, but maybe someday when this war is over.' He was a perfect gentleman as they danced to two tunes together then he thanked her, 'I should return you to your date.'

They re-joined the group as Ned's father was telling them that his sister had just given birth to a daughter.

'Have they chosen a name yet?' Tannis asked.

'Clara.'

'Nice name.' Jack nodded.

James turned to his best friend then told them all, 'He was hoping for a boy, they told him they were gonna call him Ned after him.'

'Well Captain Franks, maybe you'll have a son of your own one day,' Reno consoled him jokingly, 'you too, Captain Weatherly.'

'Not me,' James held his hands up, 'I want a daughter, that way I'll always have a girl in my life who loves me no matter what.'

'It's true,' Ned Snr piped up, 'he's even chosen a name for her, from one of those history books he's always reading,' he nudged his friend 'tell 'em, James.'

Tannis looked at her father now who shrugged awkwardly, 'These people don't want to hear all this.'

'Oh, go on,' Reno laughed, 'tell us, it can't be as bad as my old man. He wanted Euphemia for my sister, thank God for mom.' The whole table laughed, 'So come on Captain tell us.'

James looked a little awkward. 'Ok,' he surrendered, 'Tannis, I like the name Tannis.'

Reno raised his glass, 'Well, here's to Ned and Tannis, and may they never see war, only peace.'

They all raised their glasses for the toast, only her teammates noticed that Tannis put the glass to her lips but didn't drink. Ben squeezed her hand under the table and saw she was trembling, she looked at him and made to speak, but Ned Snr got there first, 'Lucy, would you dance with me?' She accepted; she didn't care it was Ned's father, she just wanted to get away from her own.

'You're a lucky man,' James said to Ben as they watched Ned Snr dancing with Tannis.

'Yes, I am,' he smiled, but it was an honest smile.

'You gonna marry her?'

It was Ben's turn to feel weird now, 'We're already engaged,' he told his future father-in-law, 'How about you?'

James smiled, 'No, like I told Lucy, duty calls now, but when I do, I want what you've got.' Ben frowned a little, not sure what he meant.

'I mean I want my girl to look at me the way she was looking at you when you were dancing together earlier, you're all she sees, she'd follow you anywhere,' he raised his glass to Ben, 'that's what it's all about.'

The dance was over now, and Ned Snr returned Tannis to Ben's side and thanked her again. Jack had left a few moments earlier to be outside to tail Reno; where inside he turned to James and Ned Snr 'You should get some rest, gentlemen, busy day tomorrow,' he said his goodbyes and left. Then it was time for Ben and Tannis to go.

'Goodbye Lucy and thanks for the dance,' her father shook her hand.

'It was good to meet you,' she fought to keep her voice even. Ben shook hands with both men and took Tannis by the arm as they left.

She waited by the door while he went to check their coats, a short way behind him he could hear James and Ned Snr talking.

'Wow, that Lucy was hot,' Ned Snr told his friend, 'Not like you to let a gorgeous gal go by.'

James looked surprised, 'You make me sound like some Casanova.'

Ned Snr raised an eyebrow, 'C'mon James, you practically have to fight the women off.'

'Yeah, and how many dates have I had?'

'Hmm, well yeah, true,' his friend mumbled.

'She's out there, we just haven't met yet' James sighed.

'I'd say Lucy must've come pretty close,' Ned Snr grinned.

'Someone like Lucy but not her, she's gorgeous yeah, but well, it was like dancing with my sister or something, I dunno,' James shrugged.

'If your sister looks like that, you gotta introduce me,' Ned Snr perked up.

'You're not going anywhere near my sister, and I didn't say she looked like her,' James laughed, 'c'mon we've got work to do tomorrow.'

Ben couldn't help but smile as he collected their things. He joined Tannis now and they stepped outside. It was a cold night, but she welcomed the crisp, fresh air as they walked towards the car park. He put an arm around her, 'Some night?'

She leaned into him and exhaled slowly, 'Let's get out of here!' They rounded the corner and saw Reno walking towards his car; Jack was already in theirs waiting close by, he motioned his head towards the tree line over to their right; someone was waiting in the shadows. Ben discreetly acknowledged his CO and leaned back against the wall, pulling Tannis to him; she nuzzled his neck as he did the same to her, allowing him to keep watch on whoever waited in the shadows. Reno smiled to himself as he saw them kissing, 'Lucky son of a gun,' he muttered as he unlocked the car door, that was when the figure in the shadows made their move. It was a male dressed in a Navy Ensigns uniform.

'Hicks,' Ben whispered as he saw the man hurry towards their mark. Jack saw too and jumped out of the car.

Reno turned as he heard the Ensign approach. 'What is it?' He hoped there wasn't a problem for tomorrow.

Hicks didn't get the chance to speak. Jack had a gun shoved in his back while with the other hand he showed Reno a fake security clearance. His team were there instantly, Ben dragged Hicks away to their car as Jack handed Tannis the gun for cover.

'Naval Intelligence, Doctor, we were warned of an enemy threat; we'll take it from here,' Jack explained. Reno looked over Jack's shoulder and saw Ben bundle Hicks into the back of the car and get in next to him while Tannis sat in the front with her weapon trained on their prisoner, Hicks made to speak, but she put her finger to her lips and glared at him.

'Is this to do with my work?' Reno was a little shaken.

'*Project Rainbow* must proceed as planned tomorrow' Jack said clearly.

'You know about the project?'

'We have the highest clearance, Doctor,' *more than you know*, he thought to himself, 'you're perfectly safe now, and I must ask you not to mention this to anyone.' He insisted.

'I understand,' Reno got in his car and started the engine. Jack closed the door and watched him drive away.

'Where's Richardson?' he hissed as he got in the car with his team and turned the key.

'Always have to try and rule the world,' Tannis glared, 'but you'd cease to exist too if you stop the experiment.'

He shook his head, 'Richardson was monitoring the cave before either of us knew about The Eldridge. We were working together at the time she found the power surge; we would've explored the cave with or without you. We'd even planned to take blasting gear, so we would've got out too.'

They drove out of town to a nice quiet spot where they wouldn't be disturbed, Hicks was dragged out of the car, Ben threw him to the ground, and Jack stood over him, 'So where is Richardson waiting for you?' Ben crouched on the other side of Hicks and looked at Jack. 'You know if you kill the host the parasite can't live long out here.'

'Interesting idea, Major,' Jack had no intention of playing good cop bad cop, they didn't have time, 'but I think a woman's touch is called for,' he looked over to Tannis as he whispered in Hicks' ear, 'she's taken this one personally so I think I should let her take care of you.' Hicks looked nervously at Tannis as she stood by his head but still, he wouldn't talk. 'Gave you a choice,' Jack sighed as he and Ben stood up, 'he's all yours love.'

Tannis grabbed him by the shoulder and easily hauled him to his feet, then she reached down the front of her dress and pulled out a long thin dagger, Jack gave Ben a curious look who in turn just shrugged; she was always armed. 'Tannis, you wouldn't be alive today if Kira hadn't healed you,' It was Nyra speaking.

'True,' she acknowledged, 'and I probably wouldn't be alive for much longer if you had succeeded tonight,' she eyed him, 'besides, I don't keep scores, saving a life should be done selflessly and not for personal gain or to bargain with later.'

Hicks lunged at her and went for the knife, he didn't even land a punch before she grabbed his wrist and spun him around, shoving his arm painfully up his back and marched him towards the car. Throwing him roughly over the bonnet, her teammates stood on the opposite side, arms folded and watching as without a word as she stuck the knife in his shoulder, Hicks screamed in pain. 'I know you feel the pain too, Nyra. Kira felt mine when she was in me,' Tannis twisted the blade now, and Hicks yelled out once more, but he moved to look towards Jack and Ben. Tannis shook her head 'If I see your spooky little arse going anywhere near them, I'll blast you into a very unpleasant dimension.'

'Ok, ok, I'll take you,' Hicks conceded but only after Tannis had removed the blade from his shoulder, unzipped his fly and shoved it inside, and for as much as her teammates hated Hick's they both winced, she pulled the knife out now and wiped it on his shirt before putting it back down her dress while her teammates bundled him back in the car.

As they drove away, Jack looked at Hicks in the rear-view mirror. 'You try anything, and I'll bury you out here Sgt.'

He directed them to an abandoned airfield an hour from town. It was private, non-military, with one corrugated metal hangar and a brick two-story building next to it. A lamp shone from an upstairs window. Jack killed the lights and drove as close as he dared, then they could walk the short distance to the hangar, he reached into the glove box and took out another pistol. They got out of the car and Tannis handed the gun she held to Ben, he trained it on Hicks as she shrugged off her coat and tossed it on the back seat, then she grabbed the waistband of her dress and pulled, it unwrapped from around her revealing a shorter more practical skirt, this she hitched up slightly to show her stocking tops, where she had a small revolver strapped to the inside of her leg. Ben smiled, she never ceased to amaze him, but his smile soon hardened when he saw Hicks getting an eyeful although it soon earned him a smack around the head with the butt of a gun.

'Where do you keep the spare bullets?' Jack smirked. She narrowed her eyes at him and threw the surplus part of her dress in the car with her coat; then she went with Ben to check out the hangar as Jack shoved Hicks towards the building next to it. The hangar was empty, Ben knelt and put his finger in some oil on the floor, 'It's fresh,' he walked over to the wall and tapped on some of the barrels stacked there, he sniffed them too, 'aviation fuel, a plane was here not long ago.' They joined Jack outside the brick building, and Ben gave him the details.

He nodded, 'Tannis, go round the back, come in when you hear the ruck,' she disappeared out of sight, and they gave her a moment to get in position then Jack grabbed Hicks by the scruff of the neck and threw him inside when Ben kicked the door open. Hicks crashed to the floor, his shoulder fully healed now, and stood up quickly as Richardson ran down the stairs, she froze when she saw Ben aim his weapon at her.

'Tannis coming in,' she announced herself as she walked in from the darkness of the back room. Jack motioned for Richardson to finish coming down the stairs and join them, then he turned to Tannis, 'Check it out,' she nodded and carefully made her way up the steps.

'I was alone, Colonel,' Richardson said coldly.

'You'll forgive me if I don't believe a word you say,' he replied sarcastically.

Tannis came back down, 'All clear.'

Jack had already removed Hicks' timepiece and had it in his pocket, so he waved his gun at Richardson again, 'Timepiece if you please, Doctor,' reluctantly she gave it to him. 'Now Kira and Nyra, you two can come out, and Tannis will send you back where you came from, she'll blast you quick, so you won't need your hosts, which is just as well because they have a court martial to face.'

Richardson looked at Jack in amazement, 'We can rule as Gods in this world, Colonel, you don't understand the full power we can share,' she turned her gaze to Tannis, 'and with all of the power that you possess you could rule all…'

'Oh, change the bloody record. Do you know how many times I've heard this crap?'

Nyra spoke to Tannis now as Hicks made to step closer, 'Think of what our children could be.'

'And that one too,' she rolled her eyes.

He stopped in his tracks when he heard Jack arm his weapon. 'I don't think she likes your idea of foreplay, sunshine.'

Tannis grimaced as she stepped closer to her team. There was the hum of an engine in the distance, and it was getting closer.

'Plane's coming back,' Ben looked at Jack. 'Who's the pilot?' Richardson looked nervously at Hicks, 'strange we haven't heard from Kira this evening, isn't it?' Jack looked at the doctor, 'she's in the pilot, isn't she?'

She closed her eyes, 'They've got a link,' Tannis moved to be between her team now. The roar of the engine was deafening as the plane flew overhead and rained a hail of bullets down onto the building, shattering the windows and tearing the place up. Inside, everyone dived for cover, but Jack ran outside as the plane turned to make another approach.

Hicks ran out after him, kicking Tannis in the head as he passed, he knocked her out cold. Richardson picked up Tannis' gun and pointed it at her, 'You'll be dead before you pull the trigger,' Ben warned her as he took aim. She threw the gun at him, he ducked, and she ran outside. Tannis was unconscious but ok, and Jack needed him now, he glared at the situation as he ran out into the night. The plane was heading back towards them, its guns blazing. Jack stood his ground and fired at the cockpit; Ben hurried to his side and did the same.

Hicks made a dive for Jack, and the two of them began to fight. Ben grabbed Richardson who slapped and kicked him, she was nothing like Tannis; he thought as he punched her out.

Jack was doing fine, he quickly overpowered the Sgt with a stranglehold, only releasing him from his grip as the man slipped into unconsciousness from lack of oxygen. That was when he noticed the plane, as it got closer, he saw a white form emerge from the cockpit window and it was heading straight for Jack. Kira knocked him right off his feet as she entered his body. Ben turned his gun on his friend, 'Leave him!' he ordered, but he was forced to watch helplessly as Jack stood up and put his hand in his pocket and pulled out the two timepieces, letting them fall to the ground, then Jack's body went limp, and he fell unconscious as Kira left him and entered Richardson again.

Ben checked his friend's pulse. He was alive; he sighed in relief before looking over at Hicks and Richardson who lay motionless still, he looked back at the house; it was then that he heard the change in the tone of the plane's engine, it was over revving and heading straight for the building. The pilot was probably dead, killed by one of their bullets. Ben ran as hard as he could back into the building.

Jack was coming to when he saw his friend race inside seconds before the plane hit, 'No!' he yelled as he saw it nosedive into the roof. He hurried over to the debris that remained, the whole of the upper floor had collapsed, and the tail of the plane could be seen sticking out of what was once the roof. The engine was still roaring, and the door was blocked. Jack made his way to one of the smashed windows and saw them both motionless on the floor. Ben had thrown himself over Tannis to protect her from the falling masonry and, by the looks of it, had taken a knock to the head, but that was the least of their problems as above them, just poking through the ceiling, the propeller turned viciously; the blades were bent and broken but still lethal.

Jack looked back towards Hicks and Richardson. They had gotten up now and were strapping their timepieces back on, he opened fire, but they were gone 'SHIT!' he cursed then turned back to his team, 'BEN!' he shouted, but the noise of the engine was drowning him out, 'BEN!' he yelled again, his friend began to stir, good man, thought Jack as he saw him check his surroundings first before moving; Ben slowly turned his head and looked up and then slid off Tannis and onto his back. 'This way,' Jack beckoned, 'doors jammed!'

Ben nodded and tried to pull Tannis out. The structure shuddered suddenly, and he froze as the cockpit slid closer to them, the noise was unbelievable, the downdraft blew hard on them now and Tannis began to wake, he reached his arm across her chest to hold her down. If she sat up startled, she would be sliced to pieces, the broken blades were that close now, she opened her eyes and went rigid. The building shuddered again, and the cockpit slid toward them with nothing to stop it. Tannis summoned all the energy she could, her total terror helped immensely, there was a blinding flash, and the plane along with most of the building was gone.

Ben stood up as Jack walked in through a hole that was once the blocked door. Tannis wasn't moving, 'She'll be out of it for a while,' he said as he picked her up and held her to him.

Jack was just relieved they were both ok, 'She can take as long as she likes she's earned it.'

He then went on to explain about Richardson and Hicks, 'At least if they're gone, they won't be able to leap back so the experiment can go ahead tomorrow,' Ben sighed.

'Yeah, but they'll be back somewhere,' Jack sneered as he drove them to the apartment.

As it was the early hours now, they managed to carry Tannis inside without being seen, Ben laid her on the bed and left her to sleep it off while he and Jack got cleaned up and ready to get the hell out of there as soon as the experiment was over later that day.

Tannis woke up after a couple of hours, still feeling a little worse for wear, her mood didn't improve when she found out their quarry had got away, 'Can we sod the court martial off next time and just shoot them?' She had the mother of all headaches.

Ben gave her some aspirin with a glass of milk, 'So where did you send the plane?' He asked.

'It's on Atlantis, I thought the pilot might have a family, I'll send him back and stage a crash when we get home.'

Jack nodded his approval, even when she was frightened for her life she still thought of others, typical Tannis, he thought.

'Why do they all want to rule the world?' She massaged her temples.

'Power mad,' Jack yawned, 'goes to their heads.'

Tannis excused herself and went back to bed as she was still shattered. Jack put his legs up on the couch and covered himself with a blanket. Ben slumped down in the armchair and draped a blanket over himself too. Jack respected him a great deal for that, 'Go to bed Major; you'll be knackered trying to sleep like that.'

Ben thanked his CO and walked into the bedroom. He was exhausted and a little sore from the night's events, he noticed that Tannis hadn't bothered to undress, she just lay on top of the bed, so he did the same and covered them both with the blanket he'd carried in. She was already asleep when he pulled her into his arms, and it wasn't long before he joined her.

They slept in the next day. All they had to do now was see the experiment ran to plan and it wasn't taking place until 1500 hrs, so Jack decided that they would have some well-earned R&R 1940's style.

They spent the day taking in the sights, listening to the music of the time and dining together as friends, no rank, no work, time off.

They sat in a coffee shop now reading through the day's papers, they didn't make happy reading being full of news coverage of the war. Tannis read one article in particular about a battle the Americans had won in Italy, she stopped reading and laid the paper down and stared out of the window instead. Ben looked across curious as to what she had been looking at, she pointed to the story and looked at them both, 'Will's there right now.' They both felt for her as she sighed, 'No one is the master of time, we're all slaves to it.'

The time came for the experiment. They didn't want to be in the Navy Yard so, using their clearance, they watched from a piece of scrubland close to the harbour. A chain link fence was the only thing that separated them from the yard itself.

They stood in silence as they watched the crew make their way on board. Tannis stood between her teammates as she usually did. She grasped the fence when she saw both her and Ned's father walk up the gangplank and go inside. She chewed her lip as the ship left its moorings and moved away into the harbour. It was eerily quiet; the experiment had begun, the well documented green mist appeared around the ship then there was a big blue flash, much bigger than when they made their leaps, but the same colour and The Eldridge was gone. 'Bye, Dad,' Tannis whispered as a tear ran down her cheek.

Ben took her hand from the fence and held it in his, 'C'mon, it's done,' he looked over to Jack who nodded, 'Yeah let's go home.'

The two men linked arms with her as they turned and walked away down the slope towards the derelict building, they had agreed to use to make their leap from, and were almost at the bottom when they heard the screams and the sirens; The Eldridge had returned. Neither man had the chance to react as she pulled herself free and ran back to the fence, she got there a little ahead of them; her knuckles were white as she clung to the wire, her eyes wide in horror.

'Bleedin Christ,' Jack was by her side now and saw what she saw. Ben stood behind her, on The Eldridge men were jumping overboard, badly burned and screaming in pain, then as they looked closer, they saw the dead and dying, their bodies somehow joined to the bulkhead and the deck.

'I'm sorry,' she whispered, 'I'm so sorry,' as the tears ran unchecked down her face.

Jack grabbed her wrist, 'Not this time love, things are different now, this was my command.'

She swallowed hard and nodded, 'Thanks Jack.'

He let go of her and walked away, getting his first insight into the guilt *DE-173* had felt, yes, he had made this happen.

Ben put his hand gently on her shoulders and whispered, 'Come back to me.' Tannis released her grip on the wire and turned to him, he held her tightly then they walked away together and didn't look back.

Two days after their return to Atlantis, Ben and Tannis were married in the little white church on the hill. It was a small wedding, Ned and his family, Jack and his family and, of course, the Admiral and Dr O'Brian. They made a stunning couple, him in his dress uniform and Tannis in a white flowing Grecian-style gown. Her headdress was made from local flowers as was her bouquet. Ned gave the bride away, and Jack was the best man. When it came time for the exchanging of the vows, the whole congregation leaned forward eager to hear Tannis' words, she smiled as Ben winked at her, even he didn't know what she was going to say so in her clearest voice, she promised to love honour and obey. The ceremony was complete, it just remained for the words you may kiss the bride to be said. Their lips met, and the congregation applauded, Ned dabbed a tear from his eye.

As they left the church, the five white crosses that marked her brother's and sister's graves were all decorated with the same flowers that made up Tannis' headdress. The guests threw confetti and wished them well, and after the photographs, they all made their way back to Ned's for the reception. Of course, Ned's idea of a small reception involved most of the town and the Eldridge teams, 'Well, they all wanted to wish you the best,' he told them as they saw hundreds of guests making their way to the house. As tradition dictated, the bride and groom led the first dance which Ned chose as *Never Tear Us Apart* by *INXS*, after which they slipped away for a moment together on the beach.

Alone now, he took her in his arms, 'Happy Mrs. Rhodes?' 'Couldn't be happier, do I call you Major Rhodes again now?' she teased.

'Ben will do just fine,' he pulled her to him and kissed her again. They turned to the house as they heard cheering, the guests had all come outside to toast them. The bride and groom waved, and then Tannis took his hand in hers, and they were in Avalon.

Chapter Nine

Tannis was waiting in the hold for her teammates to return, they had gone back to the real world to collect the last of Jack's belongings from before *The Wind Dancer* that he'd kept in storage, and were due back any second now, no doubt laden with boxes. Blink, there they were, but something was wrong, Jack was supporting Ben, 'Medic!' He yelled as Tannis ran over to them, 'My God, Jack what happened?'

'Hit and run; the bastard never stopped,' Jack struggled with his unconscious friend. She grabbed them both, and they were in sickbay.

'Where's O'Brian?' She glared at the medic in front of her.

'On leave, I'm Dr Wilson, I can assure you I am fully qualified,' he said assertively as he had the nurse shove them out into the passage while he made his assessment, 'prep him for surgery, he has internal bleeding,' they heard him say as they left.

Tannis sobbed in Jack's arms, 'He's got to be alright; he can't leave me.' Jack fought to control himself, she needed him now, and it was going to be a long wait.

Ned and the Admiral came down to join them and watched as Tannis paced up and down, 'I can go back, tell me where and when Jack, I can stop this from happening.'

Jack took her hands in his, 'He shoved a kid out of the way of the car, if you go back the child will die, you know Ben couldn't live with that, and I know you couldn't.'

An hour or so later the doctor came out to them, 'The operation was a success, but we need blood, AB negative, and I know the two of you share the same rare blood group Tannis, so come with me.' She grabbed Jack and hugged him then followed in the doctor's wake, he led her into the infirmary and through to the recovery room, she gasped as she saw her husband lying there with all the drips and pipes attached to him. He looked so pale; she touched his face gently, 'Come back to me,' she whispered.

'Tannis, please,' the doctor tried to hurry her. She willingly lay on the bed next to Ben's as the medic pushed the needle into her vein and her blood flowed straight into her husband as she reached out and took his hand in hers, closed her eyes and prayed.

She was feeling sleepy now, but the doctor assured her that was normal, and he went to check Ben's dressing. He had already changed a blood-soaked one; he smiled as he looked under it, 'Your blood is healing him,' he looked over to her, but she was asleep.

'What the hell is taking so long?' Jack got up and leaned against the wall and turned as he heard someone hurrying down the passage, it was Dr O'Brian, the Irishman was a little short of breath when he came to a stop, 'I just heard, what happened?'

Hennessey filled him in on the situation up to and including the part where Tannis was taken away to donate some blood.

'But we've plenty of blood stocks AB negative included,' he looked worried now, 'why the hell is he taking from Tannis?' He smelled a rat as did Jack, and the two of them hurried inside followed quickly by Ned and the Admiral. They raced through the infirmary, but the door to the recovery room was barred from the other side. When they looked through the window a horrible sight greeted them, Tannis was still hooked up to the machine draining blood from her, her skin was grey, her lips almost blue, Ben, on the other hand, was a normal healthy colour.

Jack kicked the door down as Dr Wilson hurriedly tried to grab the extra bags of blood, he had harvested from Tannis and snatch Ben's timepiece, but they slipped from his grip as Ned lunged for him and knocked him out cold with one punch. O'Brian hurried over to Tannis and yelled for a nurse from the next room to attend to Ben. He disconnected the machine and checked her pulse. It was faint, but there was something there thankfully, he quickly attached drips and monitors to her now, calling over his shoulder, 'How's the Major doing?'

The nurse gasped as she checked the wound, 'He's completely healed.'

'I thought as much,' O'Brian looked at the three men as they stood by Tannis' bedside now, 'I doubt Major Rhodes' accident was any such thing, it was all staged to see the healing effects that her blood could have, I've turned down countless requests for more tests on her. I should've known they wouldn't let it go,' he worked quickly on Tannis, but it wasn't looking good, collecting the bags of blood Dr Wilson had failed to take with him O'Brian started giving it back to her, 'Ok sweetheart, you saved your husband now concentrate on saving yourself.'

Once she was stable, the doc had them both moved to a private room, then went to his office to meet with Jack, Ned and the Admiral.

'Who is responsible for this, Doctor?' Hennessey was furious.

'Oh, it's not military Admiral, be sure of that. The coalition is very respectful towards Tannis, but there are some private concerns involved, those are the ones I'm talking about. I've had requests for blood samples to be sent to private labs for their research. I have the letters on file; I'll let you have them,' O'Brian offered helpfully.

'Thank you, Doctor, at least that will give us somewhere to start,' Hennessey would be grateful for the task to occupy him.

'You think they're trying to clone her?' Ned thought of Gunther.

'I really wouldn't know what those unethical bastards have in mind, but I can tell you this when I ran Tannis' blood tests for her routine medical, I found that her blood would never make itself compatible with another, even that of the same blood group. The powers she holds in her DNA won't live outside her body, it's as if it recognises foreign DNA and won't mix with it.'

'So how come Major Rhodes has healed?' Jack's voice betrayed his anger at the situation.

'Well, the only theory I can come up with is that her body doesn't see his DNA as foreign,' the doctor replied.

'You've lost me there, Doc,' Ned looked confused.

'After nine children, you have to ask?' O'Brian chided.

'Oh, right,' Ned clicked on.

Ned and Jack took turns sitting with the unconscious patients over the next twenty-four hours, they read to them and talked to them about the events of the day but to no avail.

Jack came to take over from Ned now to do the night shift, 'Any change?' he asked, Ned just shook his head, 'Still waiting for Ben to wake up and Tannis can't hold her own without the machines,' he sighed. It was getting to him now, he had never seen her like this before, sure she'd been hurt plenty of times, but she'd always bounced back, 'Jack, I don't know what I'll do if she doesn't pull through,' he choked.

'Mate, I haven't known her as long as you have, but I know she won't give in,' Jack consoled him.

Ned just stood and nodded silently as he left the room.

'C'mon you little fighter,' Jack leaned closer and whispered in Tannis' ear.

It was about 0200 hrs when Jack's eyelids began to droop, demanding that long blink that would allow him to drift off to sleep. Instead, he almost jumped out of his skin when Ben gasped and sat bolt upright, wide awake, 'It's ok, Major, you were in an accident, but you're fine now,' he helped his friend to lay back down.

'I remember the car and the child,' Ben tried to piece things together in his mind, 'you brought me back here, I heard Tannis,' he looked at Jack, 'where is she?' he didn't like the look on his CO's face, 'where's my wife?' he demanded sitting up again, as he did so he looked across to the bed next to his and saw her lying there attached to the machines, 'what the hell happened!' He jumped off the bed and stood by her side; she had been fine when he left.

Jack told him the full story as Dr O'Brian walked in the room, he had heard voices and guessed the rest, 'She's gonna be ok right Doc? I mean she'll heal, won't she?' his voice wavered.

O'Brian gave it to him straight as he always did, 'I don't know, Major, she lost a lot of blood, and I'm not sure we even got to her in time, and even if we did and she heals herself, there's the risk of brain damage,' he gestured to the machines, 'these are all that's keeping her alive at the moment.'

Ben sat down heavily on his bed, his head in his hands, 'Why can't they just leave her alone?'

'Hennessey is on the warpath, he's ordered a full enquiry, whoever's behind this is finished,' Jack tried to reassure him.

Ben wouldn't leave her side; he spent the night in the infirmary with her, talking to her, hoping for a sign. Morning came, and so did Ned and Jack. They sat in silence not knowing what to say that hadn't already been said. O'Brian came in to check her vitals; he had been dreading this moment, but there was no skirting around the issue, 'She's not responding, I'm sorry.'

'No,' Ben stood up, 'she just needs more time.'

'Major, she's clinically dead, the machines are the only thing keeping her alive. I can't get her back; her physiology is more than ours, she needs something, and I don't know what it is.'

Ben stood at the end of her bed as the doctor walked back to his desk, 'You don't turn it off!' he yelled.

Jack stood by his friend now, 'Give her more time Doc.'

'And would she want to be kept alive like this?' O'Brian raised his voice, frustrated at the whole situation. He looked at Ned who just dropped his head; he knew she wouldn't, they all did.

'I have no intention of turning off life support, Major, as next of kin I would have to ask for your consent, and as you are aware I have not!' the medic snapped, 'but Tannis has a living will and at some point, we must respect that.'

Ben had never felt such rage building inside him; he was physically trembling as he turned to look at her, 'God, damn it, Tannis, wake up!'

'Major!' Jack cautioned him.

He shook his head, 'No, it doesn't end like this!' he pointed to her, and a huge surge of energy flew from his finger hitting her in the chest, all the monitors she was attached to shorted out, even the IV bag burst. Ben froze and looked at his hands but only for a moment as everyone's attention turned to Tannis. She'd sat up, pulling the lines and feeds from her body, and then she fell backwards choking on the oxygen pipe that had been breathing for her, the doctor ran over to her. 'Tannis, it's Dr O'Brian. Try to relax, and I'll get this out of your throat.'

Ben was at her side now, she reached out to him, but her body went limp as the doctor administered a sedative, 'She would've arrested, we needed to calm her down, she still needs to finish healing.'

'But she's gonna be ok now right, Doc?' Ben dared to hope.

O'Brian nodded, 'It would seem Major that the two of you have a knack for saving one another.'

Ben grinned and looked at Jack and Ned, they were both smiling too. *Time to make some calls*, Jack thought to himself as he made his way to the desk.

'Now Major, while your good lady wife rests I think we should run some tests on you, see what else you got from that transfusion.' O'Brian raised an eyebrow; this should be interesting.

Tannis slept for another 24 hours without sedation. Ben had lost track of time as he sat with her. He had fallen asleep in the chair, her hand in his. He woke as he felt her move, she was looking at him smiling drowsily, 'Hi,' she tried to speak, but her mouth was dry. Ben gave her a drink of water and stroked her face softly, his eyes full of tears.

'I thought I'd lost you,' he whispered.

'I thought I'd lost you; Dr Wilson told me I had to give you as much blood as I could, or you would die,' she croaked, her throat still sore from the O2 pipe. He closed his eyes tightly at the thought of what could've happened and kissed her, 'I love you so much.'

'I love you, Ben,' her eyelids drooped, and she slept for another hour; he didn't care, she was back with him now.

That afternoon Hennessey stopped by to see how they were doing, he brought Tannis a bouquet of flowers and was relieved to see her looking much better. Not long after that, Ned and Jack poked their heads around the door. Jack had bought a laptop with some movies for them to watch while Ned carried a hamper of food, Tannis eyed the latter warily. 'Oh, don't worry,' he said in mock offence, 'Elea made it all.'

'You're looking much better today; love,' Jack sat on the edge of the bed.

'Be even better when I get out of here,' she lowered her voice in case O'Brian was around. She liked him a lot but not his workplace.

'Know what you mean,' Jack agreed then looked over to Ben, 'so has the doc found any more of your superpowers, Clark Kent?'

Tannis looked puzzled, 'What?'

'Oops,' Jack hadn't realised she didn't know, 'Ben got a little more than your healing power when you gave him your blood,' Jack told her all about it.

She looked at Ben, 'You saved me.'

'I think that was a two-way street, Babe,' he smiled.

'Have you tried anything else?' She looked worried now, but he just shook his head, 'Been a bit preoccupied.'

Alone again the two of them sat on her bed watching a movie. Tannis leaned into him as he slipped an arm around her, but twenty minutes in, he felt her leaning heavier on him, he looked down, 'Are you asleep again, Babe?' he stroked her hair, 'that's ok,' he settled down and watched the movie as she slept in his arms.

Jack called in again on his way home, 'She still falling asleep?' he asked, full of concern.

'She's doing fine; Doc says she can come home tomorrow.'

Jack nodded, 'Do her good, see you later,' he left as quickly as he had arrived.

The next morning O'Brian discharged Tannis with a clean bill of health, she hugged him and kissed him on the cheek then grabbed her clothes and hurried off to change. Ben shook his hand and thanked him, 'Not so fast, Major, I think it's time we checked on your inheritance, don't you?' The doctor led him over to the treatment room and offered him a seat. It had already been prearranged as Hennessey and Jack were there.

Tannis came looking for him; she stood in the doorway in her own clothes now, 'What's going on? I thought we were going home?'

'Now that you are both fit for duty, we need to ascertain the extent of Major Rhodes' abilities,' Hennessey told her calmly.

'Tannis, if you'd care to take a seat, I'll need your help for this,' O'Brian pulled a chair around so that she could sit opposite Ben who whispered, 'Welcome to your world?' as she sat down.

'Now they have two performing monkeys' she muttered.

'How would you like to proceed, Tannis?' The doctor asked.

She was not in the mood for this, so she picked up a scalpel and cut her thumb and let the blood run, then stuck it in her mouth, after a few seconds, she withdrew it, and it was healed. Ben did the same, and with the same result, he grinned at his wife. 'Do you feel any different Major?' The doc asked.

'Yeah, I feel like I could take on the world, like a kid that's had too many E numbers, I just need to be doing something, but I don't know what,' he said quickly then looked at Tannis, 'how do you make a leap?'

'Whoa, if you're gonna try that I'm coming with you,' she grabbed his hands.

'Let's do it,' his eyes flashed with excitement.

'Ok,' she held his hands tightly, 'close your eyes and concentrate on thinking of the time and place you want to go to.'

He did as she asked, slowing his breathing down. He focused on his task and suddenly his eyes flashed open, and he flinched, 'What the hell was that?'

Tannis gaped, 'You saw them didn't you, you saw the portals?'

'I saw something,' he tried to describe it, 'like a dark room lit with, I dunno, like thousands of suns being eclipsed except one that was like a wormhole, I guess I was heading toward it,' he shook his head.

'That was the one you needed, they're what we all travel along when we make a leap, you just don't see it with a timepiece,' she took his hands in hers once more, 'try again just let yourself go towards it.'

'Hold on,' Jack was wearing his timepiece for such a test, 'give me the time and place, I'm coming with you.'

'Kefalonia, 2020 bc 0900 hrs,' he saw his wife smile, 'Ready?' He looked wary, but he trusted her, so he closed his eyes again briefly, opening them as he felt the warmth of the sun on his face, 'Yes,' he yelled as he hugged her to him, 'this is fantastic, is this how you feel all the time? It's so cool!' he picked her up and spun her around then remembered himself and put her down and grinned at Jack, 'Sorry, sir.'

'Let's get back, shall we?' Jack had an uneasy feeling.

Ben took her hands in his again and closed his eyes, 'There are more portals now, but they're lit with red, not white light. One of them is strong, it's pulling me in,' he screwed his eyes tight as he tried to concentrate.

'No, Ben, open your eyes, stay away from it!' Tannis yelled, 'Ben!'

He gasped as he looked at her, 'What was that?' he eyed her cautiously.

'Tannis, what's going on?' Jack frowned, 'what did you mean stay away from it?'

She shook her head and stepped away from him, letting go of his hands, 'Bad places, other dimensions, evil places, monsters,' she shuddered involuntarily.

'Monsters? Come on, love!' Jack raised an eyebrow.

'Monsters, Jack, where do you think our legends and horror stories come from? There's evil out there. I've seen it, and I was lucky to survive.'

'Ok,' he raised his hands in surrender, 'c'mon, let's go.'

She retook Ben's hands, 'Just stay away from them,' she looked genuinely frightened as she spoke to him. He nodded and closed his eyes; they were back in the infirmary.

O'Brian was reading through the results from Ben's latest blood tests when they returned, 'Well, Major, it seems that your fun will be short-lived; your body is taking back over. I'd say within ninety-six hours you'll be like us mere mortals again.'

'Tough luck, Superman,' Jack slapped him on the back. Ben couldn't help feeling a little disappointed.

'Finally,' Tannis sighed as she closed their apartment door and leaned her back against it, 'so, what do you want to...' his lips were suddenly on hers with such passion as he pushed his body against her. She returned his kisses with her desire, he picked her up and carried her into the bedroom, they quickly undressed one another and lay down together. Their lips met again; this was the first time they had been alone since they had both almost lost their lives; they needed to be as close to each other as possible. They made love with a heightened sense of passion then lay breathless just looking at each other, their desire sated for now.

She rested her head on his chest as he stroked her hair, 'Tell me about the darkness behind the portal.'

'Evil lives there, you must've sensed it,' she shuddered.

'I felt something like when the hairs on the back of your neck stand up, or you know when you're being watched, yeah.'

She looked at him now, 'I went through it once when I was a child, I was curious,' she wrinkled her nose, 'in hindsight I should've followed my instincts and stayed away.'

'What happened?' he asked softly.

'It was fine at first, the people welcomed me, and I played with some of the other children too. When it started to get dark, I thought I should go home, it was my first leap to another dimension, and I didn't realise I needed to rest before I could return, they said it was too dangerous for me to leave in the dark and I should stay with them, and they would try and get me home in the morning. I had no choice, so I stayed in the attic with their two children.'

He could feel her physically shaking as she recalled the details of that night. 'Hey, c'mon, it's ok I've never seen you like this before, what happened?' He held her to him.

'The monsters came,' her eyes brimmed with tears, 'we could hear the parents downstairs screaming, then it all went quiet until the attic door burst open and two of them came in.'

'Two of what?' he frowned.

'I don't know, they were like humans, but their skin was grey, and their eyes looked black and dead. But it was their teeth that really scared me. Their mouths were full of razor-sharp teeth,' the tears ran down her face, 'they grabbed one of the children each and ripped their throats out, all I could do was make a small leap into the branches of a tree outside and hide like a coward.'

He sat her up and looked into her eyes, 'How old were you?' he soothed.

'Nine.'

'Exactly. You were a terrified little girl, not a coward; no one could ever accuse you of that,' he held her to him again.

'Stay away from them, Ben, I'll be glad when this curse has worn off.'

He'd never heard her call her powers a curse, he knew she hated being treated as different, but he liked his and would be sad to see them go.

Next day on The Eldridge the team were called to the briefing room. Ned and Hennessey were already there as usual, but they had been joined by someone else who appeared to be a civilian from the real world. They took their seats; Ben sat on Tannis' right as their guest was in his place. Hennessey made the introductions, 'Alpha team, this is Dr Jonathon Blair. He is a civilian contractor for the coalition and has expressed an interest in the alternate dimension that was brought to our attention when Tannis and Major Rhodes were testing yesterday.' Blair was a slimeball in a suit Jack thought to himself a demon in the boardroom but bugger all use in their world except to slip a knife between your shoulder blades.

'What about it?' Jack had let it go when Tannis had been so upset about it, but now he could smell trouble.

'The coalition would like me to investigate it,' Blair spoke smoothly.

'I take it you read my report, Dr Blair?' Jack eyed him warily.

'I did, yes, Colonel.'

'Well, you must've missed the part where Tannis told us to stay away.'

'The figments of a child's overactive imagination, Colonel, is no reason to pass up on an opportunity to explore a dimension that we were up until now unaware of,' Blair said bluntly as he looked at Tannis.

'It wasn't a figment of my imagination,' she leaned forward glaring at him.

'She's right; I was there when she got back. She was in shock, couldn't speak for two days,' Ned spoke up.

'It's irrelevant. I won't take you!' Tannis folded her arms across her chest.

Hennessey smiled to himself, that was good enough for him, he was against the mission anyway.

'I thought you could control her?' Blair's tone showed no respect.

'Control Tannis?' The Admiral's back was up now, Blair could go to hell as far as he was concerned, 'is that an oxymoron?' He looked at Jack.

'More like an impossibility sir,' his officer replied as he too folded his arms across his chest, 'she can be such a minx.'

Tannis wasn't stupid, she could see they were backing her up, but still side eyed them both with a raised eyebrow, then glared at her brother when he put in his pennies worth.

'Her gum chewing insolence during the teenage years never wore off, she just ditched the gum,' Ned didn't even look up from his paperwork.

'Just as well you won't have to then,' Blair cut in, looking at Tannis, as he produced a letter from his briefcase, 'I have orders here for Major Rhodes to take a team through. I understand he still has his powers for a few days yet!'

Tannis' hands were facing palms down on the table, and her teammates could see the static charge building under them as she glared at Blair who in turn was looking slightly nervous now; Jack and Ben put a hand each on hers and gently pushed them down, 'I feel the same way, but we must follow orders,' Jack calmed her.

'It would be best if you accompanied your team, Tannis. If the mission runs over, we will use you to return,' Blair closed his briefcase.

'You know I will follow my team,' she hissed.

'Excellent, there will be two others joining us, that won't be too taxing for you if we have to rely on you to bring us back, will it?' He sounded so business-like.

'There won't be that many coming back,' she snapped as she stood up and left the room.

'You know, Dr Blair, you should show Tannis some respect, you may find yourself in need of her help out there,' Hennessey said gruffly.

'Oh, I have read the mission reports, Admiral. She would lay down her life to protect her team, almost has,' he looked at Ben who returned his look with a sneer.

'Yes, she would,' Hennessey said proudly, 'but you're not on her team, and you just really pissed her off,' he added bluntly.

Ned stormed off angrily as Blair followed him, 'I need briefing material from you.'

Hennessey spread his hands out in front of him, 'Like you gentlemen the ropes are invisible, but my hands are tied,' he confided in them now, 'I wouldn't be surprised if he didn't have something to do with the past few day's events; this is too much of a coincidence, so watch your backs out there.'

Ben leaned forward now too, 'Tannis told me what happened when she went there, it wasn't a child's overactive imagination, she's terrified of the place.'

Hennessey nodded his understanding as he explained that Ned had filled himself and Jack in earlier and they were all of the opinion that Blair believed her too. Scientists, Jack thought to himself, the only one he respected was O'Brian.

They both knew where to find Tannis when her teammates went looking for her. She was up on deck looking out to the harbour; they stood either side of her as always, 'Well, at least this time you don't have to wear a corset,' Jack looked across at her.

She couldn't help but laugh, 'Always a bonus.'

'We should be getting ready,' Ben took her hand, she nodded and took Jack's too, and they were gone.

Alpha team were joined in the hold by Blair and two other scientists, one male and one female, Dr Rickman was a studious-looking man in his mid-fifties, Dr Kelsey was in her early thirties about the same height as Tannis with brown hair; neither looked as if they would be much use in a fight, Tannis thought. They all wore military issue greens; her teammates carried their semi-automatic weapons, side arms and knives and no doubt other armaments stashed about themselves. She wore her trademark leather and along with the usual arsenal she now carried a semi-automatic weapon like her teammates, but also had a sidearm on each thigh, and two pump-action shotguns crossed on her back.

'Err, are we going into a war zone?' Dr Kelsey asked Tannis as she walked past her to stand with her team.

'Absolutely,' Tannis replied and fastened her ammunition belt around her. She said her goodbyes to Ned and prepared for the leap; then she stood in front of Ben, 'Concentrate; It will draw you to it like before. Just go with it, it will pull you in fast, so your landing might be a bit rough,' she blinked hard.

He squeezed her hand, 'I'll see you there.' Tannis took Jack and Dr Kelsey's hands; Ben grabbed Blair and Rickman by the wrists, she heard him gasp a little as he was pulled in, that was her cue to leave too.

'Oof!' Jack groaned.

'Sorry, Jack,' Tannis had landed on top of him again as Dr Kelsey fell hard on her arse next to them.

'All part of the service, love' he lay still for a moment, winded. She rolled off him and saw Ben's travelling companions getting up from the ground and dusting themselves off. Her husband sat against a tree feeling the same way she did. He looked across at her and smiled, she smiled back but didn't bother trying to get up yet.

Jack finally got to his feet a moment later and secured the area. They were in a copse; green fields lay ahead of them, and the sun was low in the sky; it was late afternoon and not warm. Winter, Jack thought to himself, it would be dark soon.

'From what I can remember the settlement is about a mile that way,' Tannis pointed across the field in front of them.

'You described it as like early settlers?' Dr Kelsey looked at Tannis who just nodded; she was in a high state of alert looking all around.

Ben joined them now, and Tannis put a hand on his arm, 'You, ok?'

He nodded, 'Yeah, hard work that time though.'

'It'll be dark soon,' she gave him a nervous look.

'Let's move, people,' Jack set off in the general direction Tannis had pointed out, 'Major Rhodes, Tannis take the rear.'

'Sir,' Ben acknowledged as he and his wife dropped back to follow the group while Jack walked point.

He called a halt a discreet distance from the settlement and took out his binoculars, 'Looks like they've upped the defense's a bit since you were here last,' he offered Tannis a look. Ben had his own, and he could see the small town had now surrounded itself like a colonial fort with substantial timber walls and a solid wooden gate which was open at present. They could see people hurrying inside, still dressed as Tannis had described. They walked on; the sun was going down fast now.

The gates were locked by the time they reached the fort, Jack banged on a metal hatch; it slid open and nervous eyes peered out 'What do you want?' a man's voice half whispered.

'Shelter for the night,' Jack held up a leather pouch, 'we can pay.' 'Too late, once the gates are closed, they don't open again until sunrise,' he slammed the hatch shut as the sun fell behind the horizon and darkness began to surround them; the only source of light flickered down on them from the burning torches on the battlements above.

Tannis flinched and raised her weapon when to their left the corn in the field began to sway.

'Twitchy,' Blair mocked.

Her teammates took aim with her as Jack mimicked Blair's sarcastic tone, 'There's no breeze.' Then there was a high-pitched yell from within the cornfield, which began to part as the sound got closer to them.

'Hold your fire,' Blair called out, 'we're here to observe only.' Tannis was trying to slow her breathing as Jack and Ben took their positions either side of her, their weapons still trained on the approaching noise.

Two human forms burst into view from the corn and ran towards them, 'Jack?' Tannis wanted permission to fire, it was a tricky situation as they had to be sure there was a threat first. The two figures slowed to a walk, their skin and eyes were as Tannis had described, their mouths, however, remained closed. They came to a stop in front of Dr Rickman, and he moved slowly towards them. 'Run!' Tannis' voice was barely a whisper, it wouldn't have made a difference if he had heard her, the two 'monsters' as she called them grabbed the doctor and opened their mouths; their lips seemed to be able to peel back to allow huge razor-sharp teeth to protrude as they ripped and chewed at his throat. He struggled weakly before death took him.

'Now!' Jack gave the order, and he and his team opened fire on the two attackers, the bullets hit their targets, and they fell dead. The corn began to shake again, and the noise soon followed, 'Get behind us,' Jack yelled to the two remaining civilians and watched Blair shove Kelsey to the ground as he hurried to hide behind Alpha team; she quickly got up and took her place.

'What in God's name are they?' Kelsey cried out.

'Figments of a nine-year-old's overactive imagination,' Jack threw back at Blair.

'How could we know she was telling the truth?' he cringed.

'You knew, that's why you're here, weapons research, is it?' Ben sneered, 'well, congratulations, it looks like you found what you were looking for.'

They backed closer to the gates, 'Short controlled bursts,' Jack ordered.

Two more appeared from the corn now, then two more and then three more. 'I don't suppose either of you feels up to a leap?' Jack looked from Tannis to Ben, they both shook their heads while keeping their eyes on their targets who were getting closer. There was a clunk from behind them, and a different man's voice shouted 'Inside! Hurry!' The gate had been opened slightly, and they all rushed through and helped shove it closed as their would-be attackers ran for the opening. Alpha team secured the safeties on their weapons and looked around them.

'Thank you,' Jack nodded to the man who had opened the gate, a small crowd had gathered.

'Where are you from, because you're not from these parts; we know our neighbours, and no one travels for more than a day, so how did you get here?' the man asked. Jack explained that they were from more than a day away and had been part of a larger group but had come under attack, and they were now the only ones left. They seemed to buy it, and with their superior weapons, they would be a useful addition to the night's defense's. The man introduced himself as Thomas and Alpha team, and their hangers-on were made welcome. They were given a brief tour and apologetically offered a barn to sleep in, which Jack assured them was fine, they were just grateful to be inside. Along with their accommodation, they were brought food and drink by the women and children who were then hurried away to the safety of their locked cellars for the night while the men took shifts on the battlements.

As they ate their food, the conversation turned to the *Nightwalkers* as the settlers called them. They had been part of their world as far back as anyone knew and the settlement had been there for at least 250 years. It seemed the *Nightwalkers*, as their title suggested, only came out at night to feed on anything that moved. They had a bloodlust that couldn't be satisfied, but they also had some intelligence because if their hunts went badly, they would turn on their own and eat them, sometimes depleting their numbers substantially. When that happened, they would then hunt humans only to bite them and pass on their infection, once bitten, there was no cure, and the victim was turned within 24 hrs.

Blair and Kelsey stayed with some of the settlers near the barn, no doubt finding out as much as they could about the subjects of their mission while Alpha team took position on the battlements. They looked down to where they had stood earlier, the body of Dr Rickman and his two killers had been dragged away into the cornfield; there was no one out there now, but they knew they were being watched.

The corn began to move again, and the yell followed. One of the sentries on the battlement called out the alert, then turned to Alpha team, 'The Nightwalkers are hungry, and they won't give up easily, will you stand with us?' Jack nodded, and his team spaced themselves out and took aim. Noticing as they did, the settlers were only armed with blades and axes.

The attack came swiftly; a line of *Nightwalkers* ran from the safety of the corn with two more lines behind them. They tried to climb the walls by standing on one another's shoulders and jumping over each other like ants, others had fashioned ladders from wood no doubt cut from the nearby trees. Alpha team picked their targets and opened fire. A ladder appeared close to Ben, and a sentry leaned over to push it away but was grabbed by the climbing *Nightwalker* who bit his throat out and dropped him to the ground below where others tore him apart like a pack of rabid wolves, then the *Nightwalker* made it onto the battlement and another quickly followed, Ben saw him in time and opened fire, killing it instantly, but the second was on him as he tried to reload, his strength was better than usual it seemed, and he could hold the beast away from his throat; But another climbed the ladder now and then another, one grabbed Tannis and threw her off the battlement to the ground below in the fort and jumped down after her. Ben overpowered his attacker and threw him back over the parapet, but there was still another behind him. Jack saw it, 'Down!' he shouted, Ben dropped to his knees, and Jack opened fire; it was dead before it hit the floor. Ben got to his feet and looked down to where Tannis had landed; she'd lost her weapon in the fall and didn't even have the chance to grab one of her others. The attack was so full on; it was all she could do to keep the beast at arms-length.

Jack shoved the ladder away from the battlement along with the two *Nightwalkers* that were still on it, 'Help her!' he shouted to Ben as he fired a few more rounds at the force below. Ben ran down the steps towards his wife, the *Nightwalker* had managed to get an arm free and landed a lucky punch knocking her to the ground, and it quickly moved in for the kill, Ben was too far away to get to her in time, again, he felt the rage build up inside him and went with it this time. He shoved his hands out in front and sent the *Nightwalker* flying backwards into the wall, he had a clear shot now and took it then ran over to Tannis and helped her up.

'Major!' Jack crouched on the battlement and looked down at them, 'stop showing off and both of you get back up here,' he said a little tongue in cheek.

They joined him again and carried on fighting. The *Nightwalkers* seemed to give up after a while, content to eat their fallen, even some of them that weren't quite dead judging from the screams coming from the cornfield. They remained at their post until the last scream faded as the sun began to rise and the sentries left to make their way home.

In the barn, Jack kicked Blair's boot to wake him up, 'What is it?' 'Your watch,' Jack said bluntly as he made himself comfortable in the straw and leaned his weapon against a nearby post.
'Colonel, I have hardly slept with all of the commotion outside,' Blair protested, then looking over to where Ben and Tannis lay in each other's arms he pointed, 'and that is not protocol I must say.'
Jack jumped up and grabbed Blair by the collar, and marched him to the barn door, 'We haven't slept because we were up all night helping defend this place,' he dumped him outside and went quietly back to his nest in the straw, noticing as he went Dr Kelsey picking up a pitchfork and taking her place at the door.

A few hours had passed when Blair barged back in, 'Wake up!' he yelled, the three of them sat up instantly, their sidearms trained on him. Seeing no danger, Ben sighed and pulled his wife back down in the straw with him as they stowed their weapons. Jack glared at him, 'You trying to get yourself killed, Blair?' he asked as he too secured his weapon and lay back down. Blair trod carefully now as he went and sat next to Jack.
'I've been talking to the local people; they tell me there is an abandoned city about three hours walk from here.'
'That's great Blair, but if you keep waking those two up,' he motioned toward Ben and Tannis, 'they won't be up to making a leap. And I don't know about you, but I'd like to get out of here as soon as possible.'
'Colonel Marsters, we must look. If there is a city, there'll be records, we could find out what happened here; find out where these monsters came from.'
'Thought you said there was no such thing,' Jack closed his eyes.
'Colonel, we may be able to help these people, and find out if any of this is a threat to our dimension,' he was insistent now.

Jack rubbed his hands over his head as he sat up, 'Ok, but when I say it's time to leave, we leave, understand? Because you WILL be left behind!'

'Absolutely,' Blair turned to Kelsey who still stood watch at the door, 'be ready to leave,' he said bluntly.

Hmm, Jack thought, at least one of them had some backbone, he wasn't sure how much use she'd be with the pitchfork, but her heart was in the right place.

'Major Rhodes, Tannis, up you get, Dr Blair wants to go for a little walk,' he sighed. A few minutes later they stood outside the barn ready to leave, a few grateful settlers brought them food and water for the journey and bid them hurry back before dark.

'Couldn't we just leap the city?' Kelsey asked.

Jack shook his head, 'Our timepieces don't work in other dimensions, and until my teammate's recharge their batteries, we're on foot, so, let's get a move on, shall we? We'll be cutting it fine getting back before the land sharks come out again as it is.' They walked on in silence and broke rations halfway but ate as they walked. Time was against them, but there were open fields all around so the team could relax a little as they could see for miles.

Jack dropped back to walk with his team, 'Well, I think we can safely say you conquered your fear last night,' he looked across at Tannis; she was still unusually quiet, subdued even, 'so, what's still bugging you?'

She shook her head, 'This place is, it's all wrong, I have a bad feeling, and it involves the four of us.'

'Four?' Ben looked at Blair and Kelsey, Tannis nodded. 'Blair, I don't trust him, he means to do us harm.'

'You sure you're not just pissed off because he forced the mission on us, cos I am,' Jack admitted.

She smiled, 'No, just don't turn your back on him,' she warned as they carried on. A short time later, true to the words of the settlers, they came to the abandoned city. It was overgrown, and some of the buildings were crumbling, the wide roads were grass covered and indistinguishable from the pavement. As they walked up a small incline, Ben let out a gasp, 'Oh, my God, that's Capitol Hill! This is Washington DC.'

'But it doesn't make sense,' Dr Kelsey thought aloud as they made their way to the Library of Congress, if there were going to be any records, there was a good place to start. 'Why are the settlers living like that when they were far more advanced, what looks like centuries ago?'

'Because something bad happened here,' Ben spoke quietly.

'Stay out of the shadows,' Jack warned, 'perfect hiding place for Nightwalkers.' They found the library after a while and Alpha team secured it before allowing the two scientists inside. The books were so frail that most of them disintegrated as they touched them.

'We're not gonna find anything here, let's get back,' Jack nodded to his team to move out.

'Maybe it was a rift in the dimensions that brought the Nightwalkers through?' Kelsey spoke to Tannis.

'It's possible if they had no Philadelphia Experiment there would be no one to spot the rift and stop it, that or we're all dead,' Tannis agreed as she walked toward the exit.

'Comforting thought,' Jack muttered to himself as he followed her, 'c'mon Blair we're leaving!'

'But we still have a little time left; we should try and find something, anything,' Blair protested. Jack turned and walked back toward him. He had taken just a few steps when the floorboards creaked loudly and gave way under his feet. Ben tried to grab him, but Jack had fallen through. They all stood close to the edge and looked over.

'Found something,' he groaned. He was flat on his back covered in dust and rotten wood, but at least he was ok. Ben jumped down to the floor below and joined him, it wasn't a long drop. Tannis stayed above to keep watch on the two scientists.

Jack reached up and helped Dr Kelsey as she lowered herself down, Ben just watched as Blair dangled himself and dropped awkwardly to the floor. Tannis took a quick look around where she remained above then walked over to one of the large bookcases and pulled a metal framed ladder from its runners and lowered it to Ben, she didn't use it though she jumped down and landed silently by his side.

Blair frowned at her, 'What was the point in that?'

'You want to get out, don't you?' Jack shut him up. They all shone their torches and looked around, it was bare brick except for a small button flashing red. Where the hell was it getting power from? Blair walked up to it, 'Blair No!' Jack hissed but it was too late, he pressed it.

Alpha team raised their weapons. The room shuddered a little, showering them in dust and large splinters of wood, then the wall that was home to the button slid across to reveal two glass doors. No doubt safety, Jack thought as he touched it. There was a corridor on the other side, empty but lit, 'Any ideas?' Jack was open to suggestions. There was a small keypad numbered zero to nine to the right of the doors, Blair walked over to it and pulled a small electronic device from his pocket, which he attached to the numbered panel with small clips, the doors slid open shortly after.

Jack raised an eyebrow and looked at his team; he could see they were thinking the same thing. Namely, how did he know to bring something like that along? Footsteps from the room above and the tell-tale yell of a *Nightwalker* made the decision for them. They all hurried into the corridor, and Blair secured the inner doors just as the *Nightwalker* jumped down into the room they had vacated. It began to yell and shriek as if communicating with others of its kind. The shrieking got louder as it saw them and charged at the doors, smashing into them time and again, its blood smeared the glass so relentless was its attack, but still, it stepped back and made for another charge, one that was denied as the outer doors slid shut.

Jack led them cautiously down the brightly lit passage. It turned sharply to the right ahead but then just continued down a gradual incline as they headed deeper underground.

As the end of the passage came into view, they were faced with yet another door; this, however, opened automatically as they approached. Alpha team went in first to check it out, it was a large lab, still lit, with all its equipment looking fully functional. It was as if the technicians had just stepped out.

There were three rooms off the main one, Alpha team took one each and checked them out.

Jack's room was mostly storage, just shelves of equipment and a small desk inside. He satisfied himself it was clear and left, closing the door behind him. The room Ben took must've been used to keep the lab animals in; there were empty cages all over, some small but others large enough to hold a man in, *what the hell went on here?* he thought to himself. Whatever it had been used for, it was empty now, so he too closed the door and left.

Across the room, Tannis was trying to open the door to check out her room, but a red light was flashing above it.

'What does this mean?' she asked Kelsey before she tried to open it. Kelsey walked over to a desk close by, 'It needs venting; the air inside is poisonous, it looks like a termination chamber.'

Tannis looked aghast at the woman, 'They shove things in here and gas them?'

'Yes, in fact whatever is in there should be perfectly preserved,' she hit a button on the computer keyboard, 'when the red light goes out, and the green one comes on, the door will unlock,' Kelsey explained as she went back over to where she had been tapping at another terminal. The light went green, and the lock clicked. Tannis opened the door cautiously, her weapon at the ready, but she lowered it as it fully opened, and she looked inside. Her teammates walked over to her from the other side of the lab to see how she was doing.

'Clear?' Jack called to her, but there was no answer, 'Tannis, clear?' He called it louder this time. The two men raised their weapons and hurried towards her as they saw her step over the threshold. She was staring at something on the floor, and as they drew closer, they saw what she was looking at, three bodies lay dead at her feet. Ben lowered his weapon and pulled her into him to hide her face as he stared down at them, 'Christ!' Jack whispered. It was them, dressed as they were now. Jack lay dead on his front; his head turned slightly to the side while Ben lay on his back, Tannis had fallen across his chest. 'Get her out of here,' Jack ordered as he stared at their alternate selves.

Ben led her out and across the lab into the room he had just cleared. Blair and Kelsey went to see what was wrong, Kelsey's hand went to her mouth, and she turned away. Blair showed no emotion, just went back to his computer terminal and carried on. Jack closed the door and leaned against it, 'I should get their timepieces, could cause more trouble for this place if someone found them,' he sighed as he turned to go back in.

'Let me, Colonel,' Kelsey stepped forward, 'you shouldn't have to.'

'Thanks,' he gave her a nod as he stood to one side to let her pass. She quickly returned and handed them to him, 'Thank you, Doctor,' he said as he shoved them into his pocket. She was turning out ok after all.

Ben stood with his wife in the empty room, holding her tightly. She had been spooked from the start of this mission, and now he knew why, he took her face in his hands, 'Look at me,' she opened her eyes, 'what's the only thing that's real?' he asked her firmly.

'Us,' she whispered.

'Say it,' he held her face close to his.

'It's only a mission; we're the only thing that's real,' she focused on him properly now as he smiled and kissed her tenderly, then held her again as Jack came into the room.

'You, ok?'

Tannis nodded, 'I'm sorry, Jack, but I knew I had a bad feeling about this place.'

'And now we know why,' he nodded, then moved closer to them and lowered his voice, 'I get what you mean about Blair now too, watch him, he knows too much about this place. Someone killed our other selves out there, that was no accident.' They left the room and joined the two scientists, 'Anything yet?' Jack asked as he tried to look over Blair's shoulder.

'I've found something interesting,' Kelsey called him over and stepped aside to allow the three of them to see the screen, 'the schematics of the facility; it appears there's another way out through the back of the lab animal storeroom,' then she looked sheepish as Blair chastised her for not concentrating on her brief.

'Good work, Doctor,' Jack approved, 'no point in getting what you came for if you can't get out again,' he jibed at Blair without looking at him, but Ben was 'Sir,' he motioned to the scientist who was now downloading some files onto a memory stick. 'Seems you've found something too, Dr Blair, and what would that be?' Jack didn't trust him as far as he could throw him.

'Just technical data for our records back in our dimension,' he dismissed. Dr Kelsey frowned and moved over to his terminal; he pushed her aside. 'That will be all, Dr Kelsey,' he snapped.

'Actually, that won't be all,' Jack fronted up to him, and the two men squared off against each other, It would've been no contest for the Colonel to beat him to a pulp, but the situation never arose, sadly in Jack's opinion, as Blair backed down when he noticed Ben and Tannis had their side arms aimed at him. Kelsey stepped over to the terminal now and read through the files he had been downloading.

'My God, all of this was man-made. A Nightwalker came through from another dimension, and they caught it and tried to assimilate its strength and agility for use on humans in the battlefield, but all the subjects when infected became Nightwalkers. The genetic strain was dominant and couldn't be controlled,' she looked at the team now, 'it was also found to be contagious, passed on from a single bite. Subject 2387 broke free and infected the lab techs, and it ends there.'

'And the last entry was made 947 years ago,' Tannis exhaled and looked at the ceiling, she was pissed off now.

'There's more,' Kelsey looked at them nervously, 'your other selves… Dr Jonathon Blair activated the termination code.'

Jack raised his weapon, 'You bastard, you're doing this in our dimension, aren't you? That's how you know so much.'

'What subject number are you on?' Tannis asked coldly.

'You're mistaken. I've no idea what you're talking about,' he lied.

'Liar!' Kelsey rounded on him, 'you knew all of the passwords and codes to open these files.'

'How far along are you?' Tannis aimed her sidearm at his knee, 'how many have you murdered?'

'It's hardly murder; most of them are homeless, nobody misses them,' he said without emotion.

'How many?' Jack glared, 'or she pulls the trigger.'

'1745,' Blair was afraid now.

Ben pulled the memory stick out of the computer, dropped it on the floor, and stamped on it. 'Delete the files,' Jack ordered Kelsey who nodded and went to work. It didn't take long.

'Sir,' Ben secured his sidearm and picked up his semi-automatic, he had been looking at the security monitor which focused on the doors from the library. The *Nightwalkers* had breached them and were on their way down the corridor.

'Move!' Jack yelled as they headed for the room with the back door. Once inside, he and Ben shoved a desk against the door and braced themselves as the *Nightwalkers*, who were now in the lab, tried to push their way in. Tannis joined her team, and with her strength, the intruders were held at bay for now. Blair knew where the switch was for the hidden door and he soon opened it, making sure he was the first one through, he made to close it, leaving the others trapped, but Kelsey ran after him and floored him with a swift kick in the groyne.

'Hurry!' she yelled to Alpha team as she stood making sure the door stayed open.

They knew they wouldn't make it if they let go of the desk and ran for it, the *Nightwalkers* were too fast. So, they grabbed their weapons and opened fire as they walked backwards toward their exit. They killed everyone that came through but there were just too many of them, and they kept coming. Their semi-automatic weapons were running low on ammunition as the bodies stacked up, 'I'm out,' Ben shouted over the noise; they were only halfway across the room.

'Me, too,' Jack threw his weapon to the ground as Ben had done. Tannis stepped a little in front of them, and they grabbed a pump action shotgun each from the holsters on her back. In seconds, they were once again moving back towards the way out, they were almost there as Tannis ran out now too and un-holstered both her sidearms. As soon as they were inside the exit tunnel, Kelsey hit the button to close the door, but a *Nightwalker* threw itself halfway through the opening. Although it was crushed to death, its sacrifice left a gap big enough for others to get through. Everyone ran along the passage; it was not as well-lit as the others they had come along earlier. This one had been cut from the earth and was roughly shored up with wooden beams. Jack hoped they were stronger than the floorboards in the library. The team turned and opened fire once more, killing a few, but the numbers were just too many.

Blair was a short distance ahead of them and once more knew precisely how to get out of there, he shoved at one of the beams propped against the wall. It fell to the ground to reveal an opening that he hurried through, but the beam he had moved had been helping to support the roof; the other supports were old and rotten; they couldn't take the strain and collapsed, bringing part of the roof down. A falling beam hit Tannis, and she dropped like a stone.

The *Nightwalkers* were getting closer as Ben dragged his unconscious wife out of their grasp. They were metres away now; he looked behind them, it was blocked. He knew he wasn't up to making a leap, so he used what power he had and thrust out his hands, bringing the roof down in front of them. It cut them off from the *Nightwalkers*, but now they were trapped.

From the rockfall behind them, they heard Blair as he hurried back down his escape route to find the tunnel blocked. 'Help me!' He screamed, then came the cry of a *Nightwalker*, they heard him beg for his life as the hunter stalked its prey, 'Help me!' He screamed again.

Kelsey turned and faced the rockfall he was trapped behind and yelled back, 'You sowed the wind, Doctor, now reap the whirlwind!' They heard him choking on his blood as his throat was torn out, then nothing more, but now they had problems of their own. From in front and behind they heard the *Nightwalkers* digging their way to them, and by the sound of it they wouldn't take long.

Jack leaned closer to Ben and whispered, 'How many rounds left, Major?'

'Five,' he checked his sidearm.

'I've got four,' Jack told him then added, 'save one for each of you. I'll take care of the Doc and me if it comes to it.'

Ben nodded and shook his friend's hand, 'It's been the greatest part of my life.'

'Mine too,' Jack tried to smile as he thought of his family. Ben looked down at Tannis, probably best if she didn't wake up. Dr Kelsey sat terrified next to Jack, he opened his arms, and she moved into them, clinging to him. The three of them sat and listened as the *Nightwalkers* got closer, they were almost through now. Ben kissed Tannis one last time and put the barrel of his gun to her head; his hand was trembling. Jack too held his gun to the back of Kelsey's head, but she took his hand that held the weapon and guided it to her temple then looked up at him with her eyes full of tears, 'Thank you Colonel,' she whispered.

Ben was cursing himself for not being strong enough to leap when it hit him, 'Wait!' he shouted, 'the timepieces from our other selves, they should work fine in this dimension.'

'Bloody Hell!' Jack gasped as he pulled them out of his pocket and gave one each to Ben and the doctor. He strapped the other on himself, 'the barn at the fort, go,' he ordered.

The first *Nightwalker* broke through the rubble and let out a yell; maybe it was one of disappointment, because there was no one there.

Back in the barn now, Ben lay Tannis down in the straw and sat next to her with his head in his hands as he thought about what he had almost done, Jack and Kelsey sat nearby, both thinking the same thing. The silence was broken when Tannis began to stir, she sat up quickly and looked around her, 'It's ok, we're back at the fort,' Ben told her as she leaned against him then she flinched back a little and touched his face gently, 'Don't feel guilty for something that never happened.'

Jack knew she had sensed her husband's torment at what he was going to do back in the tunnel.

'Well, we're all back safe and sound thanks to your husband,' he went on to explain what had happened.

'So, Blair got what was due to him then,' she said bluntly.

'It's happening back in our world now though, and we have to stop it,' Jack looked at all of them.

'It will be stopped, Colonel, don't worry about that,' Kelsey told him, 'I was assigned to watch Blair by the coalition, they knew he was up to something, and now I have the proof they need to shut the whole thing down,' she reached in her pocket and pulled out a memory stick.

'You're a dark horse! I knew you'd had some training when you pulled up the schematics and found us a way out,' Jack grinned, 'enjoy your work in the real world?'

'Not really, I'd like to work on Atlantis, but that's not on the cards.'

'Why not?' he frowned.

'Oh, you know they ask you; you don't ask them.'

'Oh, they'll be asking, Doctor.'

She grinned, 'You think so?'

'I know so, we need people we can rely on, and don't lose their heads when their backs are against the wall.'

Tannis stood up now, feeling better, and she walked over to the barn door as Ben collected their weapons. The sun was going down again, she was remembering the first trip she had made there and saw herself as a young girl playing with the other children, and she smiled.

Jack was behind her; he rested his hands on her shoulders, 'You feeling better?'

She nodded, 'Told you there were monsters,' she put a hand on one of his.

'We never doubted you, but there was more than one kind of monster at work here,' he turned to Ben, 'You ready to leave, Major, or has your Kryptonite kicked in?'

'No, I can still manage, sir,' Ben looked across at his CO trying not to laugh. Tannis took Jack's hand, and Ben grabbed Kelsey's wrist, and they were gone.

Chapter Ten

The coalition training facility was not a place Tannis frequented, being a self- confessed gym dodger. And after being stuck there for two weeks of dancing and etiquette lessons, she avoided the place like the plague. Both Jack and Ben used the facilities for sparring practice mostly and the occasional workout. Although as Tannis had pointed out, they got enough hands-on experience in the field with the number of missions they had pulled lately and they had been training hard all week learning horseback Sabre techniques, which they had passed with flying colours thanks to her help. She was a natural, although she had modestly insisted that it was only because she had been doing it longer.

So, that morning she had decided to take Jester out for a ride while her team went to the facility.

As the two men boxed, there was an unarmed combat training session being held close by. No one on Atlantis was a raw recruit, but this group had just joined the programme. They were military trained, of course, but this job required a little more.

Master Sgt Hendricks' voice boomed as he chewed out one of the female newbies, 'Lt Jenkins, what the hell was that?'

The young woman flinched as he bellowed in her face, 'I was trying to disarm Master Sgt,' she sounded back. Her partner for the exercise, also a Lieutenant but male, sniggered, she had tried to take a knife from him, but he had knocked her to the ground in a single shove.

'You find it amusing, Lt Robson?' Hendricks glared at him now, 'I doubt you would if Lt Jenkins here had been assigned to watch your back because right now there would be a knife sticking in it.'

'Sorry, Master Sgt,' the cocky young Lieutenant looked at Jenkins now, 'maybe she should have an easier partner to spar with?'

Hendricks rounded on him, 'Son, you must think you got a pair.' Jack and Ben stopped what they were doing and watched; this was going to be interesting.

'Oh, big mistake,' Ben whispered.

'Yeah, Hendricks is gonna make him pay for that one,' Jack agreed. Both men knew the Master Sgt and thought he was one of the best. He trained his recruits well and had the best record for giving them the skills they needed to stay alive out there. He had been hand-picked for the job, he was in his early fifties now but could still handle himself in any combat situation, always proud of the US Marines uniform he wore and had been decorated countless times for bravery. What hair he had left now was shaved close to his scalp and greying a little, but his physique was still in excellent condition.

'Jenkins, back in line,' he dismissed the young woman, she would scrub up; she had the right attitude to the job, just needed the proper training. The cocky Lieutenant that stood in front of him, however, was another story he was going to get himself and his team killed on his first trip out if he didn't have this arrogant attitude knocked out of him.

As if right on cue, Tannis walked into the room, much to the surprise of her teammates who exchanged curious looks as she gave them a small wave and stood quietly by the door, even more unusual was the fact she wore sweatpants and one of Ben's old khaki Marine Corp t-shirts over her vest top, her hair was tied back in a pony-tail high on her head. Hendricks acknowledged her with a nod, 'Please join us ma'am and thank you for your time.'

Tannis walked over to where he stood with Lt Robson. Hendricks looked along the line of his group, 'Jenkins, front and centre,' the young woman stepped forward and stood in front of them, none of the newbies had met Tannis yet, 'demonstrate again,' he ordered. They took position and Jenkins lunged at Robson once again, and once again, he threw her to the ground and pressed the fake weapon to her throat, then he got up, leaving her to make her way to her feet. Tannis offered her a hand up and she smiled as she took it, getting to her feet slightly embarrassed, 'Back in line,' Hendricks barked, then turned to the group, 'well, you have all attempted to disarm Lt Robson and failed, any ideas why?' The line remained silent 'Anyone?' He looked at Tannis now too, inviting her opinion.

'Failure to spot your opponent's weakness?' she said a little nervously, not used to such circumstances.

'Exactly,' The Master Sgt barked at his group.

Ben removed his padded helmet as Jack had already done and began to take off his gloves when Jack frowned, 'He's eyeing her up!' Ben followed his CO's gaze and saw Lt Robson undressing Tannis with his eyes.

'Son of a…'

'Now, Major,' Jack gave him a friendly warning as they continued to listen.

'What weakness, Master Sgt?' one of the men in line spoke up, 'he can take us all.'

'Well, I do have a soft spot for blondes,' Robson winked at the group.

'Oh, I can see where this is going, Hendricks is good,' Jack sniggered.

'Humph saves me a job,' Ben muttered.

'Very well,' Hendricks stepped back, leaving Tannis facing Lt Robson.

'Oh, I don't know Master Sgt, I've never really done this kind of thing before. I told you that earlier,' Tannis looked nervously at the instructor.

'Oh, don't worry, gorgeous. I won't bite,' Robson grinned, 'hard,' he wouldn't mind pinning her down on the mat, he thought.

'You secure that, Lieutenant!' Hendricks ordered.

Tannis looked back at her team who both gestured for her to go for it, so she shrugged as she turned around, 'Ok.' She stood in front of Robson but didn't move, just waited. *Too easy*, he thought to himself and lunged towards her. In one fluid movement, she kicked him in the groyne, and as he fell to his knees, she kicked out, knocking the weapon from his hand into the air, catching it on the way back down.

'Overconfidence in your ability will get you killed,' Hendricks barked once again as he took the fake weapon Tannis now handed to him, 'dismissed.'

The line disbanded and moved away, Robson limped along behind them, 'Lt Jenkins, remain,' Hendricks called out. *God, what now?* Jenkins thought as she walked back.

'Tannis has kindly agreed to help bring you up to standard with your training. I'll leave you to make the arrangements,' he turned to Tannis, 'thank you again, ma'am.'

Tannis smiled 'No problem, Master Sgt. It's nice to know someone who recognises what's in front of them.' He nodded curtly and left the two women together, saluting Jack and Ben as they walked over. Jenkins stood to attention as her superiors joined them.

'As you were, Lieutenant,' Jack nodded to her.

'Permission to speak sir's, ma'am?' Jenkins stammered. Jack nodded his consent,

'You're Alpha team,' she said in awe, 'Colonel Marsters, Major Rhodes and Tannis.'

Jack brushed it off in typical Tannis style, 'Not today; it's our day off,' he wiped his face with the towel around his neck, 'so, what's going on?' He looked at Tannis now.

'I thought you were taking Jester out?' Ben added.

'I did, but the Admiral called and asked a favour,' she looked at Jenkins, 'you have excellent qualifications; you just need to work on your self-defence, I know how you feel, I was the youngest in our lot too.'

'You mean *DE-173*, I can't wait to meet Ned, I've read his file, he's awesome!' Jenkins enthused.

'Well, he's something,' Tannis pulled a face.

'Ah, you must be the military historian the Admiral mentioned,' Ben looked at the young woman in front of him. She was brunette and had a small build, not unattractive, but not his type either, then again, he was biassed he thought as he looked at his wife; and Jenkins did need her help. It looked like a strong gust of wind would knock her off her feet.

Tannis excused herself from the group as her phone rang, 'Hey, Ned, what's up?'

Her teammates made polite small talk with the Lieutenant, but both men kept one ear on the conversation Tannis was having with her brother.

'Ned, calm down, well, how far back have you gone?' She paused to listen to his reply, 'Really? Wow,' she turned and looked at her team, 'they're both here with me, we're at the gym.' Ned must've made a sarcastic comment as she tried to look behind at her own butt, 'It's not that big,' she stopped when she realised they were all looking at her, 'Ok I'll be right there, no point in dragging us all in until we trace the threat,' she ended the call.

'Phoenix?' Jack raised an eyebrow.

'Looks like it,' she sighed, 'I should go and help Ned, he's trying to trace it, but they're covering their tracks well on this one.'

'Just gimme a chance to change, I'll come with you,' Ben didn't want to spend his day off without her.

'Me too,' Jack called back as they headed for the men's locker room.

'It's supposed to be your day off, guys,' she called after them. 'One in, all in,' Jack said over his shoulder.

Tannis went with Lt Jenkins to the female locker room to change, and they arranged their first lesson for a few days' time. Then she went to meet her teammates outside; they were already waiting for her.

'Women,' Jack tutted in mock disgust,

Tannis narrowed her eyes at him and was about to say something when Lt Jenkins ran over and saluted, 'Sirs, ma'am.'

'What is it, Lieutenant?' Jack wanted to get going.

'I thought maybe I could help with the problem sir; I mean that's what I'm trained for.'

'Couldn't hurt,' Ben shrugged when Jack looked at him for an opinion.

'Ok,' Jack agreed.

'We should get going, Ned'll have his French knickers in a twist by now,' Tannis said as she took Ben's hand in hers, then Jack's in the other.

'Ma'am, I should warn you I have only made one leap, and I threw up,' Jenkins confessed.

'Don't worry Lieutenant, Tannis is much more refined, you won't feel a thing,' Jack told her as he grabbed her arm and nodded for Tannis to make the leap.

Lt Jenkins blinked, and they were in Ned's office, 'Wow, this is unreal,' she laughed, 'was your first leap with Tannis like this, sir?' She asked Jack.

'We were in a bit of a rush, and the landing was a bit hard,' he gave Tannis a sideways look.

'Well, my landing was nice and soft,' Tannis grinned as she went on to explain.

'Hello,' Ned waved sarcastically, 'time changes going on, shall we take the trip down memory lane after we've saved the world?'

Tannis stuck her tongue out at her brother, 'This is Lt Jenkins,' she introduced.

'Ah, the history buff,' he smiled.

'How did you know that sir?' Jenkins was surprised.

'He's not a sir, and I'm not a ma'am, and you can't do anything around here without someone writing a report on it,' Tannis informed her.

'So, what have we got so far?' Ben sat down at one of the empty desks and put his feet up.

'Oh, you'll love this one,' Ned looked at them all as he went on to inform them that England was now ruled by the French as was the USA although it was now called the Union Des Francais. The room was silent for a moment, Tannis wrinkled her nose and looked at Ben, 'Better cancel that table for tonight,' he nodded and sighed heavily as he folded his arms across his chest.

'Ok, so what would Phoenix gain from this one?' Jack asked the room, 'other than to ruin our day off!' The time screens updated now showing the Russian Revolution never happened because Napoleon defeated the Russians in 1812 and went on to invade China in 1820. It seemed they were the greatest power in the world with no opposition.

'I guess Phoenix are parlez vousing a lot of Francais,' Ned looked at the screen. 'Oh, and Montauk is up and running after a thwarted attack in the 1980's. It would seem world domination is on the cards for this chap, the new French President,' he clicked his remote, and an image appeared on the plasma screen behind him.

'Dick!' Tannis rolled her eyes at the fat faced balding arrogant image of Jefferson. Ben sneered, he and Jack had acquainted themselves very well with the images and information that they had been given on Phoenix.

'So, does it follow that he would be the one who went back and changed the past?' Jenkins was keen to learn.

'Not always the case, they usually work in two's though,' Ned told her, but he was looking at his sister, he'd thought this was all over, and now she had to face them again. 'Anyway,' he cleared his throat, 'I've got as far as Medieval France, found a couple of things to look at but probably nothing and I've still got England and the US to get through, so please dive in.'

'I call the US,' Ben sat up and began to trawl through the files on the screen.

'Rule Britannia,' Jack smiled as he sat down at the next desk and switched the computer on.

'Mind if I take the States, too?' Jenkins asked Tannis; after all, she was American.

'Go for it,' she shrugged and went to sit with Jack.

A couple of hours passed, and the UK and the US had almost covered two hundred and thirty years. Ned had taken a break to go and get them all something to eat and drink and returned now with a huge tray full. Jack stood up and stretched then cleared a space for Ned to put the tray down on top of a large filing cabinet. The Lieutenant got up too and rubbed her eyes, then she walked over to the tray and stood next to Jack, 'Coffee, sir?' She held the pot out.

'No thanks, Lieutenant,' he picked up the teapot and poured two cups. Ned had already helped himself and gone back to his desk. 'The Major will have a cup of sludge with you, though, black and no sugar,' he carried the two cups back to his desk, giving one to Tannis who was still trawling through the files on her screen, then went back and got a selection of fruit and sandwiches which he put between them both, Jenkins did the same for her and Ben.

'Thanks, Lieutenant,' he said as he leaned back in his seat to drink his coffee. Tannis too stopped now and picked up her tea and began to drink, she slid down in her chair and rested the cup on her chest then closed her eyes for a moment.

Ned groaned, 'Well any further back and I'll be in prehistory, and no one dabbles in that, too unpredictable.'

Tannis' eyes flashed open, and she sat up slowly, put her drink down and grabbed the mouse, clicking back through the pages she'd already scrolled through, 'You onto something?' Ned switched the main screen on to show Tannis' as she flicked back through the centuries showing nothing but the monarchy.

'They're all Catholic,' she muttered as she carried on.

'Wasn't everybody back then,' Jack knew his history.

'Yes but,' she paused the screen when she arrived at the Tudor dynasty and moved slightly forward to Henry the Eighth, 'we might be able to cut out a huge chunk if Henry still broke from Rome,' she clicked the mouse and there on the screen was the proof they needed, Henry's six wives, 'Yes!' she smiled and continued forward to the Stuarts, past the civil war and came to the death of Charles the second, who was succeeded by his brother James who had a long and happy reign. She stopped there and looked at her brother who winked at her.

'Well done, little sister,' he looked at the others, 'don't let the blonde hair fool ya.'

'Yeah, I'm not as dumb as you look.' Tannis fired back.

Ned got to the point now, 'Charles The Second had a childless marriage, although he sired many children from various mistresses, so when he died, the throne went to his brother James, but James was a Catholic and to cut a long story short, bit of a scuffle and James got chucked out very early on in favour of his Protestant daughter Mary and her husband William of Orange, but as you can see here, James remained on the throne, and his children went on to unify with France.'

'Well, that's narrowed it down a bit,' Jack grinned as he shoved a sandwich at Tannis, 'eat!' She took it from him and got back to work while everyone else switched their screens to the same era.

'Both Anne and Mary married French prince's,' Jack read aloud. 'William of Orange was killed at the Battle of Seneffe in 1674,' Ben added.

'It's John Graham,' Ned concluded.

'But I thought Bonnie Dundee wasn't a known Jacobite until William and Mary were on the throne?' Jenkins piped up.

'Yes, but Graham was in William's army at Seneffe, he saved William's life, even got a promotion for it,' Ned brought the relevant file up now and read how serving as a Cornet in William of Orange's guard, he was present at the Battle of Seneffe in 1674 where he rescued the young prince when his horse fell in marshy ground. As a reward for his actions, Graham received a Captain's commission in the same troop.

Ned brought up the altered timeline now and read on, 'He's mentioned on the roll call up until 8th August 1674. The battle was on the 11th, so somewhere between those dates he was removed from history.'

Jack looked at his team, '1674, anyone?'

Tannis shot a quick look at Ned, 'Bags I go back as a bloke, I can strap my boobs down, it worked when I fought for Wellington.'

Ned thought for a moment, 'You could be there for days this time. Your cover won't hold for that long, Waterloo was ok in the confusion of battle. Besides Jack and Ben will be officers, you'll need to be with them not in the ranks.'

'And what if we have to go into battle?' She shot back.

'You can put a uniform on then, but let's hope it doesn't come to that,' his tone of voice told her the conversation was over.

'Ah, corsets,' Jack understood her outburst now.

'Well, you three can enjoy what's left of your day off, I'll borrow Lt Jenkins for a bit longer if that's ok, Jack?' Ned didn't look up; he was already getting down to the details of the mission.

Jack nodded, 'I'll clear it with Hennessy,' then he looked to his team, 'I'll see you at the briefing.'

It was after two as Ben and Tannis walked along the quayside, his arm around her shoulder, hers around his waist. They went back to their apartment and made love. As they lay in each other's arms, Tannis asked him, 'How does Caroline handle it? Jack going away like this, not knowing where he's going or what he's doing or even if he's going to come back for that matter.'

'She's a Colonel's wife, it's what they do. Besides, she would've known what she was in for when she married him,' Ben spoke softly.

'Well, I wouldn't like it,' she pulled herself closer to him.

'I would,' Ben said honestly, then continued, he knew she would soon take the bait, 'knowing you were safe at home waiting for me,' he laughed as she hit him with a pillow, then quickly pinned her down and kissed her; soon, their kisses grew more passionate, and they made love again.

Jack had returned home now; it wasn't time for Caroline to pick the kids up from school for another hour. He opened the front door, 'Caroline, you home, love?' he smiled to himself. He was thankful every day for the second chance he had been given to be with his family.

'In the kitchen,' she called back, she was washing her hands and judging by the fresh vegetables in the wicker basket by her side she had been picking them for dinner tonight, 'Have a good workout?'

Jack moved across the kitchen and stood behind her, wrapping his arms around her waist. He kissed the side of her neck as they both looked out of the window at the fantastic sea view. He could feel the warmth of her body through the thin material of her dress, he let his hand slide towards her breasts as his lips caressed her neck. She tilted her head back and closed her eyes as he lifted her dress and undid his trousers. She could feel his hardness, his desire for her had never dulled; he pulled her panties to one side, she turned her head, and their lips met as he entered her, 'Oh Jack,' she cried out as he made love to her, he could feel her tremble as she climaxed.

He wanted to see her now, so he turned her around and laid her on the oak table and was inside her again. God, she felt so good, he thought as he pulled the front of the dress down to reveal her breasts and took one in his mouth. She cried out with pleasure again, and this drove his passion more; he shoved deeper inside her, 'I love you,' he whispered as he came. They had intended to shower and change, but as they walked past the bed towards their bathroom, he pulled her down onto the cool fresh sheets and made love to her again. They lay together quietly now as he stroked her face, 'How long will you be gone?' she whispered, he pulled her into his arms, and she rested her head against him.

'Three or four days, maybe,' was all he could say, she knew better than to ask anything more.

The briefing room was crowded when Alpha team arrived, not only were Ned and Hennessey there, but they had been joined by Lt Jenkins and Delta team too, so Ben had to forgo his usual seat, instead sitting next to his wife.

Hennessey, of course, headed the meeting, 'Delta team has been read into the situation,' he looked at Jack as he spoke, Delta team were all personally chosen by Jack; they were led by Major Tom Hutchinson SAS who was joined by Captain Harry Chapman, Royal Marines, and Captain Zac Phillips, a Canadian who served as a Royal Marine. A lethal combination known affectionately as MI6 due to their sophisticated manner, good looks, and sharp dressing when off duty.

It had been decided that two teams would be needed for the mission should they be forced to engage in battle and because this would be their first encounter with Phoenix since they had been set free from their alternate dimension prison. They had been very quiet, no doubt planning this and as Ned had pointed out the ones that had come back hated each other so it would take a lot of negotiation to agree on their chain of command.

They opened their files and read in silence; Jack was to hold the rank of Captain, as was Ben, to allow them access to all areas when in the camp. The two men flicked through the pictures of the clothing they would be wearing and studied the weapons they would be using. Delta team would be lower ranked as Cornets giving them easy access to Graham.

Tannis read her file and paused halfway down, 'It says here I'm travelling with my sister and her husband?'

'I told you that you were going back as a woman,' Ned frowned.

'I know that but who's my sister?'

'Lt Jenkins will be your mission specialist. She will pose as Major Rhodes wife,' Hennessey explained, 'Lt Jenkins came up with the idea. Should you go into battle, her input on the day's events will prove invaluable.'

Ben and Tannis exchanged uncomfortable looks.

'Sir,' Jack wasn't sure about this one, he'd seen the look on his teammate's faces, 'Lt Jenkins isn't mission ready, and this is a definite Phoenix threat.'

'Of that, I am aware, Colonel. That is why she will pose as Major Rhodes' wife, that way she will be protected at all times,' Hennessey nodded to Ned to continue.

'Ok let's move on, shall we?' Ned began, 'Now hopefully you will neutralise the threat before the battle, but as I'm sure you've read about our past encounters with Phoenix they nearly always work in two's. If you stop the first attempt, be assured, they won't leave it at that. The protection detail of your mark will be down to Colonel Marsters. However, should you have to go into battle you should be prepared,' he glanced at Tannis but wouldn't hold her gaze, his stomach churning at the thought of her facing Phoenix again, 'It will be nothing like the warfare you have encountered so far, swords, sabres, muskets and cannon will be par for the course.

You have been given rank and put into the cavalry, Tannis included should the need arise. I know you have all been trained in horseback skills but, well, nothing can prepare you for it. Tannis, you were at Waterloo,' he gestured for her to jump in.

She shrugged uncomfortably with the attention, 'You must stand even though you're lined up facing ridiculously close to the enemy, then the order is given to open fire and you aim at the man opposite and pull the trigger, men either side of you will fall, but you still have to stand until the order is given to march toward the enemy, then you're being shot at and the enemy cannon are firing at you, eventually the line will move forward; but by then the noise is deafening and you can't see your hand in front of your face for the smoke. Then, if you manage to survive the advance and get under their guns; you get pounded by your own,' she sighed, 'and be aware the bodies of the dead and wounded pile up, don't trip over them and don't stop to help them or you'll be finished yourself.'

'Seneffe will be no exception,' Ned took over, 'there will be more than one hundred thousand men on the battlefield that day. Your side will have forty thousand infantry, twenty-two thousand cavalry, and seventy guns. The French will have thirty thousand infantry, fourteen thousand two hundred cavalry, and sixty guns. And after ten hours of fighting, it will be declared a draw. The French suffered ten thousand dead and wounded, but William's side was hit hardest with ten thousand dead, fifteen thousand wounded, and five thousand captured. It's going to be rough out there, not only do you have to protect your mark, but you must stay alive in order to do that and as you can see the odds are against you. As soon as Graham saves William, get out of there Phoenix won't try the same trick again once they know we're on to them.'

Hennessey looked at them all one by one, 'Digest the information in your files well, I don't need to tell you how important this is. All teams report to the hold in one hour ready to leap,' he then stood and left the room. They all sat in silence and read what was in front of them. Ben looked at his wife, and she met his gaze, each knew what the other was thinking, and each knew it was pointless to even raise the subject with the Admiral.

They stood together in the locker room now ready to go, Ben wore a scarlet knee-length coat buttoned down to the waist with pewter buttons, underneath was a loose fit white shirt with a green baize waistcoat, cravat, sea green breeches with white hose and black square-toed shoes, topped with a black felt hat with a low crown and a wide brim trimmed with silver braid. His crimson silk sash with silver fringe was tied at his waist over which he wore a leather baldric to hold his sword, this too was trimmed in silver and velvet. He looked stunning, Tannis thought to herself as she ran her eyes over his outfit for any mistakes.

She wore a green and gold brocade gown with a long bodice and low waist, as was favoured in the day, with elbow length sleeves and a narrow skirt. She didn't like the feeling of having her shoulders uncovered as they were, but the dress wasn't likely to budge though thanks to being trussed up in the loathsome corset. Her hair was tightly piled up on her head with a long ringlet hanging down either side of her face.

The last person left the locker room, and they were finally alone when he put his hands on her waist and pulled her towards him, he kissed her softly and held her to him. There would be time to worry about the battle if it came to it, but he knew this wasn't the only thing on his wife's mind as she looked up at him. He kissed her again, then the tannoy called them to the hold but he wouldn't let her go, he just wanted her in his arms for a while longer, she looked up at him and smiled, 'It's time.'

He sighed and nodded, 'This is gonna be a weird one.'

'It's only a mission, we're the only thing that's real,' she nuzzled his neck; he smiled now, snapping himself out of it, God, he was lucky to have her, their marriage was set in stone as far as they were both concerned, she trusted him completely as he did her. He recalled a comment Jack had made to Major Harmon one time when they had all returned from a trip to the real world. Tannis had stayed on Atlantis, it had been the stag night of an old friend from Iraq. As they were walking down the gangplank after their return, Tannis was in Ben's arms straight away, and they walked home together a few metres in front of the others.

Ben had heard Harmon when he muttered, 'She didn't even ask him what he'd been up to, did she know it was a stag night?'

Jack simply replied, 'If she had to ask, what would be the point? Same goes for him, they have a trust between them you would never understand Major.'

They were all in the hold now ready to leap, all the men in uniform and Lt Jenkins dressed in the same style as Tannis.

Ned hugged his sister as he always did before a mission, 'Don't play with them; this is not the time for revenge, make it quick and get out,' he was irritated, 'this should not be happening. It was over; they were finished,' he stepped back as he saw the look in his sister's eyes. He knew she was pissed off too, 'Follow Jack's orders,' he told her, as he stepped further back and stood at Hennessey's side.

She smiled at her brother and used their old saying from the days of *DE-173*, 'Light the fuse,' she held her head high in defiance.

'And cue the music,' he nodded knowingly.

'Alpha team, Delta team, good luck,' Hennessey nodded.

It wasn't difficult to mingle with the brigade due to the camp being busy and crowded with over sixty-two thousand people milling about, Jack lucked out and managed to get lodgings above a tavern for his team and Jenkins. Although truth be known, it was mainly because he had bribed the innkeeper very generously; Delta team had joined the troops in the tents, thousands of them covered the nearby fields. The priority was to find Graham, and it wasn't easy; the old saying of a needle in a haystack came to mind, but under the guise of taking the ladies for a stroll the couples went their separate ways and covered a lot of ground.

It was Ben who spotted him, and under the pretence of asking for a drink for his wife, they made as much small talk as possible between a Captain and the lower ranks. This gave Delta team the chance to see their mark and make plans to be close by, Jack saw and led Tannis away; they might have to stake him out later. He led her back towards the tavern; it would soon be time for dinner, 'You seem a little tense, my dear?' He was in character for eavesdroppers.

'I was hoping to see some old acquaintances, Captain,' she replied in kind.

'Oh, I'm sure you'll bump into them sooner or later,' he nodded a greeting to another passing couple.

'I was hoping sooner.'

He knew exactly what she meant, he wanted out of this place; there was going to be a slaughter here in a few days' time, and he didn't want his people anywhere near.

Dinner was a subdued affair as they couldn't talk freely in a room full of other officers and their wives. Ben had already had a few enquiries about his sister-in-law from some of the single officers, so to fend off any unwanted attention he told them that Jack was paying court to her, and their engagement was imminent.

Tannis was on the alert as they ate, her eyes discreetly checking everyone in the room and all those who entered. When it was time for the ladies to retire upstairs, she changed into her Cornet's uniform and was about to leave when Jack let himself in quickly and closed the door. He knew she wouldn't just go to bed quietly, 'I thought that uniform was for emergencies only,' he gave her a stern look.

'Jack, I can't lay around here all night like a spare part; I should be out there doing my job.'

'Delta team have got Graham covered for the nights,' he thought for a moment, 'still, I suppose it wouldn't hurt.'

'Good, see you later,' she said as she moved toward the door.

'I suppose it wouldn't hurt if we both went,' he still blocked her exit.

'Could be a waste of time,' she tilted her head to one side.

'Well, I couldn't think of anyone I'd rather waste time with,' he opened the door. Ben saw the two of them on the landing as he was making his way to the room he shared with Jenkins, his frown said it all.

'Just taking an evening stroll,' Jack looked over Ben's shoulder to another officer walking their way, as he passed Jack patted Ben on the shoulder, 'goodnight, Captain, don't keep that lovely wife of yours waiting,' Ben looked at Tannis, she had stopped to salute the passing Captain as she was ranked lower than all present; the man returned her salute and carried on his way.

'I would like to come with you, it would be nice to meet up with old acquaintances all together,' Ben pushed.

'You should be with your wife,' Jack put an end to it.

'Yes, I should,' he looked at Tannis. He hated this; he should be out there with his team, not babysitting Jenkins. 'Goodnight,' he said bluntly as he opened the door to his room and went inside.

It was a warm August evening outside, so the pair spent a good couple of hours wandering around the camp. But it was to no avail, so they were forced to return to the tavern. Luckily, everyone was asleep; making it easy for Tannis to slip upstairs to her room, she undressed in the moonlight and lay naked on her bed and thought about Ben across the hall sharing his bed with Jenkins. She knew nothing was going on, but she wanted to be with him, since they had been married, she had never slept alone.

Her thoughts turned back to them now, had he in his sleep, thought the warm body next to him was her? Did he hold her in his arms now? Was she laying her head on his chest? She thought of the nights when he reached for her half asleep, how they would make love. Tannis sat up now, got off the bed and, wrapping herself in the sheet, stood looking out of the window, resting her head on the cold glass and mentally chastising herself for having such stupid thoughts, it was going to be a long night.

She could have no idea that in the room across the hall Ben lay awake too, Jenkins had rolled over in her sleep and put an arm over him; he had woken with no doubt as to where he was and had carefully detached himself from her and rolled her back onto her side of the bed. He then shoved a bolster pillow between them and tried to go back to sleep, but it evaded him now as he lay thinking about Tannis. He knew she would be fine with Jack, and he should concentrate on the mission, but it wasn't easy. After another sleepless hour, he gave up and sat in the fireside chair.

The next morning when Jenkins awoke, she looked over and saw Ben asleep in the chair and stole an admiring glance at his body. His trousers covered him from the waist down, but she could see his toned torso and wondered what it would be like to be held in his strong arms, she lay back and allowed herself to fantasise for a moment; he was a very handsome man, there was Tannis but she was out of the equation at the moment and, besides, she'd never had any problem in the past getting any guy she wanted; she could replace Tannis no problem.

Getting out of bed, she began to dress as best she could, while she was doing this, he stirred and stretched as he woke up and walked over to the nightstand, poured some cold water from the jug into the bowl and splashed it on his face. Jenkins watched like a bitch in heat as the water ran down his chest before he wiped himself with a towel, she had her skirt on now but needed help with her bodice. 'Would you mind?' She turned her back for him to lace her up and held on to the bedpost as he pulled the laces.

'Is that too tight?' He heard her gasp.

'No, that's fine, thank you,' she had gasped when she felt his breath on her bare shoulders as he tied the lace at the small of her back.

'You should go and help Tannis when you're ready,' he told her as he continued to dress.

Jenkins left quietly and walked to the door directly opposite and knocked, Tannis opened it and let her in, 'Did you sleep well?' she asked cheerfully as she laced Tannis' gown.

'Not really, no' she replied truthfully, thinking the Lieutenant clearly had.

There was a knock at the door a short while later; it was Ben come to escort them down to breakfast. He didn't go into the room but waited in the hall for the two women. Jenkins came out first and took his arm while Tannis followed behind them in silence.

Jack was already downstairs waiting for them and stood as the ladies drew closer. When they sat, Ben looked over to Tannis, 'You look tired, didn't you sleep well?' He forced himself to adopt a neutral tone.

'New surroundings take a little adjustment,' she said as she looked directly at him.

'Well, not to worry things, will soon be back to how they should be,' he returned her stare. Tannis looked away quickly as Jack told them to end the conversation by offering her some bread.

After breakfast, the officers were called to a meeting nearby to discuss the forthcoming battle so the ladies were forced to stay in their rooms as they couldn't wander the camp without an escort. This frustrated Tannis as she wanted to be out there; the attack on Graham was imminent now. She consoled herself that Delta team were watching him, but none of them had ever come up against Phoenix except her, and she felt as if it were her responsibility to make the kill and keep them out of it. So, she bit her tongue and sat in Jenkins' room as they should. Jenkins, being the married woman, held seniority over Tannis, who now paced the floor like a caged animal, she was so frustrated and to add insult to injury she had been forced to listen to Jenkins talk about herself and Ben as if he was her husband. That was fair enough downstairs with the other wives, but Tannis had soon put her in her place when she had tried to continue the conversation when they were alone together in her room. *Great, I have all of this to think about, and now Jenkins has a crush on my husband,* she thought to herself.

After the meeting, the two men returned to the tavern and went straight upstairs to the room Ben shared with Jenkins, but they were not alone. The Captain whom they had seen in the hallway last night had joined them. Ben walked in ahead of the group, Tannis made to go to him and froze as Jack and the other officer followed, Jenkins stood up, walked over to Ben and took his hands in hers, 'Husband, you should've sent word you were bringing a guest,' she stood dutifully by his side.

'Captain Harker had his pistol cleaning kit stolen; he's just borrowing mine, that's all,' Ben forced a polite tone.

Jenkins went to their travelling chest and took out the kit, handing it to her husband who then passed it to the Captain who thanked them graciously and left promising to return the equipment as soon as he had made use of it. Tannis looked at the two of them standing there together; the last straw was when Jenkins took his hand and leaned into him as she looked Tannis in the eye and then looked at the bed, Tannis rushed past them to the door as Ben shrugged Jenkins off him.

'I need some air,' she glared at Jack who quickly followed her out into the hall. They took yet another very long walk around the camp and still turned up nothing, so after a very tense dinner they retired to their rooms for another sleepless night.

After breakfast, the following day Jack and Ben once more went to a meeting, Tannis refused to spend any more time sitting idly with Jenkins in her room, so volunteered to join some of the ladies in the surgeon's tent preparing for the battle. Her teammates dropped her off and later collected her after their business was finished for the day with the intention of also picking up Jenkins and taking yet another stroll looking for Phoenix.

They returned earlier than expected to the tavern and while Jack and Tannis waited outside Ben went in to fetch her. It didn't take long for him to reappear alone, Jenkins was not there, 'Where the bloody hell has, she gone?' Jack fumed, she had been told to stay put, under no circumstances was she to leave the room.

'I'll go up and change,' Tannis offered, 'at least that way we can split up and cover more ground,' Jack nodded his consent as he silently seethed at the situation, all she had to do was stay in her room, add to that she was supposed to be a historian and knew fine well a lady shouldn't be walking alone. Now he had to waste valuable time looking for her and not Phoenix.

Tannis soon returned dressed in her uniform, they agreed their search pattern and set off in different directions to return at a prearranged time. Tannis wasn't that bothered about finding Jenkins; she was more for sniffing out Phoenix, if Jenkins turned up along the way so be it. Jack was of the same mind too, as was Ben, and after a fruitless search with the sun going down, they all three returned to the tavern. And who should they find sitting quietly in her room 'Jenkins!!!' Jack hissed, 'where the bloody hell have you been?' he glared; he couldn't vent his full wrath as the noise level had to be kept down.

She jumped up out of her chair, 'I just stepped out for some fresh air,' she said, looking like a rabbit caught in headlights. Jack disciplined her as much as he could, threatening her with more when the mission was over, so once again dinner was a tense affair; Tannis was regretting her offer of help with Jenkins' training, quite frankly she felt like flattening her herself, Ben too felt trapped being tied to her for most of the time on this mission. Jack was making a mental note for his return to The Eldridge; no more useless spare parts on missions like this one, his team were crippled carrying a lame duck with them.

It was their turn to watch the mark the following afternoon, they walked in their respective couples as they followed Graham back from his sword practice in the woods. When he paused for a moment and looked behind him, Ben stopped and pulled Jenkins into him and looked down at her, but she pushed it too far and turned her head up to his, put her arms around his neck and kissed him, he couldn't push her away; their cover would be blown. Graham smiled to himself and walked on.

'You know, if you squeeze my arm any tighter it's going to drop off,' Jack spoke through a false smile as Graham passed them by. Tannis released her grip as she watched Ben shove Jenkins away from him; that was when she saw him coming from the west, dressed in a Spanish officer's uniform, 'Gunther,' she hissed, 'or a clone at least,' he hadn't seen or sensed her yet; She turned to Jack, 'Mind if I work off a little angst?' Jack was impressed; he had wondered how she would react when she came across a Phoenix agent after all that had happened. She had respected his command and asked permission, so he inclined his head, 'Make it quick and clean,' he said and looked around, apart from the clone they were alone. It would do her good to be off the chain for a bit, too. Jenkins was a real pain in the arse, and he thought it might bring her back in line if she saw Tannis at work. He turned to speak to her again, but she was gone, so he made his way over to Ben and Jenkins. They were ignored by the clone; whose mind was on his prey, Jack could see by the look on Ben's face that he had seen Gunther, too.

'Where's Tannis?' Jenkins asked.

'Oh, she's wound up tighter than a hunter's trap at the moment, so I thought I'd let her blow off a bit of steam,' Jack shot her a stern look.

They watched as the clone stalked his prey along the tree line, waiting for Tannis to make her move. From the trees above she dropped silently behind the clone, put a hand over his mouth, and with the other dragged him into the thick bushes, Graham carried on his way, oblivious. A short time later she re-joined her group, 'Just a clone, he refused to give anything up,' she reported to Jack.

'Body well hidden?' Was all he asked, she nodded as she handed him the clone's timepiece and they walked on.

They all walked back to the tavern together, 'You know there's another one out there,' she sighed.

'Yes, and if he makes a move tonight, we'll be ready for him,' Jack hoped it would be the case.

'He won't, Jack, now he knows we're on to him, he'll do it undercover of battle tomorrow when we're most vulnerable,' she looked at him, 'but you knew that didn't you?'

He looked from her to Ben and nodded as they went inside.

That night at dinner wine was served as usual because the water was unfit to drink. Alpha team as always drank sparingly, but Jenkins seemed a little the worse for it. She wasn't noisy or out of line, but it was apparent she had already been drinking in her room. 'You'd better get her to bed,' Jack whispered to Ben as he glared at the young Lieutenant, 'and find the bottle.' Ben helped her to stand and led her towards the stairs; she nuzzled his neck as they walked.

Tannis watched them leave then looked at Jack, 'care to take a stroll?'

'Excellent idea,' he was hoping Phoenix might try something tonight and thanked God Tannis could remain professional; he was already his best man down babysitting a drunken idiot.

Up in their room, Ben helped Jenkins towards the bed, where she swayed and put her arms around his neck then purposely fell back onto the bed pulling him down on top of her, her lips on his, he grabbed her arms and pulled her off, 'Remember yourself,' he snapped.

'She need never know,' she whispered.

Ben glared at her and in an angry whisper said, 'Tannis is my wife and the only woman I want, and this isn't real!'

Jenkins lost her temper now, she had never been turned down before, 'How can you love her? You saw what she did today, what she's capable of, she's not even human, for God's sake.'

Ben controlled his rage and sat in the fireside chair with his back to her, 'Sleep it off,' he snapped again; he wouldn't even dignify her last outburst with an answer.

A few fruitless hours later, Jack and Tannis returned to the tavern, and he saw her to her door. They both knew what the next day would bring, 'I'll see you in the morning then,' he half smiled resigned to the fact that going into battle was their only option.

'Goodnight, Jack,' she kissed him on the cheek, as she opened her door, Ben stepped into the hall. He had wanted to talk to her, but she didn't even look at him. She was looking behind him then without a word to either of them she went into her room, slammed the door shut and locked it. Ben gave Jack a puzzled look, but he too said nothing, just barged past his teammate, into his room. He turned to follow his CO and saw the reason for Tannis' actions. Jenkins was standing naked behind him, Jack grabbed her by the wrist and pulled the sheet off the bed, 'Cover yourself up and get to bed, you stupid little girl!'

Ben made to leave; he wanted to see Tannis, 'Let her be mate,' Jack warned, 'she's had her nose rubbed in it for the past few days, but she's not stupid.'

The two men left Jenkins snoring face down in a pillow and went downstairs for a drink. It was quiet down there now; all the women had gone to their beds, and the few men that remained were now drinking themselves into oblivion, no doubt to block out any thought of the impending battle. Jack and Ben drank in silence, but for different reasons. Jack thought of his family; he knew that no matter what happened tomorrow they would be safe for the rest of their lives and for that he would be eternally grateful to Tannis, not that she would ever want to hear of it. He wasn't a religious man, but at this moment in time, he was silently praying he made it through tomorrow and went home to see them again.

Ben was in torment not being able to see his wife before the battle; there was so much to say, and if things went badly, he might never see her again. Jack finished his drink and called for another; he knew what his friend must be going through, 'Things shouldn't be left unsaid before a battle, you should be with your wife.'

Ben leaned forward and put his head in his hands, 'I'm sure she'll be asleep,' he said dryly.

'I said you should be with your wife,' Jack stared at him.

Ben looked at his CO and smiled, 'Thank you.'

Jack just nodded and drank his drink.

As he made his way up the stairs and along the hallway, a fiddler began to play a tune; the sound drifted intoxicatingly up the stairs. As he stood in front of her door and knocked softly Tannis opened it and stood looking at him; she was in her nightgown, which had slipped from one of her shoulders. Neither spoke, she just let go of the door handle and stepped back into the room, her eyes on his, he walked in and closed the door behind him.

As she continued to back away, he walked towards her; she stopped as her back came to rest against the wall. He moved even closer to kiss her; she pulled back slightly, he stopped and looked into her eyes as he took her hand and placed it over his heart. Then his lips were on hers as he unlaced her nightgown and let it fall to the floor. She untied his shirt and lifted it over his head, and he pulled her to him needing to feel her naked flesh on his, his lips were on her neck now, and down her throat, she held her to him as he took her nipple in his mouth and ran his hands down her body, then he lay her on the bed and hastily removed the rest of his clothes and was next to her stroking her naked body, he kissed her tenderly.

'I love you, Tannis,' he whispered.

She smiled up at him, 'I love you, Ben.'

His lips were on hers again as he raised himself over her, she was wet and warm with desire for him, and he groaned with pleasure as he entered her; it could never be like this with anyone else, she was everything. He made love to her, taking his time with every part of her body, she shuddered as she climaxed the first time and called out his name, then he pulled her on top, and she made love to him. When she came this time, he sat up and held her to him then it was his turn he lay her down and pushed harder inside her then the release came.

They lay facing each other now, wrapped in a sheet, he stroked her face gently as a tear ran down her cheek.

'Hey, c'mon, let's not think about tomorrow until it happens,' he whispered, knowing exactly what was going through her mind.

'Please, Ben I have to say this now,' her voice wavered, 'there's a really big chance of not making it tomorrow.'

'No,' he put his finger to her lips, he wouldn't hear it.

'Please, Ben,' she moved his hand away as she steadied her voice, 'we're bound to get separated in battle, and I don't want you looking for me; you must concentrate on taking care of yourself.'

'Tannis, I can't hear this,' his voice cracked.

'My life began when I met you, Ben Rhodes,' she was crying now, 'if I don't come through tomorrow …'

He couldn't take anymore; his lips were on hers again, hard and determined, 'We're both gonna make it tomorrow, you fight and stay alive, and I'll find you, I'll always find you.'

Morning came too soon; they rose and dressed, Tannis in her Cornet's uniform this time. She tied back her hair and stood in front of Ben as he inspected her, Jack knocked and came in, his stomach knotted as he saw her standing there in her uniform; she looked like a young boy small and vulnerable, he wondered why he hadn't seen this the other night, but realised it was because the other night she wasn't facing death. He looked at Ben now, 'Go and tell Jenkins the rendezvous,' Ben left them alone for a moment; he knew Jack wanted to say his goodbyes too. Her CO stood in front of her now and straightened her sash then nodded, 'Just remember to get the job done and get out.'

She hugged him tightly, 'I love you, Jack, you made my life a lot better.'

'I love you too, darlin, and you really did make my life a lot better,' his voice wavered as he pulled away from her, he looked into her eyes and kissed her hard on the lips. It was not a lover's kiss of passion but a kiss from the love of the closest of friendships, and then he was gone.
Ben came back for her; it was time.

They stood in their respective lines of cavalry; Delta team were close to Graham near to the back. Tannis had drawn the short straw and was placed in the front row of the first column ready to advance, she glanced back and saw her teammates in the distance watching her through their telescopes; she gave them a brief nod and turned to face the thousands of French also lined up ready for battle, 'Lionheart,' Jack was in awe of Tannis' courage as she stood and faced the enemy. Ben drew on every ounce of inner strength to stay calm as he watched his wife staring straight ahead, ready to attack, his guts were in knots.

Then looking at his watch, the commander gave his signal, and the cannons fired, soon to be retaliated by the French. Tannis had been right; the noise was deafening as either side's artillery pounded the other. The two men were amazed how the ranks held as they were blown apart but forced to wait for the order to attack. Then the trumpet sounded, and they watched helplessly as Tannis' troop trotted slowly forward until they built up speed into a full gallop, sabres raised into the fray.

She was fighting hard when the smoke from the cannon fire obscured her from view, and it was time for Jack and Ben to attack.

They were soon separated in the chaos. Jack had William in his sights; they might try and kill him now, while Ben charged after Graham, he saw Delta team fighting for their lives surrounded by the French but couldn't see his wife; he came under attack from a French cavalry officer who had fired his pistol and missed so now charged in with his sabre.

William seemed well protected, which was fortunate as Jack was riding hard when a stray cannonball burst through the trees killing his horse. They both went down together, pinning Jack's leg under the beast. He struggled to pull himself free, but it was useless; then he noticed the pain in the top of his arm and the warm blood that ran down it. Some flying debris had hit him, he reached for his pistol and fired as an enemy trooper ran toward him. The man was killed instantly, but this left Jack a sitting duck with only his sabre to defend himself with.

A pack of troopers closed in on him ready to make the kill; one slightly braver than the others drew close and raised his sabre. This is it, Jack thought, but he wouldn't close his eyes, he would stare in the face of death, a pity for the Frenchman that he too didn't keep his eyes open, as from the right a horse reared and kicked him to the ground. Jack looked up to see Tannis jump from her mount and finish the unconscious man off, then she rushed at the oncoming attackers, dispatching one with her pistol.

As another got closer, she grabbed the dead man's sabre and pulled out her own and fought him two-handed; he didn't stand a chance, she stuck both sabres in his chest. As he fell to his knees, she pulled his pistols from his belt and shot the two men either side of him, then she pulled the sabres from the dying man, shoving him to the ground with her booted foot, 'And what?' she raged at the three others who remained. Jack could see she was full on and ready for more, 'You want my officer, you go through me!' She yelled at them.

Unable to agree who would attack the crazed Cornet next, they backed off and disappeared into the smoke. Tannis hurried over to Jack and helped him get free of the dead animal, 'You're hurt,' she checked his arm, tearing a piece off her shirt, she secured a bandage around the wound.

'It's fine,' he winced as he limped over to a tree and leaned against it, his leg hurt more than his arm did. Tannis walked over to where her horse waited; she had thrown the reins into a bush to hold it when she had dismounted, she gave her wounded CO a leg up and, when steady, he offered her his arm, 'Come on.'

Tannis shook her head, 'You'll be faster alone; don't worry about me,' she patted his leg and walked over to a dead Dutchman and picked up his musket; it was still primed, he must've been killed before he could get the shot off, 'save the world, Jack,' there was no need for her to pick a target, because one chose her; a French cavalry officer charged her down as Jack rode away.

He turned to see her calmly aim as the officer galloped towards her. She pulled the trigger, and the horse slowed down, as it passed her, she pulled the dead man to the ground and mounted his steed without stopping it, 'She's off the fuckin chain,' Jack shook his head as he rode back into the smoke.

Ben was hacking his way through a horde in search of an enemy officer's scalp to brag about later when he saw the Phoenix agent stalking his prey, it was Rafe, musket primed and aimed at Graham. Ben took out a pistol he had saved for this very moment and aimed. It was then he saw Tannis riding hard, she crouched on her saddle as she came close to Rafe, the musket discharged but missed its intended mark as Tannis jumped on the agent, distracted for the moment, Ben missed the rifleman taking his aim and knew no more.

Tannis and Rafe fought hand to hand, 'So, my lady, you sensed me before I knew you were there, I'm impressed.'

'Don't be,' she sneered, 'anyone can smell shit a mile off.'

'Oh darling,' he landed a lucky punch and split her lip, 'why must we always fight like this?'

She kicked him in the groyne bringing him to his knees, 'Believe me, if I had a gun, we wouldn't be fighting like this.'

Rafe was dressed as a Colonel, so typical of him, and from his vulnerable position on his knees, he smiled a ruthless smile, 'Oh dear, attacking a senior officer and in front of witnesses,' he looked toward the three Cornets who now stood behind her, 'take this rogue away,' he ordered. But the three men, dirty and battle weary, moved to stand by Tannis and raised their weapons at Rafe; it was her turn to smile now.

'Thank you, gentlemen, aim for the head,' she showed no sign of emotion.

'Ah, so is this the rest of Alpha Team, or would you be Delta?'

'I knew that cow was up to something,' Tannis fumed 'well, you've just lost your little spy, I'll kill her.'

He dismissed the threat, 'Feel free, she was too easy to turn and is of little use to me now.'

Cannonballs began to rain down from their side, all of them dived for cover and could only look on as Rafe made the leap, 'Shit!' Tannis rolled onto her back when the bombardment had stopped for a moment, 'Thank you chaps; the mission is over, you should get back to The Eldridge, tell Hennessey what just happened.' After much insistence from Tannis that she would be fine and the security threat must be reported immediately, Delta Team made the leap.

The battle was over, the guns had fallen silent; all that could be heard now was the mournful cries of the wounded and dying. The women who had made their way onto the field and into the woods could occasionally be heard screaming when they found the mangled body of a loved one. And of course, there was the scourge of the battlefield, the men and women who robbed the dead of anything of value, it was one such who came across what they assumed was a dead Captain. The toothless hag rummaged around in his pockets, taking his watch and purse, but she got more than she bargained for when he sat up quickly and put a knife to her throat, she dropped all that she had taken from him and slowly moved away, then broke into a run as Jack stood up. His arm throbbed painfully, but his leg was still the worst; he couldn't bear much weight on it.

He looked around trying to get his bearings then baulked at the sight as far as the eye could see were bodies with the most hideous of injuries. He thought he'd seen it all before, but nothing could've prepared him for that. He couldn't remember what had happened to him; he was just grateful to be alive. As he scanned the area around him, he wondered if his team were out there somewhere and if the mission had been a success.

A few stragglers were making their way back to camp now, so he headed that way too, using a discarded musket as a makeshift crutch.

He had hobbled for about half a mile when in the distance, he saw a Cornet shifting bodies, apparently looking for someone, Jack could tell by the way the Cornet moved that it was Tannis. He went towards her as quickly as he could, she turned as he got closer and ran to him, almost knocking him off his feet as she hugged him tightly; he kissed the top of her head and thanked God.

'I can't find Ben,' she was worried, so different from the killing machine he had witnessed earlier; job done, she was Tannis again.

'We'll look together,' he put an arm around her shoulder and leaned heavily on her, 'did you find the other agent?' He had to ask.

'It was Rafe,' she said dismissively, her mind clearly on finding her husband; 'the mission was a success, but he got away, Delta team helped me then I told them to get back to The Eldridge,' she went on to explain the conversation she had had with Rafe.

'Bitch!' He spat.

Tannis was scanning the horizon now, 'Yes, well I will kill her when we've found Ben' she said, very business-like.

'She has to go back for questioning,' Jack winced in pain.

'So, did Richardson and Hicks and we all know how that one went,' she reminded him. As they came to the next motionless man in a Captain's uniform, she stopped for a moment and then moved on, Jack gave her a puzzled look.

'This man is dead,' she explained, 'Ben is alive, or I would know it.' He didn't question her; he was sure she meant it. They carried on the search for another hour and were resting Jack's leg while he sat back against a tree when another group of stragglers came into view. Tannis had her back to them, checking Jack's wounded arm, when she smiled at him and turned quickly, 'It's him,' she called over her shoulder as she ran down the small embankment they had been sitting on. Ben saw her and hurried over, Jack looked up to the heavens, 'Thanks,' he whispered as he saw the two of them in each other's arms.

'I've been looking for hours,' they both said at the same time. Ben didn't care that she was still in uniform; he kissed her and held her close. Dried blood showed how his head wound had bled severely, she touched it gently, her tears of joy mingling with those of sadness.

The three of them sat under the tree now in silence. Tannis leaned into Ben as he put an arm around her shoulder; it was hard to find the words to describe the sheer carnage and senselessness of it all. Eventually, they all told of their experiences and laughed when Jack described his shock at being woken by an old hag rummaging through his trousers.

'Sounds like Ned's stag night,' Tannis giggled.

They sat in grateful silence for a while until Jack was ready to move again.

As he stood and leaned on his team for support, he thought back to when they left The Eldridge, 'What music?' he looked at Tannis who, in return, looked at him as if he'd lost the plot, so he rephrased the question, 'Light the fuse and cue the music.'

'Oh,' now she got it, 'Will was a huge Mission Impossible fan, so when he made a leap that's what he used to say,' she thought for a moment before adding 'and as you know most of our missions were damn near impossible.'

The sun was setting as they made it into camp, Ben had been told about Jenkins' betrayal, and they now needed a plan to get her timepiece before she escaped. So, on the way back to the meeting place Jack had arranged that Ben would go to her first and somehow try to get close to her and get the timepiece, Tannis was not happy about the idea. So, when they walked into the prearranged place in the woods where they had come across the clone, Ben smiled as Jenkins hurried over, 'I was so worried,' she said as she moved towards him to throw herself into his arms. But Tannis stepped in front of her husband before it could happen and head-butted her. Jenkins fell unconscious to the ground, blood pouring from her nose and mouth.

'Or you could just do that,' Jack shrugged; Tannis was owed that one.

They made sure no one was around, and in the blink of an eye, they were gone.

Chapter Eleven

Tannis was with Ned in his office, drumming her fingers on the desktop. He was trying and failing miserably to ignore her, Jack and Ben had gone back to the real world with Hennessy for some big meeting with the Joint Chiefs of the Coalition. Tannis had also been invited but was unable to attend as she was covering for Ned at the time. He had been on leave with his family, and as they had gone to Avalon, Tannis had to remain to bring them back on time, which she had done, and was now waiting for her team to return, drumming her fingers louder and louder.

Ned stopped typing and looked up, 'Tannis, they're not due back for another three hours! For goodness sake, go and find someone else to annoy!'

She stuck her tongue out at him and jumped down from the desk she had been sitting on. She was almost at the door when Major Charles burst in, 'Tannis, leap us to a safe place on the island! We need to talk urgently, you too, Ned!'

'Is Ben, ok?' It was her first thought.

'As far as I know, but please we must hurry,' Charles told them. Ned nodded and walked around his desk to join them. Tannis grabbed both their wrists and made the leap. The Major had no idea where they were, but from the pile of bricks in the field, Ned did.

'Now, Major, what's got you all worked up?' He frowned.

'I came to you as soon as it was confirmed. The coalition is pulling out of Atlantis, the whole lot, orders from the Joint Chiefs, effective immediately, the operation is shut down,' he couldn't believe his own words.

'What about Jack and Ben, they're in the real world?' Tannis' mind raced.

'They're to hand in their timepieces and will not be allowed to return; the same goes for all of us when we are back in the real world,' the Major told them.

'It's Phoenix, got to be,' Ned thought out loud, 'they've somehow managed to find the Joint Chiefs and are controlling them.'

'My thoughts exactly,' Major Charles sneered.

'I have to find them, they're in danger,' Tannis looked at the two men.

'No!' Charles said louder than he meant to, 'if this is Phoenix your team already knows, and so do the agents. They'll use this to draw you out. You must remain on Atlantis.'

'But what can we do stuck here?' Tannis didn't like feeling helpless; she wasn't the helpless type.

'I will try and contact your team and Admiral Hennessy when I get back to the real world. Let us take care of it,' he touched Tannis' arm lightly, 'we cannot risk losing you; if we fail, you are our last hope.' Tannis looked at her brother for advice, but he just nodded.

'You must take us back now; I am due to leave very soon,' he sighed.

Tannis did as she was asked. They had only been away a few minutes but when they returned The Eldridge was a hive of activity. Before she released her grip on the Major, she looked at him 'Good luck, Major, and if you find my husband tell him I will see him soon.'

Charles smiled and said, 'God bless you both,' and then he was gone.

Ned put an arm around his sister, 'So, first last and only again…again, what's the plan, rescue your team and the Admiral, save the world and terminate some Phoenix agents with extreme prejudice?'

'Absolutely!' she glared at the situation.

An hour or so later they were both in the hold to see the last of the coalition troops off. Major Charles had left some time ago, and the only one allowed to stay was Dr O'Brian, as he was needed in the infirmary; he had a patient too sick to move. It was a member of Echo team who had been injured on their last mission, O'Brian had left his sedated patient and headed for the hold where he now met up with Ned and Tannis as they were waving off the last of the crew. 'Phoenix will be behind this make no mistake,' his voice rang out behind them.

'Now all we have to do is work out a way to put them back in their box,' Ned scowled.

'Preferably a wooden one,' Tannis added.

Four hours earlier in the real world, Hennessey, along with Jack and Ben, had been driven to the meeting with the Joint Chiefs. None of them had any idea what it was about, all they had been told was that it was urgent they attend. The Coalition wouldn't be happy Tannis couldn't join them, but then again it was last minute, so what did they expect, Hennessey thought to himself as they got out of the car and walked up the stone steps to the impressive Georgian manor house. Jack and Ben just looked at one another; neither man liked this sort of thing, they were soldiers and liked soldiering, not politics. Once inside they were shown into a large meeting room where they were asked to sit and wait. A few moments later, the high-ranking officers that made up the Joint Chiefs entered the room.

Ben and Jack stood to attention until they were told to stand easy and take a seat.

'Where is Tannis?' one of them, a British Brigadier General asked. Hennessey explained the situation, surprised they were so put out that she wasn't there.

'I'll come straight to the point,' a US Air Force General spoke now, 'it has been decided that all operations from Atlantis shall cease forthwith and all personnel shall be recalled immediately and ordered to hand over their timepieces. Which is what we require of you now gentlemen.'

'I must protest,' Hennessey stood up, 'this is insanity, we are under constant threat from Phoenix.'

'As you were, Admiral,' the British officer said calmly, 'we have assurances from Phoenix that they have no interest whatsoever in controlling time. They were the ones putting things right; it was *DE-173* trying to alter time to suit their family in the future.'

'Sir, have you read the mission files? Even in our short time on Atlantis we've had to stop Phoenix trying to change the past!' Jack forgot himself.

'That will be all, Colonel. You will all three hand in your timepieces and report to the nearest military base for fresh orders,' he snapped.

'Sir, Tannis is my wife, I need to return to Atlantis. Colonel Marsters has family there too,' Ben looked at the man who sat opposite him.

'Not our problem, Major, you fraternised with an Atlantean. Besides, I'm sure she will come looking for you,' the man now looked at Jack, 'as for your family, they have no place in this world. I suggest you make arrangements with Tannis; also, I take it she will know where to find you?'

Ben shook his head, 'No, how could she?'

'Well, I'm sure she'll work it out for herself, orders have been sent to The Eldridge, personnel will be pulled out imminently.'

There was nothing more anyone could say. The three men handed their timepieces in and left, but they didn't go to the nearest base. Hennessey took them to an apartment in town that he had kept on, and once safely inside he turned to his men, 'Gentlemen, it would seem that the Joint Chiefs have been compromised.'

Jack nodded, 'Phoenix must be controlling them somehow.'

'They'll be watching us,' Ben walked over to the window and looked down into the street, sure enough, a car was waiting below, 'that's why they wanted Tannis here today, so they could finish it all in one go.'

'Yeah, and Tannis being Tannis, they'll know she'll come looking,' Jack sighed.

'If The Eldridge is being stood down, she will know already. She's not stupid she won't just charge in,' Hennessey said as he walked over to a large, padlocked metal chest, 'is there anywhere she would look for you, Major?'

Ben shook his head, 'No sir, I had no idea where we were going today.'

Hennessey unlocked and opened the chest. It was full of weapons, semi-automatics, handguns and shotguns, all with ammunition, 'Arm yourselves, gentlemen, we have a job to do.'

Jack and Ben exchanged a look of surprise.

'I'm not ready for my pipe and slippers yet,' the Admiral said as he reached down and picked out an AK47.

The three men chose their weapons and sat down to form a plan. 'We have the advantage of knowing where the Joint Chiefs are and from what we know about Phoenix they have to be close by to control them,' Hennessey was silenced as simultaneously Jack and Ben glanced at the door. The two men stood and walked over to it. Ben grasped the handle as Jack got in position then nodded to his teammate. In one swift movement, the door was opened, and Jack lunged forward and dragged the eavesdropper inside.

Major Charles landed on the floor with a thud, his hands raised as the three men aimed their weapons at him.

'Had a feeling you'd be here,' he smiled at them as Jack offered him a hand up. They sat and listened as Charles retold the events from The Eldridge, telling them that no one wanted to leave but they had to follow orders.

'So Tannis and Ned are alone now?' Ben looked at the Major. 'O'Brian is still on board for now, Sgt Flyer from Echo team was still too sick to move.'

'Does Tannis know you've come here, Major?' Hennessey asked. 'No, sir, I only know of this place from a conversation we had previously. I didn't tell her about it because I knew she would come looking for you and I figured that's what Phoenix would want.' 'Good thinking,' Hennessey nodded, 'we must try and resume order without risking Tannis and Ned; if we fail then it will be their turn.'

Ben showed Charles the weapons chest, and he made his choice.

The Eldridge was eerily quiet as Ned and Tannis sat with O'Brian in the briefing room.

'I don't even know where to look. It was all so secret, how am I supposed to find them?' Tannis frowned.

'The only lead we have is the destination they left in the log, but from there they could've gone anywhere,' Ned sighed.

'Let's look around the destination area and see what there is. It's worth a try,' O'Brian began typing, and the screen on the wall lit up, different buildings in the surrounding area appeared. He flicked through them, but it was useless, they could be anywhere. The Georgian building her team and the Admiral had been driven to flashed up on the screen, and the hairs on the back of Tannis' neck stood up.

'Stop!' she stared at the image, 'that's it,' she said confidently. 'How do you know?' O'Brian asked.

'Because that's Jefferson's family home,' Ned told him and smiled at his sister, 'clever girl.'

'I'll need a copy of the plans,' Tannis was already plotting her attack.

'Err, I'm coming too, we've no idea how many of the bastards are behind this,' Ned piped up, 'and don't even bother to argue; if I don't come with you, I'll just follow.'

She opened her mouth to speak, but O'Brian jumped in, 'And that is exactly what Phoenix will be hoping for; you two are going to need back up!'

'First, last and only; we are the backup Doc,' Ned shrugged. 'No,' the doctor leaned closer, 'there are others.'

Tannis wrinkled her nose, she could think of no one.

O'Brian looked from one to the other, 'Tannis, you are the ruler of time,' she made to protest, but he raised his hand for her to let him finish, 'like it or not you have the power to make time work for you. You can travel back for your help.'

'Who?' Ned frowned, 'you know we can't go back for *DE-173*; it's impossible, we were there when they were killed. It would cause a paradox if we showed up with ourselves already there, not to mention cock up the present.'

The doctor shook his head, 'No I don't mean your brother and sisters, I mean your parents. We know they went to destroy Montauk in the 80's, go back before they make the leap to the future and get their help, I think they owe you that much.'

Tannis sat, open-mouthed, 'But that's against the rules; we could alter what they do in the future. What if one of them is killed?'

'Bollocks to the rules,' Ned banged the table, 'our folks left us this mess and since when did Phoenix play by the rules?'

'That's my boy,' O'Brian said proudly then looked at Tannis, 'what do you say?'

She grinned, 'Cool, family road trip.'

Inside the Montauk facility, half of the ceiling had collapsed, and the lighting hung down flickering, there was a strong smell of smoke and blood. As Ned and Tannis made their way along the corridor, they stepped over bodies, noticing that a few were Gunther clones. 'Looks like the folks have been busy,' Ned whispered.

Tannis nodded. 'Let's hope we're not too late.' They both crouched in silence as they heard voices drawing nearer. Then slowly stood when they recognised their respective parents; unfortunately for them, their folks had just left them as a nine-year-old and a thirteen-year-old and therefore didn't recognise the two adults standing before them. Tannis was in her trademark leather, Ned also in black leather. Their parents raised their weapons to open fire as Tannis called out 'No, wait, don't shoot!'

Her father looked closer, and he seemed to recognise her, 'I know you from somewhere.'

Ned Snr stared at her too, 'Yeah, I've seen you before.'

'You were there in Philadelphia, 1943. The night before the experiment,' her father frowned trying to remember, 'Lucy?'

Tannis and Ned both stood with their hands raised, 'Yes, I was there, I was sent back on a mission, but my real name isn't Lucy it's...'

'Tannis?' Her mother sensed her more than recognised her.

'Mum,' she smiled and lowered her hands as her mother hugged her.

'But you're only nine, baby,' her mother tried to take her features in.

'Mum, things have changed, I can't tell you anything that might affect the true timeline, but we need your help,' she looked at her father and Ned's too, 'all of you.'

'My God, son,' Ned Snr recognised his boy in the man that stood before him, the two of them embraced.

Tannis' father looked at her now, 'I knew there was something familiar about you that night.'

They quickly explained the situation as best they could without giving anything away about the future or the past. 'Darling, we have to follow Phoenix from here, some of them have made a leap into the future, we have to stop them,' her mother was adamant.

Tannis was getting angry now, 'No, mother, you can come back here and make the leap when you've helped us!' She snapped.

From the shadows along the corridor a wounded Phoenix agent stumbled towards them and opened fire, Tannis was still arguing with her mother, she didn't even break the conversation, she just thrust her hand out and sent their attacker and his hail of bullets into another dimension. Her parents, along with Ned Snr, were stunned into silence, 'So, are you going to help us or not?'

'Your powers have grown with you,' her father smiled at her, 'are you sure you need our help?'

'There are others involved, and if Phoenix are controlling them, we won't be able to handle them all. The innocent must not be harmed; only Phoenix must die,' Ned explained it was so hard having to watch every word.

In the real world, Hennessey and the others made their way back to the manor house. It was getting dark as they approached and bowing to Jack's experience the Admiral let him take the lead; except for the part where Jack suggested he remain at the apartment. He refused, saying that his country needed him, and it was the least he could do in its hour of need, so now he waited at the perimeter with Jack while Ben and Major Charles went to recon the area. They reported back that security was tight; guards patrolled the grounds and CCTV was apparent. But it would be easily overcome if they timed their movements and went while the cameras were facing the other way.

They waited and timed their way in perfectly. Once inside the grounds they made their way in through one of the cellar windows, it was too old to close properly so it couldn't be adequately secured. It was pitch dark inside and, without modern technology in the form of night vision to help them, they had to go old school and wait for their eyes to become accustomed. Hennessey had used the internet to gain access to the plans and layout of the building, so they knew which way to head for the back stairs.

Once at the foot of the staircase they split into two teams. Hennessey was with Major Charles; he didn't want to split up a winning team in Jack and Ben; they had worked closely together on many missions now and could almost second guess one another.

So, they climbed the stairs silently to the next floor as Charles and Hennessey checked out the ground floor; they found empty rooms mainly, all the guards seemed to be outside on patrol.

Upstairs Jack and Ben checked each room cautiously. They were all more or less the same; either empty or full of furniture covered with dust sheets. On the landing, which overlooked the hall downstairs, they heard the arrogant voice of Jefferson, 'Colonel Marsters, Major Rhodes, show yourselves and come down or your friends will die,' he sneered, 'your choice, I don't care either way, but you know I can make it very unpleasant for them.'

'Shit!' Jack cursed as he looked at Ben; they both knew they had no choice.

'No!' Hennessey called out, 'you have your orders.'

'And we've seen these guys at work, too, sir,' Jack replied as he and Ben walked down the stairs with their hands raised.

Jefferson marched them at gunpoint toward a room at the back of the house. Once inside the four of them saw the Joint Chiefs sitting at a large table with their eyes closed, like robots waiting to be switched on, Jefferson motioned with his gun for his new prisoners to move to the far side of the room then gave the order for Ben to open the large double doors. He did so, and they all walked inside what must've been, in years gone by, a ballroom but its new use was apparent as manacles hung from the walls and six Gunther clones waited, armed and ready.

Once the four men had been securely chained, Jefferson placed his weapon on a nearby table and sat down, 'And now we wait,' he smiled as he looked along the line of captives, 'for your teammate to try and fail to rescue you,' he played with his gun again, 'and when she is dead, you shall all die too; then nothing will stop us.'

'You'll be lucky, she doesn't even know where we are, remember? It was all top secret; she wouldn't know where to look,' Jack said as he pulled on his manacles, they wouldn't budge.

'Oh, I have fought *The Eldridge Brats* for many years, Colonel, and despise them as I may, I know they are resourceful and cunning. You have Tannis' loyalty; she will lay down her life for her team, mark my words,' he grinned.

'I don't suppose you want to tell us how you found the Joint Chiefs and managed to compromise them?' Jack changed the subject.

'I don't think so, Colonel, it may be needed in the future.'
'Always works in the movies,' he shrugged.

'I thought you wanted Tannis as a baby factory?' Ben hoped to buy time for her if she showed up.

Jefferson rolled his eyes, 'Not us, that's Rafe and Gunther's fantasy.'

So now they knew two agents were absent for this power play. 'We will content ourselves with wiping her interfering life off this planet,' a woman's cruel voice rang out as into the room stepped the blonde-haired figure of Elsa, Tannis' aunt. She walked over to the men chained to the wall and looked at them one by one before coming to a stop in front of Ben, 'So, you're the one who married her?' She looked him up and down and noted she did find him attractive, 'you shouldn't waste your time on a little fool like that; you need a real woman.'

Ben said nothing as she looked closer at him, probing his mind. He gasped in pain, and a small trickle of blood ran down from his nose, she released him from her power and laughed. Then moved on to the others' giving them a small taste of what she could inflict.

She turned to Jefferson, 'I'm bored; I think I shall play with one of our guests while we wait.'

Jefferson just shrugged, 'Well, don't kill any of them yet, we want her scared for their safety, not so pissed off we get blasted to Christ knows where!'

Elsa sat on the desk opposite her captive playmates and closed her eyes. The four men didn't have to wait long to find out which one of them she was targeting as Ben threw his head back, eyes closed, and groaned with the pain. It started like hot knives being forced into his skull then his whole body burned, he looked down and saw the flames licking at his legs; he writhed in agony now as the flames got higher. Just as suddenly as it started, it was over, he looked down again; his legs were fine, nothing had happened.

Elsa looked thoughtful, 'Now let's see something personal,' she grinned maliciously, but her expression changed instantly as she turned to Jefferson.

'Playtime's over,' he smirked and picked up a remote control from the desk and aimed it at the huge TV on the wall. It flashed to life and showed a live feed from the front gates as they now lay mangled in the driveway; the cause of their destruction stood in the opening they had once protected. Tannis was holding two PP2000 Russian-made submachine guns, with her two pump-action shotguns on her back and ammunition wrapped around her. There was no point trying to sneak in as she knew Phoenix would sense her coming, which they had.

Four guards ran at her, and she opened fire, killing them quickly as she headed for the front doors, these she kicked open and without breaking pace, walked the length of the entrance hall. Her fingers were firmly on the triggers, spraying either side of the room with bullets, killing the seemingly docile clones who barely had a chance to react.

Dropping her spent weapons to the floor and retrieving one of her shotguns from the holster on her back, she moved into the room where the Joint Chiefs sat as dormant as before, giving them a quick glance, she carried on toward the doors at the far end of the room. As if on cue another clone came from a side door and barred her way; this one was different to the others; he seemed more skilled, and his eyes showed no emotion.

He gave an evil sneer as he dropped his gun to the floor and removed his other sidearm, dropping that too. Then he slowly drew a dagger from his belt. Holding it in one hand, he beckoned her to him with the other, 'I want to see your eyes when I stick it in,' he leered.

Tannis raised an eyebrow, she didn't have time for this, so she cocked her weapon and shot him. Stepping over the body, she reached out for the door handle that led to her quarry.

A clone beat her to it from the other side and opened the doors wide on Jefferson's instruction, a mistake for the clone. Tannis shot him too, although he was quickly replaced by another who aimed a sidearm at her while Jefferson spoke, 'Drop the weapons,' he said as he aimed his gun at Ben. Tannis glared at him as she laid down her arms, well, the ones on show, at least.

'Bring her,' Elsa commanded.

The clone, which now walked behind Tannis, shoved the barrel of his gun in the back of her head then proceeded to push her forward. She moved slowly, checking everyone chained to the wall was ok. The clone shoved her harder, and she turned her head, 'Do that again, and I will kill you,' she warned. As if in defiance he shoved her again; in one fluid movement she turned, grabbed his weapon, breaking his wrist while doing so, then as he bent his knee and cradled the open wound on it with his good hand, she stepped up on his bended knee, wrapped her legs around his neck, choking the life out of him while she took aim and shot Jefferson and then Elsa in the head, the clone fell dead, and Tannis expertly stepped clear.

'That was too easy,' Jack whispered as Hennessey raised an eyebrow, 'That wasn't off the chain?' the Admiral questioned.

Tannis side-eyed the pair of them as she moved over to the desk. She looked up as Ned entered the room seconds later, 'Well, I know I'm good, but the kids could've taken care of that lot,' he carried a hessian bag with him.

'Clones,' Tannis tutted, she found what she was looking for and turned to face Ben and the others as Ned walked over to the door to collect her discarded weapons and ammo belt. A shot rang out, and he flew backwards as blood burst from his chest, 'No!' Tannis yelled as in through the doorway walked an Asian man and woman whom Jack and his incarcerated companions didn't recognise, but it seemed Tannis did as she made to draw on her power to dispatch them.

'Oh, I wouldn't if I were you,' the woman waved a small handheld transmitter, 'I press this button and your friends here fry.'

Tannis stood herself down, 'I guess Cole made his deal with you and just took your timepieces for show,' she forced herself to control her rage.

'We assumed he'd changed his mind,' the male spoke now, 'we've been monitoring the world's communications for the past three years trying to make contact with other agents.'

He walked over and picked up the hessian bag Ned had brought with him, 'now we have a bag full of timepieces for our new army,' he opened it up and looked inside, raising his eyebrows at the number, 'impressive hoard,' he begrudgingly complimented.
'Gunther won't be happy you've been playing in his toy box,' Tannis motioned to the dead clones.

'We don't care for their stupid plots; we have our own agenda,' the woman cocked the shotgun again then looked at the prisoners one by one, 'and, how sweet, you married one of them,' she sneered, 'I tell you what; we'll let them live if you stand still like a good girl and take a bullet like your brother,' she waved the transmitter again, 'your choice.'

'No choice,' Tannis looked at the four men, who were all in their way telling her to blast the agents to hell. She tried to force a smile but failed, as stepped close to Ben.

'Hands behind your back for your tearful farewell,' the male spoke as his companion mockingly wiped a non-existent tear from his eye.

'No,' Ben struggled with his chains, 'Tannis, Babe, don't,' his voice cracked.

'It's only a mission,' she whispered, then kissed him slowly.

'Enough, we've got a world to rule,' the male's voice was filled with boredom.

Tannis pulled slowly away from her husband looking into his eyes.

'Tannis, blast these bastards! That's an order,' Jack shouted. It all happened so fast, as soon as she turned to face the agent the woman opened fire, hitting her full on in the chest. She fell backwards, blood spattering the men chained to the wall.

'I told you they wouldn't stand a chance if we took these prisoners; they could never have known who they were up against,' the woman stroked her companion's face as he smiled.

'That's why they didn't come alone,' Catherine, James and Ned Snr walked in now, 'we just needed to know how many of you there were,' Catherine's eyes glowed in hatred.

Jack looked across at Ben. There was about to be a hell of a fight, his wife lay dead at his feet, and he was, what was he doing? Checking no one was paying attention to them Ben looked at his CO as he pulled a small key from his mouth and passed it to a stunned-looking Major Charles who passed it on to a just as confused looking Admiral, it was the key to the padlock that would free their chains. Tannis had passed it to Ben with her last kiss, Jack surmised.

He looked down at her. He never thought his heart could break again, but he was given more of a jolt than if the agent had hit the switch to fry them when Tannis opened her eyes and winked at her teammates.

'Catherine, you can't be here, how?' The woman faltered.

'What, no hugs, Sam?' Catherine folded her arms, 'Or you, Sarah? After all, I trained you both, not well enough though I see. You both failed to grow a conscience.'

'And breaking away from the pack too, tut-tut,' James shook his head, 'they're gonna want to kick your ass,' he looked at his wife, 'maybe we should hand them over; give your sister something to play with.'

'Thoughtful as ever, darling, but I think we should kill them now, we're in a bit of a rush,' Catherine smiled.

Ned Snr grabbed the bag of timepieces away from Sam as Jack passed the last of the chain through his manacles as silently as the others had; they were now all free but remained where they were taking their lead from Tannis and Ned, who, apparently for good reasons, hadn't moved yet.

James aimed his weapon at Sam while Ned Snr pointed his at Sarah. That was when a panel in the wall slid open to allow eight more clone agents through; four Sam's and four more Sarah's. Catherine and her team wasted no time in attacking, although it was more defence with such numbers.

Tannis jumped up now, 'Let's even it up a bit, shall we?' She looked at her husband and friends as she pulled the blood bag from between her top and bulletproof vest and ran over to join in the fray.

Ned sat up quickly and discharged his weapon into one of the Sam's, killing it outright as Tannis jumped on the back of another snapping its neck. Jack, Ben and Major Charles also dispatched a clone each with swift precision, then Tannis turned to the Admiral as she picked up a shotgun from the floor and threw it to him, 'Would you mind keeping an eye on the Joint Chiefs, please, Admiral? Once we've finished this lot off, they should wake up.'

The Admiral nodded, cocked the weapon, and moved into the other room, still trying to watch the activities in the one he left, he was immensely proud of his people.

Catherine and her team all made a kill, but while doing so, everyone else noticed those with powers paused for a second as if sensing something, that was when two of the attackers made a run for it and closed themselves off behind the open panel in the wall, a Sam and a Sarah, clearly the originals. Tannis picked up the bag of timepieces and ran to the Admiral, 'Mum can you stop Sarah's control over these men?' She handed the bag to Hennessey as the Joint Chiefs began to wake up.

Catherine had managed to block the mind control for now, 'Hurry, Tannis, I can't stop it for long,' her mother called.

'Admiral, get them out of here quick,' Tannis yelled over her shoulder as she ran back to her team.

'I'm guessing there's more to this than two agents playing hide and seek?' Jack picked up a weapon and checked the ammunition.

Ned pulled his blood bag out and dropped it to the floor, 'We won't be the only ones looking for them and judging by the look on Aunt Catherine's and Tannis' faces, I'm guessing more agents have just arrived.'

Hennessey had given the Joint Chiefs a timepiece each and made the leap with them. Tannis moved over to be with her husband now and hugged him, he held her tightly; this wasn't the time or place for anything more.

Jack touched her shoulder, 'Trying to give me heart failure?' He smiled.

'C'mon, Jack, you know I'd never roll over without a fight,' she grinned at him.

'The happy reunion will have to wait, Sweetheart,' James picked up a weapon and looked at Jack and Ben, 'you were there back in '43 with Tannis too,' he frowned, 'all this need to know alter time crap is annoying,' he walked back to stand with his team.

'I don't understand,' Tannis looked at her mother who explained to them all, 'The five true agents have gone, but they have left a fully formed clone of themselves, well four of them have at least.'

'Obviously, Rafe would never allow himself to be cloned,' Ned rolled his eyes.

Catherine concentrated once more, 'They have no mind powers but are still lethal, be warned.'

The front doors exploded, announcing the imminent attack, 'Hide and seek it is then, Major Charles, with me. Tannis with Ben, Ned…' Jack looked at his friend.

'I'll stick with Dad,' Ned took his place by his father's side, and they all headed in their different directions as the power was cut and the house fell into darkness. It was now only lit by the moonlight coming in through the windows with open shutters.

Tannis and Ben had crept along the first landing and now stood in a small alcove; he pulled her to him and kissed her softly, 'We're the only thing that's real,' he smiled and kissed her again. They stayed holding each other in silence listening to the sound of footsteps drawing closer, Tannis nodded she had sensed a clone. Also, knowing Ben needed to work off a little pent-up rage, she let him deal with it. He did so quickly and quietly but was a little disappointed it was a Jefferson clone and not

Sam or Sarah. Job done, they moved along the spacious landing and began checking out the rooms off it.

From the floor above them, they heard a small scuffle and a gentle thud. Jack and Major Charles must've come across one, too. They walked out of an empty room and back onto the landing when Ben groaned in pain, Tannis turned to him, 'Run,' he struggled to speak as the tell-tale trickle of blood ran from his nose, Tannis' eyes filled with sadness, but she had to leave him; he was going to try and kill her. She ran along the landing and up the stairs to the next floor looking for Jack and the Major; she saw two dead agent clones as she made her way, they had been hard at it.

Behind her, she could hear Ben making his way up the stairs, she turned and hurried on her way stopping abruptly when Jack stepped out in front of her, 'Jesus, Jack, now who's trying to give who heart failure?' She backed off; there was the trickle of blood from his nose. 'Shit!' She turned and ran straight into Major Charles, who had suffered the same fate as Jack. With little choice, she punched him in the face and ran, but Ben was heading her way, so she ducked into the nearest room. Its furniture was covered in dust sheets, she decided to hide under one. The three men entered soon after, and Jack began to pull the coverings off the lamps and tables and other bedroom furniture while Ben and Major Charles blocked any exit.

Tannis held her breath as he got closer to where she hid, his hand grasped a sheet and pulled, revealing an Elsa clone that instantly sprang to life and attacked him. Ben and Charles ran to help, Tannis seized the moment and ran past them, but not before putting a bullet in the clone's head, she still had to protect her team.

Out on the landing, she saw her mother hurrying toward her, 'Sarah is controlling your father and the others. I've taken their consciousness and tied them up, but I can't keep them under control and your team too.'

Tannis thought quickly, 'You find the agents; I'll take care of my team.'

'Fine, the only thing I can do for you is weaken her hold on them, they will all be in her control but should only function one at a time.' The two women nodded and hurried off in different directions. Tannis marched back to her team, her husband walked briskly toward her and tried to grab her around the throat, but she blocked his attack. She wouldn't fight him; she didn't want to hurt him, but it soon got to the point where she had to land a few blows as his attack was relentless and he was an excellent fighter. Then presently she had no choice but to use her power and throw him back against the wall where he dropped to the floor unconscious.

Tannis stood catching her breath as Jack moved on her, he was just as skilled as Ben and landed just as many painful punches. She blocked as many as she could, but he managed to land a good one that sent her crashing backwards into a table that broke apart on impact. She grabbed the leg of the broken piece of furniture and as she jumped back up hit him around the head with it. He was out for now too.

'C'mon, Mum,' Tannis winced in pain as she spoke. Major Charles was stepping up for his turn, and an already weak Tannis took another beating as Charles grabbed her and threw her across the landing. She crashed into a chair this time; her face was bruised and blood poured from her nose and from a head wound she had sustained. It took all her strength to stand now, but she did it and held a piece of the broken chair in each hand, ready for the next round. Her heart was in her mouth now though as both Jack and Ben stood too, but she wouldn't back down.

Ben rushed towards her; she drew a breath and raised her makeshift weapons, 'It's me, Babe, I'm back,' he looked around at the other two men, 'we all are.'

Her legs failed her, and she dropped straight onto her arse; Ben knelt quickly and held her to him, 'I'm so sorry; I could see everything that was happening but couldn't stop it,' he pulled her gently away from him and looked at her face; he was wracked with guilt as was Jack and Major Charles who crouched down in front of them.

'Why didn't you attack, you only defended?' Jack tilted her chin up gently and saw the extent of her wounds, 'I'm so sorry, love.'

'I feel so ashamed of my actions,' Major Charles hung his head. 'Didn't want you beaten by a girl,' she tried to smile, 'mum went to stop Sam and Sarah, make sure she's ok for me.'

The two men left Ben with his wife, 'I hurt you,' he choked on his words as he wiped the blood from her face.

She took his hand, 'You saved me, Ben, if you hadn't been strong enough to fight it and tell me to run, you would've killed me.'

He kissed her gently.

Jack and Major Charles found Catherine and Sarah easily enough, they just followed the noise. They headed downstairs and into one of the rooms at the front of the house where the two women were slugging it out. To the trained eye, it was clear Catherine was purposely dragging the fight out to inflict more pain and humiliation on her prey.

'Ah, Colonel, Major, glad to see you're yourselves again although I must say you look a little worse for wear, would you mind killing Sam for me? The little wimp ran off into the attic,' she punched Sarah to the ground and stood over her, 'oh and if you would be so kind as to pop next door and untie my team for me, please?'

'If, you're sure?' Jack inclined his head and led Major Charles out of the room, 'and I thought my mother-in-law was scary.'

They went into the next room and released the unhappy captives. 'Christ, what happened to you two?' Ned was shocked at the sight of them. Jack didn't want to answer, 'Sam's hiding in the attic, let's go.'

James rubbed his sore wrists, 'Where's my wife and daughter?' 'Tannis is upstairs with Ben, and Catherine is kicking the crap out of Sarah,' Jack explained and was backed up by a loud crash and a muffled scream from the room next to them. James sighed, 'She gets the bit between her teeth with these guys when she's...' he searched for the word.

'Off the chain?' Jack ventured.

'Tannis, too?' James shook his head, 'I assume something bad happened to make her that way,' he knew he couldn't ask what.

They all headed upstairs, Catherine joined them as she had gotten bored and killed her opponent. She sensed the cowering agent, powerless to use his mind control while she was present, he wasn't as strong as Sarah and impotent with no timepiece to leap with, 'His only other power is self- healing,' Catherine sneered as she looked around, 'he's in another part of the house now; he's using hidden passageways in the walls.'

'Not surprising, this is Jefferson's old family home,' Ned piped up as they headed for the door, 'we'll be at this all night, let's get Tannis and Ben, I have an idea.'

The eight of them stood outside at the end of the long driveway. 'Is he still hiding in there, Aunt Catherine?' Ned pulled a transmitter from his pocket as she nodded.

'Jefferson is going to be so pissed off,' he pressed the button. The whole house exploded in a ball of flames; there was nothing left but the foundations, 'a little something I prepared earlier,' Ned grinned.

The parents turned to their children now to say their goodbyes. 'We'll tidy up at Montauk and make the leap from there,' Tannis' father told her then grabbed her tightly, 'I love you, sweetheart,' this was their farewell.

'Take care of each other,' Ned's father hugged him.

'You know this has to happen,' Catherine held her daughter close, 'we will see each other again,' she looked at Ben now, 'and I expect grandchildren when we do.'

Then three little blue flashes and they were gone.

'Fuck!' Ned kicked the nearest tree, 'I'm sick of this time travel bullshit.'

Tannis just nodded as the tears ran unchecked down her now healed face. Ben took one hand, and Jack gripped his arm and took hold of Major Charles' wrist. As the sirens of the emergency services got closer, Tannis grabbed Ned, and they were gone.

Back on The Eldridge, Hennessey and the Joint Chiefs, along with Dr O'Brian, were waiting for them. It was almost back to normal, as soon as they had returned, they had ordered the immediate recall of the crew.

'People, please report to the briefing room,' Hennessey said as the Joint Chiefs took their place ready for a leap.

'And who the hell happened to you?' O'Brian gave the three men the once over before allowing them to leave.

'It's a long story, Doc,' Jack nursed his sore ribs.

Once in the briefing room, they all took their seats and waited, Tannis fidgeted awkwardly with the strap on her wrist blade.

Hennessey walked in, 'The Joint Chiefs have gone back to the real world, but measures have now been put in place so that this can never happen again,' he looked directly at Tannis, 'was it your idea to bring your parents and Ned's father along for back up?'

She didn't want O'Brian to get into trouble so was prepared to take the blame; she drew a breath, but Ned piped up, 'It was my idea; I take full responsibility.'

Tannis didn't like the idea of her brother being punished either. 'No, he's just covering for me, he's the sensible one, remember; I'm the one who broke the rules last time.'

Hennessey raised his hand for silence, 'No rules were broken; you didn't change time, whoever it was, it was an act of genius. The Joint Chiefs wanted to commend them, that's all.'

'Really?' Tannis looked at her brother, and they both said, 'It was Dr O'Brian.'

'Cunning sod,' Jack grinned.

Hennessey was given a full verbal report of the events that had happened after he had left with the Joint Chiefs. He listened attentively, and when they had finished, he stood and addressed them, 'You all performed your duties exceptionally today. I am proud to have you under my command, Tannis, Ned, your parents are owed a great deal. It must have been hard for you to see them again and let them leave to be trapped in the future, but know this; they are valued,' he dismissed them all then for a week's leave.

That night, Tannis undressed Ben and cried when she saw what she had done to him. His ribs were bruised, and she had drawn blood on his back when she slammed him into the wall, he also had a black eye and a split lip. He held her to him as they lay in bed, 'It wasn't real, it was just a mission,' he whispered.

She kissed him gently on the lips, 'We're the only thing that's real.'

Caroline was shocked at the state Jack returned home in, 'This wasn't just from observation, Jack,' she frowned as she looked at his body when he undressed, both his eyes were black, and his ribs were cut and bruised, and a huge gash ran down his back, 'who did this to you?' He knew she didn't expect him to tell her, but he smiled to himself as he imagined her face if he did, he pulled her close and held her all night, grateful to be with his family again.

Ned slipped his long thick nightie on and went to bed early, pleading a headache. His chest was bruised from the gunshot blast, and he had a lump on the back of his head from the fall, but that was nothing to what Elea would do to him if she knew the truth.

Milton Keynes UK
Ingram Content Group UK Ltd.
UKHW020828050923
428087UK00016B/1107